The Harvester

Jon Biddle

Published by Inspired Books

Edited by Casie L. Williams and Paul Hobby

ISBN: 978-1-9164582-5-3

This is for the one person that will never read my book!
To my beautiful wife, Samantha.
So pure is her energy that the words in this book would taint her glorious
white light forever.
For you, the girl that saved my life, these words you shall never read,
are for you.

Forever in my heart.

The first law of anesthesia,
All surgeons are cunts.
There is no exception to this law.
Anon

1

Rain fell freely, bouncing off the inky black tarmac. Everything took on a shiny, new glow as the drops settled. The patter of the rain in autumn, beating the welcome drum of longer evenings, nights in, wrapped up warm with wriggling, cozy toes created a feeling of anticipation for the oncoming season.

Shop window mannequins, swathed as though winter had already set in, hinted at Christmas through their color palettes and textures. This change of season was Lucy's favorite, along with the heady scent of the end of a decent warm summer, moving soon to Halloween, onto bonfire night and quickly motoring towards Christmas; by far, the best time of year.

Colchester was unusually quiet this Saturday night; Lucy guessed it was due to the football game on the TV, Chelsea Vs Barcelona and of course, the Strictly series returning. She loved watching Strictly, but wanted to go out with friends; she pondered whether her boyfriend Harvey would watch it with her as she wandered earnestly through the rain.

Her boyfriend Harvey was glued to the TV watching the game as she'd suspected, although she couldn't understand, since he was a lifelong Arsenal supporter, why he was happy to watch other teams. Lucy had never understood nor cared for the game; her father and brother were rugby fans, which seemed more sensible to her, in a nonsensical way. Her father had said football was a man's game played by thugs, and rugby was a thug's game played by gentlemen. Comically, the language that came out of Harvey when watching a game, perfectly demonstrated that daddy was right. Regardless of these foibles, she utterly loved him and everything that went along with him.

She left her friends at around 11pm. The Wagon and Horses felt like the inside of a packet of jelly babies. Full of scantily clad, brightly dressed chubby girls hoping to get lucky.

Her friend Zara, who was a little more plump than herself, had such a way with words. She'd decided to wear a luminous green tight sheath dress that was way too short. Every bump and lump was accentuated by the sheer brightness of the color, which screamed, 'I'm having sex tonight, first-come first-served'. Lucy was instantly attracted to and had admired her boldness when they started university together. She would say, "Do you really want to wear that?" And Zara with her northern carefree attitude, just shrugged away the comment and carried on.

With a head slightly fizzing from a mix of flavoured gins and cocktails, Lucy left earlier than planned, before the inevitable tipping point where soberness and alcoholic oblivion collide like a crash test dummy. A hangover was the last thing she wanted on a Sunday, the day before she started her first shift as a midwife at Colchester General Hospital.

Three years of training finally completed, Lucy's brain was fuller than when she started. The physiology of women and babies, life long friends and an eagerness to change the world with her new found skills. Just being a midwife was not the long-term goal.

The car was parked in St Johns Walk behind Culver Square, the retail shopping goto destination of the town. First she had to navigate the drunken binge drinking statistics along the high street. Her purple empire dress was flowing in the stiff breeze coming up the high-street. Driving the rain even harder into her face, it was getting cold.

Two weeks ago, it was warm. She held her clutch bag to her face as though it was a peak from a baseball cap, shielding her face from the rain. Ignoring the whistles and catcalls from the drunk soldiers hanging about outside the bars. She ducked down Pelhams Lane turned right and immediately swung left onto Trinity Street on to her favorite part of the town, Sir Isaacs Walk, the old part of the town where beautiful boutique shops sold the most attractive things that she could not afford right now.

She raced through the tunnel to the top of the stairs with a brief hiatus from the rain that sloshed out of the overfilled iron guttering, splashing her as she raced, the stairs lead down to the car park.

Her coat and slip-on sketchers were in the backseat of her car, then a quick run down more steps to the Gala Bingo taxi rank on Osbourne Street. Hopefully, Mohammad, her favorite taxi driver was on, to whisk her home to Harvey.

Mohammad always took her back to her student digs without the meter running. It was the least he could do after Lucy was there when his youngest, now two, Jamil was born. It wasn't a stressful birth for his wife, but nonetheless, he was convinced they were a gift from Allah himself.

Lucy was a petite woman, naturally athletic, blonde hair, fuller lips and an almond shaped face, slender, smooth legs that had the perfect color. She was a head turner, which irritated Harvey.

He was insanely jealous and protective of his girl. He loved her with all of his heart. It was almost an unbearable feeling and Lucy knew, that while he was watching the game, he would be worried about the attention she would be drawing from the soldiers out on the town.

Another reason to get home early. Curl up and catch up on the social media feeds. The standard regretful WhatsApp messages from her closest friend Lilly had already found a man for the evening. Once finished Lucy would have to deal with Lilly's texts. I hate myself. He only wanted me for my body. Why can't I have a decent boyfriend messages. When all Lilly had to do was stop sleeping around. Perversely, she enjoyed what Lilly got up too. There was nothing that Lilly hadn't done and Lucy almost envied the freedom she had. Fifty Shades of Grey Lucy grinned. That book was boring compared to a coffee break with Lilly.

Although security and stability was a more significant draw. It's what Lucy needed to focus on achieving whatever there was to accomplish in her exciting new world.

However, she enjoyed receiving them and sharing them with Harvey. Although a little prudish, he was still a guy and his internet search history revealed a lot!

The car was parked under one of the street lamps in the car park, by the stairs leading to Osbourne Street. No accident. Lucy would run into town the next day and pick up the car. It was also under the only working street lamp in the car park as she always did. Although today, the light wasn't on.

She noticed it, but it didn't alarm her. Lucy's car, was still visible from the shop signs on the lower level of Osbourne Street.

Harvey had told her too. She could hear him now "babes, at night, always park under a street light. You'll see 'em coming, and the CCTV can see you" jokingly he always added.

"At least if you get snatched by a perv, there'll be evidence" which followed a laugh. One of those jokes that would endure a lifetime of marriage and missed whenever it wasn't said but still didn't need to be told.

As Lucy approached the car. Striding with confidence even though slightly intoxicated in her high heels. She loved the sound of her heels on the tarmac. It was a sexy sound. She was hoping Harvey had left the umbrella in the backseat. She knew her coat was hanging up on the door at home, a decision of now regret while the rain hammered even more. As relying on Harvey was an even bigger, poor assumption.

It felt as she was walking on the underside of a colander, the rain was smashing hard into the ground. She noticed a van parked right next to her mini with a tall slim fit man. He was leaving, the van blipped as the indicators in unison on all four sides flashed to tell the whole town, this van was now locked.

As she approached her car the man tripped, spilling the contents of his messenger bag all over the soaking wet floor. "Fuck" the man cried, the thump on the tarmac was painfully audible, augmented by the standing water on the black concrete. Lucy, always willing to help charitably ran the final five steps to the guy that had fallen, and crouched. Her skirt hitched up, as she realized when she squatted with her knees clamped together. She stuffed the excess material of the skirt between her legs. "Oh my gosh, are you okay" Lucy asked. "Yes" the man replied. "These new shoes, so slippery." The man's accent was a well-educated. Mid-forties, he was cute and very muscular under the clothes he was wearing.

"That thump on the floor made me wince, are you sure you're ok let me help with your things before they get soaked," Lucy said as she was quickly snatching at the contents of the bag that was already soaked.

"You're so very kind, I can't believe I was so stupid." The man was on his knees watching her grab his things oblivious to the water running off his angular Germanic features. She was perfect, beautiful, sexy. Everything he had hoped for, Lucy was a perfect specimen!

Lucy realized after a minute or so the inconsistency of the moment. She was grabbing the items while the guy was...watching.

She looked up while her hands were feeling around for more bits and pieces, he was looking at her, with piercing eyes, and a small smile in the corner of his mouth. "Nice to meet you, Lucy, I have been..." Lucy heard him say, then his mouth was moving, but there was no sound. She was grabbing around the soaking wet floor, and although her hands were moving, she couldn't feel them, her arms started to flail her legs collapsed from under her.

Lucy went to scream but nothing went beyond the thoughts. She was entirely conscious, but the conscious and unconscious thoughts remained were they were, just thoughts and not actions.

Her mouth was watering, to the point of dribbling. She could feel the saliva falling out of her mouth. Instinctively, she reached for her mouth. But again, nothing. She had no control as her bladder voided. Mortified yet impossible to stem the flow as her bladder squeezed as her muscles relaxed. The warm urine ran down her legs, the cold wet surface of the tarmac replaced with warm wetness.

Suxamethonium was now one hundred percent in control of Lucy's depolarised muscles. Normally, Lucy's muscle would depolarise and then repolarize to complete a muscle action. The man had brushed against Lucy's hand as she helped him with his things. She didn't notice the small subcutaneous prick of a very finely gauged needle, on the thicker part of the underside of Lucy's left thumb.

Once in the tissues, the drug quickly absorbed into the vein and quickly found its way coursing up the arm and on its way to the heart. The Clapham Junction of the vascular system, drug arm to brain time around thirty seconds, she had no chance, rendering her completely conscious yet paralyzed.

In one minute, forty-five seconds later, Lucy is lying on the ground. Unable to speak. Her brain was screaming GET UP GET, GET UP, SCREAM. She went to do it, but nothing.

The final phase of a complete motor block as the muscles suspended in the depolarised state. As calcium flooded in the sarcoplasmic reticulum of her billions of muscular cells, her body shook uncontrollably. To the uninitiated in modern anesthesia, it would look almost epileptic.

But these fasciculations are an indication to the administrator that the person is completely paralyzed.

The man stood. In his pocket was a pocket face mask that doctors use on patients in the hospital. Attached to a small dual gas canister with a balloon in the middle of the tubing. He had to move quickly, Lucy's muscles would quickly regroup and return to normal function in under ten minutes.

She needed to be moved without damaging her beautiful body. The mask fitted snugly and with elasticated loops placed around both ears, the canister was light. Custom designed for this purpose. Once secured the man twisted the pressure regulator to two, opening the canister exposing the liquid, that at ambient temperature became unstable and converted to a gas.

Lucy, so confused. Was paralyzed, unable to move, could feel everything, yet, nothing, nothing worked.

In her training, working in the operating room. She recognized the smell coming out of the facemask. It was pungent, unpleasant, yet it made her feel warm. Made her stiffening aching painful muscles relax, like getting into a warm bath on a cold day, weirdly nice considering what her conscious mind was screaming. It was the unmistakable smell of sevoflurane, a widely used anesthetic inhalation agent to maintain hypnotic anesthesia. Mixed with oxygen, unconsciousness was a guarantee. He squeezed the balloon and she felt her lungs inflate then deflate.

She was desperate to protest but there was nothing. Looking up the man was holding the mask and stroking her hair with his free hand. His lips pursed, as though he was shushing a child as they drifted off to sleep. Her ears were ringing, the sound of the rain became so loud like a drum. The final sense an anesthetized persons loses is hearing.

She could hear the number 23 bus leave the bus stop. She could feel the thud her own heart beating in her throat and thumping in her ears, the rain beating in time with her heart. Lucy felt her consciousness slip away, drifting to an oblivion of a painless involuntary sleep there was nothing she could do.

The man apparently experienced in administering anesthesia, inserted an airway that stopped Lucy's tongue falling back and blocking her airway.

The canister, rested on her chest, and the man cradled her head with his right arm placing his left hand under her knees, in one action he was to his feet, she hung from his arms like a rag doll, lifeless and empty, he was strong. Quickly, he swung round looked to the back of the carpark and stairs where Lucy had just approached from, nothing. All the surveillance cameras watching at this car-park and Osbourne road were out of action.

The man had seen to this the day before, knowing that it would be months before any bureaucracy would pay for their repair. He paused and waited, he was counting to thirty. Eyes were on stalks searching into the darkness of the car-park. The rain was running off the tip of his nose, eyes wide and unphased by the falling rain. His ears, tuned closely into the moment. Lips apart to equalize the pressure in the eustachian tubes to allow the faintest of sounds to get through to the eardrums, sirens, shouting to the witnessing what they may have just seen. Anything that could cause the implementation of plan B. It was a painfully long thirty seconds. The man, prepared for this. Every eventuality was taken care of. He slowly turned purposefully and effortlessly, he walked to the van, the side door clicked, the door protruded from the side and then in a moment of engineering perfection, slid back and a light inside flickered on.

The man climbed into the aperture of the van. It was tall sided. His six-foot powerful frame could stand upright in the inside. It looked like an ambulance of the future. Spotlessly clean, the best medical equipment that money can buy.

Anaesthetic machine, defibrillator, consumables such as dressings, bandages, casts, syringes, drugs. With his elbow, he pressed a rubberized black button on the side wall inside. The same smooth action of the door silently slid to close the vehicle, the man waited without looking for the high-quality click of the locking mechanism as the door slid home.

On the cue of the click, knowing the door confidently was now closed he deftly lay Lucy's unconscious body on the gurney. The time this had taken from Lucy collapsing to putting her on the stretcher was less than four minutes. He glanced at his watch. He still had six minutes until the suxamethonium had worn off knowing that the drugs potency was running out, he had to work quick.

Grabbing her left wrist and on the forearm, wrapped a pink rubber strap which had grabbed from the drop-down compartment in a large array of cubby holes on the side wall of the vehicle. Like a tourniquet, the pink strap retarded the return circulation of Lucy's blood. Caused a dilation of the vessels in her arm. Lucy was fit, cardiovascularly perfect, her veins as if on cue rose up like a loaf of bread rising in the oven. With a smooth, trained action, her skin covering her swollen veins, cleaned with a swab soaked in chlorhexidine. A sizeable bored cannula smoothly entered into the vein flashing back in the chamber telling the man he was in the right spot. With a dressing the man attached the drip that was already prepared in advance, two tubes ran into the junction that was screwed tightly into the cannula. He reached over her body, and two syringe pumps nearer Lucy's head were waiting patiently for the operator to press GO, he could smell the perfume she used, Jimmy Choo Flash. He knew her intimately, he studied everything about Lucy Hodges. He looked down at her face as the pumps whirled in the same smooth action of the door, albeit much quieter. Her skin was floorless, the slight bounce of her carotid arteries on each side of her throat was pulsating, rhythmically, she was at peace, the pumps pushing a concoction of Propofol, Remifentanil and midazolam into her veins keeping her deeply asleep. He looked at his watch, one minute to spare. The man sighed heavily. The hardest bit done.

He slumped back on the small chair attached to the wall under the black rubberized button, he could feel sweat under the rain-soaked skin. Her body connected to a monitor that showed Lucy's vital signs. He noted her vitals, pulled out his phone. Tapped a heart icon. Waited while the smartphone connected to the WIFI in the van. It only took three or four seconds. The same monitor layout appeared on the phone, then a second later, the smartphone duplicated Lucy's vitals. Precisely the same as the monitor fitted to the other side of the wall of the van. Blood pressure 116/69 - normal, oxygen saturation was 99% - normal, respiratory rate was 12 - normal, temperature 36.7 - normal, heart trace 65 beats per minute - regular and normal, carbon dioxide that was expired 4.5% - low but expected seeing as Lucy, flooded with hypnotic drugs. The man was satisfied.

He rose from the chair, rechecked Lucy's straps, covered her with a blanket.

Positioned himself at her head end, took the mask off, grabbed a metal laryngoscope. Inserted it into Lucy's throat in an upward motion, revealed the opening of Lucy's Trachea. Grabbed a breathing tube, inserted it into the hole, inflated the balloon to securely seal the airway, attached the breathing circuit, and hit vent on the anaesthetic machine. The mechanical ventilator kicked in like Darth Vader, Lucy's chest rising and falling in time with the sound.

Rechecked the vitals. Checked the air entry on both lungs with a stethoscope, he was happy.

Every space was utilised effectively, which meant he could freely move about the vehicle, he opened the door that connected the front of the van to the rear, eased himself into the drivers chair, set the satnav to Kings Stag, Dorset. The satnav already knew where he was going.

Pressed start, and the van clattered to life, he placed his smartphone in a holder by the gear stick, Lucy's parameters hadn't changed she was stable. Selected first gear. The Mercedes Sprinter lurched into life, and the man negotiated the van out of the car park. Turned right onto Osborne Street, slowly, and with purpose, drove to the T junction of Head Street. Turned right, at the top of the hill.

Traffic lights were red, the pub the Wagon and Horses on the left seemed to be spilling out onto the street. The man noticed a couple. She was shouting at what he thought was her boyfriend. The pedestrian light was green. He smiled, the guy is in trouble he thought. But he then thought that the women wearing that luminous green tight dress was far too overweight to wear that.

The light changed to green, the van lurched and stopped suddenly. As the girl went walk across the road thinking the green man was still giving the green light for her to pass but stopped as the van stopped.

"FUCKING HELL, Watch where you're going dude" she shouted. Waving her arms frantically as she carried on walking. This van wasn't going to stop her. The boyfriend shouted "ZARA....ZARA", she ignored him and carried on walking... The man in the van pursed his lips and bit his left cheek. A habit from childhood, as she passed, he raised his left foot and pressed his right foot. The clutch and throttle responded and the van slowly advanced. Gathering speed, across the junction, past the pub, and down the hill, the sign said railway station and the A12 link road to London, as the rain carried on falling, the red lights of the van disappeared into the wet night with the other cars on the road leaving the drunk calamity behind.

Lucy was gone.

2

The alarm burst into life. Resting on the radiator, vibrating through the hot steel. The exquisite sound of high-quality duck-down rustled as Alex, slowly stretched, separating her tired limbs, feeling that satisfying resistance right to her toes.

Her left hand exited the piles of material covering her slumped prostate body, fingers eagerly searching for the phone, like a spider trying to find its way across a wall. The fingers were finally touching the violence. A vibrating phone made all the worse by being amplified by the radiator fixed to the wall. It was for a reason. Alex had a strict morning routine that required her to wake, one hour earlier than usual. That included weekends, and Sundays are no different to Monday when Alex treated this hour, as her lifesaver.

Nonetheless, waking before the whole of suburban London, on the Sabbath, required a conduit of stimulation, and that conduit being the radiator.

Her fingers purchased the slim chassis of the phone, without looking out from the heavenly mounds of the duvet, and her thumb intuitively pressed STOP.

Alex immediately swung her legs to the floor. As her upper body reacted in an opposing way by sitting her upright. Eyes still closed, her tangled hair stuck to her face, and sticking up, running both her hands through the riotous strands attempting to smooth the mess down. It looked as though Alex, if a picture were taken, would seem as if she was upside down.

She exhaled, pursing her lips together, blowing out the air in an apparent attempt of protest.

"Jesus Alex" a voice came from under the duvet in a muffled almost groaned tone, "can't you make any more noise." Alex yawned and stretched at the same time as replying to her husband "sorry lovely, sore head?" she asked. Her husband Simon was out with the boys, Barcelona and Chelsea playing last night in the Camp Nou.

He woke her at precisely 2:45 AM, smelling of lager, kebabs and of course, cigarettes...which will be a sore conversation mentally scheduled for about 4 PM this afternoon.

"Yeah, just gonna lie here for a little longer", he moved, his right leg swung out from under the inferno of the duvet, and slammed into the top side of the covering. "I think it's your turn for coffee," he said.

At least that's what Alex thought he said with his head buried in his pillow. Alex leaned back, and tenderly patted his exposed right buttock cheek, "coming up, go back to sleep."

Alex shuffled into the kitchen still yawning, the cold tiles replacing the warm fibres of the carpet, this time, as though she was on mute, she still couldn't appreciate how tidy the house was. The house was silent.

Their two children were both at university. When they were home, the house was chaotic, messy yet…full of life. Now there was order and peace, that screamed louder than the chaos.

She loved it and hated at the same time. Her morning routine dictated that she should live in the now and appreciate the space around her. That's what the therapist said anyway.

Alex was a 'D' type personality. Driven, dogmatic and determined in everything she did. She expected nothing but the best from herself and her subordinates. Although expecting it from the head-shed, rarely got it. Getting her into hot water on lots of occasions. She often came across as acerbic, giving people the wrong impression of her. Once you got to know her, she was a strong ally, steadfastly loyal and a protectorate of the team. The dichotomy of her approach to life was that Alex was enormously spiritual, a passionate woman that loved life. A solitary hedgewitch, she found true healing in herbal remedies and pagan rituals, not really believing in the hocus-pocus of modern medicine. She questioned everything, even the kids rolling their eyes when something was amiss in a shop, Alex was ready to challenge everything that unfolded in front of her.

The first order of the day, meditating, get the coffee on, then go back upstairs and read her book while Si sleeps off his drunkenness. Meditating only took ten minutes, via an app on her phone. What did we do without mobile phones she pondered. Flicking to the right screen on her phone, located the icon of the meditating app.

A manila folder that Si had brought home was on the table. The A4 print out caught Alex's eye. The word Rocuronium was showing at the bottom corner of the report. It had idly slipped out. A drug name that came from a previous life when Alex was an anesthetic nurse in the army, before transferring to the military police in search of a bit more excitement.

That excitement transferred to the Metropolitan Police when the children got older.

The drug itself is pretty specialized and shouldn't be on any report that Si should have. Considering his vocation was Food Hygiene and Trading Standards. Curiously she opened the folder, and at the same time, raised her eyebrows in a comedic way. Looking alarmed, to ready the eyes to focus without the standard contact lenses.

The document was a meat processing report, a spot check audit of a food recycling plant at the Tilbury Docks, East of London. She only assumed that the drug administered to animals. But in the food chain, why?

Her knowledge from a previous world, coupled with the inquisitive mind of now. Her police murder squad suspicion was kicking in, although on extended sick leave. The shrink had diagnosed post traumatic stress disorder after a particularly brutal murder case that went horribly wrong. She was 47 years old, had turned to the London suburban housewife life.

It didn't fit. Pottery, yoga, meditation and skinny lattes with almond slices with her lady friends in the mornings. The pull of the job was growing daily in her mind. The pottery, yoga blah blah blah just wasn't her.

Soon, she would disappoint Simon. He was hoping she would get a taste of the good life and give up the force. Maybe that shouldn't be brought up when she bollocks him smoking!

The morning routine was for these precise exercises, leaving her the rest of the day to contemplate.

However, the file had intrigued her. With her left hand she caressed the pagan tree of life pendant always around her neck, her right index finger underlining the words as she struggled to read the report.

The kettle thumped its completion, which made Alex jump instigating a sense of guilt, no morning routine toda, she tutted under her breath, hearing her mother's voice chastise her yet again.

Alex got up, and gingerly padded over to the kettle, poured two cups of instant joe. Si is going to hate this she thought. He only likes filter, but she forgot to get a new bag while shopping. She poured the steam swirling out of the cup, her gaze swung slowly over to the file on the table "Food of Unknown Origin," "rocuronium," she said, seems odd, this wasn't right…!

She grabbed the cups in each hand and padded back to the hallway, the manila folder coming into her peripheral vision. She paused, looking up through into the hall. With a sigh she turned, padded over to the kitchen table. Reached across, and grabbed the folder, stuffed the thin wallet under her arm.

Alex came into the bedroom like one of those Chinese game shows…awkwardly. Si opened one eye, he smiled "CRACKERJACK" he shouted which was muffled in the pillow as only half his face was exposed. A '70s game show for kids, if you didn't respond back, as a forfeit you received a cabbage...only '70s kids know this apparently!

She chose to ignore it!

With a clunk and a slop of coffee, unavoidably running down the sides making a small moat circling the cup on Si's side. He looked up by propping his body on his elbows. For a man in his late forties, he still has definition. His back was chiseled, individual bulges of muscles around the shoulder blades and flanks, "ooooh" Si said, "That's just the ticket."

He flipped his lithe body over, Alex observed not in a way she would do it. In three stages of groaning and inflexible limbs protesting to their limit, her movement was almost agricultural.

As Alex shuffled around their bed, Si complained "eww, instant." Alex mouthed the words as Si said it. "Sorry love," with her free hand she flipped her side of the duvet over and lifted her right leg, perched on the side of the bed, cupping the cup with both hands. Si could see, in the sunlight probing through the wooden blinds, balls of suspended water in the steam of her cup, he loved the mornings with his wife.

"You found my file" Si said while motioning with his head. He knew Alex would have an opinion when he did the spot audit at the plant.

"Have you read it" Si asked, smelling his coffee, sipping it and then using the bottom of his lip to stop the predictable dribble of coffee down the side of the mug. Alex loved Si the moment she met him while she was in the military police. He had little quirks that just made her smile, this was one of them, sometimes while at work she would do the same, both children did it too, making her laugh on family holidays when all three would do it almost in unison. When will she see that again she thought.

"Yeah I read it briefly" Alex replied, "what's the deal," she said while sipping her drink.

"We don't know. Its meat of an unknown origin, that means it's not part of the farming five". Alex looked at him.

"Farming five?" she asked.

"Umm," Si replied, interrupting his sip, "Yeah, the farming five" he held out his hand "chicken, turkey, beef, lamb and pork," with each meat, he raised his thumb and fingers in unison to the meat. Alex frowned, "what does that mean?"

"It means we don't have scope to test this meat out, compoters don't check others like alligator, kangaroo, and… monkey" his soft almost nonexistent Norfolk accent still on some words like computer.

"MONKEY" Alex blurted, she stared at Si, "who eats monkey, like, I mean, I haven't seen that in the meat aisle at either Waitrose or Sainsbury's" she said.

"Lidl's sells it," Si said. For a moment Alex was considering the truth in that, her friend Sally had cooked her a beef casserole, and the meat was tough as old boots. That meat was from Lidl's, but they, at the time thought it was a donkey. Laughing as they tipped it in the trash while ordering pizza! She noticed another idiosyncrasy of Si when he was joking with her. He forced his lips down in an attempt to stop smiling.

"Gross, even if it's MONKEY" Alex overemphasized the word, "I don't know what this drug is doing in the food chain, period."

Si cupped his right hand over his nose and mouth, and pulled down wiping away the drunkenness and sleep from his face.

"What do you think, we are about to close this down because we don't know where it is from, there's no evidence of anything other than the fact that this a weird test result, there's no governance issue here because we don't know whose door to knock on." There was a pause, "the meat has been disposed of correctly, and we are confident the meat is not in the food chain, it's just the company hasn't followed the right disposal regulations," Si looked at her…

"Have you still got the meat" Alex asked.

"Probably, I'll have to make a call though. There's a chance it's already binned. I only want your take on it Alex. I don't want you to get involved in something that's not there" Si said, knowing the stress that Alex was under, and having to look after her after her final murder case that had gone horribly wrong.

"It's okay lovely, if you can get me a sample of the meat. I will get a contact in a path lab to test it. Knowing its origin may help you, I mean."

Alex laid down, looking up at her man, "if there's some impropriety going on, or some weird religious group eating things they shouldn't, then you've done good right."

Si knew Alex was right. He needed to close the loop. The file had been bothering him, for no apparent reason, other than the fact that Simon was a perfectionist. Liked things finished. He grabbed his phone, opened it and was looking for Ed's message history, so he could text. "I didn't mean now," Alex said, her hand sliding down Si's abdomen, feeling his soft pubic hair and the smooth shaft of his manhood, gently retracting the skin back, instantly feeling the definite swell.

She looked up, he was still looking at his phone, he felt her gaze, Si looked down at her while still typing, paused as the right chemicals in his body filled the right cells releasing the right enzymes, making him think of the most erotic thoughts. He breathed out deeply. Another idiosyncrasy Alex noticed as Si narrowed his eyes. She could feel his fire in him. This turned her on even more. As Alex slowly went back and forth on his shaft and locking her want into his eyes and smiling. He tossed his phone, pulled the duvet back, and with a groan, he feasted on his wife.

3

The service station McDonalds was springing to life, the sweet smell of fast food being ruined by teenagers. Weekend punters were coming in thick and fast for coffee and pastries.

To Twickers, fetes, kayaking, air-soft and divorced parents running across the country to spend a couple of hours with their children, every customer was heading to different locations yet having one thing in common, the toilet or a refuel with a piece of carb heaven.

Broc was outside, under the poplar trees, sipping a hot coffee on a wobbly picnic set. The wobbly table dug into the soft earth and all but ruined the surrounding grass. The table was awash of pigeon poop, empty fast food wrappings and cups. The ground littered with spent cigarettes.

The drive from Colchester in the rain was slow and onerous. He was tired. He chose local roads circumnavigating the M25, the ring road that borders central London from the rest of the United Kingdom.

Checking road traffic conditions, road works were almost at every junction during the weekend. Being snarled up in a road closure, or an accident wasn't worth the risk. He joined the M3 north of Fleet, near Aldershot, where he gunned the van at a quicker pace knowing the service station wasn't far. He rubbed his eyes longingly for some respite, but there was none when his hand left his face. He could see the van. Always in sight of his prey. Lucy was the 27th victim Broc had kidnapped.

Nestled in the lorry park, in the shadow of the tall trees, the view from the picnic area Broc was sitting had a view of the filling station, where traffic police always sat eating bacon rolls and sipping hot tea spying the approach road to the main carriageway, checking out the cars leaving.

By day, he was a celebrated, gifted general surgeon, dealing with the liver, stomach and pancreas as well as renal and hepatic liver transplantation surgery. Working as a consultant part-time in London, with a long waiting list of patients with an equally long list of satisfied patients that had survived their encounter with either cancer addiction-related disease or genetic malformations at his slick surgical hand.

Broc was well known in the Royal College of Surgeons and for good reason. His seminal paper, published twelve years earlier had changed the face of liver surgery and had brought accolades to the institution.

Broc loved lecturing the new aspiring young surgeons in anatomy, going into great detail of every aspect of the structures dissected out on cadavers in the cutting rooms in the bowels of St. Bartholomew's, in the King George Suit, under the shadow of St. Paul's cathedral in central London.

His opening lecture on anatomy was titled Human Beings Are Identical: The Only Thing that Separates us is Upbringing and Education.

Students and surgical trainees came from all over the world. In some cases, to work for nothing, just to be mentored by the Great Broc, the liver supremo.

Rumour had it, he was general surgeon to the Windsor family but was never substantiated. Even so, Broc, like his father before him, was destined for greatness and a knighthood before his 50th birthday.

By night, however, he had an alias. Broc was called Saunders. Kevin Saunders, who kidnapped women, that fit criteria for transplantation and removed their organs.

The transplantation world is rigorously controlled by strict policies and procedures that protect both the donor and recipient, along with government legislation. Money for transplantation is strictly forbidden. The downside of this, people have to join lists. People with money and the right contact skirt around the vulgarity of waiting.

So the very rich in America, China and the United Arab Emirates pay and circumvent these policies by paying into an underground transplantation organization that procures the right specimen for the right patients and of course, for the right price. The super rich can muscle their way to have exactly what they want. David Rockefeller, had undergone no less than six heart transplants in 38 years. Where your average Joe, if they were lucky, had one, when that failed, that was that. A hole in the ground beckoned.

The organization worked exclusively, for decades on the black market, now with the internet and the dark web, the organization has expended.. Their tariff was simple, when a donation was required the parameters were sent to the key surgeons; Broc was one of five surgeons globally.

Historically, the surgeon would wait for a patient that was suitable to come into their practices. There, they would, if possible, come to an arrangement and remove a partial segment of liver, or kidney. If the patient was near death, wait until natural causes took them and then removed the required organs. It had a tremendous failure rate, with wealthy patients often left dying before the organ was located, or dying of a massive failure within the organ after it was transplanted. The providence of the organ was often omitted by the surgeon. Patients, such as women who had died of breast cancer, would usually have a metastasized tumor markers in the liver. When a wealthy Texan oil billionaire or a Russian oligarch died of breast-related cancer in the liver, it left the coroners scratching their heads.

Broc was different. Much different. His organs were of the highest quality. Fresh, young and pathology free. No one asked why, or where he got them from, he just delivered on his promise.

Sometimes it took a while. Sometimes it was quick. In Lucy's case, the request came six weeks earlier. Plumbing the genetic markers and hemodynamics into his phone along with age, sex…he preferred women. Not for sexual needs, but for other reasons. Females were often statistically more fit than men, the complex female anatomy excited Broc, and women readily visited their family doctors more frequently than males, especially for fertility issues such as aches, pains and conception challenges.

All these require the family doctor to perform a full blood count, which incidentally, included the necessary parameters for transplantation, again by design. The health authority was creating a database called HAEMOmatch. Clinicians could access patient genetics and hemodynamic markers from possible transplantation if the patient in question was involved in a traumatic event. Clinicians had instant access to the data, pairing the right recipients for donation, the research paper that addressed this issue, created an international ethical debate. Thus, creating a business plan to implement the strategy. Within a year of the article by Broc. D et al (2009) the HAEMOmatch program was up and running pushed relentlessly by Broc, then allowing Broc, anonymously to have access to the network.

Any person that matched the criteria on the national blood sampling unit would send a push notification to Broc's phone. There, Broc would investigate the requirement of the blood sample. It could be a hospital admission because of trauma such as road traffic accident or picked up for being drunk on a Saturday night. As long as the specimen was fit, healthy, female and wasn't a cancer risk, Broc would take the investigation to the next level.

A man of detail, he would locate the specimen and then spend at least three weeks tailing them, he knew Lucy was about to start a new career as a midwife. He also hacked into their social media profiles and any other online systems they may be on and got to know them. Where their family lived in proximity to the victim, would they be alerted if the women were taken, what was their work route, what public transport did they take, where their car was parked, which day they went to the supermarket. In a previous case, he registered with a dating app where a victim was frequently promiscuous. Matched the corresponding data, arranged a meet, went on a date, to a high-end restaurant. They had sex in the back of the car, in her house, all night long, and then on a separate occasion, kidnapped her and murdered her then removed all of her organs. Her begging still gave Broc goosebumps.

In some cases, he paid homeless drug abusers to burgle the houses, and steal anything of pertinence. By the time Broc had planned the kidnap, he would know every aspect of the specimen's life. He knew that Lucy's boyfriend, Harvey, would be pacing uncontrollably around the house right now. He knew that Harvey would have received a photo of Lucy that Broc would have taken on Lucy's phone. Then he would set her phone to low power, secure it in a forensically cleaned envelope posted to the Aberdeen post office. When she was officially declared missing the police would track the phone to the sorting depot of the central post office at 38 Ashgrove Road, Aberdeen.

The video Broc sent to Harvey was explicit and for a good reason. On her knicker line was a tattoo of Snoopy, a regretful moment in her first year of university. He messaged the video to Harvey's phone. The message read I think we are done Harvey, I met my old boyfriend Peter tonight, I am going back to Scotland with him now, this will be the last time you see this!

The message ended, followed by close up video of her tattoo and finishing between her legs.

Broc had to send the video, in order to stop Harvey going to the police, making the trail as cold as possible when the police went searching. Broc knew Harvey would be rounding up all her friends, colleagues and those she went to school with; old boyfriends and even go into fits of rage where he may injure himself, delaying the police report even more so.

Lucy's hemodynamics were a good fit, almost all of her organs were going to a Chinese businessman, who was 65. He didn't need the organs. Apparently, he had the notion that if he had younger organs, he would live longer, what an idiot Broc thought. Lunatic he pondered. Who's the real lunatic here. He drained his coffee, checked his phone, Lucy's vitals were stable. Heart rate was elevated which was most probably a full bladder, he'd rectify that in a minute, he flipped to the camera app in his van, Lucy was safe and sound, probably awake at this point. Still unable to move as the paralyzing drug had now changed to Rocuronium. It had the same effect as the suxamethonium, the onset of the drug was slower, but the result was much longer. Typically a 50mg dose would last more than an hour. The syringe driver was trickling in a target controlled amount of 50mgs over 50 minutes, guaranteeing paralysis. He rose from the table and wandered towards the van and considered how he got to this point in his life.

As a child, Dale Broc was emotionally ruined by his father, a neurosurgeon, who was internationally renowned for his practice. His father abused Broc emotionally and sexually, cruel with his comments, and lived in a state of perpetual negativity. Nothing was good enough for his father unless he had absolute control of everything in his life, including his wife and child.

The sexual part of the abuse wasn't penetrative, but in a way that removed Broc's sexual development. Broc didn't sexually develop in a way any healthy child with a healthy upbringing would experience. To that end, Broc didn't know if he was heterosexual or gay. Men sexually excited Broc as much as women, but having meaningful relationships was impossible as Broc experienced chronic impotence; this could have also been from his schooling at Eaton. Housemasters abused their powers, sexually degrading the young in their care, no one cared. The authorities were part of the problem as they were often there abusing the children along with the housemasters.

It made him angry, leading to awkward encounters while at medical school. The women in question were always 'understanding' but nevertheless, sexual gratification, achieved only through extreme pornography and the use of chemical adjuncts, such as Cialis or Viagra.

While going through Broc's surgical training in London, Broc immersed himself in the underground sex scene. At the time in the late 80's and early 90's, sex clubs were frowned upon. Secret networks where only the willing, who were robustly vetted could attend. Broc had passion and a thirst for inflicting pain on young women. Coupled with an abundance of cash gave him a season-pass in the most tawdry and seedy of venues.

The clientele were wealthy, obese businessman. Unhappy with their annual blow jobs and lean sex lives. Sat in dark, dingy basements of affluent hotels that were filled with the smog of cigar smoke, escort girls prowling around naked, serving drinks, any girl could be sexually used at any point in the room, the drugs the girls were forced to take saw to that. The room would have annexes to the main room where the real perversions occurred. Public school boys that had a taste for the young and the weird, parliamentary officials, and celebrities that abused their positions, anything went, children, mature, animals, no one ever questioned one's perversion.His mentor in the sex scene was a well-known minister in the government that had taste for boys just barely legal.

He mentored Broc in his perverseness. He slapped Broc on the back at the bar "What's one man's perversion is another man's normality, eh?" he snorted. Broc remembered seeing this minister on the news a few hours earlier. Seemed wrong, there was even access to snuff movies, these commanded the highest price, to watch a girl get brutally raped then murdered would set you back £500 in 1990, weirdly, these can be viewed for nothing on your smartphones now.

Murder or underage wasn't his style, he didn't like it, nor agree with it, the inside of the human body is the most sacred and beautiful piece of art anyone can cast their eyes on.

Broc went to these events so he could vent his fetishes of BDSM. He enjoyed the company of young girls, not so young that would attract the suspicions of the law, yet young enough to ruin the future of the girl in question. There the girl would be tied to a sawhorse, where the same overweight men would repeatedly rape the girl at both ends, Broc would watch in the corner mostly horrified but sexually stimulated. He would finish by whipping the young girl's flesh until she bled. This was his ejaculation. He didn't need the muscular spasm in his groin and the spreading of his seed. He just, for that moment, when her blood flowed, and she writhed, shackled to the sawhorse in agony, ejaculated in his mind.

He tried boys, didn't like them. He tried men. Equally, he hated the experience. Dated young female doctors from sensible backgrounds, the kind of women that were shamelessly paraded for a suitable sire in the pages of Country Life by the women's parents were as much of a turn off as fellating another man in the public toilets in Waterloo railway station.

What excited Broc, was anatomy. The human body in it full artistic glory. Finely dissecting the layers of tissue, revealing the delicate structures, through the skin into the fascia, then through the muscles, exposing the vascular structures, the nerves, and how they interact with the tissues and the organs.

While on a fellowship in Springfield, Illinois he met Gunter Schwab, MD. The liver surgeon had a private practice at the lakeside of Lake Decatur 40 miles east of the state capitol.

A small isolated industrial town with a large lake. Schwab would hold parties in his boathouse near Moose Country Club. Similar to the parties Broc attended in London, but not so extreme. It was here that both Schwab and Broc were approached by Tao Ng, a Chinese businessman that worked for an underground organ transplant syndicate. Broc remembered Ng being so matter of fact and intimidating.

Schwab, money driven not patient centred, Broc, seeing this as a business opportunity and a reason to slake his thirst on the vulnerable agreed to join the syndicate and answer to Ng who paid them a retainer for their services. The arrangement was perfect. The retainer secured their silence, while their connection to a well connected Chinese thug that was part of a triad gang would result in them, their families and anyone that cared to be involved with Schwab and Broc being killed. Not to mention the syndicate kept detailed accounts of evidence, including the conversation they were having at the time.

Broc perfected his skills, he was creative with anything mechanical, he worked his skills on designing the perfect instruments for his trade. Used modern technology that was freely available on the high street. Paid tutelage to young computer hackers to understand intrinsically the proliferation of secure networks. There was no secure network he couldn't enter. It took a few years to hone these skills and find the right location, but he made his first job work seven years earlier. She was a young female specimen called Victoria, he harvested all her organs and sent them via courier in packages specially designed. So perfect and efficient was his operation, that Ng prioritized the orders to Broc, in London. Once the specimen was harvested, he would dissect every aspect of the living corpse. When finished, the entire body and anything left of it was fed into an industrial meat mincer and disposed of.

Broc got to the van and opened the driver's side. It smelt clinical in the truck. He disarmed the disablement device as it was connected to an oxidizing incendiary device that would incinerate every aspect of the van. It would be the type of fire the fire brigade would cordon off, and wait until it had died out, as nothing could extinguish the flames. There would be no trace left, including any evidence, nothing. This device made Broc nervous, it could be operated from his phone, but the detonator proved difficult to perfect. The app on the phone clicked green, telling Broc the device was now disarmed.

Broc looked out through the windscreen, pausing to survey the view in front of him, the van was positioned equally as strategically where he had sat drinking his coffee. Broc could see the whole building and truck park, the vegetation at the rear would have made it impossible for anyone to gain entry into the van. Also, anyone coming would have to approach in full sight of Broc.

Once clear, with his right hand, he deftly felt for the latch to the connecting door, his fingers located it, turned it, and in a swift, smooth, action, he was through the door and into the rear of the van.

The lights flickered on, making that heavy click of the starters of the true-white fluorescent light spark to life. Lucy was motionless. Under her blanket, she was still in her dress.

Her shoes tossed casually underneath. Broc straightened them. Her heart rate was 95 beats per minute. He leaned over her carefully. Her heart rate spiked to 120.

She was present!

4

Lucy was staring up at the van ceiling. She could feel everything. Lucy's lower back was painful, like when you would spend too long in bed on a Sunday morning, the low light to her right, had sounds emanating from it. Lucy went to move her head in the direction, but her thoughts just remained like that, just thoughts. She was confused, her muscles were screaming, as the lactic acid was rising. What was going on, she thought?

She remembered the previous evening, walking to her car, she remembered the man in the car park, she remembered falling and wetting herself, then him placing the mask over her face and the familiar smell of the anesthetic gas. Lucy felt weirdly warm, not cold considering the alarming state she thought she was in, she felt safe.

There was no doubt she was in a van. She could see the fittings in the thin roof. There was a whirling circular contraption, she guessed was the other side you see when a builders van goes past, driving fresh air into the rear of the van, spinning in the wind.

There was a sound from outside. She felt someone approach the van. All her muscles remained dormant. Dead like, she couldn't scream, she was trying to tense up, but nothing, she couldn't sit up, she couldn't even use her hands to protect her modesty. The van clunked and then the familiar sound of a security system was bleeping. The same sound she remembered last night.

The driver's door opened, she could hear the scrapping of the man's shoes on the tarmac outside. The man heaved himself in, there was manly grunt as he did, the van dipped momentarily on its suspension and then the door slammed shut. There was a pause, then the switching of levers and the audible sound of computerized devices. Her hearing, augmented, could hear everything, even his breathing. It was laboured. The inner door latch made a noise, and the door opened and the lights, like razor blades cut through Lucy's eyes as the irises in her eyes narrowed rapidly, as the brilliant light started burning the back of her retinas. Her autonomic thoughts screamed at her to raise her hands to shield her eyes, nothing moved. Her eyes in a fixed stare, unable to move, she was desperate to see the man that had taken her. Without her eyes moving, it didn't take long for him to come into view, she could feel him manipulating draws and pressing buttons. Lucy felt him come into her space. Felt his hands on either side of her body, resting on the trolley. His face came into view, she smelt the coffee. Lucy wanted to scream. His face was calm and gentle, with solid features, but her predicament argued with her rationalizing how the man looked, she was paralyzed on a trolly in the back of van, THAT THIS MAN HAD DONE! WHY, WHY, WHY...The man lowered his face nearer Lucy, she thought he was going to kiss her, she tried to reel back, but nothing, she had no clue where this encounter was heading, but where ever it was going, Lucy knew there was nothing that she could do to control the situation.

"Lucy, my name is Dale Broc." He adjusted himself to not lean on her delicate body. He moved closer to her ear, his breath hot, not unpleasant, the coffee strong. In her mind's eye, her eyes widened in abject horror. "I have taken you. This will not end well for you. In the next 48 hours, I will harvest all of your organs and then end your life. I know your feeling confused right now." He went on, "There will be no going back for you now, you must come to terms with your situation, I will try my best to make sure you don't feel anything."

Broc lifted himself up, looked into her soul, and paused. He held her gaze. He swore he could see her pleading in her eyes. It did nothing to Broc in his conscious. Lucy stared back at him, trying to fathom what he had just said. On balance, she felt like she preferred being raped and dumped. What the fuck did he mean, harvest my organs? she thought.

Broc looked down, "Your heart rate is elevated, Lucy because your bladder is full, so I am going to catheterize you. This will make you more comfortable." Broc started assembling some items that were needed. Lucy thought, this guy has just told me he wants to kill me, yet he's taking care of my basic needs, she was confused. "Although you can't feel that now, I need you to be comfortable." Broc said out of sight. There was a coldness to his tone, a matter of fact. Lucy's situation couldn't get any more surreal. She felt him tug at her knickers. The shame Lucy felt as Broc defiled her dignity. The knickers finally gave and snapped in his hand. He cursed. Raised her right knee with her foot firmly on the trolly surface, and let it gently fall to her right. Lucy felt compromised in an unprecedented way. She heard the familiar snap of sterile gloves. She was paralyzed, yet conscious and about to be catheterized in her bladder from a person that had just kidnapped her, not 60 seconds earlier, the same man that had told her life was now over.

Broc picked up a swab from the catheter care packaging already soaked in sterile water. With his free hand, he parted her vulva to expose the inner labia, the vaginal orifice was visible. She wasn't a virgin. Above that was the tiny urethral opening, the hole in which Broc was looking for, he mused for a second. Lucy's anatomy wasn't ruined by the ravages of childbirth, nor will it ever.

With the swab, in a downward motion, wiped Lucy's innermost parts. She consciously winced, she could feel the heat of embarrassment seep from every pore in her body and the drag of the cold swab on her vagina, it felt like wet hands on rhubarb, scratchy and uncomfortable. Lucy could feel Broc's fingers probe her femininity, the coldness in his action wasn't sexual in any way. It was clinical and hideous, as though one of the old matrons on the labor ward were doing it. Broc then inserted the latex catheter. Lucy had catheterized many women in labor, as the catheter slid in, she felt the thicker part about an inch from the tip scrape through the opening, it felt how she imagined while performing catheterization herself. The catheter went up to the hilt of the channels at the other end, 20 inches or so. Then Broc inflated the balloon with a syringe. His knuckles pressed into her vagina as he pushed, causing pain to Lucy. He then tugged on it and felt the resistance as the inflated balloon inside the bladder bounced freely off the urethral opening on the inside. Broc knew the catheter was in the right place. At the same time, clear urine flowed freely from Lucy's body into a catheter bag fitted to the end of the pipe. Lucy was violated in a way she could never imagine, this whole process seemed almost funny, yet horrifyingly real.

Broc lowered her leg, stood and removed his gloves. "That should make you feel much better, Lucy." he said in an almost caring voice. Lucy felt compelled to thank him.

Broc checked the drugs, her vital signs, fluids, now the catheter, she was a regular temperature still, so no artificial warming. He leaned over Lucy again. A tear seeped out the corner of her eye, Broc noticed. "There's no need to cry, Lucy." Broc said, with a tissue, he retrieved from one of the drawers, wiped the tear away. "I shall make your harvest as painless as possible, I can't guarantee though, but you are going to serve a higher purpose." he said.

A higher purpose, Lucy thought. She was about to start her dream career, waiting for Harvey to get down on one knee. Have a couple of kids. Live a free and happy life. This jerk tells me I am for a higher purpose; Go fuck yourself, she thought, more tears and they flowed more freely now.

He leaned further, Broc looked down again, he saw the tears, guilt never entered his psyche, all emotions relating to guilt, embarrassment, dignity were wholly absent from Broc's mind and Lucy could feel the fuzziness she felt before, cloud her head. Broc was adjusting her blankets, "Just some sedation, Lucy. We have at least another two hours to your final stop, I don't want you to be concerned." The remark almost felt like a joke, but Broc wasn't joking. Lucy's consciousness drifted to oblivion and total hypnosis. Broc covered her eyes with dark-like swimming goggles, to preserve the moisture in her eyes. Meticulously, Broc rechecked his phone. Vitals normal, heart rate had dipped to normal beats again. The catheter had done the trick, he checked the securing straps, made sure they were not causing any tissue damage to Lucy's delicate skin, he was happy.

Broc entered the driving compartment, in the time that he was in the rear with Lucy, more than twelve vehicles of different sizes had come to the carpark, to his right, a man in a fluorescent vest was approaching, motioning a circular movement with his hand. Broc instantly wound his window down. "Can I help?" Broc asked.

The man, portly, mid-fifties, with florid cheeks and an unshaven face, his face was full of self-importance, his belly was hanging from his untucked ill-fitting shirt like a tongue on a comedy cartoon caricature. "You need to move your van, mate!" he shouted, he stopped at the van, out of breath, Broc thought this man probably calls everyone mate.

"Your van should be parked in the other carpark, this apron is for the artics." he jerked his right thumb to the trucks stationary behind him.

"I am just leaving," Broc said. Bewildered as the carpark wasn't even a third full. The man was trying to see into the back of the van as Broc was speaking, weaving his head from side to side, Broc matched his head movements, like mating swans, the man got the message.

"I was looking for you not ten minutes ago, how did you get into the van without me seeing you, mate?" the parking attendant asked, still shouting, and still out of breath. Broc nodded his head to the rear of the van "I was in the back, just securing my load." Broc engaged first gear, "OK" the man said, "In future, park over there." He pivoted on his worn-out work boots, the steel toe cap glinting in the sunlight through the leather. Pointed over to the grassy knoll where Broc had been sitting and through to the main car park."Sorry for your inconvenience." Broc said, "Thank you as well for your advice, I'll remember that on another occasion, you have a pleasant day kind sir" Broc finished, lifted the clutch. The man turned to Broc and nodded while pursing his lips, posh toff, more brains than common sense he thought. "No sweat, mate," he remarked hiding his real thoughts. His face told Broc what the man was thinking anyway. Broc joined the cars snaking their way out of the service station and on to the carriageway. Broc looked in his rearview mirror. The man was standing still, watching him leave, that was the second time that same man had approached Broc. Have to change my route Broc thought, I can't risk this jobsworth clocking me again.

The man watched the van slowly ebb its way to the main concourse to the carriageway, the wind picking up, lifting his shirt higher above his exposed belly, he knew he had spoken to the guy before, the next time he's getting a ticket, poncey bell-end he thought and turned about to seek some other parking infringement.

Broc joined the carriage way. The satnav said 90 miles, one hour and 58 minutes. With no traffic restrictions, he settled in. Broc clicked play on the smartphones music library. Clicked back to Lucy's vitals, vitals -normal. The opening intro to Penny Lane by the Beatles came to life; two hours, then he'd be home comforted in the knowledge that the kidnap phase would be over, then safety and dissection, Broc tapped his finger in time to the music, following the sun to the South West of England.

5

The game had finished, Harvey was watching the endless replays of his favorite team Arsenal; Sucking air in and shouting obscenities at the screen as his team in his opinion, blundered around the pitch. Concerned that Barcelona had beaten the Chelski scum on the first round of the European Championship, now the Gooner's had to face Barca at Camp Nou as well, he would have a preferred a London derby final in the Stade De Paris in the summer, probably be a Spanish affair that had become the norm. Valverde's team was looking good this season, Wenger's side wasn't going to make it through, he just knew it. Half the Barca team was made up of previous Gooner players anyway.

Harvey had scoffed his frozen pizza grilled to cremation and drained a fair few Stellas. The lids littered the kitchen and the empties lazily hung around the coffee table. He had that mellow Saturday night-in feeling. Tonight, after a few pink gins and cocktails, Lucy will be in no state to stop him from doing as he pleased. She liked it. He loved it. It wasn't anything weird, just adventurous.

He received a text from Lucy at nearly 11 pm. The text said she was leaving in a couple of minutes. In about 35 minutes, he would be exploring her drunken naked body right on this couch. But nothing came, 45 minutes later his phone vibrated. As Broc had predicted, Harvey was pacing. He had sobered up slightly. Feeling insecure and anxious, where the fuck was she! he thought. He picked up his phone, a message from

Lucy, probably at the taxi rank, bloody Mohammed is busy. Why can't she use another taxi he thought?

Harvey went red "BITCH" he shouted and threw his phone down. The video playing over and over again, "Fuck, Fuck!!" Harvey's mind was racing. She's leaving me, "Who's this fucking Pete?" he picked his phone up again.

Lucy's tattoo was visible, the small mole on the left side of her labia fully visible, and the unmistaken hand that belongs to a man, the hand was strong, long fingers, the nails weren't that of a working man. His mind raced, recalling, like a hard drive, all the conversations that he had had with Lucy, past lovers and sexual conquests.

The standard confessions couples make when they go steady. He was trying to remember a Pete. There was a Pete, a Scottish chap, Lucy had said. They didn't have sex, but Lucy said that he was a perfect man, until Harvey came along. At the time, Harvey thought Lucy was lying. He could see there was a spark there when she mentioned his name. This video and message, I can't imagine, fuck!

He double clicked the home screen, found Lilly's number.

"This better be good, Harvey." the voice said on the other side, Harvey could hear she had company.

"Where's Lucy, she just sent me a text, she's just fucking binned me, the bitch got an old boyfriend fingering he…" Lilly cut him off.

"What do mean Harvey, are you pissed, I left Lucy at the Wagon and Horses, she was coming home for a bit of action, what are you talking about, she's binned you?" Harvey could hear her move about and a guy's voice, muffled, "Who are you with?" Harvey enquired.

Harvey had forwarded her the same two messages he had received, the text and the video. "I have messaged you." he stated.

There was a pause, Lilly was accessing her phone, the guys' voice again, a little clearer, "Who's on the phone?" a strong voice said, probably a soldier, Harvey mentally checked that he shouldn't ask Lilly who she was with!

"I've got it." Lilly proclaimed, "What the fuck, Harvey?" she had seen it. More shuffling, "Hold on a sec," Harvey heard a closing of a door, and then the opening of another, Lilly's voice had become slightly echoey, "I saw Lucy, not more than an hour ago Harvey, I don't under…" Harvey cut her off "Did you meet this, Pete?" Harvey demanded.

Pete, she thought, what had Pete got to do with this "Once or twice." Lilly said, she was searching the same portal of hard drives as Harvey, just from a different perspective.

"He was Scottish infantry, he was on a course, based in.." she paused, "Cyprus" she found the data needed, "based in Cyprus." Harvey could hear in her voice, she was concerned.

"Lilly, did Lucy tell you anything, anything at all?" her concern was now mirroring on to him.

"No!" she replied, she was confused, her normality had shifted on her paradigm.

"Pete was here for about six weeks, he was on some airborne course." Harvey could see her her thinking, "It was a fling, he went back to Cyprus. She was kind of upset when he left. They had some moments, nothing special though. She got over it pretty quickly." Harvey heard her voice falter, as though she was going to cry, Lilly and Lucy shared everything. She didn't mention anything about leaving tonight, nothing about Pete, if anything she was nauseatingly gushing about going home to Harvey.

"Why are you crying, Lilly?" Harvey urged. "She told me everything Harv, literally everything…I am so confused." Harvey heard the door knock on Lilly's end, heard her get up, there were some muffled voices.

A man's' voice boomed into Harvey's ear "Mate, Lilly hasn't seen Lucy, we left her at the bar in the wagon, have you tried anyone else?"

"Who the fuck are you?" Harvey demanded, how does he know Lucy!

"That's not important bro," the voice said, "but you're disturbing my night with Lilly, now be a good boy, and fuck off." With that, the line went dead.

Harvey stared at his phone in astonishment, he double clicked the home button again, found Zara's number and clicked call.

"Aye pet, what's up?" the Geordie accent, unmistakably Zara.

"Have you seen Lucy?" desperation in his voice, engaged Zara's attention immediately, Harvey heard the TV mute.

"Noo, I haven't pet, left her at the bar, me shag let us down, so came home watching a bit of the Googlebox" Her Geordie accent, stronger after a few drinks, "Why's that, pet?"

"She's gone." Harvey said, the realization, Lucy had gone, his voice cracked.

"Don't be daft, man, she probably stuck waitin for a cab, bloody packed up the toon," she said.

Harvey found the messages from Lucy, pushed forward, the same message he sent to Lilly, "I have sent you two text messages." There was a pause, he heard her fumble with her phone, her breathing audible, and regular.

"Fooking hell man, what's that about?" she blurted watching the video. "Hev yes been drinkin, gan tee drive yor screeve."

Harvey didn't know what she meant, "Sorry Zara, in English."

"Nee bother, ah meant can ye drive, 'ave ye bin drinkin."

Harvey filled the gaps, he understood, can he drive. "I smashed a couple of Stellas, definitely over the limit, plod everywhere in town, not worth..."

Zara cut him off, " Nee bother, going to get a cab, I'll be at yours in an hoor," Harvey heard her gather some things, "Try callin debs, or her Mam, see yee in a tick, pet." The line went dead.

Harvey slumped down on to the edge of the sofa. His phone dropped to the floor at the same time. He stared blankly in front of him, empty, angry, how could she do this, he thought! It didn't feel right. The phone flashed into life, text!

Harvey bent down, picked up his phone. It was Lilly.

Just been on Pete's Facebook profile, the guy is in Cyprus, he's just posted a picture of himself in Limassol, whoever that hand was, it wasn't Pete!'

Harvey reread the text. He didn't know what to do. He only knew Lilly and Zara, the rest of her friends were transient. Disappeared after their three-year course had ended. Whoever she knew now, including the growler he spoke to on the phone was anyone's guess. Facebook, why didn't I think of that, he thought.

Harvey found the app on his phone, he wasn't a regular Facebooker, more a stalker, like most men. He had a profile, and the only images he had on there were of Lucy, his brother and a couple of mates from work who had tagged him, he never got it, more intrusive than anything else. Harvey didn't quite get that today, your whole life is on show.

Although, he spent time viewing Lucy's facebook page closely, passively policing her movements and the people that she encountered. There where so many posts and pictures just in the last two weeks. He clicked her friends' list...how can you have more than one thousand friends, Harvey thought. The friends Harvey had, counted on one hand, where do you start.

His phone rang, it was Lilly.

"Harve, sorry babes, Tom's a bit of gruff, he's had a few and had plans, I've left him sleeping it off." Harvey felt relieved, another ally willing to help.

Lilly asked, "What's happening, what's going on?"

"I dunno, I've spoken with Zara, she's coming over." Harvey said, Lilly, amazed that Zara wasn't pre-occupied, there's a wider story there she thought, that'll have to wait for now. "OK, I'll call some of her friends, I don't get this video, saying it's Pete, when in fact it's not Pete, this seems so bizarre, Harve."

Harvey opened his curtains, looked out into the darkness, the inky black punctured by the yellow hue from the old street lamps, like upside-down funnels, guiding the way up the road, he saw headlights approach. "Lilly, I don't feel good about this, I think we should call the police."

Harvey was feeling sick to his stomach, none of this felt right. Loads of girls had dumped him, it never felt like this, but he truly did love Lucy, maybe that's why he felt so sick.

Lilly's voice became softer "Harve. Lucy was gushing about you all night. I was sick of it, and jealous. Dude, she loves you more than you know, this isn't right. I think the police tomorrow morning if we don't get to the bottom of it tonight, I know what they are going to say." Harvey was rubbing his face with his free hand, he saw the car approach, slow and stop. The inside light illuminated the interior, it was Zara, being driven by Mohammed.

"Lilly, I have to go, Zara has arrived, she's with Mohammed." he didn't wait for the reply, he clicked end. Lilly heard the click of the hang up before she registered what he said, she put the phone down on the table, perched on the end of her sofa, knees clamped shut, hunched over her small frame, with both hands cupped around her mouth, Where the hell are you Lucy!? Lilly thought.

Harvey tossed his phone, in his shorts, tee shirt, and white socks, ignoring the cold and damp outside, he padded up the short footpath, out the gate, ignoring the small stones and gravel particles inflicting pain under Harvey's feet.

"MOHAMMAD!" Harvey shouted, he scooted up the side of the van, Zara peered out the back window, with her arm extended to the center console, paying for her trip.

Mohammed wound his window down, "Hello, sir." Mohammed enquired suspiciously. "Have you seen Lucy mate, it's important?" Harvey clamped both hands on the sill of the open window of the car, Harvey's feet, in the soft, moist earth, ruining the color of his white sports socks, he ignored it!

Mohammad, a kind man, with a kind face, Lucy said he was the gentlest soul she has ever met, Harvey agreed with that assessment. His balding features and a large nose was unmistakably Arabian by nature, where precisely, Harvey didn't know. With his soft voice "No Arvey, Zara ask me already, she texts me about 11, I waited for twenty minutes, I had to take a customer to Layer Road, went back, again nothing, I had one more customer, then Zara called me."

Harvey's shoulders slumped as he pushed his weight into the sills of the door frame, his strong frame momentarily moving the car.

Zara got out the car. She closed the door. Her hand tenderly stroked Harvey's back, he lifted his head, looking to the sky for inspiration, Mohammed staring up at his face.

"Ah hev been through facebook, pet?" Zara looked around, she turned on her feet to look behind, while looking in the other direction she said "Where's her screeve?" Harvey looked at her, she turned and faced him, paused and then raised her eyebrows in anticipation of the answer.

Still leaning on the car, Harvey said "What's a screeve, Zara?"

Mohammad spoke, Harvey turned, with the look of astonishment "She asks where is Lucy's car." Mohammed paused "I lived in Newcastle when we came to England."

Zara piped up, nodding her head in the direction of Mohammad "He's reet pet?"

Harvey thought. "I know where she parks her car, she always parks in the St. John's Walk car park, by the step going down to the taxi rank."

"That's fair specific, pet?" Zara said inquisitively.

Harvey straightened himself, "She always parks there, she feels safer, it's under the streetlight, and covered by cameras, it's what she's always done," shrugging his shoulders and holding the palms of his hands out.

"I'll drive you, my night is over, get in." Mohammad demanded.

"Let me just get changed first guys." Harvey spun on his heels, and sprinted back to the house, Zara got back in the car, she opened her phone, messages. Found Lilly, We are going to find Lucy's car, pet. The car isn't at the house, Harvey is distraught, any ideas pet' Zara hit send, the message was immediately received and read.

Harvey came back out the house, jeans, black tee shirt, trainers, a light rain coat and a scarf, he was wrapping the scarf as he ran to the car.

Zara's phone flashed, a message from Lilly, Keep me informed, stuck in West Mersea, skint, and Tom is too pissed to drive, I'll wait by the phone, should I call her mum?

The car surged forward. The diesel engine sounded as though it had driven around the world ten times. Like a bag of spanners being jangled, as the car increased speed. The fan belt screeched up the road into the haze of the damp September evening. The early hours giving an eerie silence to the 110,000 souls of the last census comfortably wrapped up in their beds, three people traveled through the town, looking out of their windows in total silence.

Zara, face illuminated by the screen, hit reply to Lilly I dunno, I think dis doesn't feel right, but callin her mum will create an issue, if this is innocent 4 whatever reason Lucy will go ape shit, wdyt, Zara ended the message with a raft of emojis, hit send, delivered, received.

Zara was most of the time impossible to understand, her text speak was even worse.

Lilly was replying. The message delivered I am feeling sick, this doesn't feel good, Debs is away, she hasn't heard from Lucy, do we go to the police? More emojis.

Zara replied What would 5-0 say?

Lilly had a headache, she knew that the police wouldn't be interested, she agreed with Zara text that the police would say that she's an adult of sound mind, and has the right to do whatever she felt. Though the facts to her friends was saying something else.

The car entered the car park. Lucy's car was sat, lonesome in the dark. A couple of homeless people were milling around the stairwell Lucy had descended to enter the car park. They were illuminated by the car's headlight, they scattered in all directions like mice in fear of the police moving them on.

Mohammd parked the taxi in front of Lucy's Mini Cooper. Harvey didn't wait for the car to stop, his door was open, with a grunt, he quick-stepped out the car, and ran over to it. The vehicle gave Harvey hope as the car was Lucy's prized possession. Seeing something that contained the energy of Lucy gave Harvey an emotional lift, as though he was seeing her in the flesh. Using his hands and the inbuilt torch on his phone. He looked inside, wiping the wetness from the glass like a Squeegee, it ran down his wrist as he cupped the glass to gain more acuity in the dark cavernous interior, the car was empty. Her coat and sketchers still on the back seat. He knew she hadn't made it to the car, her usual routine after a night out was to get out of her heels at the first opportunity. Sometimes, when they were on a night out together, he would massage her feet waiting for a cab, the memory caused Harvey pain.

He turned to the cab, Zara looking from the inside, pale faced, clearly unwilling to venture out into the cold. Harvey shrugged his shoulders and shook his head. Mohammed stepped out, walked past Harvey, to the rear of the Mini, placed his hands on the wrought iron fence and peered up and down St. George's street, scanning the doorways and dark shadows between the streetlights.

"I am going to retrace her steps," Harvey said. He turned to Mohammed, "Tell me mate, you sure you haven't seen her?" Mohammed came away from the fencing. Walking towards Harvey "My friend," his accent heavy, but gentle, place his hand on Harvey's shoulder, "we will find her, this will turn out ok, I can feel it, she is a gift from Allah." Harvey looked at him. He felt Mohammed's compassion, he reciprocated and patted Mohammed's opposite shoulder.

Zara was now hanging out the window, "Shall we drive to the boozer?" Harvey looked at Mohammed for translation, "Shall we go to the pub Lucy was at?"

Harvey looked down the road, Lucy wouldn't have walked the main roadway, he knew she would cut through the high street. It was a predominately pedestrian walkway.

"No," he walked back to the taxi, inadvertently kicking an idle stone on the tarmac, it clattered under the chassis of the car. "She would have come from there." he motioned to the stairwell and looked down at Zara, "Whatever happened, it was between here, and there." with his head, he motioned to the stairs.

Harvey's phone rang, it was Lilly. "Anything??" she said as soon as Harvey pressed the green button. Her voice was almost as though Harvey had been looking for Lucy, found her and expecting to hear something derogatory from him, what she got was the opposite. Harvey replied in a melancholic way that unsettled her, "Nope, nothing." was all he said.

6

Broc turned off the main road, on to the B3143 from Sturminster Newton and approached the final destination in the quintessential rural village of Kings Stag, in the heart of Dorset. The village was predominantly agriculture, cattle, peppered with commuters from the financial powerhouses of Bournemouth such as Chase Manhattan or Barclays Bank and steadily increasing with the affluent haves from London that could afford such idyllic weekend retreats.

The downside of this, was the village became almost deserted during the week, it also had a detrimental effect on local businesses and eateries. The locals resented the newcomers, blow-ins, Broc smiled at this term... Broc wasn't considered a blow-in, him being in the village was by choice, and entirely of his own making, the community welcomed Broc back from such a long absence as he had adopted an entirely new identity for his dissection and harvests. Not even Ng and his organization knew, so good was the deception.

Prior to his first victim, only visiting the farm once, Dorset would have never been on Broc's radar. A city boy, a lover of the metropolis, the only time he ever ventured in the country, was cross-country at Eaton and that wasn't country. The Berkshire countryside was too well manicured compared to this. Nonetheless, the mist hung heavy over the village, almost comforting Broc; strangely, it felt like home. He noticed the chocolate box houses with plumes of steam swirling from their vents. Warming the families in their beds, the morning was shaping up to be a beautiful autumnal day. Walking the dogs, kids playing in the leaves, the middle classes with new money from Bournemouth and London would rub shoulders with the Dorset aristocracy in the Green Man Pub. The landlord was cashing in on the blow-ins fortune, quaffing £50 bottles of Merlot and warm ales priced at £5 a pint that would give most newcomers catastrophic bowel movements six hours later. The same beer was served to the locals at a fraction of the price. His comforting feeling evaporated at the thought of these happy people with their happy lives and perfect John Lewis kids. Compared to the horrible upbringing he had endured. His face hardened, like a hypnotist snapping their subject out of their trance state, looked at Lucy's vitals, as he did habitually every five minutes…all in normal range.

Broc, nine years earlier, had a patient called Kevin Saunders, a proud military man, who had fallen on hard times after leaving the army, like a large number of veterans who struggled in the civilian world. Saunders turned to drink and at the end of his military career, making it through the day without a drink was impossible. Pigeon holed in an admin job in London, looking after the Queen's Troop administrative needs while they went about their business guarding the number one tourist attraction in Britain, the Royal family. This job, given to senior soldiers that were gathering dust in the operational battalions and were poised to return to the life of civvy street.

By the time Saunders met Broc, as a patient in his liver clinic, he was yellowed with jaundice, had the worst ascites, giving the impression of the third trimester of pregnancy, almost homeless being looked after by a local authority somewhere that was nowhere in London.

Broc formed a platonic, innocent, and genuine friendship with Saunders. He was a decorated Guardsman in the Coldstream Guards. On leaving home, Saunders purposefully joined the most northern infantry regiment he could, to escape the influence of his parents, in particular, his father Pete, who behaved abominably towards his son.

Learned behavior passed down the generations of emotional abuse and an assumption that after all that abuse, he would take over the reins of the family farm. Nope! Saunders escaped Dorset, joined the army and served in Northern Ireland, Kuwait, Bosnia Herzegovina, Kosovo, Iraq and Afghanistan. He briefly saw action in Somalia but couldn't talk about that.

Saunders and Broc chatted for hours about his exploits, Broc genuinely interested and excited by the war stories. Broc wanted a military career, but unlike Saunders, did as he was told and went to medical school on his father's instruction. He admired Saunders for that for a 17-year-old boy to be so desperate to leave home, and never return one of the bravest things Broc thought. Their upbringing similar with the abuse, but Broc never having the courage to go.

Saunders' drinking continued, having more admissions into hospital, when Broc diagnosed him with stage 4 liver cirrhosis, the only hope of survival was a transplant.

Broc discussed this with Saunders on many occasions, after finally coming to terms with his addiction and mortality, as do most, he agreed to go on the transplant register.

With the great Broc as his surgeon, he didn't have to wait long. Prepped for surgery, Broc consented Saunders and went through the usual risk the surgeon consults all his patients. Saunders reached out, with his blackened nails, saggy yellow skin, like a corn-fed chicken, touched Broc on the arm.

"If you can't do it, or things start to fail, let me go, Dale." he pleaded. "I've had a great life, there's nothing out there for me now."

Broc looked down, placed his hand on top of Saunders, "I'll do my best, Kevin. You're in good hands, my friend." he said gently, he meant it, he didn't want Saunders to die.

The risks though, were stacked against Saunders making it through the surgery and that was the easy bit. He had months of rehab ahead, with an already active alcohol addiction coupled with regular medication to keep the rejection symptoms down, he didn't feel that the outcome was going to be good.

The delivery of Kevin's calcified liver went on without a hitch, as if the body helped Broc remove it from its bed, marginal blood loss, the liver looked more like a loofa left to dehydrate on the side of the bathtub. Johann Sebastian Bach was playing serenely, St. Matthew's Passion on the stereo in the corner of the theatre, the choir almost in unison with the medical professionals going about their business in silence like a ballet troupe of choreographed dancers. Organ donation is an exceptional occasion. Treated with the utmost respect for both patients. The donor, in this case, was unidentified, for reason of confidence, to protect the anonymity within the transplant service. A 25-year-old male, who, as with any change of weather, collided at speed after slipping his 1200cc Yamaha with a brick wall. Brought to the hospital, with multi-organ dysfunction, massive terminal brain damage, the only viable organ in the victim's body was the liver function test with a blood chemistry analysis, he was a donor, and therefore viable, the chemistry matched Saunders.

Broc went to the cold box that had been brought to the theatre via courier. Blue lighted their way from Southampton University Hospital. As the choir was singing solemnly, he raised the rich, dark red tinged with a bluish purple, perfect in its appearance; touching it, Broc felt the exquisite smoothness of the organ, his loins tightened, the most incredible organ in the human body. It puts up with everything that we throw at it, drink, drugs, poor diet, helps fight infection, processes blood and eliminates cells, produces bile to break down and emulsify fat, synthesises proteins and detoxifies the body.

On the other side of the operating table was Broc's registrar, Mr. Squibb, a particularly gormless no-hoper from Westminster School for boys, educated in the Nottingham medical school that was once a polytechnic. Morbidly obese, Broc hated him. He nodded to Squibb, passing the liver to him to transplant.

To Squibb, the most amazing time in his life, he would remember this moment forever, in crystal clear detail, his grandchildren will be told of this moment when he worked with the great Broc and allowed him to plumb a liver in, while being tutored by the great man himself.

What Squibb didn't realize, as part of the grand plan, Broc had resected the portal vein too short, with already calcified vessels surrounding the organ, there was no way even the Great Broc would be able to join together.

Squibb seated the liver in place, Saunders according to the anesthetist was stable, Broc noted that Squibb was savoring every nanosecond of this experience, it took him back to his surgical training, the room full of medical students, standing on stools and tables to gain a good view of the procedure. The hepatic artery was anastomosed, without any complications, they both checked the patency of the vessel, and it didn't leak. All that was left was the most challenging vein to join together, the portal vein.

Squibb releases the DeBakey clamp and instantly lost control. Broc didn't have to resect the portal vein too short to frame Squibb in his incompetence. The incompetent fool had released the clamp prematurely. The clamp should have been released once the anastomosis was completed. Squibb had had a momentary lapse of concentration, as with most inexperienced surgeons, was three steps ahead of the procedure.

"SHIT, SHIT, SHIT!" Squibb cried, as the toneless, slippery vein, like a gift that kept giving to Broc, he was calmly suctioning the blood away from the wound, watching while Bach's Wedding Cantata echoed around the room. The suction container for the blood, 100mls, 350mls, 500mls, 1000mls, the room collectively was holding their breath, 1500mls, Broc stepped in.

"You useless fat piece of shit, Squibb!" Broc snapped, Squibb, tears in his eyes, peering through his mask and surgical glasses, covered from head to foot in Saunders' blood and other blood from charitable donations from the blood bank. Broc worked his magic. The bleeding was slowing, but alas, the dip Broc heard in the heartbeat coming from the top end, where the anesthesiologist sat. Not in this case, the anesthesiologist and her anesthetic technician were working furiously to fluid resuscitate Saunders. His blood pressure was so low, which accounted for the slowing of the blood coming out of the portal vein. Another pair of hands was procured by the techinician to squeeze more fluid into Saunders. The beep quickly increased, Broc, in a mess of blood, tissue, and fat from the surrounding areas, was working with the most utter focus and with the slick economy of movement, he heard a whisper behind him, one of the medical students had said something. The students engaged even more, as a loss of control of the liver is one of the most dramatic surgical intervention one can witness, this was truly exciting.

"GET OUT!" Broc barked to the room, without hesitation, like zombies, the students shuffled out, shocked, traumatized, and excited in the same breath to what they had witnessed, did immediately as they were told.

"Dale, tell me some good news?" the anesthesiologist asked.

"I still haven't got control, bleed has slowed on my end, but I think that's his blood pressure."

The anesthesiologist peered over the patient drapes, like a neighbor looking over a garden fence, "He's running on empty, I can't get any more into him, he's going to arrest any…"

Saunders dropped his heart rate, ventricular fibrillation, and erratic abnormal heart trace screaming in Broc's ears, he stood back, knowing that the crash team would enter any second and start chest compressions and electric shock therapy of the heart.

They crashed through the door, the anesthesiologist held up her hand, Broc was glad, he knew what she was going to say.

"STOP!" she bellowed. The team stopped in their tracks. "This patient is in stage 4 cirrhosis, liver transplant, the surgical team…" Everyone stared at Squibb, who had started actively sobbing. "We have used 20 units of blood, cryoprecipitate and FFP 's, Tranny acid and fibrinogen, his blood gas is catastrophic. There's no way we can bring this chap back."

As soon as the anesthesiologist said that, the trace went into a gentle wavy line, the words ASYSTOLE flashing in red blazoned across the top of the screen. The wavy line indicated some electrical activity in the body and around the patient, such as electrical interference, often confused as a sign of life.

"Squibb, get out of my sight, you're finished in this hospital!" Squibb, dutifully, still sobbing, ran from the theatre, tearing his gown and mask from his face. "I'll be speaking to the College ABOUT YOU SQUIBB, DON'T THINK THIS IS OVER!" Broc's words echoed around the room and hit Squibb square in the back as he exited the theatre.

Broc felt nothing.

Broc at first didn't think this was a plan until he had started dissecting Saunders ruined liver. Saunders words still resonated in Broc's thought process that he wanted just to die. Broc was satisfied that dying was what he wanted, he would never make it through the rehab, anti-rejection medication and the worse of all, the disease of drinking. Broc, knew the cancer of alcohol addiction would be the most significant battle Saunders would've faced, this liver is wasted, should have gone to a more worthy recipient.

After dealing with Saunders' death, his funeral was only attended by Broc and the undertakers.

The acid test of Broc evolving plan. He advertised Saunders' death in the Daily Telegraph on three separate occasions. The final obituary notice gave the location of the funeral, The City Of London Crematorium, close to Stratford, amongst the regeneration in preparation for the 2012 London Olympics.

Broc, on the bright sunny day, held his breath when just himself and the few members of the crematorium were present and the priest Broc had brought in to give a sermon and say prayers. Saunders was cremated, when Broc received the ashes, he kept them.

Following the funeral, he went to Kings Stag, to the farm in Dorset, discovered the news about Saunders' father, and even more good news, Broc discovered Saunders' mother, Emily, had become reclusive. Part of Broc's relationship was to glean everyone for information about Saunders' upbringing, using social media to identify the people he was talking about.

School friends, family members, local dignitaries, there was nothing that Broc didn't know about Kevin Saunders.

Although Emily was from Dorchester, about ten miles to the south of Kings Stag, she was still considered a blown-in. Following farmer Pete's death, Emily had become reclusive in her old age. Never venturing out of the house, only for the basics from the small general stores in the town. After a few years, the house became run down and shabby, Emily just keeping herself to the confines of the kitchen and main bedroom upstairs was awoken strangely in the night, with the oven kitchen timer beeping.

She turned and tried to ignore the incessant beeping, thinking it would switch off, then she smelt the unmistakable aroma of a banana loaf, Kevin's favorite. Her interest became too strong to ignore. Maybe he was home. The feeling of hope swept across her heart making it skip a beat. He was back, cooking a loaf for when she woke in the morning, she was sure of it.

She got up, put on a nightgown, found her slippers, and shuffled towards the door, she saw light leaking from the gap under the door, her pace quickened as did her heart, it must be Kevin. So many years have passed and the years Emily was alone were the longest, her heart heavy with the memory of her life and how it turned out, she opened the door, the aroma of the baking even stronger, the feeling of regret, spreading like cancer through her body.

By the time Emily had reached and opened the door, she had created a story in her head. Kevin had come back to reinstate the farm to its former glory and take care of her in her old age. Maybe grandchildren too, she shuffled to the top of the stairs, peered down in hopes to gain a glimpse of the son she had missed for so long. Wronged by his father, and not strong enough to love her son as a mother should.

As she took the first step, Broc stepped out from the darkness behind. With his strong hands, with one swift, clean shove, pushed Emily down the long, bare wooden stairs and at the bottom, Broc insured her death by placing some stacked chairs.

Emily bounced, rolled down, head, shoulders, hips audibly cracking as she came into contact with each step.

Broc calmly walked down the stairs after her as she fell. She hit the chairs, clattering them across the floor, further fracturing even more of her bones. Broc stepped over her body and sat by the door on a chair.

She was tough, Emily lay on the floor while Broc watched her try and crawl to the kitchen with her one good arm. Her body was a tangled mess of limbs. Facing in different sickening directions, some sharp shards of bones exposed with the gelatinous ooze of blood dangling from them. Covered in her shit and piss, she was unaware of Broc's presence, always staying out of sight, he watched as she took her last agonal breath 15 hours after pushing her down the stairs. Broc's face didn't change once, he was now fully committed to the plan.

It was a further four weeks before she was discovered by the newsagent that was chasing her for her unusually unpaid paper round fees. The police entered her property. Stepping on the scattered papers and unopened mail in the hallway. Emily's putrid corpse, horribly bloated with the central heating on full. Sweating at the bottom of the stairs. Eyes bulging, the local plod urging, and vomiting, trying to walk closer to her rotting carcass.

Broc previously lodged power of attorney with a local solicitor under the guise of Kevin Saunders. He had the driver license, passport, military documentation, expunged his medical records, knew the history if challenged and for all intents and purposes, on paper, Broc was Kevin Saunders. The only person that would realize he was an imposter was Emily, Saunders' mother and he had seen to that.

In London, he received a letter two weeks after Emily was discovered, took a deep breath and went home as Kevin Saunders.

The approach to the village, lined with million pound properties and wealthy farmsteads, in the heart of the town, with a traffic-calming measure right outside, was the twin petrol station. Broc always mused as he drove into the village that the station owner sidelined in two other businesses, machine tool hire and cattle hire. The guise of the cattle was soft pasture, to keep the grass down and fertilize the ground. The actual reason was the cattle were used as a tax deception.

There were more than two dozen farms, taken over by tech companies. Motor racing teams and farmers doing other things that didn't comply with the ridged covenants the farms were under. When inspectors came to visit said farms, the owners would hire the cattle to aid the deception that the farm was indeed, a working farm.

The station owner saw an opportunity and grabbed the enterprise with both horns, "bloody crazy these people are, come from London and Manchester spend a packet on these gert farms and have no choice but to pay me an 'ansome price for me cows."

Broc negotiated the traffic-calming measure in the road in the Mercedes van, as he guessed, the petrol station closed on Friday evening, and will be opened again sometime Monday morning. Time has stopped in this part of the world.

After the gas station, was a turn, heading towards Hazelbury Bryan, one-quarter of a mile down the road was Blackmore Vale Farm, on the right, the farm belonging to the Saunders family and had been for the last 110 years.

Lucy had come to her last stop.

7

It was early, the morning shift was leaving on foot and in their cars, the waft of deodorant and aftershave thick in the main entrance to the Colchester police station. Mohammad had parked his car at the drop-off point and told them that he would wait, police being curious souls, all looked into the vehicle, appraising Mohammad and the taxi he was driving.

The fumes were belching out like a 70's chimney pot and the rattle of it didn't sound too clever. He thought it was wise to turn off the engine. So the fresh face coppers about to start their law enforcement duties wouldn't be suspicious enough to stop and have a chat. He knew the MOT had expired two months ago, he wanted to get it done someday, but he also knew that someday was not a day in the week and it indeed wasn't this month either!

The trio walked gingerly into the police station, the detritus of the saturday night were either waiting for someone to be processed or themselves having to be processed.

The room was drab, dimly lit with yellow lighting making the walls look nicotine stained. The smell of cheap lager and cigarettes. Advice posters hanging off the wall, with a couple of Have You Seen… pictures of people, bikes and weirdly a laptop. The room was supposed to be like this, unwelcoming, Harvey thought if it were a beautiful place, everyone would come here!

"Move along Deirdre, there's people waiting behind you." The seasoned police sergeant said peering over his glasses with an air of disdain. Essex accented, droll, and dry. The kind of tone if it had a color, would be beige. He wore spectacles, the kind you grab in the pharmacy by the till. He was unattractively thin, with an Adam's apple that bobbed up and down involuntarily, as though he had swallowed his policeman's helmet.

Through the stained window, protecting him from the clientele that plagued the front of the police station at this time of day, he was alone with an array of drawers, phones and radios. It would have looked brilliant in 1990, which incidentally, according to the plaque on the wall, was when the station was opened by the mayor of the town in 1990. Next to the phones was a bottle of kitchen cleaner and a cloth.

Deirdre turned and looked at the trio that stood there. She smiled, a bit unstable on her feet. Bedraggled and filthy, yellowed skin, deeply lined from a hard life, poor lifestyle choices and poor education, hair so greasy that it could be a fire risk, the unmistakable aroma of stale tobacco, cider, and urine hung over her like a smog of desperation.

She said something and stepped towards Harvey. Lilly, the consummate nurse, stepped forward to block her path, into the invisible exclusion zone of odor, oblivious to it. Both Zara and Harvey in unison took a step back. "Wot did ye sa, pet?" Lilly asked, putting a hand on her back, ignoring the greasy feeling on her hand. She said something else, but Lilly couldn't quite catch it. Lilly looked over her crooked back, towards the crisp, clean sergeant behind the glass. Raised her eyebrows as if she asked the question. The copper behind the glass, stood, motionless, arms folded asking, "She yours?".

Lilly rubbed the old lady's back and shook her head.

Her question that she asked with her eyebrows raised was answered.

"Nar don't know, hor." Lilly replied, horrified that a public servant would objectify another person so publicly. "Yee cannit speak to hor like that yee animal." Lilly said crossly.

The policeman, still motionless, looked at Harvey and Zara for input, there was a pause.

"What did she say?" the policeman finally asked, nodding towards Lilly.

"She asked if you knew the lady…" Harvey stated,

"…and that's no way to speak to someone" Zara added.

The policeman unfolded his arms, nonchalantly gathered up papers on the desk, sighed slowly, "She's here everyday, looking for food, coffee, or the toilet, she needs to go across the road," he gesticulated to the wall, as if the the three of them had X Ray vision, "… to the Salvation Army, this is a police station, not a social club, she ought to be properly looked after…What can I do for you?" he asked, indicating to Harvey that he was elected as spokesman, as all men the sergeants' age would.

Before Harvey could answer, Zara, took a step towards the glass, "We want to report a missing person, our friend has gone missing, and it's totally out of character."

The sergeant filed the gathered papers into a tray marked IN, he pulled out a drawer, took a seat on the high stool, removed a biro from his breast pocket, Zara was waiting for him to lick the end, he didn't. But the whole episode took longer than it needed.

"Name?" he said, with the pen poised at the top of the page.

"Zara," Zara said as she went on her tiptoes to get a better view of the paper he was writing on, face pressed against the glass.

"Face off the glass please," he said, as he was writing. He looked up, indicated to the kitchen cleaner, "everyday people try and spit through the speech hole, we have to clean it up." Zara moved her face away as though she was dodging a flying object, "But some of the scrotes that come in here leave their manners and behavior at the door." He returned to the form.

"What's Zara's surname?"

"I am Zara, our friend that has gone missing is Lucy…Lucy Hodges." Zara turned and looked at her friends, they came closer, the policeman looked up at them, apparently irritated by their presence and now having to correct the form, with a this-is-going-to-be-a-long-day look about him.

He put the pen down and leaned back in the chair. It creaked, "What's the story?" he inquired.

The three of them recounted the story, every detail, with them translating in some cases with what Lilly had said.

Finally, he said, "So, let me get this straight, your friend went out last night, frequented a couple of bars. Had a good time, you two were with her," indicating to Zara and Lilly who were eagerly nodding. "She left the Wagon and Horses at approximately 11 PM alone, and walked to her car, she was due home approximately 30 minutes later, and she never arrived home?" indicating to Harvey, who was shifting on his feet.

The anxiousness evident on his face, he nodded.

"You, then received a text from her with some video clip you won't tell me about..." he paused to see if they had changed their minds, "...and that's about the whole story?"

He waited intentionally to deliver his sage advice, waiting for any input from the three of them, but then there was none. He then leaned forward, folding his arms on the counter, his writing done with this inquiry. "So, to summarise, your friend, was of sound mind last night, had the capacity, and not drunk?" Zara agreed. "Then there's nothing we can do" he said curtly. "Your friend is an adult, of sound mind and can do whatever she wants. We can't send out the dogs, find her and kick the doors in on your say so, because there's no impropriety or evidence of a crime that's been committed. There's every chance she has buggered off to Scotland as you say. We can file in 24 hours, a missing persons form?"

He looked at the clock on the wall to their right, "If she hasn't pitched up by 11 PM tonight, might I suggest you come back in the morning and file a report as we will be dealing with the usual suspects at that time of night. If she turns up, we will speak with her..."

He was interrupted by Harvey. He was fizzing and the girls about to cut in, shaking their heads. His pause in talking brought them back, "...if she turns up, we will speak with her and then and only then, if she agrees we will tell you." He filed the paper, back in the draw, and replaced his biro and the phone rang, he reached for the phone "This happens often, you don't know what she may have been up to, this may have been her plan all along!"

"Do we come and speak with you" Zara asked, trying to keep her cool.

"Hopefully not" was all she got, he then spoke into the phone, the conversation, terminated!

They shuffled over to the corner, by the plastic chairs bolted to the floor, the old lady was sitting in the corner rocking.

"Blokes a fucking jerk!" Harvey said, he was shifting backward and forwards.

Zara was looking at the floor, "she said nothing. I have a bad feeling about this. She shared everything with me."

A pang of rejection fired through Lilly like a missile, always jealous of their connection, "She nivvor said nowt to me either." Lilly added for effect.

Zara brought back to the awareness that she might have crossed a line with Lilly, they were all close, she tenderly stroked Lilly's arm and looked at Harvey.

"Did she have anything with her, bag, passport, have you checked the bank, building society, is there anything that's out of the ordinary?" Zara asked.

"Like leaving?" Harvey churlishly said and slumped on the chair opposite to Deirdre, he could smell her, he shot her a loathsome glance, she felt it and sat back. "No, nothing, she was wearing what she was wearing, her trainers and jacket were in the car, they were still there when we got to the car." he looked up at the girls.

Zara thought she looked terrific. She was with her when she brought the purple dress. "Gosh, she looked gorgeous in that purple dress she had on."

Deirdre made a sound, incomprehensible ramblings that seemed to be noises and squeaks, they looked at her.

Harvey was looking at Deidre, thinking of Lucy's image in that dress last night, "She was smoking hot when she left." he said, the picture blocking the thought process of what was in front of him.

Deidre began to sob, she had become upset, while sitting. Steadily growing hysterical, she looked to the sky, her mouth open, as though she was looking for divine intervention. Her teeth resembled a vandalized graveyard, blackened, crooked and some broken, snot coming from her nose.

"Hey pet, what's up, wot are yee tryin to say?" Lilly took a seat next to the old lady, took her cold, yellowed hand. The old lady looked at Lilly, said something, lifted Lilly's hand to her mouth and kissed it. She uttered another sentence when two burly coppers entered the room, called her name and approached her. She became even more unsettled, as they grabbed her by both arms.

"Steady on." Zara shouted.

The desk sergeant shouted through glass "Deidre, you have got a spell in the drunk tank, sober up, and we will get you..." His voice was drowned out by the shrieking and screaming coming from Deirdre. She kept shouting "PURPLE, PURPLE, VAN."

The three of them went to leave, Lilly turned and walked backward following her friends looking at the desk sergeant, with her thumb and forefinger, created a circle, held it to her forehead, and mouth dickhead to the sergeant, he dismissed it with a wave.

As they got out, the fresh air hit them, like a wave of sunlight.

"What the fuck was that about, she was screaming purple?" Harvey said, looking at his phone, he was flicking through the contacts, found Lucy's parents landline number and hit call, they all stopped walking, they looked at each other, as though communicating telepathically.

"We need more support." Harvey said with the phone against his ear as they got into Mohammad's rattling car.

8

Broc drove the van around the farmhouse. The lights were already on. Immediately behind the house, was a barn. The barn was cladded in worn wood, giving the exterior of the barn an old, aged appearance. The interior of the barn, however, was the polar opposite.

Broc positioned the van, with the rear of the van doors facing the double door of the barn. On Broc's phone, he flipped through the app screen, found the house file app, clicked it, revealed some sub apps, found the app labeled barn and clicked it. The door instantly juddered and the smooth engineering kicked in as the doors simultaneously parted.

The cavernous interior of the barn was empty, in the middle of the barn, was a metal square post, that stood approximately five foot in height. It was spray-painted yellow and black, on the top was a keypad and a large red button.

Broc reversed and positioned the van, with the keypad at an accessible height for the driver of the van to operate. He pressed the large red button and the motors of the double doors closed silently. As the van became draped in the darkness, white fluorescent lights blinked on, giving an entirely different feel to the interior of the barn, more like a distribution warehouse than a barn.

Once the lights clicked on, Broc, keyed in his date of birth into the pad, the ground immediately behind the van raised, and lowered simultaneously, becoming a ramp. Once the mechanical action completed, Broc engaged reverse in the van, with the rear view camera screen on, he reversed on to the ramp and descended to the double doors at the bottom. He killed the engine and got out. Broc stretched, his muscles ached, he needed to work out.

He walked towards the double doors that opened automatically, the security pad on the opposing wall inside was flashing. He opened it, keyed in his mother's date of birth, then activated all the lights in the secret facility, the hum became more audible, the turbines of the air cleaning blowers whooshed into life, sounding like an airliner taking off.

After his lab came to life, Broc made his way to the van where he opened the back-double doors finding Lucy still secure on her trolley. He climbed inside after unclipping the floor and creating a ramp. Once inside he went about the tasks of moving Lucy; disconnecting the monitoring, unclipping syringes – noting they were near empty and finally reaching beneath the trolley to locate the keypad that controlled it. He then disengaged the brake and pressed drive on the keypad. The trolley kicked to life, Lucy swayed with the movement while she slept. He followed it as it made its way down the ramp; its gears, brakes, and differentials worked to keep it from running off the ramp and smashing into the wall. Once off the van, the trolley found its way in the complex to a large door which slid open revealing a large white room.

The trolly positioned itself in the middle, the brakes engaged and with a clunk, the trolley was in place.

The room was cold, stark and clinical. The walls covered with white plastic, there was no joins in the ceiling or floors, the room had no edges so the air could freely circulate without being buffered. The floor was marble-like but springy underfoot and shiny. Two enormous operating lights were suspended from the ceiling now hanging over Lucy's unconscious body.

Broc hit play on the old iPod on the docking speaker, Roxy Music blared into life 'now the party is over, I'm so tired, then I see you coming.'

It seemed odd, such an old device that stood out in such a modern environment.

Broc wheeled an anesthetic machine over to her. Connected her oxygen supply to the dual pipes coming from the machine. Dialed the oxygen to 100%, and made sure that the inhalation agent was full. He re-filled the syringes on top of the anesthetic machine labeled Midazolam and Remifentanil replaced the exhausted syringes Lucy had been receiving throughout her journey. Once connected, he adjusted the doses, and hit run. The monitor was showing 99% oxygen saturation - normal, blood pressure 114/79 - normal, ECG trace 69 - regular rhythm and normal rate, end-tidal carbon dioxide 4.9 mmHg - normal.

During the journey, Broc was unable to account for one aspect, how anaesthetized Lucy was. This calculated be a predictable measure of the minimum alveolar concentration, or MAC.

He place a strip of electrodes to her head, and the monitor transduced Lucy's electrical activity in her brain, the lower the number the more anesthetized she was, this bispectral index system was widely used in modern anesthesia.

Jealous Guy was now playing on the stereo 'I was swallowing my pain, I was swallowing my pain, I didn't mean to hurt you' Bryan Ferry was singing, Broc wasn't aware he was whistling to the tune or the poignancy of the lyrics, he went about his macabre business, well drilled and rehearsed, when happy, he took a step back and drank her in.

Now naked and clean, the whole event took about an hour. Connecting Lucy to the life-giving machine, cut her clothes away, and placed them all in a yellow clinical waste bin, drained her now full catheter bag, replaced her empty bag of intravenous fluids with a warm bag of Ringer's solution.

With soap and water infused with tea-tree and lavender essential oils he washed her down thoroughly, he paid attention to her feet and in-between her toes, her groin and buttocks were thoroughly washed as well as her hands and in between her fingers. He shaved her entire body, the hair being placed in the same bag as her clothes. Her hairless skin glistened, tanned, all but her pubic region and head, that was a stark white in comparison after being shaved. Her muscles rippled. Makeup removed with gentle cleansers, she was stunningly beautiful.

One of the best specimens he had chosen. She was going to be perfect for the harvest and dissection. He ran his hands over her warm, supple body, still whistling to Jealous Guy. Broc felt her entire body, flexing the legs, checking her joints in the knee and hips. There was no sound of crepitus or grinding of bones, her arms the same. Her soft flat abdomen, with a small amount of downy blonde hair on her navel spiralling up to her into button.

Broc cursed, he twirled his fingers in the hair, he decided he liked it and left it.

When feeling the abdomen, it revealed no anomalies, he cupped her face with both hands, staring into her eyes that were involuntary open, he bent and kissed her on the lips. They were full, warm and inviting. He darted his tongue into her. Lucy's mouth was moist, her tongue soft yet lifeless. He kissed passionately and loving, she gave him nothing in return, but it didn't matter. Tomorrow she will give Broc everything, every part of her will be given to him. Lucy will have a ringside seat to watch the great Broc carve her body up as he takes all her organs and much more than what Tao Ng will need.

Satisfied that Lucy was safe, he covered her in a warmed blanket, changed the monitoring app on his phone to the monitoring in the operating room. He then changed the parameters on the phone, Lucy's temperature levels and the rest of her monitoring limits. When the phone synced, he left, switching the lights off leaving only the large operating lights in the middle of the ceiling.

Before leaving the room, he stopped, turned, and took a final look at her; She looked as though she was on a stage.

Broc mused to himself That's why it's called an operating theatre; for him, this was his theatre. A theatre that no one would ever see. A performance that no one could ever understand or enjoy, the iPod playing on repeat the 5000 songs downloaded onto it. Lucy will be safe, warm and entertained.

He left and went to the house.

9

Broc left the building via a hidden door, to the left of the main double doors. Exhausted. The kidnap phase had taken nearly thirty hours, all he wanted was a shower, bed, regenerate and then in the morning, attend to Lucy.

He walked across the block-paved courtyard, heading towards the back door of the farmhouse, he could see Carmen, Kevin Saunders' wife's face at the window, waiting for him to come into the house.

"KEV, there you are!" said a voice from behind Broc. Startled, Broc spun round in surprise, he heard laughing "I scared you!" said the approaching man, Broc knew him as Saunders' friend from school, a meddlesome estate agent called Trevor Hussey.

Hussey had never left the area, working as an agricultural estate agent, Broc had noted how closed minded Hussey was, his education just about reaching average, married with children, overweight, large reddish cheeks and small piggy eyes that was a characteristic of a fairly substantial inbreeding habit in this part of Dorset. Hussey approached Broc, his checked shirt lazily tucked into his moleskin mustard trousers, the buttons of the shirt straining to retain the man's girth.

"I saw you arrive in your van." Hussey said.

"Van?" Broc replied.

"Yes, I saw you come down the lane. Where the devil have you parked it, Kev?" Hussey was looking about the space,

Broc hated nicknames and name shortening, especially Kev. It jarred his noble sensibility, it was up there with tattoos and mindless swearing.

"In the barn." Broc replied. Hussey stopped looking and nodded in agreement.

"I tried to get into it, its shut up like Robyn Damment's knickers, you remember that old dog from school." Hussey said, with a chortle.

"Yes, your right. I modelled the security of my barn to the exact specifications of her knickers. It was a job to do. Even the Crown Jewell's aren't as protected as those knickers."

Broc struggled to make light of the small talk but made a mental note of the name and persona so he could bring her up in a future conversation, furthering cementing his integration into the community.

"Joking aside Trevor, you know who I work for, they spec'd out the barn for security… you understand." It sounded like a warning, and it was.

Trevor tapped the side of his nose, and winked, "Secret's safe with me, Kev."

Hussey remembered the conversation he had when his long lost friend returned from the army, telling him that he was now working for a government weapons development department, nothing spectacular, but everything he did required a level of security making certain parts of the farm off limits.

Hussey respected that, although unusual. Everybody in the village lived in each other's pockets. It was a weird concept, but with the arrival of these tech companies to the area, where the whole farm estate now closed from the public. They didn't even mix with the locals, that was an even bigger crime, thought Hussey.

"I wanted to catch you Kev, I need to talk to you urgently." Broc looked over his shoulder. Carmen was still at the window, she waved.

"Ah, sorry." Hussey observed over Broc's shoulder, "You bin away for a bit then?" he asked.

After a long pause, Broc felt he had to respond to it. "Yes mate, I have, ten days traveling around Europe, visiting military bases. Been a bit of a slog, I have just driven from Poole Docks, the crossing was a bit tiresome." Broc said. "Can it wait…your urgency?"

"Yes of course mate. Yes up and down, I hate ferries, remember that trip to Brittany?" Hussey said with another laugh, linking their past.

"Yes, but really, can we do this maybe over a pint tomorrow?" Broc suggested,

"It's just that it's September, we need to chat about the Rotary fireworks and Halloween events in the village, just divvying up the work, wanted to know what you and.." He motioned to the window "…has to be fair what everyone does; I know Carmen is keen to bake some things."

"You spoke with Carmen?" Broc inquired, suddenly uneasy, he felt the needed to change tac so that he didn't sound either jealous or angry. "You better watch her baking, our oven is like the crematorium in Dorch."

Hussey laughed deeply, "She did warn me." he looked over Broc's shoulder again.

She was a filly alright, ten years younger than Broc and supple like a tender tree branch Hussey thought lucky bastard.

"Of course, tomorrow, in the Green Man." Hussey said, feeling that this conversation was now over, Broc went to leave, he hesitated. "Trevor, don't sneak up on me like that again." Broc held the pause for effect, the atmosphere suddenly became awkward.

Hussey felt uncomfortable. Broc's eyes pierced him. He sensed something. But his blinkered thought process would never be able to crack the reality of who Broc might be.

He deflated the atmosphere with an awkward laugh "yes, sorry mate, I won't again, I'll call you to see if it's convenient." Punched him in the shoulder in a friendly way.

Broc smiled, "Six o'clock tomorrow then, Trevor." he turned and walked towards the door, his friend shouted after him "Trev, not Trevor, only my mum calls me Trevor, makes me feel I have done something wrong" still laughing.

Broc kept walking, held up his thumb in acknowledgment, he would never resort to Trev he thought, what a horrible thought.

He opened the door and was suddenly startled, for the second time in as many minutes. Carmen, a whirlwind of hair, arms, shrieks and kisses flew at him, encasing her arms around Broc's muscular body, he had only been gone three days.

Trevor saw the door close, heard the shrieking, suddenly even more jealous of his school friend, Kev is indeed a lucky man, he thought.

Broc prized Carmen away from him. He placed her petite frame on the kitchen island. The house was warm, inviting, tastefully decorated and extensively modernized to a high spec. He glanced as he always did, to the hallway at the bottom of the stairs and the memory of Emily's mangled and shattered body at the foot of the stairs still present in his mind. The house smelt homely, of fresh coffee, bread and furniture polish, it felt safe to Broc.

He felt a twinge of pain. His bratty girl Carmen twisted his nipple through his shirt to gain his attention, "Ouch, you little slut!" Broc spat.

He grabbed her by the throat and squeezed. She gasped for air. She was smiling, while still trying to suck air in. Unbuttoning his shirt, she kissed him, Broc still squeezing, she was turning a dusky shade of blue. Partly unbuttoned, ran both hands inside and around his barrelled chest, thick, solid and muscular, "Oh daddy," she said breathing out slowly. Carmen licked the bottom of her lip, Broc suddenly released and instantly with a big inhale of air, her complexion pinked up.

"Fuck me daddy, please, now. I have been up all night edging, my pussy is aching for you, I need to feel your body." Her voice was low, almost out of breath.

He took a small step back, looked at her nakedness, she trusted Broc with her whole being, he was her daddio, protector, sire, Dom, whatever you wanted to call it, he was it.

Always calling him daddy, respecting the boundaries of the dominant and submissive lifestyle.

She had long thick locks of curly hair, a beautiful innocent face that was full of mischief, small pert breasts, tiny waist and long slender legs. She was a bratty baby-girl because she craved his punishment. The more severe, the better, she loved nothing more than to weep in his arms, bleeding from the pain of his love.

He stepped closer, parting her legs, and pushed his groin into hers. Broc stroked along the tops of her thighs, to her small waist, up the sides of her torso. Cupped her breasts momentarily and squeezed, she giggled, then his hands making their way to her face. Cupping it, she leaned back with her arms resting on the cold surface, she bit her lip, lifted her legs, making herself as wide as possible, Broc looked down, she was swollen, wet and very red. She indeed had been edging herself all night.

"I need to eat." Broc said, interrupted by another giggle, "And that doesn't mean you slut. Make me something," he kissed her.

A frown of disappointment shot across her face, and as Broc kissed her, she tried to dart her tongue in his mouth, but he peeled away and walked to the kitchen table. "Arrrg, daddy, stop teasing me," she pleaded.

Carmen jumped off the island without any effort, her feet landing silently on the warmed tiled floor, and filed in behind him, she knew what he wanted, eggs and bacon, with a piece of fried bread.

"You seem tired, Dale...more than usual." reverting to the reality, using Broc's name, she opened the cupboards and grabbed the things she needed.

Broc sat and watched his naked girl go about the business of his breakfast. She had the economy of movement like a surgeon. He loved it. She was so light on her feet. Bouncing around the kitchen like a ballet dancer with only sounds of her bare feet slapping the kitchen floor, and the soft close of the Italian kitchen cupboards, every movement deliberate and considered.

He felt lucky she was in his life, he wished he could give her more, but with the past being the past, that was impossible.

Carmen, who in a previous life was Tracey Burgess, was 32, or so she thought.

Brought up in the tough Manchester social care system, bounced from foster home to foster home.

At a time when checking foster parents' history was rarely made. She was repeatedly abused, and sexually destroyed by the time she hit puberty.

Naturally beautiful, if under different circumstances, with the proper parenting, she would have either been a model, or made it in business, either way, she would have been incredibly successful. Such a waste, Broc thought. She did, however, make sex a business that was equally as successful for her.

Around her 14th birthday, Tracey boarded a train for London, headed for the big lights and big dreams and fell off the radar in Manchester. In reality, she was turning tricks for a fiver along the stretch of road between Euston and Kings Cross station for a year or so, when a club owner spotted her. The kind of club owner of the clubs that Broc frequented.

The owner, a brutal man, called the Zookeeper, offered her food, some money, and board. To work the floor as a pet-girl of his club. He made no bones or lied to her. She was to be used for sex, and in whatever capacity the clientele would choose.

Pet-girls were sex objects that were used as sexual vessels only. It attracted a girl that was from a background that was as a result of sexual, emotional, or physical abuse.

The abuse was so systematic, without reprieve throughout the girls' childhood, their sense of normality, utterly destroyed. The sexual gratification of man or women in some cases was all they knew.

What came with this was an understanding that if the man wanted to hurt the girl, then the girls would allow it. There were no safe words in this lifestyle.

The aim simply was to make the daddy or dom happy.

The attrition rate of a subculture controlled by violent gangs and brutal pimps, kept the scene deep underground.

In many cases helped by the patrons of high authoritative offices such as police chiefs, MP's and senior civil servants. Girls often had to rely on drugs to suppress the memories and emotions of their childhood. With the hideous sexual practices of often very cruel and sadistic men these girls ended up being hospitalised for mental health reasons, or in most cases, found dead.

The average age of the girls was 16. Over this age, the usefulness diminished in a rapidly decreasing circle. The older girls were more experienced and more accepting of their position in life.

Realizing a way off the streets and maybe a chance to bag a whale, she agreed. She quickly became his best slut.

There was no let-up if the club wasn't on, the girls, bussed to private parties in and around London. Fed mind-bending drugs so that not only were they pliable and willing, but their holes could be used for whatever.

Fat businessmen and celebrities would pay a handsome price for a gaggle of sluts that were for just a bit more than a bit of sex.

Their imagination was left to run wild and some girls paid the price, emotionally and physically ruined, once past their prime, they were cast out and left to the mercy of the streets and addicted to booze and drugs. They often didn't last long.

Carmen was numb to anything sexual, her upbringing revolved around abuse and her understanding of it made her a harder nut to crack.

She would never take drugs or drink, sex for her was a means to control men, and control a situation. Sex was as normal as taking a breath to her. There was no connection or notion of love attached to any sexual encounter she had experienced. If a situation became out of control, like a dog, Carmen would become a submissive pet and drop to her knees. Most men, she realized didn't know what to do when this happened. The ones that didn't would beat her, have their way with her, then console her for her gift. This was what she aimed for, the tender caress after a beating. She saw these parties as a game, this was her life, submission and to serve sexually.

Broc knew how to get the best from her and he was different. Ferociously dominant. He loved playing with Carmen. He would seek her out to play with her all night long. He never wanted sex either, never really achieving an erection, only ever penetrating her once, he climaxed as he pushed himself home. Blaming her for ruining his orgasm, she savored the punishment after.

It felt different with Broc, all he wanted was to whip her, then love her and that's all she wanted.

At the time she wondered if this was what love was like, when she thought about it, she was confused.

Broc became her protector and sire. At one time, Broc was late for a party and she was commandeered by a banker from the city.

He was a young-gun, rich, full of attitude and ego. He had no idea who Carmen was or how to handle her. She behaved particularly bratty that evening, disappointed that Broc hadn't appeared like he said he would. The banker took exception to her brattiness and beat her severely.

Broc dragged the banker off Carmen, while he was beating her with a cane, Carmen shrieking in pain as the man lashed her. In a fit of rage, Broc grabbed a £9000 bottle of Chateau Latour 1989, smashed it over the banker's head while choking him with one powerful hand and with the sharp shards of glass Broc was still holding in the other hand, stabbed the man repeatedly in the face and throat. Broc didn't stop until he was dragged away. The banker left slumped on the floor, his face a mangled mess of broken glass, tissue, muscles, eyes, bone, blood pumping out of him.

The man was taken and left in a dark alley somewhere in London. Broc was asked to leave and never return, when leaving, he grabbed Carmen's hand and without question or permission from zookeeper took her. The club owner wouldn't dare stop Broc, he knew what he was capable of, and that was much more than what he had just witnessed, he sensed it.

From then on, Carmen had allied herself to Broc. She knew what he was about, knew what he did outside of his work. But for the first time, someone vouched for her. It was at that time, Broc, screaming in the banker's face, stabbing him, calling him the most profane names, she knew that her life was to be with him.

She followed him to Dorset as the wife of Kevin Saunders, she thought it was exciting, and living in such luxury. She looked after the house. Maintained the illusion while Broc was away doing his army job, did housewifely things such as flower arranging, cooking or taking old folks to the local hospital. Weirdly, she loved it. It felt healthy and good. She finally made something of herself, not only the good life but to share it with her daddy was even more special.

She also made a promise to herself that she would never orgasm again, as Broc was unable to ejaculate like a normal man, she would chain her sexual urges, she edged herself every night, masturbating herself raw. Up to the point of orgasm, five, six, eight times a night. One day, the day that Broc shoots his seed, she will climax over the event herself.

The breakfast took a couple of minutes to whip up, chatting endlessly to Broc, he was mesmerized by her beauty and even the innocence underneath the abuse was electric to Broc. He beamed as she spoke, he had no idea what she was saying, it didn't matter, he was home.

Lucy can wait…

10

The Monday morning commute to the East End nick near Mile End in London was a chore. The crowds of the unwashed, coupled with the fresh face office yuppies, all en-route to the city. Alex didn't appreciate the long greasy hair of a man flicking it three or four times in her face during the short tube journey. She felt this ought to be a crime in itself. One thing Alex thought, that being off work, although it was needed, she felt a sense of purpose again, the last case took it out of her. Familiar things that gave her comfort on the commute also fired memories of that case, excitement mixed with anxiousness was difficult to fathom. She considered the evidence. The Royal College of Veterinary Surgeons had got back to her when she was leaving the house. She pulled out her phone to read the email:

Dear Madam,

The college can confirm that in some cases, paralyzing drugs such as aminosteroid non-depolarising neuromuscular blockers are used in veterinary practice, but this isn't considered normal. Usually, suxamethonium and a drug formulated explicitly for veterinary practices is a drug called Decamethonium. The amount mentioned in the report would constitute a dose too high to be considered normal in veterinary practice. The drug on a molecular level is similar to Rocuronium, but there are slight chemical differences in the makeup. One thing is for sure that any drugs would not be present in any meat before slaughter. The regulations are too stringent. Any infringements on these robust regulations ought to be reported to the appropriate authorities....

Alex knew the moment that the email dropped into her inbox, would contain words to that effect, like a dog with a bone, she sensed that this was something big, she forwarded the email to her partner in crime Ricky Lambert.

Alex entered the police station and went straight to the murder squad's team-room on the third floor. The room was bright, people littered about, phones ringing, text message notifications, the clatter of keyboards and the smell of fresh coffee everywhere, that wave of anxiousness washed over her again fuck off Troll she thought.

She has been absent from the team for a while now. No one looked up. No seemed to care. She saw Ricky, sat at his desk, she headed towards him.

"NO, NO, NO! You can't be here Alex, turn around and go back home." she was intercepted by her boss, Frank Chivers.

He looked like a typical 70s murder detective. Divorced, getting fatter and most probably needed a couple of whiskeys before getting out of bed in the morning. To the people that didn't know him, he looked threatening, to the people that did, he was committed to his job, with a genuine sense of responsibility, he was a great boss.

He had a sizeable blonde mustache, with deep amber stains on the cupid's bow of his lips from years of smoking roll-up cigarettes. He was in beige, with a kipper tie, as if someone had bet him to wear the clothes to work, but in truth, this was all he wore. Alex loved him, he was godfather to both of her children, not for any spiritual reasons, but to tell him how much she thought of him and give him a taste of parenthood, this was the biggest gift she could give him. Reluctantly, he had accepted all those years ago.

"I need to speak to you Frank, I have a feeling this could be urgent." she said. He held up his palms in protest.

He grabbed her arm, "You're on sick leave until the jelly-head doctor gives you a green light." he tapped her head with his nicotine-stained finger, a cockney to the core. He'd seen it all, nothing shocked him.

"Ricky has filled me in on what you texted him yesterday, I think you're barking up a tree that doesn't need barking up. Admit it Alex, your work-sick?".

"Work sick?" Alex frowned.

"Yeah, it's like being homesick, but the opposite, you need to be at home and stop looking for something that isn't there." he added. He gently had hold of her arm, "Go home."

"GUV," they both turned, Rick, was sat at his desk, phone against his ear, he stood, motioning them to come over. They walked over, looking at him.

"Yeah, I'll hand you over to her, she's just walked in, mate." Ricky said.

He was a six-foot black man, ex-paratrooper, and fanatical Crossfitter. He joined the Met, following Alex, after spending six years in the Paras, he transferred to the Royal Military Police, ended up in SIB, the plain clothes unit of the RMP's, similar to CID in the civilian police. There, he spent a few years investigating human trafficking, drugs and sex abuse in the military with Alex, in central Germany. The British Army at the time was withdrawing the military resource from West Germany, so their workload was nonexistent, with much control being handed over to the German police. They formed a close bond, they were best mates and in turn, their families became best mates. He was as close to Si and Alex's kids as he was to her.

"Who is it?" Alex asked, taking the receiver.

"James, forensics."

"For fuck's sake!" Frank cried, "You have already involved the gimps, do you know how much this costs the department?"

The gimp nickname for the white all-in-one coveralls they wear at crime scenes.

Alex pulled a face and looked at Ricky. Her face saying thanks for that, he shrugged and smiled. "I wished you'd stop calling them that boss."

"James, how are you doing?" Alex said.

"I am excellent, I heard Frank," James laughed, "we do need a better superhero name, tell him. That sample you sent, it's human, it's game on." He said it so matter factly, as though this was normal.

Alex stared at Frank, "Come again?"

"It's human, I haven't run it through the spectrometer. But I know for a fact this is human tissue. Because it's you, and that I suspect it's human, bumps it up the work schedule. Give me until about lunch time, I will tell you sex, the approximation of age, if there is, maybe a forensic tag attached, this was 99% crime…" he paused, he sensed he had lost Alex, "You there?"

"How do you know its human if it's not passed through any machines?" Alex asked.

James, bulking at the ignorant use of the term machines. "It doesn't smell like anything from the farming five…you know what that is right?" he questioned.

"Meat from the food chain, I know what that is," Alex said, suddenly feeling nauseous yet smug, James was impressed.

"Yeah, when you say forensic tag, you mean a DNA match, right?" Alex still staring at Frank.

"Yeah, that's right if they're a known gangbanger or a wrongun dealt with by a gang, and or if they have been tagged in the last couple of years by your lot, we should get a name and last known."

"James, thanks, get me on my mobile, I owe you."

"I think it's I, who owes out of the two of us" the previous case involved James, he felt a pang of guilt, his screw-up with the Troll guaranteed support when ever Alex needed it "no sweat Alex, speak later." The line went dead.

Alex replaced the receiver, "It's human."

Frank looked around the room and rubbed his eye. It still had sleep in it "What are you thinking Alex?" Frank asked.

He taught Alex to use her intuition when considering a criminal case, the hunch was often right, Frank chose women primarily to work the murder cases, they could sense and feel far more than any man could. They worked without ego and saw detail like no man and Alex was the best.

Not one of the best, but the best.

"James said what I initially thought. Maybe just an efficient way a gang gets rid of someone, an addict that needs to disappear. One of the informants that have been rumbled. It's clean, efficient, easy, and who's going to give shit?"

Frank listened to what Alex was saying, "I sense a but?" Frank said, he sat on the corner of Alex's desk.

"I dunno guv, I have thought about it over the last 24 hours, I am not so sure, I just have this niggling feeling."

That was enough for Frank.

"Ok, go…go to the processing plant, take Tonto with you, CHECK IT OUT! That's all, and come back, and then brief the team, we'll take it from there."

Ricky grabbed his jacket from the back of his chair, smiling, he squeezed through the two of them, "I'll go and grab Silver" he said, Alex smiled, the car was silver in color, there was no malice in the name Tonto, just an old-fashioned way of doing things.

"My office now." Frank chided, Alex filed in behind him, she looked around the room again. Still, no one was looking up.

She walked into the small office, surrounded by glass. Some old police photos that adorned the wall, one at a jaunty angle, he stood waiting, holding the door open twitching his stained moustache, "SIT!"

Alex did as she was told. The door closed and he walked around his desk and took a seat.

"Si know you're here?" he asked, leaving it hanging.

"Course." Alex knew that Frank was aware of the situation, he knew that Si wanted Alex out of the force, she seemed safer reading those PI files for Shaun Talbot.

"So if I call Si, he will know that you're here and potentially opening a can of worms?" Frank started assaulting his keyboard, one finger smashing, like an elephant tap dancing across the keys, he got his password wrong, he looked at Alex.

"Thought you said this wasn't a tree that needed barking up, Guv?" Alex reminded. Her phone beeped, she pulled it out. A text from Ricky, she fingerprinted her way into the phone, "Needed was the operative word, i.e., you don't need to get involved, as you can see, this place is still here. It hasn't fallen apart in your absence, this investigation can be handled." He gave up trying to do two things at once pushing the keyboard away. "The Troll case nearly broke you" Frank was sincere.

"Tonto is waiting" Alex waved her phone, she got up, and went to leave, she stopped. "I appreciate your concern Frank. I know you have my back, to be honest, I am going batshit crazy at home. This housewife shit isn't my thing. I need to be kicking doors in," she paused, "I'm gonna ask" she said, opening the door. "You in my place, I think we would be having the same conversation."

"Maybe," Frank said, "I can neither afford to lose you as an officer or as a friend, but if I were to choose, I'd rather you be a friend, tread easily."

"Frank, I am fine, just going to the processing plant to ruffle some feathers and then hand the rest over to you guys, I'll sit on the sidelines" Alex raised an eyebrow, a tell, Frank knew it was a lie.

"First sign of trouble, get out and call it in."

Frank reached for his phone, "I am putting the RPFU on standby, don't be a hero today please?" Alex nodded " I think the cannons will help" and left.

"Get me the Roads Policing and Firearms Unit, I need a team on standby, we have a job on." Alex heard him say as the door closed.

She walked through the department and still the drones didn't look up. Alex vaulted the stairs, cleared through the front desk took two steps at a time to the big-engined silver Ford Mondeo, Ricky was plumbing in the address to the satnav.

"Buckle up boss," Ricky said, engaged the gears and sped off.

11

Harvey arrived at the police station at 7AM. After a fraught night with Lucy's mother, he hadn't slept a wink.

Both Zara and Lilly had to start their day in their new jobs and as a group, they all felt that Harvey should go to the police with her mum. They had graduated with Lucy and were all going to start at Colchester General Hospital.

Harvey entered the same waiting room, slightly busier than the day before, but clearly, the place had seen a lot of traffic that night. He urged Lucy's mother to sit on the polyprop orange chairs, bolted to the floor, opposite Deirdre, who was asleep, leaning against the wall in the corner.

Isabelle was always suspicious of Harvey. She thought that he wasn't right for her Lucy.

She felt he was too controlling and although, promised by Lucy that Harvey had never laid a finger on her, there was always an underlying tension in him. Lucy had been brought up as a free spirit, to buck the trend, fight against the machine and always live a life of promise and virtue. Cohabiting with Harvey seemed the opposite to the sort of guy Lucy would go for.

Lucy had said that Harvey's upbringing had been difficult. His father was a drunk and womanizer and he treated his mother with no respect whatsoever. Finally, his mother had left the family home. Abandoning Harvey and his father and he never saw her again.

When the time came, he left home as early as he could and vowed that he would cherish the woman he chose to marry and would do anything to keep her. Lucy knew he was a rough diamond, and like most rough diamonds he just needed a bit of tender loving care.

When Harvey had phoned last night, her upset and worry aside, she sensed a genuine love for her daughter from Harvey, something she hadn't realized until now. Inside, her guts were churning, but with Harvey as her knight in shining armor, no harm could be brought upon her daughter. At some point that morning, in the early hours, she suddenly saw why her daughter would go for Harvey. Underneath the bluster and Essex boy charm, was a sensitive, gentle soul, that genuinely loved her daughter.

Her face ached from all the crying she had done throughout the night, her sinuses were so swollen, it was as though she was suffering a cold.

"Sit here Isabelle, I'll speak to the desk sergeant." Harvey was pale and disheveled. A look not befitting an Essex boy. Exhausted, trawling through the town all day and night, leaving message after message on Lucy's phone. He had never felt so powerless.

Why had she done this, what had he done for her to leave him were the only questions he could ask himself.

He wasn't comfortable going to the police on his own but understood that the girls had to be at work on their first day, they discussed it. Although gripped with worry themselves, how could they not turn up to their first day. If Lucy turned up at some point on Monday, how were they going to explain the absence.

He struggled with confidence, articulation not being his strong point, resulting in his attitude being mistaken for aggressive behaviour, he took a deep breath.

The same sergeant was on the desk, crisp and clean, Harvey thought he had just come on shift, there's no way he's been here for nearly 24 hours.

"Can I help you?" the sergeant asked sardonically,

"I was here yesterday morning," Harvey said, leaning up to the window.

"Don't get too close to the window, it's more of a spit shield, and I am not in the mood for a game of Guess Who." said the sergeant.

He had seen so many people in varying states of distress and abuse, that he genuinely had no idea of Harvey and the girls that had come yesterday.

"So how can I help?" the sergeant repeated.

"I want to report a missing person. Her name is Lucy Hodges. She's my girlfriend" Harvey had to clear his throat as his emotion was trying to get the better of him.

"When were the last known movements of your girlfriend?" the sergeant looked Harvey up and down while he removed the same form from his desk drawer.

There was a pause, the sergeant still not looking up, poised with his pen, he looked up at Harvey "AND" the sergeant said.

"Oh, yeah, sorry, she was supposed to be home around 11:30 Saturday night, but she never really made it home." Harvey pulled his phone out, scrolled through his messages with Lucy.

"What's her full name, and her particulars?" the sergeant said more softly.

Harvey went through the events of the night, and what he and her friends had done since. He omitted the text message and video that he had received from Lucy, realizing this would slam the brakes on any investigation that was about to start. Harvey thought half the Essex police would be out looking for her in the next thirty minutes.

"Right," said the sergeant, filed the paper in the tray to his left, "Someone will take a look at this, she will be recorded missing in the next 24 hours. If we come up with anything, we will let you know." The sergeant replaced his pen in his breast pocket, "Is there anything else I can help you with?" he said, in finality.

"Is that it?" Harvey scolded, "Are you guys going to find her or what?"

"Or what-what?" said the sergeant "Your girlfriend was out on the piss Saturday night, the chances are and sorry if this touches your sensitivity in any way, scored and is holed up with another guy…or girl for that matter. State of the world and all that." The sergeant was getting up and grabbed his coffee cup.

"YOU FUCKIN PIG!" Harvey shouted, "I just told you my girlfriend is missing and that's out of character, and all you fuckin think is she screwing another guy, you're a fucking spastic!" Harvey stepped back, clenching his fists, "Why are you not taking this seriously?"

"Right, sunshine, firstly, calm down," the sergeant's efforts to pacify failed in the first sentence.

"PURPLE, PURPLE, van!" Deirdre had woken up with the commotion inside the room, she was flapping and gesticulating in the seat, Isabelle was visibly horrified by the thing in front of her.

"FUCKIN calm down!" Harvey booted the wall under the window, he realized why the window was there.

"If you don't calm down, you're going in one of the cells," the sergeant said. "Listen, go home, I will file the paperwork and expedite this, more often than not, there is always a simple explanation. Happens all the time. We have lodged four missing persons in the last five days, three of which have turned up." He pulled the form from the tray, held it up, "This has a simple explanation written all over it. I have your number, now go." The sergeant paused with the form held in the air. "Deidre, shut up, or you're getting kicked out!" he shouted.

"I came yesterday, and you fobbed us off. Now I am here today when you said, and you're still fobbing me off!" Harvey was florid with anger, he wanted to pick one of the polyprop chairs up and hurl it through the window, "Fucking go an' find her, do your fucking job!"

"Whats going on?" a middle-aged man in a clean, crisp suit had walked in and placed his hands on his hips.

"The gentleman is reporting the disappearance of his girlfriend sir." the Sergeant said, who had now made his way into the waiting room.

"Is this true?" the man turned to Harvey, who was breathing heavy and still at DefCon 1, his fists clenched.

"Yes, totally out of character, she disappeared Saturday night." Harvey was struggling to string his words together.

"She disappeared Saturday night and you come in on Monday morning?" the man in the suit said, Harvey then glared at the desk sergeant, without looking at the suited man.

"I came in yesterday. This twat told me to come in today if she still hadn't surfaced."

The man in the suit looked at the desk sergeant, looked at Harvey, sensed the tension between them. It wasn't the first time that members of the public had a run-in with sergeant Dowd.

The suited man got Harvey's attention, "My name is Simon Cuthbert," he held out his hand, "Detective Inspector Cuthbert."

Reluctantly, Harvey grabbed his hand and shook it, the grip from Cuthbert was warm and strong, Harvey instantly felt at ease.

Cuthbert, with his thumb, indicated to Dowd to the interview room, to the left of the sergeant's' desk, silently asking if it was free, Dowd nodded.

"Why don't we go in there. Have a quick chat, get some details and I will put your girlfriend on..." he turned to sergeant Dowd, ... "the National Reporting Form, would you be so kind to get them for me?" he then threw Dowd a look that said that he was in the shit!

"And sort Deidre out, its Monday, she should be out of sight." he demanded

"Can I grab Lucy's mum?" Harvey turned, "Isabelle, come on." Harvey said.

Cuthbert opened the door to the interview room, waited, holding it open, shook Isabelle's hand, "How do you do madam?" Cuthbert said.

Harvey and Lucy's mum sat, Cuthbert walked around the table and took a seat.

"Right from the beginning?" he said.

Harvey regaled the story. He even added the text message and video to the interview. Cuthbert took everything down, repeated what Harvey had said and then was thoughtful for a moment.

"Look, what Sergeant Dowd had said is correct."

Harvey sat back and sucked the air in, Isabelle, patted his arm.

"But," Cuthbert flicked through his notebook, "this doesn't sound right and we have a duty of care towards Lucy, I'll make some calls, see what we can come up with." he closed his notebook.

Harvey and Isabelle felt reassured, they shook Cuthbert's hand, Cuthbert tried to sound nonchalant about the discussion that he had just had, but something was up.

What the detective inspector had left out of the interview, as not to fan any flames of suspicion, the town council had reported on the Friday previous, all the CCTV cameras in the carpark and Georges Street had been hacked and then corrupted, making them inoperable, which was odd.

Cuthbert thought that Gala Bingo was going to get robbed, but this was no amateur hack. It was sophisticated and efficient, more like a high-end bank job, the sort of people that hack systems like the cameras on Georges Street were professional. There was nothing on the route of the damage to the cameras, only the carpark. There were no jewellers, no cash machines, travel agents, nothing of note. He was going to view the rest of the CCTV, up the point of the damaged cameras, but his alarm bells were loudly ringing.

12

Broc left the house as the sun was rising in the east. The clouds hung in the brilliant blue sky, like lumps of pale rose quartz. The sky was beautiful. Broc felt buoyant. It was the best time of day, the air had a tinge of cold, the leaves started their predictable turn to orange and amber, soon, the trees will be bare and the winter will take hold. That didn't matter. He had Lucy to attend too.

Throughout the last 24 hours, Broc had monitored Lucy through his phone. Her bispectral index value never changed, the physiological parameters remained stable and in the normal range. The surface that Lucy was on adjusted regularly protecting her pressure areas. Broc quickly ran intravenous nutrition through the IV line.

He had spent the day, snuggled on the sofa in front of a fire, with his naked pet, Carmen, listening to a mix of chill out tunes and classical music, mainly Bach, she nuzzled him, caressed him and loved him.

They turned in early after a scrumptious Sunday roast. She tried to stimulate him, but his flaccidness wouldn't stiffen. He wanted to penetrate her but using his limp penis was like trying to push a marshmallow through a slot machine. It was impossible, in frustration, he beat Carmen to within an inch of her life. He strangled her, used his belt as a noose. She turned different shades of blue for the three hours Broc abused her. Pulled her hair, punched her, stretched her intimate parts with his fist, her body was red, bruised and bleeding, yet she loved it. It turned Broc on and all she was, was to serve, nothing was more important than to serve her daddy.

Sobbing, Carmen waited for the best part, when Broc was exhausted, he carried her to the bath and bathed her in his favorite foam bath of citrus scents. He made her stand in the tub and he cleaned her down like she was a dirty five-year-old, with a giant sponge. She just grinned at him. He caressed her while she soaked in the healing warm water. He then dried her, and carried her to the bedroom. He placed her on the bed, tucked her in and then cuddled her, until she fell asleep, not a word uttered.

Spooning her, he held her tight, telling her that she was special and that he loved her. Her body relaxed, the muscles becoming toneless, her shallow breaths told Broc she was fast asleep.

To Broc, the essential part of dominance was the aftercare. He valued Carmen's gift to him, and made sure that there were no shortcuts with restoring her psychological state, he was told by his mentor, 'ignore this stage of dominance at your peril.'

He was wearing his sweatpants and a tee shirt. Once inside he would change into disposable scrubs, but first, Broc had to ensure that he wouldn't be disturbed.

The Harvest, for a surgical team in a hospital, would take no more than 60 minutes, draining the donor of blood as the final act of the harvest. He had his harvest down to just over one and half hours, first the liver, then the heart and lungs, followed by the kidneys, pancreas and finally the large bowel. The rest of her would be dissected for his amusement, then disposing of her through a catering grade meat mincer that he had purchased in Germany when he first started working for Ng.

What was different here, was that Broc derived sexual gratification from the dissection, the victim would be awake throughout the whole event and watch the Great Broc, strip the body of its organs.

Broc entered the complex. The ramp closed from the outside world, anyone entering the barn wouldn't know that there was a ramp or a subterranean level. Both Lucy and Broc was locked in, and only Broc would leave.

Broc walked into the operating theatre. Lucy was in the same place, quiet and peaceful. The sound was making her chest go up and down gently. He removed the blanket and exposed her naked body. She was still comfortably warm, he busied himself, arranging equipment around, emptied her catheter bag, selected a mix and clicked play on the stereo and the rich tones of Bach started. 'Couldn't be more perfect,' Broc thought.

The trolley Lucy was on, was mechanical and could be manipulated to place her in any desired position. He strapped her in, supporting her knees, hips, arms and shoulders, secured the head in a head restraint, then stood her upright. Cello Suite No.1 in G Major vibrated throughout the room as he stepped back and marveled at Lucy. She was exquisite, arms at her side with her palms facing up. She was perfect, the best Broc had ever had. His groin tightened at the sight.

With a sponge, he washed Lucy's skin with an iodine solution, around her neck, throat and abdomen. She went from amber tanned skin to a deep bronze color. He remotely tilted her head forward, separating the vertebrae in her neck. Using his fingers, Broc felt the individual bones in the upper neck and located the first cervical bone, at the base of her skull, and counted down until he reached C5 and C6 just above her shoulders. A sudden rise in Lucy's heart rate proved she felt the thin needle puncture her skin.

"Shhh, Lucy." he whispered. "This won't take long my love, it'll make you feel more comfortable, the injection will numb you from the neck down."

"And there it is, the pop." He was in the dural space, the next pop, was the subarachnoid space, then suddenly, the straw coloured fluid that bathes the brain and spine slowly flowed out of the needle, "There we are Lucy, all the pain will go away now. We can wake you up in a minute." Broc soothed.

Broc began the spinal injection process. First, he used a larger syringe with a local anesthetic and diamorphine which would completely numb Lucy within ten minutes. Next, he inserted a smaller tube through the hollow needle, connected it to a syringe driver and then removed the needle. He taped the small tube in place, switched off the anesthetic gas, but increased the paralyzing agent, and watched as Lucy's bispectral index value increased. She would soon be awake."

Lucy could sense her environment. She could feel the breathing tube in her throat. She still felt paralyzed. Her mind then took her back to the carpark. The man was falling, helping him, then remembered him standing over her. Placing a mask on her face, the next memory was lying flat, in an ambulance, the man's face vivid in her mind. Then she remembered the indignity of the man inserting a catheter into her bladder. With her legs splayed, she felt the flush of embarrassment, what was happening she thought. I am so confused.

Then Lucy remembered the smell of the man. His aftershave was earthy, almost woody. She thought it was a provocative and expensive scent, she liked it, she could smell the same smell now, was this a memory, or is he here.

"Lucy....Lucy, are you there?" Lucy could hear the voice, it kept coming from the dark, she latched onto the voice, she recognised it, it was the man from last night, still confused.

"Lucy, listen to my voice. You're just waking up, what I want you to do, is simply open your eyes." She tried, but her muscles weren't complying.

"Open your eyes, my love, everything is ok, you're safe, you shouldn't be feeling any pain." the voice said. Lucy, tried to speak, she couldn't speak, although the tube was in her throat, her jaw just wouldn't move.

"Lucy, I want you to relax, and just open your eyes."

She tried again, she could feel a finger or thumb on her eyelid, Broc slid the eyelid up, Lucy's pupil instantly reacted, he let go.

"Shit!" Broc said, "I am so sorry, the light is so bright. Give me a second, Lucy."

Lucy's eyes, bathed in bright light, it was agony, she wanted to scream, but nothing came out. It was as though she was disconnected from her body.

She felt the man's fingers again, the eyelid raised and in the low light, her eyes focused, she saw the man's face from last night. She went to speak, but again, nothing. She saw his hand and the fingers that manipulated her left eye, then the man stood back, Lucy could focus on him clearer.

"There you are, welcome to my theatre," the man said.

Lucy was in a state of panic, he was wearing surgical scrubs, there was no one else in the room, it was an unfamiliar room.

She had been in all the operating theatres in Colchester General and they looked nothing like this room. What the fuck is going on, then the man moved out of the way, to Lucy's abject horror, she saw herself in the mirror. Upright, secured by straps, completely naked and shaved. A breathing tube secured to the side of her mouth. She couldn't move, the only emotional response she could manage, was tears. She cried, hard, eyes watering like an overflowing drain.

The man came into view, stood behind Lucy, he leaned in, his face next to her right ear, she could hear his breathing, he was grinning, perfect teeth, he smelt so good, his hands came round her waist, Lucy wanted to scream out and get away, get as far away as possible, but she couldn't.

His hands moved up her flanks, and then cupped her breast, he squeezed both of her nipples, she felt nothing, "There you go babygirl, you feel nothing," the man said.

He ran both his hands down her abdomen. She tried to make her body moved. She knew where he was heading, her sense of violation palpable, he stopped, grinning even wider. "What do you take me for?" he chuckled.

"I am not a monster, Lucy. I have no interest in your sexual being. My needs run much deeper."

He was looking at her, her skin crawling, she watched, agog to the most surreal encounter of her life, mixed with fear, horror, and vulnerability, nothing about this was making sense.

She then remembered the man speaking to her in the van. "My name is Dale Broc, I have taken you, this will not end well for you, in the next 48 hours, I will harvest all of your organs and then end your life, I know your feeling confused right now."

The tears came again, with a renewed vigor.

"Can you remember what I told you in the van?" Broc asked, "I am going to harvest your organs, none of this is your fault, other than circumstances, you weren't chosen at random," the man said.

"I have put a drug in your spinal cord, in the base of your neck, the whole event will be completely painless for you." Broc disappeared from view, she could hear his clogs clipping the floor.

Lucy had so many questions, but was unable to speak. Why, why was this happening she thought of Harvey. He must be worried sick about her, her friends, she could see them scouring the town looking for her, her mum and dad, this will destroy them. How could I be so stupid to be abducted and then end up here, this guy is Satan, the devil, every kid's nightmare.

Broc wheeled two trollies into view, they were covered in a green sterile drape. He disappeared and returned with a weird machine. It had gas cylinders on, wires, tubes, a ventilator and switches, and levers.

Broc then stood in front of her, "This machine is called ECMO, it will oxygenate your blood, this means I can remove your organs while you watch me. I have to attach your vascular system to this machine." He motioned to the machine behind him.

Panic surged through Lucy when Broc, coldly, showed her the scalpel. Her body's natural fight or flight mechanism entirely suppressed. Lucy was powerless.

Lucy's eyes pleaded as Broc smiled and finding the right spot under her collar bone, deftly sliced through her skin.

Lucy heard a buzzing sound, "Don't be alarmed by that noise, babygirl."

Broc came into Lucy's view wearing a surgical mask, a cloth cap, and a green gown. He showed her some tweezer-like device, which had a wire coming from it.

"This is diathermy, it stops you from bleeding by sealing your blood vessels so that we won't be too messy." his eyes narrowed giving way to the smile hidden under the mask, as though this was an ordinary event.

Nothing is fucking normal here, Lucy thought.

Using scissors and forceps, Broc made light work of the tissue layers, locating the correct veins and arteries. He found the brachial artery, hooked the ECMO cannula to oxygenate the blood when the heart and lungs were placed on bypass. He worked his way across her chest exposing ribs and other structures. Lucy watched in fascination. She felt movement, but felt no pain as Broc worked. He was an expert and apparently a well-practiced surgeon.

As Broc went deeper, he exposed the large subclavian vein, the vein of the blood needing oxygen.

Broc looked into Lucy's eyes, "Ok, take a look."

He adjusted the light, Lucy looked, she could see under the right collarbone, completely dissected, showing a myriad of veins, arteries pulsating, nerves and muscle tissue, to Lucy this was incredulous, she closed her eyes.

"OPEN YOUR FUCKING EYES!" Broc screamed.

Lucy struggled, and complied, tears started to roll down her cheek again. With the long tweezers in Broc's hands, he demonstrated to Lucy what the structures were and which ones he was going to use to place her on this ECMO machine thing. She zoned out. It was pointless listening to the ramblings of this deranged lunatic. There was nothing she could do, trapped in her own body, completely at Broc's mercy.

A long hollow needle with a red end punctured the brachial artery. Threaded the tube into the artery, he looked at the ECG. He knew he would be in the right place because the ECG trace would alter. It did, he knew the tube was in Lucy's right atrium of the heart, the tube had measuring markings. He withdrew the tube about 5 cms. The heart trace returned to normal.

Then Broc, with the slightly bigger blue needle, inserted it into the subclavian vein, he repeated the steps. Broc quickly sutured the two cannulas into place.

Broc switched the machine on. Attached the tubing, he adjusted some dials and switches, then turned to Lucy.

"Right baby girl, this might feel a little odd."

Like an air stewardess during the obligatory safety brief, Broc showed her the machine.

"This machine will act as your heart and lungs, so I can remove your organs while you are still with me, after that, you can watch me dissect the rest of you for my studies. Then I will switch you off, and then that will be that."

Broc looked at Lucy, he grinned, there was no guilt or emotion.

You rot in hell Broc Lucy thought, go fuck yourself!

Broc turned, unclamped the tubes, the dark blood from Lucy's body, the blood returning to the heart to rid the system of the carbon dioxide, the other tube then started pumping the bright crimson oxygen-rich blood back into Lucy's body. The extracorporeal membrane oxygenator Broc had received from Ng was a godsend for his criminality.

He could harvest all the organs, and keep the victim artificially alive, the longest specimen he kept alive was six days, with just a head to communicate with. The body completely amputated from the neck down, and disposed of in front of the victim's eyes was a particular delight for Broc.

Finally, Broc placed a flat disc like device on Lucy's throat. The device would pick up the vibration of Lucy's vocal cords when she spoke. Synthesised to a software program embedded into the operating room. When Lucy spoke as there was no air in the lungs she would have no voice. The device would subliminally broadcast Lucy's voice through the speakers in the OR

Now time for the harvest.

13

The Ford Mondeo found its way into a deserted industrial estate. Tilbury, the official port of London, primarily imported paper into the UK and exported grain. It was a place of massive industry, even today, with the decline of industry in the UK, major blue chip companies still used the London Port Authority docks for import and export.

Part of the industry is the growing recycling plants. From paper to plastic, metal and food. The food recycling area was on the furthest eastern aspect of the docks, mainly for the smell and the vermin it attracted.

Ricky and Alex had spent over an hour in traffic, the sprawling east London traffic never letting up. They didn't have to search for the recycling plant. They just had to follow their noses, the smell almost intolerable.

"I think that's it, there, Rick." Alex said, looking around with keen eyes, the satnav had stated that they had reached their destination, at a crossroad, they could see a large yellow secure trailer skip, behind that, was the unmistakable livery of London's finest.

"Frank sent some uniforms for us?" Ricky asked, nodding behind the yellow skip.

Alex peered through the windscreen as if she had X-ray eyes, "Doubt it, he would have said."

Alex pulled out her phone, hit messages and found Frank's message thread, you sent uniforms to this location boss? Pocketed her phone.

"Ok Tonto, let's take a closer look." Alex clicked her tongue like she was on a horse.

Ricky drove beyond the skip, the two uniformed officers having a crafty smoke before getting back into their car.

"T-bone their car, Ricky, I want them to stay here."

Ricky complied and pulled the handbrake. The two uniformed officers straightened up, stamped their cigarettes out and approached the Mondeo.

Alex got out, brandishing her warrant card "Stand down tiger, Sergeant Brown from the Mile End nick CID, what are you doing here, constables?"

The approaching officer stopped in his tracks, understanding why Sergeant Brown had parked her car there, he thought he was in the shit.

"Sorry sarge," He shuffled uncomfortably on his feet, "Just thought we would have a quick fag before heading back into town." He waited for the impending bollocking.

"Like I said, stand down," Alex replaced her warrant card, "I asked what you were doing here constable…" Alex waited for the name.

"Constable Irving, Sarge…" The use of familiarity with title sarge grated on Alex, went against her sensibilities and military discipline, "…And Watkins, we're here on the job." he indicated to an equally guilty looking fresh-faced young officer.

Alex interest roused, Job?" She asked.

"Yeah, the boss and a clerical assistant here went hammer and tongs apparently. A member of staff dialed 999 and called us in." He pulled his notebook out, Alex noted that it wasn't an old dog-eared notebook like hers or Ricky's. Irving flicked through his pages, Alex waited. Thrusting her hands deep into the pockets of her coat, looked about, she noticed CCTV cameras looking at the skip, which had the vilest smell emanating from it.

"An hour ago, we got dispatch on the blower, sent us here to deal with a disturbance, we got here 35 minutes ago, nothing else to report, we entered the office, the parties involved in the fracas had resolved their differences both apologising to each other in front of us, we then left, sarge."

"Ok..." She looked at Ricky, he knew what she was saying, they were going in, he walked in ahead of her, in his casual, yet confident saunter, looking about the walls and surroundings. Old habits die hard.

"Ok, hang around officer Irving, we may need you." Alex went to walk off.

"We have another job on, sarge, we have to go." Irving said looking at her.

"I don't give a shit Irving, you get on your blower and tell whoever grinds your organ, that Sergeant Brown from the murder squad at Mile End has collared you, copy that Irving?" Alex took a step towards the constable.

Irving suddenly feeling unsettled, he agreed, "Sarge." He said.

Alex knew she had him. She went to follow Ricky, "Oh, and one more thing constable," Alex turned and half faced Irving. The officer, turned to face her, his complexion returning to a normal shade of pale. "There are only two forms of sarge in this world," He frowned, he didn't know where Alex was going, "Mass-sarge and saus-sarge and I am neither a masseuse or particularly into sausages, understand Irving?"

The officer's complexion reddening again, "Sergeant" Irving said, coming to attention.

Alex turned and followed Ricky. They got to the yellow painted metal stairs together. They had noticed cameras everywhere and the stairs led its way in two flights to a portacabin at the top, they could both hear voices.

Alex's phone beeped, she pulled it out, Frank had backed the constables story up, he hadn't sent any uniform ahead of them.

"Obviously not yet sorted boss." Ricky said, "I'll go in first, Alex. Follow me in." Ricky took the stairs, two at a time, Alex's breath becoming labored as she reached the top, Ricky waiting by the door, waiting for her.

"I'll wait till you catch your breath, Alex." Ricky was smiling.

"Fuck you, Rick!" She said, breathing heavily. She turned and surveyed the plant. It was big, ugly and very smelly.

"Kick it in, Ricky." Alex said.

Ricky turned the door handle and stepped into the office, Alex followed. A young attractive girl stood filing her nails, wearing high stilettos and the shortest of skirts - not what one would call office attire. She stood over a grey-haired man whose chin wobbled as he spoke to her while picking up papers strewn about the floor.

The man stopped speaking and looked at Ricky and Alex, "The office is closed, as you can see, we are in a bit of mess." He indicated to the room with his arm.

"Police," Ricky said, "I am DC Lambert, this is..." He waited as Alex walked in and was looking around "DS Brown." He was now showing his card, the girl turned, almost alarmed. Then she saw Ricky, smiled and walked around her desk, sat and just gazed.

"The police were here, fat lot of use they were. No idea why they sent plain-clothes officers here. Haven't you got more important things to do than chase up domestics?" The man carried on picking up the papers around him, Alex stepped forward.

"We are not here about your domestic..." Alex surveyed the room. It was shabby, looked like a set on Only Fools and Horses, dated, the computers were old, the carpet tired and rucked up in places, it had an unpleasant feel to it.

The guy was still clearing up the evidence of the paper cannon that had just gone off in the room, "What is it you want, then?" He inquired without looking up.

"It's about your audit with the Trading Standards and Food Standards Agency." Alex was trying to curb her irritation.

The man carried on, "What's that got to do with CID? I passed that inspection." He stopped, he was out of breath, or he needed to concentrate, or both Alex thought.

"You did pass. We want to talk to you about some aspects of the report."

Alex looked around the room. She had the attention of three office staff as well as the manager.

"Do you need a warrant?" He said, resting his hands on his knees.

"Do I need to get one, sir?" Alex replied. "And if I do, this place will be shut until I have one. Which will take at least..." Alex sucked in the air, looked at Ricky, "What do you think constable…" She asked.

Ricky sucked in the air, mimicking Alex, "…24 hours gov, at least."

"For fuck sake," The man got up. He needed the aid of the nearest office table, he made a huge effort to get to his feet. "My knees are shot to bits." He exclaimed.

"You need to go to a gym. sir." Ricky said, staring at him.

The man turned about and walked towards a door in the corner, as he approached it, both Ricky and Alex followed him, "GET THIS PLACE CLEANED UP!" He shouted.

Alex turned to look at the room, no one moved. She looked at the pretty girl at the desk who had been looking at Ricky, "I have milk and no sugar" Alex said to the short skirted girl, nodding her head to Ricky "Sweet-cheeks that came with me has one sugar, be a love," The girls face dropped. "Chop chop" Alex demanded. Something about her Alex thought.

Alex followed them into the office. The door had a plaque on it, worn out. Gordon Gormley - Managing Director it read. As Alex entered the room, Gormley had already taken a seat behind the biggest desk Alex had ever seen. Ricky was mooching around, peering through the windows that were on two aspects of the room. The room was cladded in beige wooden panels, that looked awesome in the 70's, a picture of the queen hung on one wall, the other wall, was a full-length window looking out onto his secretary, who was still filing her nails

Alex indicated to the door, " I take it your Mr. Gormley?".

"Your skills as a detective are infinite, sergeant." He said, leaning back in his chair, adopting a supercilious, over-inflated ego of himself kind of attitude. "What's this about, the report was clear, it was a pass." Alex was trying not to focus on Gormley's wobbling chin as he spoke and was watching Ricky.

Ricky was looking at files on a slanted shelf, probably the shelf was straight when it was first put up, but now, after years of use, it was coming to the end of its purpose.

"Is he allowed to do that, sergeant?" Gormley asked, holding his arm out, in Ricky's direction. Ricky looked over and carried on regardless.

"Focus on me Mr. Gormley." Alex said.

Gormley leaned forward, the chair protesting with the shifting weight, he shuffled some scattered papers on his desk, found a pink duplicate form, he passed it to Alex, Alex recognized the writing of her husband. "The guy that came, A…eerm," Gormley said.

"Mr. Brown" Alex interjected.

"Yes." Gormley looked at Alex, dismissed the feeling, but not making the connection that she was DS Brown.

"Yes, Mr. Brown, cocky twat, waltzed in here like he owned the shop, in his stereotypical suit, these fucking bureaucrats have no idea what it's like at the coal face."

Alex bit her tongue, Si worked in Trading Standards to keep shits like you on the straight and narrow she thought, and I chose that suit.

"Where did Mr. Brown take the food samples from?" Alex asked.

"Erm, the freegan skip." Gormley said matter factly.

"Freegan?" Ricky said, Ricky's body was a temple, and was religious with his food, this was a term he hadn't heard of, Gormley looked up.

"The yellow skip outside, it's for people to chuck food into, like restaurants that can't afford proper disposal or supermarkets that have gone over their quota of food wastage weight. They come and dump it inside the yellow skip, it's locked, so the freegans don't go in there an' nick the food." Gormley was looking irritated, it was a subject that he didn't like talking about.

"I don't understand." Alex asked.

"What don't you understand, sergeant?" Gormley replied.

"Well, that the skip is locked and that you enable restaurants to swerve the law and then you let these so-called freegan's ransack the skip. What are they…these freegans?" She asked.

"Firstly, I don't enable anyone. We have the skip because these restaurants that I supposedly enable, would dump their shite at the front gates. Have you any idea the vermin that we have had to deal with in the past." He lit a cigarette, "And these fucking freegans' are not tramps or homeless, disadvantaged souls, but normal people that have jobs and money. They choose to not live in wasteful society and nick other people's waste." Both Alex and Ricky looked at each other.

"The skip is locked to try and stop the worst kind of vermin…", He threw the lighter onto the desk and took a deep heave on the cigarette, "…Humans, I have it under advice from the Trading Standards."

"I noticed that the skip, front gates and immediate courtyard inside the gates are covered by CCTV cameras." Alex asked, trying to keep on track.

"Yes, we have to, security in place has to be tight for insurance and compliance reasons, why do you ask?" He took another deep drag from the cigarette.

"You know it's illegal to smoke inside a place of work." Ricky stated disgustingly.

Gormley looked up at Ricky and blew the smoke in his direction, "Sue me.".

Alex spoke "I asked because I would like to look at them. How often do you empty that yellow skip?" She stood and walked over to the window feeling queasy and opened it. There was a gush of air, the stained, yellowed curtains gracefully rose. Alex shut the window and the curtains unceremoniously fell back against the wall. The smell outside was more overpowering than the smell of smoke in the office.

Gormley cackled and started coughing. "The smell is something you get used to working here, I don't even smell it anymore." He flicked some ash into the overfilled ashtray "We empty it every Monday and Friday." He blew out more smoke "Something's telling me you need a warrant."

"Listen, show me the footage. Park me over there by the computer in the corner, I will take a look and I won't call

Trading Standards and ask them to come in with their magnifying glass. You know how these things can turn out, no matter how compliant you are, they will find something. And shut you down, for long enough to hurt you financially." Alex looked around the room, "It doesn't take the brains of an archbishop to know that may be a problem for you."

Gormley pulled a face, leaned forward and stamped the cigarette out, spilling more ash onto the table. He knew he was cornered. He pressed the intercom, "TASHA!" There was a pause, he looked at Alex, Alex looked out of the full-size window that had a good view of the leggy brunette that hadn't brought them their coffees and was still filing her nails. "TASHA, for fuck sake!" He went to get up.

"WHAT?" The girl shouted, Alex could see the girl was now looking into the window, file down and pressing the intercom, a problem girl Alex thought.

"Get me the CCTV footage of the front gates and the freegan skip from last Monday." He let go of the button.

Alex saw the girl stand and move out of sight.

Alex walked over to the computer in the corner, Gormley seemed uptight that she was now sitting at the screen. Switching it on, "You won't look at anything else will you?" Gormley asked worriedly.

"As you said, I don't have a warrant, so I can't. I only want to look at who's dumping the food in your bin." Alex said, wiping the desk with the heel of her hand, "You'll be fine, Mr. Gormley."

There were food and other dried lumps of something scattered all over the keyboard. The screen looked dirty, with a thick layer of dust along the top, Alex thought wisely to clean it.

The girl came in, followed by an attitude that needed smacking out of her. "Here." She threw a folder of CD's on to the desk.

"That'll be all." Gormley said, trying to sound authoritative.

"Whatever" Tasha stated as she rolled her eyes and walked off. Alex noticed she pulled out her phone, scrolled, found DAD, messaged POLICE and hit send.

She had some sass Ricky thought.

Gormley arranged the discs and passed them to Alex, "They're in date order, we keep the copies for eight weeks then rewrite over the top of them. Only keeping them back if there's something going on, or the Standards chaps what to look at them."

Gormley was being over helpful, which seemed suspicious. Alex was looking at him, trying to gauge what was going on, she noticed that Ricky had clocked it too, he raised his eyebrows, answering the silent question that Alex was asking.

The discs went back one full month, but going on the information that Gormley had given to Alex, she started with the previous Monday. She knew that Si had visited the plant on Tuesday, so the skip had had to have been emptied on Monday, assuming that the skip had been emptied as scheduled. Monday would probably reveal some interesting activity.

She didn't have to wait long, a high-sided Mercedes Sprinter van came into the grainy shot, two men got out, there was no livery on the side of the truck, but even more curious, the number plate, was hidden.

"Mr. Gormley, have you seen this van before? There are two chaps in it, offloading stuff in to the skip."

Alex was replaying the clip, zooming in on the men accessing the side door of the van, there was a relatively large pile of meat in polystyrene trays, thrown into the skip.

He bent down and looked, he was close to Alex's face, she was mesmerised by the flabby chin hanging like a turkey's neck, the smell of his unwashed body, coupled with stale cigarettes was overpowering.

"I dunno, Sergeant." He took control of the mouse and replayed the clip, "Never seen these guys before."

Ricky's phone rang, he answered, "Sup."

"Are you sure you haven't seen these guys before?" Alex pressed him.

Gormley shook his head, his chin catching up with the head shake eventually, "Nope, sorry."

"Boss," Ricky strode across the room, handing her the phone, "Forensics, Dr. Dugal."

She took the phone, stood up and walked to the window, Gormley sat down, the chair creaking.

"Hi James, what have you got?" Alex stared out the window. She could see the uniformed officers chatting by the car, the seagulls circling over the estuary making their choking calls, her suspicions again reinforced with a sickening feeling when James spoke.

"Glad I am on your side, Alex. We have a hit on the DNA, it's no gangbanger. Melissa Davies, 22-year-old girl, reported missing over three weeks ago from Bodmin in Cornwall, you can google her. The local news has run regular reports on her absence. Totally out of character." James was matter-of-fact. She had known him for some years now. She knew that until the case is closed, he will remain matter-of-fact throughout the subsequent investigation.

"You sure, James?" Alex asked, but it was pointless. James was a stickler for details and would've run the variables multiple times.

"Yes, she had a concoction on of drugs, all anesthetic grade…propofol, rocuronium, some sodium bicarbonate, calcium gluconate and heparin. These drugs probably mean nothing to you, Alex, but they are anesthetic drugs. Designed to keep you alive, how she ended..." There was a pause. He was trying to find the words "In this state, is up to you, I guess."

Alex did know. She had a previous life. These drugs were a regular part of her day before transferring to the RMP's. She ended the call.

She turned, "Mr. Gormley," She walked over, he was still engrossed in watching the grainy images on the screen, "You don't need to worry about Trading Standards shutting you down."

"Oh, why's that?" He was still looking at the screen.

"Because I am shutting you down. You're recycling plant is now my crime scene and until otherwise, none of you are leaving."

14

After Broc had tested Lucy's blood gasses and confirmed that the gaseous exchange essential for human life was occurring in the ECMO, he was happy to remove the breathing tube that Lucy had been relying on.

He grabbed a syringe and walked over to her, her eyes full of fear and angst.

"I am going to remove this tube now Lucy." He fumbled around the tube, Lucy couldn't make it out as it was all to close to her face. Broc found the pilot tube, inserted the syringe and pulled back on the plunger. The cuff that secured the tube below Lucy's vocal cords deflated, her body trying to start the predictable breathing pattern, but the paralyzing drugs still preventing it, she convulsed slightly as Broc removed the tube from her throat.

Lucy had the oddest sensation. She knew she wasn't breathing, but didn't feel the rising panic of trying to get a breath. She felt peculiar, but ok. There was no pain from the neck down, still unable to move and now, not breathing, her lungs remaining dormant, waiting in anticipation of the inevitable rush of air to expand them. But that breath will never be taken by Lucy, the next time these lungs will experience that rush of air, the lungs and heart will be in another human being.

"You can speak if you wish, Lucy." Broc said. He stood back, "I have taken the tube out for you, babygirl. You can speak, just try." He angled the operating table to 70 degrees, allowing Lucy to see around the room, but also, keeping her bodily fluids within her body cavity when the time came.

Lucy tried, but nothing came, her throat was so dry, it felt as though her throat was stuck together, she opened her mouth, a noise came out, then the messages found their groove, her mind fully engaging with the first thing Lucy had thoughtfully commanded since her abduction. The word came out, "WHY!" It was muffled and horse, but Broc heard the word clearly.

"Why…you say why, that's funny." He turned about and grabbed a trolley, he was in his element. "Everyone asks that question. I think it's an odd question when you can ask others."

Lucy could have sworn he was enjoying himself, of which he was. He was behaving like a child on the morning of their birthday, an over exuberant excited ten year old.

"Why?" Lucy asked again, this time becoming more coherent, with demand in her voice, Broc stopped, he sensed the tone, he didn't like it.

The excited child in him had just received a shot across the bows. Like he would have got from his father, he turned and walked up to Lucy. With the back of his hand, he slapped it into the side of Lucy's face.

The pain Lucy felt was augmented by the loss of sensation from the neck down, he cried out "Don't you fucking dare take that tone with me." Anger in Broc's eyes, Lucy never shying from an argument met them with her own. Her upbringing was the polar opposite of Broc's, she was taught to fight for what's right or wrong and anything that was worth fighting for.

Tears filled her eyes, the pain was resonating and not leaving, she couldn't touch her face, it was throbbing and she could feel the flushing of blood. Broc stood back, feeling the shame again for his anger, his anger subsided and his features became soft again, he approached Lucy, staring at him in repugnance. "Sorry babygirl." Broc caressed her face, Lucy wanting to avoid the attention, but still unable to move.

"Why?" She asked softer, more gently, the ECMO machine distinctly whirling and keeping Lucy alive.

He stared at her, finding the words. "It's never personal, Lucy. You fitted a framework that was required, your only crime…having a blood test at the wrong time, that's all."

He went back to the trolley, with the other instruments on it, "I work for an organization that pays very well." He arranged things without touching them, as he was yet to get completely sterile.

"Where there's a demand, there's a supply, it's finding the right people to do the job." He looked up at Lucy.

"You took an oath, where is your moral code and ethics? You're a doctor, even surgeon, I have been around enough of them." Lucy, still had tears in her eyes as she spoke, it hit home again how surreal this was, she was hooked up to a machine that was breathing for her, after being kidnapped by this man.

"The oath I took as a medical student was to first, not harm, my interpretation of this is that there is a higher purpose than just you Lucy; second to that, my childhood had never installed that moral compass that you have just mentioned and ethics…" Broc laughed, "I work in healthcare, where are the morals and ethics with that? Every government organization in this stinking country is morally and ethically bankrupt, if you think how can I sleep at night, I can tell you, I sleep very well."

He turned and walked up to the enormous stainless steel sink the corner, still in sight of Lucy. For five minutes, Broc scrubbed his hands and forearms, water cascading off both elbows and running onto the floor, his elbows becoming an extension of the taps, skin brown with iodine. He gowned himself up and deftly donned two pairs of gloves on to his hands.

He turned and approached Lucy. She pleaded "Please, stop. You don't need to do this. I won't tell anyone. I won't go to the police."

Broc pushed the surgical trolley in front of Lucy. He rearranged the instruments on the surface again. Lucy could see all of them, glinting in the light.

Broc picked up the large scalpel blade and turned, "It is all too late for that now babygirl, too much has been invested in you being here right now."

"Please, I beg you," She said, her voice cracking, Broc approached Lucy. The large scalpel glinting in the white surgical lights, although Lucy couldn't move, she could still feel the warmth from the light, Broc came closer, she tried to hold her breath, yet still nothing, nothing complied.

Broc placed his free hand on Lucy's chest. With the palm of his hand, her skin stretched, he was poised with the blade "This won't hurt at all, Lucy. Try and relax."

Broc looked up and saw the horror on Lucy's face. Tears were streaming down her cheeks, he paused. A moment of unease spread through him. Was that regret he thought. He threw the thought away and looked down at Lucy's chest. Nimbly felt with his fingers along the center of the chest, worked his fingers upwards and found the manubrium, the top part of the sternum, with his index finger, he hooked it over, feeling for the hard cartilage of the trachea, underneath the larynx. Lucy could feel it, she frowned in pain, a muffled cry came out "Please," It was painful, she could feel his fingers, "Steady babygirl" Broc said.

He found what he was looking for and stretched the skin. The blade cut smoothly into Lucy's flesh. Like a knife through tender lamb. This she couldn't feel, as it was just below the epidural block in Lucy's neck, in one neat move of the blade, Broc swept the knife downwards, always feeling the anatomical landmarks as he cut with his free hand. Broc's fingers found the first destination of the cut, on the xiphisternum, in the center of the chest, at the bottom of the ribs. He turned to his trolley, blood on his hands, Lucy was watching, so much blood she thought, it was at this point that Lucy had finally come to terms with her predicament, there was no way out from here, just let him get this over as soon as possible.

Broc turned and smiled at her, he now had a fresh blade, "Don't want you to get an infection, Lucy." Broc nodded to the knife in his hand, "Clean blade babygirl." He winked.

He approached her, again, from the top, with the new knife. Duplicated his initial incision and made another cut. This time deeper, his free hand had changed to the electric cautery pencil he had used earlier. Lucy could hear the slicing of her muscle and fat. The buzzing sound of the cautery gave off an unpleasant overdone barbecue smell of burning meat, she closed her eyes and thought of Harvey, how her life would've panned out, her family, her friends. She wondered if they even knew she had been abducted, they certainly wouldn't know that this was happening to her, she knew there was no going back now, her fate was sealed.

Broc was in his element, the music on, a perfect specimen to dissect, this was as close to utopia that Broc could get to. He reached the surface of the sternum quickly, something his previous surgical mentors all instilled in him was to get through the tissue layers quickly. His dissection was efficient and almost bloodless, circumventing obvious major perforating vessels in the layers and quickly cauterizing the hidden rogue ones that spurted or oozed when the knife went through them. He placed a scissor-like a device that had three-inch teeth in depth, it opened outwards and held itself open on a ratchet and gripped the edges of the wound making them stay open, he used two of them.

Broc felt from the top of the manubrium and pressed, feeling the sternum on the way down until he located the notch-like feature called the sternal angle, lateral to the second rib and the entry to the heart.

Broc turned, put the knife down and picked up the power tool, he pressed the go button and tested the blade on the device. Lucy opened her eyes when she heard the power tool start and saw Broc stood in front of her, her blood all down his gown, holding a saw in his hands, the reciprocating bladed tool making a loud noise.

Broc approached her, "I know the noise is horrible, Lucy, but it won't hurt, I promise."

Again with his free hand, he felt for the anatomical point, rubbed the nub of the notch on her sternum. Lucy's eyes wide, focused on the tip of the blade protruding from the power tool, the sight was too horrific for words, she passed out.

Broc smiled, the saw always affected everyone. He placed the tip in the notch and pressed, the saw like going through thin wood, made light work of Lucy's sternum. Once the blade was two thirds into Lucy's chest, her cheeks began vibrating in unison to the power tool's back and forth action.

Broc angled the saw downwards and guided the saw all the way down the sternum, once the teeth of the blade minced through the xiphoid, the saw naturally came out of Lucy's body. It always did that, Broc thought.

Lucy, still passed out while he fetched the sternal spreader, a weird looking instrument, designed to pull the rib cage apart, to expose the thoracic cavity. With his fingers inserted into Lucy's chest cavity, the tight sternum pressed against his fingers. With his fore and middle finger, he rubbed up and down the underside of her rib structure, freeing any nerves, vessels, and fat; once both sides were clear, Broc inserted the spreader. He turned it, the sickly cracking sound of Lucy's ribs woke her up, the sound was nauseating, "What are you doing? Please stop!" She sounded breathless.

Broc stopped and looked at the monitor, Lucy's oxygen saturation was within reasonable limits, he carried on turning the crank handle while looking at her, smiling. "This must be the most surreal thing to ever happen to you, Lucy." Broc said.

Still breathless, Lucy was trying to gather her thoughts. She thought that this week, was the start of the rest of her life. She blanked out Broc and tried to ignore him.

"I said this must be the weirdest thing to ever happen to you Lucy, don't ignore me." He chided. She looked at him and tried to find the words.

"This is the worst thing to ever happen to me."

Broc stopped, considered her comments and then looked down, the cavity, opened. The pale vascularised pericardium sack that contained the heart. Beating rhythmically with the ECG trace beeping in the background. It was an impressive sight, with both hands, Broc reached in. Cupped the sack, he felt Lucy's life force beat without hindrance. The heart with a life of its own, forcing seven liters of Lucy's blood through the ventricles of her heart every minute. Four hundred and twenty liters an hour, ten thousand liters in a 24 hour period, three million liters a year, the heart, thought Broc, was an incredible organ.

Time pressing, he needed to crack on, with the blade, he followed the contour of both of Lucy's collar bones, until he met the junction where the collarbone and the ball joints at the tops of the arms met, following first the left flank, passing the left breast, all the way down to the the top of the protruding iliac crest, at the top of the pelvis, he then turned to the right side and did the same again, he stood back, pursing his lips, making sure the symmetry was correct, feeling the protruding prominences of the pelvic bones forming Lucy's tight waist, with the blade, he sliced, transverse across the bottom of Lucy's abdomen, circumnavigating the Mons Veneris, the fatty mound of tissue above the vagina, named after Venus, the God of love.

Broc stood back, all that he needed to do was incise the thoracic and abdominal sections and meet at the top of the Mons Veneris. After that, things would get a little messy as the fatty and vascular layers, muscle and visceral fat would exsanguinate at least a liter of Lucy's circulating blood and fluid. He needed to be careful. With a theatre team, drugs and a second pair of hands the blood loss would be much lower, but it was something Broc couldn't avoid.

He de-scrubbed, cleaned his hands, went to the anesthetic machine. He adjusted some of the dials, gas flows and increased the drug delivery on the syringe drivers and waited for her blood pressure to reduce. Within five minutes, her blood pressure was much lower than usual parameters. She would now bleed less. Lucy oblivious and unconscious throughout the initial incisions.

Broc stood, looking at her, thinking what her life would have become, again that feeling of emotion swelling through his tissues and nerve endings, he closed his eyes and again, threw the thought away. He went to the sink and re-scrubbed, his phone in his back pocket kept vibrating, must be work, idiot junior surgeons not knowing their ass's from their elbows he thought.

As Broc approached Lucy, she started to rouse. Her head jerking, Broc checked the parameters, she isn't feeling pain, "Lucy, are you back with me?" Broc asked as he approached her.

He picked up the bigger knife, "This is going to get a bit messy, maybe you should keep your eyes closed while I do this." Lucy's eyelids spasmed, they weren't going to open. Broc started where he first made the incision, armed with a suction tube, he cut deep and guided the knife around the subcutaneous incision site. Blood was freely flowing covering Broc's surgical gown and splashing onto the floor like an over wet mop, the suction making a sound like a child coming to the end of their milkshake. The tubing was jerking violently, sending the waste blood to a suction canister. When all the incisional margins were met, armed now with the electrocautery device, he made light work of the fascia, and then he was through. He worked his way around her thorax and abdomen, gripping the flesh with his hand like he was ripping up carpet, the tough white tissue vaporizing into the air giving off a pungent, unpleasant smell.

As Broc was finishing, Lucy opened her eyes, "What are you doing?" She asked.

Broc stopped, looked, blood across his face and his gown saturated in Lucy's blood, "Ah babygirl, you're awake, nearly got to the main part of your performance Lucy, it will be your moment of glory." He returned to tying off vessels, and cutting more tissue with the cautery device.

Lucy felt groggy "Thirsty," She said, her voice hoarse and raspy.

As Broc was busy cutting away, her body jerking with Broc's movements "There's no need for you to drink any more, babygirl," He said, "Soon it'll be over, Lucy."

Lucy didn't know what he meant by this, she could smell the iron in the air, along with the singed aroma of burning tissue, it smelt like a cesarean section, her mind going back to her time as a student in the operating theatre, she drifted unconsciously again.

Broc worked his way through the large piece of skin that he had excised. He felt for the lateral prominences of the ribs down each side of Lucy's flank. Using a large pair of surgical pliers, forced the jaws of the instrument into the space, with a stomach-churning slice, all 12 ribs were free of the ribs protruding from the thoracic vertebrae. The whole abdominal and thoracic section including Lucy's breasts was free, the final piece of fascia coming away. Broc nearly dropped it. It was heavy. It weighed about seven kilos, Broc held it up where the collar bones would have been attached and stood back, holding up to let Lucy look at it.

"LUCY!" Broc shouted, "LUCY, look!"

Lucy roused, licked her dry, parched lips and fell unconscious again. Broc placed the flesh onto a free trolley.

Lucy's yellow peritoneal fat hung down past her knees, still attached up and behind the spleen and liver and the major vessels that perforated the fatty layer, feeding the organs.

He picked up the free fat and with his cautery device, sliced it off. A few arterial and venule vessels oozed and spurted, Broc threw the excess fat on to the abdominal skin and made light work ligating and cauterizing the corresponding vessels. He then spent the next twenty minutes cutting away the main root of the peritoneal fat, avoiding all the major mesenteric arteries and veins.

Once happy, he stood back and marveled at Lucy's body. He cleaned up and any idle pieces of tissue, cutaway.

He felt a twinge in his groin. Heart and lungs, the perfect hues of pink, bluish purple, deep and pale reds. The liver, sat in the upper quadrant, the perfect gallbladder, the intestinal tract a shade of green and pink . Slowly moving, like a caterpillar, the stomach, folded in on itself, the rugae folds allowing the stomach to fill a small space when not full of food.

He ran his hand over the organs, their warm, smooth and moist textures exciting the surgeon, he licked his lips, he tased Lucy's blood on his lips, he grinned.

Nothing was more perfect than that for this moment. He stifled the swelling in his groin, this was Broc's sexual utopia, as he was gently squeezing the small tubes of the jejunum. He then realized that his phone had be vibrating, a specific ringtone that wasn't good news. Must be important he thought, he paused, considered ignoring it, it played on his mind, he glanced over to the phone pursed his lips. He stepped away from Lucy, de-scrubbed and washed himself down in a considered, habitual way. Not taking any shortcuts, he glanced over to Lucy. Basking under the white surgical lights, her organs working in harmony, it was a delightful sight, he reached for his phone, a text from Tasha, the last message visible, 'POLICE, advise, hurry.'

15

Alex had made her way to the police station after receiving the forensic, SOCO, lab technicians and extra police. She handed the crime scene over to her colleagues from the murder team, who were busy interviewing all the staff.

Both Alex and Ricky had done a cursory search of the office and had found offensive material on the company computers, even if Gormley were eliminated from the abduction and subsequent murder of the missing girl, there was enough evidence for the Crown Prosecution Service to charge Gormley with the invasion of privacy, child pornography and inappropriate images and video footage of female staff workers.

Gormley sat quietly, pensive, looking at the floor handcuffed, he had tried to protest his innocence. Alex thought that now his past had finally caught up with him, he seemed tired of the lying and just gave up.

His behavior was ringing too many alarm bells for Alex. Each of the staff had been detained, apart from Tasha. She had left the office to run an errand before James had called and Alex had placed the plant on lockdown.

Alex entered the murder team squad room. Frank was waiting. He grabbed her by both shoulders "You never cease to amaze me, Alex, fucking excellent job." Frank spat as he said it, he saw it, she saw it, they both ignored it. Normal!

He turned in step with Alex as she walked, "This Gormley character, he's got no form. Nothing from his background, a bit of debt and a couple of unpaid's, nothing of any specific concerns." As they arrived at Alex's desk, she pulled her chair out. She was frowning as she sat. She looked up at Frank.

"It's not him," she said, she clicked away quickly on her computer, seamlessly sliding through the myriad of security checks, Frank just watched...he could never do that.

Frank shook the enviousness away, "What do mean, the guy's a scrote, his hardware is full of grott." Alex smiled at the army term for pornography, colloquially known as grott.

Alex got into police national computer database and brought up Gormley's misdemeanors. It confirmed Franks assessment. She looked up. "It's not him, Frank. He's a pervert and predatory, but actually doing what happened to Melissa in Bodmin. That's not his MO. He's weak, pathetic, probably has a small dick, submissive even."

Alex turned to her screen, tapped away, brought up her emails and checked her inbox. James had sent securely, the lab report of the meat specimen, now labeled Melissa Davies. Alex's heart skipped a beat when the specimen had a name to it. Brought on a different meaning.

She affectionately touched Frank's hand. It felt dry, gnarled and hard, though warm. Under Frank's bluster, he was a kind man. She had more than respect for the old dog.

"I want the first run at him, Frank, like now," She insisted. Frank knew when he shouldn't argue with Alex.

Frank pursed his lips, his thick moustache covering the lips as he did it, "Vice is coming over, Renton is inbound as we speak."

"Renton Davis, are you fucking serious?" Alex exclaimed, "The bloke is a sex pest himself Frank, what the absolute fuck?" she continued.

Frank looked around the room, no one looked up, "I didn't choose him. Apparently, he's the only one available. I've told them that we're still running point on this investigation. Chill your beans, Alex. You never know what these guys can bring to the table."

Alex was already up and walking, "Go easy Alex, don't put him in a corner just yet, the press is going to be over this like a bad rash," Frank said as she continued to walk, "Brass will want this done by the book."

"Rick, let's go, we are taking a run at Gormley, see what he knows,"

Ricky was sat on the desk swinging a foot, chatting to an attractive female detective that Alex didn't recognize, "Roger that boss".

The three headed down the corridor towards the interview rooms. Frank stopped in front of the one marked 'Gormley' in non-permanent marker. Alex and Rick entered.

Gormley looked up. He was ashen, fear in his eyes, a half-drunk vending machine coffee on the table, he was still cuffed, the duty solicitor, barely out of university, sat arrogantly next to him, writing.

Alex motioned to the constable by the door, "Take the bracelets off."

"Ma'am, I am not..." he was cut off.

"Take them off...NOW!" Alex said.

The constable getting the vibe, walked over, slid the key in the lock and slid the cuffs off like a magician's trick. Gormley rubbed both wrists and blew his cheeks out as he drained the last third of the coffee.

The solicitor looked at Alex, "What has my client been charged with?" the arrogant attitude was almost palpable.

Alex slid the chair back, making a scraping sound on the to lino surface, Ricky did the same next to Alex.

Both police officers were ignoring the solicitor, Alex watched as Ricky unpackaged a tape cassette, placed it in the recorder and then waited for the audible tone to disappear.

Alex spoke first, mentioned the date and the time after glancing at the wall clock, introduced Ricky and Gormley, then turned to the solicitor, "...and you are?"

The solicitor frowned, looked at Gormley, then said "Simon Spieth, duty solicitor." he returned to his writing pad.

Alex turned to Gormley, "I am going to level with you Gordon," Alex used Gormley's first name. "What we have found in your business is not of interest to us, a colleague from another department is coming over to deal with that. It's also highly likely that if convicted, you will do porridge for what we have found."

Spieth now curious, put his pen down and focussed on Alex, Gormley winced at the thought, not because of the high possibility of going to prison, but his secret life, laid bare for all to see, the worst was to come, "Officers are at your home now, searching it, your wife is aware of what's going on, she has asked us to tell you that she has gone to your daughter's until our searches have concluded." Gormley started to cry.

Gormley still looking at the floor, he was listening, some tears dripping from the end of his nose.

Alex continued, she opened a manila file and produced photos of an attractive girl, "We want to talk to you today about this women, Gordon, we haven't got the time to mess about, vice are are on their way and once they're here, I will have to hand you over to them, we are time critical."

Gormley looked up, scanned the photo, he paused, taking her in, his databanks of memory almost audible to Alex and Ricky. A skin tag flopped lazily on his left eye. Alex struggled to stop looking at it. She waited patiently for the answer.

"I've never seen her before." Gormley said.

Alex shuffled through the pictures and papers in the file, produced another photo, this time, a photo of a standard 500-gram packet of ground meat, typical of any supermarket.

Alex slid the photo next to the girl's picture, "What about this?" Alex said.

Gormley looked at the photo, "I guess, looks like something we would process, it's a standard pack of mince, we get rid of tons of it per week, I am not getting you."

Gormley looked confused.

Alex looked at him, she knew he wasn't responsible, but the next revelation to this man is going to turn his world upside down. Alex tapped the picture of the mince and then tapped the image of the girl, "This girl, is now this packet of mince. The packet you see here, is in fact, this girl." Alex pointed to the picture of Melissa Davies. "She was kidnapped from Bodmin in Cornwall the week before last. Her DNA has turned up in your processing plant as ground mince."

Gormley's face took a few seconds to process the information, the solicitor broke the awkward silence, "Are you suggesting this meat is this girl and that you have corroborating laboratory reports to support this? And are you suggesting that my client is responsible for this?"

Gormley's face drained of blood, he was pale and ashen, "I am going to be sick" he said, he wasn't lying, his shoulder bucking to rid the thoughts he was thinking. Ricky sprang into action, pushed his chair back, with a hop and skip to the waste paper bin in the corner of the room, grabbed it and was just in time as Gormley's stomach violently splurged into the receiver.

Gormley's head buried deep in the bin, the room quickly filled with the stench of vomit, "Oh my God." Gormley said, voice amplified in the bin and echoing around the room, "Oh my God." he repeated, "I didn't do this."

Spieth had pushed himself as far against the wall to avoid any potential splashback and his face scrunched up to stop the smell from entering his nasal passages, hands up in protest, he looked at Alex.

"I want the custody nurse here immediately. This interview is over until Mr. Gormley has received a clean bill of health."

"No" Gormley chimed, head out of the bin, mucous hanging perilously from his nose, "No," with the back of his hand, he wiped the snot away from his face.

"Mr Gormley, I must..." Spieth was cut off. Gormley's hand was up. Spieth went to speak again, but Gormley cut him off.

"Enough," he sat up, took in a deep breath, shoulders rising to draw the air in, Alex hadn't moved. This guy will spend some considerable time in jail for what was found in his office.

She felt nothing for him, although, she knew he had nothing to do with the girl's disappearance, Ricky sat next to her, feeling the same. Picking at this cuticles, looking intently at Spieth, wanting to rip his smarmy public schoolboy face off.

Alex sniffed, leaned forward, "Gordon, I know you didn't do this," again tapping the pictures. She looked intently at him, "but you need to look at this from our side, on your computer we have found a plethora of material that compromises your integrity and potential guilt."

Spieth cut in "It is not illegal to have pornography on one's computer."

Alex turned to look at the solicitor. "Pornography found is of underage children. Being raped and sexually abused, second to this."

Gormley muttered looking up "Forgive me."

Alex stopped, was he looking for Divine intervention she thought.

She carried on, "Second to this, we have found evidence that the ladies toilet in the processing plant had been rigged with high definition webcams."

Gormley interrupted again "please please please," Spieth was silent, his face wasn't expecting anything like what Alex was saying.

Alex continued, "The cameras set up so the ladies that work there, were seen and saved on your computer defecating and urinating. Three of the ladies seen on your computer were interviewed today at the processing plant, so we know it's your doing."

Gormley started to sob.

Alex shuffled some papers in the manila folder, "So can you see why we need to eliminate you of this inquiry accurately. Our position is this, with what we have found, unless otherwise directed, you're having this against your name, too." Alex holding up the girl's photo.

Spieth shifted in his seat, after the trauma of hearing the terrible news of the girl and then the expulsion from Gormley's stomach, he managed to regain a little bit of the smugness he arrived with.

"I don't think the possession of the…" Spieth struggled to find the words, "...girls remains constitutes guilt sergeant." he said.

Alex placed the photos down, still in deliberate view of the suspect. "Along with the other evidence, Mr. Spieth, we are compelled to follow the evidence, until there is something contradictory to the fact and under the guidance of both the CPS and vice, Mr. Gormley is going to be charged with all of the offenses." her tone was a matter of fact.

Gormley sniveled, "I didn't do this, I admit..."

Spieth cut in, "My client has nothing to say at this stage." Spieth's arm was outstretched across Gormley's chest.

Gormley glanced over to Spieth, "Say nothing until we have spoken in private and I have offered you council." Spieth reinforcing the comment with a nod. Gormley nodded in agreement.

There was a knock at the door, the constable by the door looked at Alex for approval, she nodded and the constable opened the door, a six-foot man, heavy set with a full head of hair, strolled in with more front than Brighton seafront. Renton Davis was a career vice copper, there weren't many career vice coppers, the nature of the job is too upsetting, but Renton was very different.

There was nothing he hadn't seen or witnessed. There were rumors from some of the female conquests in the Met that he was himself as depraved and perverted as some of the degenerates that he pinched, Alex didn't like him.

Her dealings with him were cursory at best, with her childhood, his world was something she didn't want anything to do with. Deep down, he was probably a decent guy, but the question remained, why would anyone want to voluntarily do a vice job, not just any vice job, but dealing with people that chose the lifestyle they chose. In truth, this case had Renton's name all over it. A missing girl, probably sexually abused during and beyond mortality and exposed to a horrific death, then fed through a meat mincer. Either to augment the perpetrator's perversion or a clever way to dispose of the body.

The body Alex thought, this isn't the first, it's to well drilled, the distances are too far. If this is so, how many more.

Alex looked at the clock, stated the time introduced Davis to the room.

Davis' voice was deep, commanding, he was a chap not to be ignored, nor was he used to being ignored, "Sergeant, can we step outside?" he asked.

Alex pursed her lips. She looked at Ricky, Ricky nodded and stood up, Alex looked at Gormley, "Interview suspended." Ricky walked past Renton. They nodded at each other. Alex followed, walked past Renton. She expected Renton to file in after her, but he didn't. She stopped momentarily, glanced over her shoulder, Renton was just looking at Gormley, Gormley's face said it all, they knew each other.

"Told you, one day you would be in an interview room," Renton said, disdain in his voice, in a low tone, dragging out the comment. "Didn't I?" he repeated.

Gormley looked at the floor. He had nothing to say.

The corridor outside the interview rooms was a hive of activity. Both Alex and Ricky pressed against the wall. Renton closed the door on Gormley and Spieth.

"You know this guy?" Alex said, nodding to the door where Gormley sat.

Renton followed the nod and walked into both Alex and Ricky's personal space. "Yeah, he's a bit harmless, just a piss-pest from some of the clubs I work on my patch. He's harmless…." he was interrupted by Ricky's hand. "A what?" he asked, Renton, looked bemused!

He jerked his thumb in the direction of the brown door, "Gormley, he's a sex-pest,"

Ricky frowned, "the bit before, piss-pest..." he paused, "you called him a piss-pest, what is that?"

Renton looked at Alex, as though Alex knew what was, "I don't know what it is either" she said shrugging her shoulders.

Renton looked up and down the corridor, as though he was going to tell them a secret. "Gormley is a guy that drifts about some of the clubs I go to. He is often at an extreme club called Club Swartz. You'll find Gormley naked, wearing only a see-through rain mac, and people urinating on him."

Ricky and Alex were staring at Renton in disbelief, "Bloody hell, I should photograph your faces." Renton said laughing.

Ricky laughed, "You had me there, Davis." Ricky said "I thought you were serious." he added.

Renton's face didn't change. He watched both Ricky and Alex. Thought to himself, these two have no idea, "I am not joking, Ricky. Gormley thinks nothing other than being pissed on, whatever your vibe, whatever turns you on, Ricky. You think about that for a couple of seconds, that's the same for Gormley, it's his fetish or kink as it's known, have you any idea why it's called Club Schwartz?" Renton asked?

Alex shook her head, "You guys probably know the place, they have a restaurant at the front of the club, that's simply called Schwartz, it's German for Black."

"We know," Ricky said, "we both served in Germany."

Renton's phone was ringing, he pulled it out, checked the caller ID, paused and hit the dismiss button. "Ah, yeah, you guys were partners in Germany, ok, Schwartz, the restaurant was made famous as it's an eatery that is in pitch black, the waiters are blind, you can't see your food or the room you're in."

Alex remembered, "Yes, yes, it was on a cooking program on the TV not so long back, you can't see anything, essentially the only senses you have are smell and taste."

Renton was nodding, "That's the place, behind there, in the same building, run by the same people is an extreme fetish club, called Club Schwartz because it's a place for scat lovers, scat is a sub-fetish in the BDSM world where people shit on each other."

"Come again?" Alex said.

"There's a room dedicated to it. There are swingers, bisexual, non-binary sexuality, greedy girls, sadism, BBC's, BBW's, you name it, and that chopper," Renton was jerking his finger again to the door, "is where you'll find him. This crime your investigating," touching the Manila folder in Alex's hands "isn't Gormley, he's essentially harmless. What you found at his place of work is probably hideous, but essentially, Gormley is extremely submissive. If he knew who was involved, he would have told you. He's here by coincidence, Alex."

"I don't believe in coincidences, Renton."

Alex looked at the floor and pursed her lips, "Where do you suggest we go from here then?" she asked frankly.

Renton appreciated the veiled call for help. He didn't rise to it. He knew he couldn't. "I know the owner, Club Schwartz. He feeds me info. He runs a seedy shit hole of a club, but he knows where his bread's buttered. He may be able to put us in touch with a real person of interest." he leaned against the wall opposite Ricky and Alex, people walking between them ignoring the interaction.

"Who would that be?" Alex replied.

Renton had his hands in his trouser pockets, he looked cool and unwavering, he had confidence. "We need a meeting with the Zookeeper, he's the daddy of the sex scene in London, I've never met him and he's been quiet of late, but Dmitry Orlov, the owner of Club Schwartz, will know something."

"Sarge" came a voice from down the corridor. A young, fresh-faced detective constable of no significance was leaning through the door. All three looked, both Renton and Alex said yes, awkwardly realizing the faux pas on both sides.

"The interviews of the staff at the processing plant has been concluded, they have been all eliminated from the inquiry, apart from one name." he looked to the reporters' notebook in his hand, scanning the names, "erm, Tasha Richardson."

Alex stood away from the wall, "The secretary, where did she go?" she demanded.

"I dunno sarge, the officers at the gate you posted before the lockdown, saw her leave, she was on foot, no vehicle." The young officer raised his eyebrows, waiting eagerly for the next play.

"Can we send some uniforms to her house?" Renton asked.

"We did, the address on her employment file is bogus. It's three bedroom semi owned by" he flicked through his notebook, "Irene and Bill Swales, lived at the address for nearly forty years, they've never heard of Tasha Richardson, nor do they know her from her photo we have of her."

"FUCK!" Alex said, she had one hand on her hip and the palm of her other hand on her forehead!

"The plot's thickening." Ricky piped up, both Alex and Renton looked at him.

Alex then turned to Renton, "I want a meet with Orlov....TODAY." She said starting to walk down the corridor, "and Ricky, throw Gormley in the cells and then find that fucking woman."

16

Ricky walked into the squad room to phones ringing and keyboards clattering. Smaller groups of coppers were sharing paperwork. He noticed a table with the standard we're in for the long haul pile of doughnuts, mini chocolate bites and the constant stream of freshly brewed coffee. For some of the old school of the squad, tea and toast were all that was required.

Going against his dietary regime he grabbed a frosted chocolate doughnut, coffee in a polystyrene cup, parked himself at his desk and took a sip of the dark drink; the coffee was strong but oh so hit the spot.

He had been reflecting since the discovery and identification of the meat.

When the squad was tasked to investigate murders, it helped detectives to distance themselves and not become too affected. Ricky just didn't know what to make of this one, it was so out of left field. Sitting at his desk he saw the picture of him and his wife. Though he wouldn't be home until very late, he knew she was safe and that helped his mindset.

He typed 'don't wait up cupcake. Something has come up, you know, a work thing, the kind of thing that will keep me busy for a while, love you,' with a string of emojis to complete the text.

He put his phone away. Not waiting for a reply, he opened the folder, looking for Tasha's contact details. Picking up the phone, he proceeded to try the numbers listed, none of the numbers worked. The mobile number was no longer in use and the landline was a number that had never been issued, let alone used.

Something Ricky knew from being on the job and Alex hit on it every time, was that there were no coincidences, only evidence related to the crimes. So having an employee from the processing plant simply disappear was not a coincidence. Tasha had made herself a person of interest and locating her became a priority.

A computer expert and right at home sifting through multiple layers of police surveillance, Ricky began the long arduous task of watching the tapes from the docks. Lucky for them, the docks were tightly controlled by the authorities - her Majesty's Taxes and Revenue services - so all the comings and goings were heavily monitored in case there may be some evidence of anything that could potentially owe the crown.

Tasha's gait out of the plant was hurried. She briefly spoke to the officers, who at this point had no reason to stop her and then walked quickly up the road, from the direction that Ricky had driven up earlier that day. She turned left, now walking around the rear of the plant, turned left again and then came to a sports coupe, Audi A5. Ricky zoomed in, odd, why would an office assistant be riding a £50K whip and why park there? There was a staff car park at the plant. He noticed her look over her shoulder as she approached the car, the indicators flashed, Tasha opened the door and climbed in, the car drove off the apron.

Ricky then launched a tracking software program weirdly named, Vengeful. He wasn't sure why it was called that, he dragged the car with the number plate into the program, dropped it on the pane in the screen, hit search and leaned back. The chair gave off a satisfying creak that Ricky enjoyed. He didn't have to wait long, the sophisticated algorithms of the program crunched millions of binary codes to spit out every camera the car hit until it disappeared. The program indicated the car had driven for 35 minutes. It had made its way to Tower Hamlets in East London. The route detailed on the screen, the road she took. The number of times the car braked, which lane, what speed and where the vehicle was left in a municipal car park, with the parking paid.

Ricky hit the last location image, which was a black and white HD video of the car, parked.

Tasha getting out of the vehicle, he highlighted Tasha and then launched another program called PAXTRAX, the program used facial recognition software to search parameters and then the tracking of the pax or person was followed throughout, if needed, Europe.

Tasha walked to Tower Hill underground, bought a ticket with cash at terminal six, CCTV footage of her searching her bag for the money had caught her. The trains she took, the carriages that she occupied, the camera even picked up the book she was reading. Bridal Wear through the ages. Then to Earls Court and 24 minutes later Tasha emerged from the tube station, turned left and walked a little way. Turned left onto Trebovir Road, walked halfway down the road and into the Empire Hotel which was located on the right-hand Side of the road.

Ricky launched TripAdvisor, punched in the hotel information, it was a two-star hotel, which reading the reviews, barely made it to the two stars. The decor was suspect and the road was a known vice area for prostitutes.

He then launched Companies House and found the owners of the hotel, they were of Arabian descent, registered office in Hounslow which wasn't unusual to Ricky, they had a string of low budget hotels but no adverse history.

This street was a breeding ground for cheap sex, safe houses for fundamentalists returning from Syria, to visit family or plot the next terror campaign coupled with affordable accommodation for Earls Court exhibition center staff and youngsters' visiting London on a budget.

Ricky pulled his phone out, had a text from his wife, but ignored the distraction. He found Alex in his recents and hit call.

Two rings in "Speak to me" Alex said, still in the car.

"Got her, sarge. Trebovir Road, looks like she is in the Empire Hotel, a shit hole about halfway down the street," Ricky was still looking at the entrance of the hotel.

"Awesome, we are still in the car, get some uniforms down there, pick her up, don't arrest her though," Alex said.

Ricky stole himself away from the screen and stared down the phone "come sarge again? You don't want her pinched?"

"No," Alex said. "She's running scared, Ricky."

"That's not what I am seeing boss. I just watched her leave the processing plant, climb into a £50K Audi and leave the car in a suspect car park in Tower Hamlets. Then tube it to Earls Court, the hotel, owned by a Saudi family based in Hounslow. I would say that she's on the run, not running scared, boss."

There was a pause Alex was impressed as always with Ricky's thoroughnesses, "Talk to me Ricky, what's your gut say?"

Ricky thought for a moment, why was a girl, with a false name, that's not coming through the facial recognition software, have a sports car parked nowhere near where she worked, then race across London. He relayed this to Alex.

Renton piped up "The Empire Hotel is a known knocking shop for businessmen using Earls Court, most of those hotels are seedy hotels offering whatever. My experience with anyone that knows these places have some involvement with the place, she won't be there when you get there. She is already gone."

Alex looked at Renton, Ricky came across the hands-free. "What do you mean, I have eyes on the entrance, they're Victorian townhouses, there's no way through the back, I have checked already."

Renton laughed, "What you can't see Ricky, is the service alley behind the houses that run the entire length of the street, where the term Tradesman's entrance comes from. She would have walked straight through, onto the alleyway, and up the street. In the process, I suspect she's changed her appearance already; she's in the wind, mate. It's a classic trick by prostitutes when being followed by toms and coppers."

"How can you be so sure?" Alex questioned.

"She's followed a path I would follow, knowing prozzies, she's a girl with a past. She's acting like she's on the payroll with someone other than Gormley, we need her name. And by that, I mean her real name. We will then be one step closer to the target, but right now, she is in the wind, I'm telling you."

"Boss, I will go down with some uniforms now, check the place out, if she's not there, then we move on to plan B, right now, I can't see how she's going to leave this place. If she has bounced, the front desk will know something."

"Go" was all he had to hear, the line went dead.

As Ricky got up, his phone vibrated, it was Alex, stay frosty was all the message said.

17

The two plain clothes police officers had entered the room not long after the uniformed officers had been called for the disturbance. It was only a spat with her boss, nothing out of the ordinary, but today he was extraordinarily irritating, Tracey Stubbs wasn't sure if it was him, or a full moon.

She had been working at the meat processing plant for a couple of years now. Her suitor compensated her meager salary with £3000 per week through Western Union.

On top of the monetary compensation, Broc had given her a new identity, Tasha Richardson and cleaned up her past to avoid any chance of it coming back around; all she had to do was report anything out of the ordinary to him and whatever it took to keep Gormley the Gormless, clueless.

Why she was there and what Broc was up to was of no concern to her. She was out of the game, being used as a sex toy by some of the most sadistic men in London. It was time to leave anyway. She was past her prime, now in her twenties, she would end up like all of the others that look like mutton dressed as lamb.

Seeing this as her way out of the game and at Broc's insistence, Tracey applied for the job. Gormley, a known sucker for a pretty girl and a regular at the sex club scene that Broc frequented, Tracey showed a bit more than just some leg and cleavage. As anticipated, Gormley hired the girl, a brain-dead socialite on minimum wage so he could letch at her all day long, order her about and maybe one day, use her for something other than office administration.

Gormley placed her by the window to his office so that he could see her. When Tracey was alone in the office, she would turn to his direction. Hitch up her skirt and spread her legs and let Gormley appreciate the show she put on. So much so, the worn carpet under his desk had turned to a shiny glass-like surface with the months and months of ejaculate being spurted on it. She would look at him dead in the eye until he climaxed. He thought she was a goddess, she thought he was pathetic.

When the uniformed police arrived, it spooked Tracey, she considered texting Broc, but then when they left without really giving a shit, she went back to her nails and Gormless bumping his gums cleaning up the mess they had both created. But fifteen minutes later two plain-clothed officers entered the office, that was a different story, instantly her blood ran cold, something was up.

The female police officer was a badass no frills don't fuck with me lesbian or whatever copper. He was a six-foot black man that was just gorgeous, even so, he had a menacing demeanor about him too, plain-clothed filth is not a good thing.

She felt Broc needed to know when she could. She pinged text to Broc, police, advise hurry and waited for the reply. Soon after the text was sent, her phone gently vibrated on her lap, nonchalantly, she picked it up and all it read was Plan B. Tracey blew air out of her cheeks, she needed to work and work quickly.

There was some post that needed posting, special delivery and marked urgent. She made her excuses to the office staff and left, quickly. The clock was ticking, she knew it.

If plain clothed officers are here, it will be for something serious. What Broc was up to was something that Tracey had thought about, but never really engaged with it, why would he use a place like this and what for she thought. What could be worth £12K a month to keep Tracey at a minimum wage job, with an entire pseudonym created for her just to keep her eyes peeled for the filth. She didn't want to hang around to find out.

She left the office and climbed down the stairs. Catching her stiletto heel in the grated steps now and again "fucking 'ell" she cursed, when she hit the bottom step, she strode with ease. Like a catwalk model down the runway. She chatted cursory to the officers outside and made her way to the car. She loathed the police, always one-sided, treated her parents like dirt and then when she was busking for tricks in central London, she would still be pinched and her cash taken by the Bobbies. The odd blow- job got her out of trouble, but nevertheless she wasn't liked by them.

The car was always parked out of the way because Broc told her to, if the police come for whatever reason, she wouldn't be able to leave the staff car park. Also, he knew what she was driving and a twenty-something leggy bird on the breadline wouldn't be driving a killer whip. Questions would be asked.

So for the last two years, she parked at the one-man-band MOT testing center which had a carport, of which she paid the owner with a little bit more than money, she didn't mind as he was quite hot.

Tracey had been a high-class prostitute in her youth after a poor upbringing. Both her parents were addicted to heroin on the council estates in Balham, South London. She had to learn quickly to look after herself. As a young teenager, she realized that the power of her sexuality gave her many fruits in life and quickly developed a confidence to go along with it. Using that to care for both of her parents she would clothe and feed them from tricks she turned with willing shopkeepers and businessmen. Before her sixteenth birthday, she returned from school to find both her parents dead from a drug overdose. It was there she dropped off the grid. She was incredibly attractive and a girl willing to do anything, she quickly came to the attention of the Zookeeper, who took her under his wing. She was an acquiescent servant to his perversions. She was compensated well for her skills, then one day, she met Broc and Tracey Burgess. They became friends, working the floors of the clubs together, sharing the profits with a kebab at the end of the evening.

Dashing, handsome, and very strong, Tracey quivered whenever he entered the room, Broc always made a beeline for Tracey. Down to earth, feisty and a bit bratty, she craved punishment from him, often making her back and breasts bleed from his belt. With her connections to the zookeeper, she had to learn to take care of herself and had become expert in evading both coppers and toms chasing her for either money for services rendered. It was something that she was very good at. She could teach the odd spook a few tricks.

She had created multiple exit routes for whatever situation that she may be in all around the capitol, this being Plan B, devised by both Broc and her, she knew she was burned and had to get out of dodge quick.

She drove the rehearsed route, not speeding, heart pounding, mouth dry and feeling sick, but she kept to the plan, nothing out of the ordinary. The only shame she thought was that this car was the best thing she had ever bought, it was a legitimate purchase and in about fifteen minutes or so, she won't ever see it again.

The car park in Tower Hamlets was a rehearsed spot, a car like this would be either stolen or set on fire within 24 hours of being left in that part of London, not because anyone would, but because someone would be sent there to do it. The point was, no one would give a shit that the car was either nicked or torched, it was Tower Hamlets!

As she walked to the tube station that was a small distance from the carpark, she surreptitiously slid the car key into the waste bin as she passed by, keeping the car open and unlocked so to tempt anyone to do as they wished. Tracey felt sad but recognized that Broc knew the bigger picture and relied on him to keep her safe. She pulled her phone out, found the contact Jamal and typed I need an exit. As she walked, she waited, her phone vibrated, Jamal was on it as she expected, when, was all he replied.

Tracey paused in her gait and typed now, urgent. The dots came up on the phone, he was reading it, Earls Court, you know the road, get there ASAP straight through. She hit the tab share location, typed A5 S Line coupe, Black, reg BL16AHR, get rid no trace. Dots again, done, she smiled, he was a useful ally, she pocketed the phone.

Jamal worked a network for under the radar services. He was the go-to guy if one needed to disappear, false papers, etc. The one-stop-shop for anything illegal that criminals needed to administer their business. Even a stolen car could be changed into your name, it was merely a matter of connections and he was connected. No one had ever met Jamal. She had heard that he was in prison and worked from there, other rumors were he was a white dude living in Essex, while others said he was a devout Muslim that hated any kafir's or authority not linked to Islam. Tracey didn't give a shit, it was a service that she paid for and paid well for. He always came through.

She arrived at Poplar Docklands Light railway station, paid cash for a one-way ticket to Earls Court from the vending machine and boarded the train. She stood, at the rear of the train as to see anyone that could approach her or possible tails. Tracey scanned the carriageway, using her phone to secretly film the people in the section of carriage she was in, her headphones in, but not on, as to avoid any unwanted attention.

Canary Wharf was busy and deafening between the tourists and serving United Kingdom's financial hub. Keeping vigilant of her surroundings,Tracey avoided eye contact by keeping her head down. She also made sure to avoid the CCTV cameras by walking close to the wall.

Tracey didn't know at what point the police would come calling, but knew that they would. At a crossroads deep under the skyscrapers of Citibank and HSBC, she paused, looking for the grey color of the Jubilee line, found it and walked to the escalator taking her lower into the ground. Standing on the right side of the elevator, she looked dead ahead, tapping her hand, listening to the pretend beats in her ears avoiding all contact with anyone. On the platform, she made her way to the rear and waited for the train. The whoosh of air racing down the tunnel told her that it was imminently coming, checked her phone nervously, no missed calls or texts, check her social media feeds, nothing out of the ordinary.

The train pulled up, the carriage was quiet, Tracey chose to stand again, waited for the doors to close and everyone entering to settle, pulled her phone up and played the video she took in the previous train to compare the occupants of this train. Only a well-dressed woman, mid-thirties, with long auburn hair, was reading a Harry Potter book. She was halfway through the book. It looked on the video clip she was halfway through the book as well, Tracy's stomach tightened, could she be filth she thought. She filmed the carriage again, put her phone away, and settled on watching the woman through the corner of her eye.

As the tube traveled to the center of London, the carriage became busier, a heady mix of tourist, school children and business people. As the train arrived at Waterloo, the Harry Potter reading woman, checked her phone, dropped her book into her cavernous Michael Kors bag, got up and strode out of the train as soon as the doors opened. Tracey breathed a sigh of relief. She was confident she had no tail.

Tracey got off the train at Westminster, considered walking to Earls Court, but decided against it. Her heels were starting to bite.

Climbed onto a District line train, replayed both videos and scanned the carriage she was in again, nothing out of the ordinary, no same person on this train. The train took the short distance to Earls Court. Tracey sprinted up the stairs and found the exit. The A3220 road was as busy as ever. Tracey turned left and pulled out her phone, there was a waiting message from Jamal. Trebovir Road, No 5, straight through, tell them I sent you.

Tracey started walking again, turned left and headed down. The street was lined with numbered pillars. Finding number 5, she climbed the steps, walked through the door and stated to the smiling pretty girl at reception without stopping, "Jamal sent me."

The girl's face changed, she reached under the counter and passed Tracey a bundle. It was clothes, a different jacket, scarf and hat. Tracey de-robed as she walked through the hotel, changing her clothes as she walked heading out the back door. The garden was messy and unkempt, a couple of wobbly BBQ's littered the overgrown grass on each side of the uneven concrete path. The nearest BBQ full of rusty water with drowned dog-ends, the rotary clothes line at a lazy angle with no washing line on, the line partially hidden in the tall couch grass at the feet of the drier.

She reached the back gate, it was locked, with a handkerchief, she unbolted the jammed bolts, after a few grunts and heaves, it slid from its home and the door creaked open.

The old cobbled, uneven path, in different shades of green moss, approximately a meter and a half wide, just enough for a barrow boy with his barrow back in the Victorian times to come down with food and supplies for the affluent houses that have now become cheap budget hotels. In the advent of CCTV, drone surveillance and increased technology, the pathway, covered in rampant Buddleia and climbing roses, with a smattering of Russian vines, commonly known as a mile-a-minute. The path was hidden from any prying eyes. It was a cheap trick of ending a police trail, the police would naturally stop the chase at the hotel reception, no warrant and with no authority to go any further into the property. The assailant or suspect would be long gone, either end of the road was a tube station, circumnavigating the major artery in and out of London, it was all too easy.

Before turning left Tracey scanned the alleyway making sure it was clear. Now walking parallel she came to an inconspicuous doorway, after walking through, she stopped to check the busy street. No one stopped or paid her any attention. Closing the door she turned right, now walking away from the tube station she had come from not ten minutes earlier. Eyeing a black cab whose light was on waiting on the traffic jam, she climbed in.

The cabby looked in his rearview mirror, the attractive woman that just got in looked at him through the same mirror, she smiled, the killer smile that makes men do anything, "Sweets Way, Whetstone, quick as you can drive" Tracey said. She pulled her phone out, found Daddy on her phone, On my way she typed, she paused, looked out of the window, I was careful, should be alone. Tracey hit send.

Dince Akran and his brother, George, were kicking their heels outside the Kentucky Fried Chicken in Tower Hamlets. Dince's phone rang a Stormyz track, he pulled his phone out, the message from Jamal, Black S line Audi A5, BL16AHR, parked at this location, no trace, there was a map and it was just around the corner. Dince grabbed George's arm, "c'mon fam, job to do brah."

They found the car park and found the car unlocked. They climbed in and in under a minute, fired up the engine and the Black A5 disappeared. Within two hours, the car would cease to exist, Dince's phone vibrated as they exited the car park. A PayPal payment of £500 dropped into the account, he grinned and showed his brother, George.

Job Done.

18

Broc was unsettled, the police at the processing plant wasn't good news, it was the last thing he needed before a harvest. Thank god for Tracey he thought. He had to compose himself. He had already begun on Lucy and he had to make sure this harvest met beyond perfect standards.

He took a swig from the glass of water on the scrub sink, re-scrubbed and went back to Lucy.

She was stirring, drifting in and out of consciousness. "Lucy, are you with me?" he arranged some new instruments on the trolley and cleared some rubbish that had accumulated. At the foot of Lucy's limp, lifeless body, a puddle of blood was forming, with the odd drip of blood running off icicle-like structures of clotted blood. Broc hated the mess.

Lucy stirred some more "Where am I, my mouth is so dry, water, please, water?" she pleaded. Broc pursed his lips, still distracted.

"Lucy, you can't have water, not anymore." The organ receptacles, neatly arranged on the side. In order, large bowel, including the stomach, followed by the liver, then the pancreas. The heart, then the lungs and finally the kidneys. He could strip her out in one hour, then stabilize her and get himself to London and sort the mess that he felt was running out of control.

With electrical surgical shears, which contained staples, Broc located the neck of the descending colon where it met the sigmoid, just above the anus and sheared through tissue, the stump of the colon flopped lazily to the side. He felt with his hands all around the large colon, to where it met the small bowel ileocecal valve, just above the appendix. Clamping, Broc sheared through the soft smooth tissue, Lucy still sleeping but conscious. He placed the bowel on the free trolley, cut the first end at the point of the staples and with his free hand, massaged the bobbly tube to expel the faeces in Lucy's bowel. The smell of shit was strong, so strong it woke Lucy up.

"What's that smell? Oh my God that stinks." she said with her eyes still closed. Her demeanour was like a girl drunk and was finally home and needed to sleep.

"Don't worry." Broc said as he was now flushing the tube of bowel with warm saline.

When done, he placed it in to the first box. Rescrubbed, cut the oesophagus away from below the pharynx, with dissecting scissors, freed up the back wall of the food pipe, pulled and the stomach came free. He pulled the remaining small bowel away from the side walls of Lucy's abdomen and cut the pancreas away from the bottom end of the stomach, cauterising any bleeds that occurred.

Broc was less careful. He knew that time was of the essence, even though, the dissection and cutting of tissue was the work of a creative genius.

Once the stomach was out, he had the pancreas and then the liver, these were big bleeders and was not for the faint-hearted. It didn't phase Broc, he was in his element. This was his gratification, the excitement, the beauty and stress crescendoed, he bit his lip and tasted blood, Broc always did this while he was deep in thought with his dissection. Lucy stirred, made a sound, talking for her would now be a struggle as all the supporting muscles around the pharynx were now cut, forever affecting how Lucy would feel.

The fish-like organ of the pancreas came away with a sucking sound and blood splashing onto the floor. It was a perfect hue of deep purples with a bluish tinge to it. It felt smooth but rough, some pancreatic fluid oozed from the Sphincter of Oddi, the opening to the organ's inner workings.

Broc smoothed the surface with a swab, cleaning the mucous and blood like an obstetrician wiping down a newborn baby. He placed the organ in its container, he turned and smiled, the best bit, the liver. Lucy's liver was exquisite, smooth and glistening in the light, the arteries surrounding its function pulsating to the beat of the ECMO machine. Although it was not the deep colors one would expect from such a healthy specimen as the heart was no longer beating. He ran his hands through the space the liver was sat in, the lungs half inflated and easily moved by his hands. He felt a stiffening in his trousers. Finally, his blood was coursing through the appendage that forever let him down. Broc wanted to bury his face in the wound and eat her liver. He would if he could but shrugged the thought away. He located all of the vessels that ran to and from the organ.

Big vessels, stiff and erect with the life flow of Lucy's body pulsating through the walls.

With the electrical shears, he cauterized as he cut the liver from the liver bed. Without too much fuss and bleeding, of which Broc marveled at his surgical prowess, the liver was in his hands. Big, heavy, full of blood, yet smooth and resplendent in all its glory. Broc's loins tightened even more, "Look, Lucy," she stirred. Her head lolled, she managed to open her eyes and look down to Broc, she couldn't fathom what was happening to her, "Look Lucy," Broc repeated. Cradling the large organ for Lucy to see, "This is your liver, look how magnificent it is."

Lucy licked her lips, with her head lolling, "Please, leave me alone," she gasped. Tired of mourning her previous life, she just wanted to head to the light and be left alone.

Broc irritated, reached up and grabbed her face, yanked her head down "LOOK YOU FUCKING BITCH!" he screamed, saliva splashing over her face, "LOOK WHAT I HAVE DONE!" Broc was incensed, he wanted to rip her throat out.

Lucy didn't care, "Fuck you and everything about you," she stammered, "I hope you rot in hell, you're beyond beastly," she said.

Broc gritted his teeth, placed the liver in the receptacle it was to be transported in and walked over to Lucy, "You fucking bitch" he said calmly, with a spoon like instrument from the trolley, he grabbed her face. Pulled her right eyelid open, the spoon followed the curvature of the eye as it slid in behind the eye. Lucy screamed, pain for the first time since her kidnapping, it was unbearable as she felt her eye ripping from her head. The optic nerve stubbornly stopped the eye from coming away, Broc pulled harder and it jerked her head violently finally yielding with a snap to Broc's strength.

Broc held up the eye with the nerve dangling from the end and showed Lucy, "I'll teach you to be so fucking disrespectful, you ungrateful whore." He turned and threw the eye into the meat mincer and switched it on.

The gears of the metallic machine ground immediately into action and made little work of the small eye, spitting it out onto the steel surface.

Broc turned, Lucy's head was hanging forward, blood running free from the backend socket. She was sobbing, so much pain and trauma for one day she thought, could it get any worse.

Broc approached her, gently held her head up, "Lucy, your behavior was unacceptable, baby." he soothed. Blood from the eye running over his hand like rivulets of rain down a window pane. "Don't bring the worst out in me again. Soon, this will be over."

Sobbing she pleaded.

He ignored her, took a swab from the trolley, unceremoniously stuffed it into the empty socket to tamponade the flow. The pain of the cotton swab stuffed into the hole was searing. She screamed. "Ssshhh" Broc soothed, he stroked her head, kissed her forehead.

He returned to Lucy's thorax. There were some bleeders oozing. With the cautery, he zapped them, the ends charing, sealing the vessels, the plume rising like a cigarette left in an ashtray, the intermittent sound of buzzing playing in unison to the music on the stereo.

The thin fascia covering the heart and the lungs were no match for Broc and his dissecting scissors, the fibrous pericardium sack exposed, and the smooth surface of both lungs, pink and moist, yet weirdly still, the ECMO doing the work of both heart and lungs efficiently.

Broc felt around the hardened surface of the pericardium, he could feel the structures of Lucy's heart. With a blade he sliced through the tough first layer, the serous straw, clear fluid ran out of the sack and onto the floor. Once in the space with his dissecting scissors, Broc opened up the cavity, Lucy's heart was a good size and healthy. No fat around the structure and good perfusion. With his fingers, he felt for the left and right phrenic nerves, then the vagus nerve. Made sure there was enough length for the recipient. He then felt for the pulmonary pedicles, isolated them with rubberized silicone strips, red for arterial and blue for venous. Broc stood back, he didn't notice his shoulders aching, he stretched while looking at Lucy, she was still sleeping.

Back to the dissection Broc, with his fingers, felt upwards following the trachea, the pipe that fed Lucy air into her lungs. He measured four inches, feeling the stiff cartilage, cut through the trachea which always gave off a foul smell. The pipe came away with a sickening cracking sound, he found the bifurcation of each of the right and left bronchus. Locating the major vessels of the pulmonary vein and aorta and isolating these in the same fashion as the pedicles. Broc then delivered the heart away from Lucy's body, it fit neatly in Broc's right hand, then he cut the vessels away, now the heart was away from its bed. He place it in to the box, quickly sutured the pulmonary vein and aorta in to the synthetic grafts waiting in the box. Once connected, he pressed to go on the inside of the box, and the heart began to beat on its own accord. The sinoatrial node inside the heart firing after being freed from the drug infusion Lucy was receiving to stop the heart and lungs from working. Sporadic at first, Broc tapped the heart with the handle of his dissecting scissors. Finally, the heart reached normal sinus rhythm. He closed the box. The heart will be good for 48 hours.

Broc return to Lucy, she was looking pale, he wanted to finish as soon possible, he felt he should be London.

He made small work of the lungs. They came away with no fuss, a little more blood than he would have wanted, he then made even less work of the kidneys. Both kidneys in separate boxes, as they would be going to different recipients.

Broc then cleaned Lucy up, cleaning her skin, flushing out the empty cavity that once held all of her organs. He traversed the operating table, so Lucy was almost in the upright position, he cleaned himself up, cleaned the floor, and brought the mirror back into view. He then woke Lucy up. She took a while to stir. She finally came to. She raised her head and looked ahead.

She recognized the person she was looking at. She couldn't quite understand what she was looking at. Her abdomen was flayed open. It looked like a Belfast sink, a deep organic, rectangular hole. There was nothing there that Lucy could recognize as normal. She struggled to find the words, she was trying to take it in, but it wasn't sinking in,

"What have you done?" the tears came, "My God," she cursed, "what are you?"

Broc came into view. He was smiling, like a painter, gauging what someone would think of his painting. "What do you think, Lucy?" he asked.

Lucy's lip quivered, "You're not human."

Broc smoothed Lucy's head, "I have to leave now, Lucy. I am going to make you a little more sleepy, I will return probably in the morning and finish off the work, then you can truly appreciate the work I do."

Lucy looked at him, "Please, just finish me off. I can't cope with this any more, you've stolen everything from me." she said, her voice struggling to hang on to any semblance of control.

Broc leaned over and increased the milk-like substance on the syringe driver and Lucy's eyes fluttered upwards, her eyes closing. Broc stood back, admired the wound again, checked the vitals, all normal, laid the operating table back to the horizontal position.

He turned to the boxes that contained Lucy's organs, sealed them up and placed them on a sack cart. He wheeled them out of the operating room, through the corridor, the door hissed and opened, the rush of fresh air hit him, Broc breathed in deeply. He walked up the ramp and left the cart next to the door.

He went to the house. Carmen was busy cooking. He went up to her, kissed her on the neck, she smiled, "You're done," she looked at the clock, he is early she thought. "You was quick," she said.

"Something's come up,"

"Oh," Carmen replied, turning to him, placing her arms around his neck, "as in" she glanced down.

"Alas no," Broc said, "Tracey S. called, the processing plant has received a visit from the police, not your regular police, plain-clothes officers, not sure what it's about, but I have sent Tracey away and needed to check it out."

Carmen suddenly felt isolated and scared. "It will be ok though, right daddy?"

Broc wasn't sure, the police turning up had to be connected to the meat, why else would they be there. He reassured her "Don't worry babygirl, keep by the phone."

He motioned to the packages out in the courtyard by the barn door, "Get Baldwins to do a pickup, they have to go today." Grabbed the keys to the car, kissed Carmen on the cheek, and went to leave.

Carmen grabbed him "Be a careful, daddy." she said.

He stopped, looked at her, "Always my love." and with that he was gone.

Carmen heard the car engine fire up, she reached for her phone and dialled Baldwin's number, Broc was gone, the engine notes fading in the distance, the phone answered, a blustered female voice answered "It's Carmen Saunders, from Blackmore Vale Farm in Kings Stag. I have a pickup, has to be today."

The line went dead.

19

Alex and Renton arrived at Club Schwartz. Alex felt nervous. It was a world that she wasn't that familiar with, though Renton seemed at ease, this was his manor. The club from the outside looked like an ordinary restaurant. The restaurant, however, had a twist.

You ate your food in total darkness, blind waiters guided you to your table and served your choices, a popular venue for Londoners and tourists alike.

Beyond the restaurant and the perceived ordinary world, behind three heavy drapes was a door. A burly eastern European meat-head sat on a bar stool, looking as though he had lost a tenner and found a pound. Both Renton and the guy exchanged pleasantries of sorts and he undid the door to a spiral staircase descending to the basement. At the foot of the stairs, the room opened into a cavernous space of deep red and purple lights, the smell of bleach omnipresent in the air.

The bar furnishings were plush and opulent, the bartender was polishing the deep mahogany bar top. All the drinks one could want, from cheap run-of-the-mill-beers and spirits to a samovar of Absinthe, expensive gins and vodkas, £60 or £70 a shot kind of drinks were available. In the middle of the space was a catwalk. All sorts of business people sat watching a couple of naked female dwarves pole dance, ten-pound notes sticking out of their skimpy thongs, their bow legged frames just seemed strange. The whole scene felt surreal to Alex. Not forty seconds ago they were walking past various businesses like Pret e Manager, Burger King, Marks and Spencer Food Hall, but now they were in the weirdest of places. And to be honest, pole dancing dwarves didn't rank high on her notion of erotica.

Renton gestured to a group of well-built men in the corner. He guided Alex's arm in the direction and as they approached, a slim, attractive naked black woman, smiled at Renton, parted her legs, "I pink inside like all the white girls, wanna have some fun?" she said in a thick Caribbean accent.

"You're alright sweetheart," Renton said, he flashed his warrant card. The girl closed her legs and returned to her drink and raised an eyebrow.

Alex felt a wash of embarrassment, she was no prude, yet this place made her feel uneasy. The atmosphere was oppressive with tormented souls and damaged people.

"Officer Davis," boomed a voice, perfect English yet unmistakably Russian, the features were Russian, the attitude was Russian. Smoke billowed from the enormous cigar the man was smoking. He was a big guy, ex-military Alex presumed, tasty with his hands to and he was a guy that knew how to look after himself. Though for appearance sake, six armed men surrounded him. To the Russians, it was all about show and tell.

"How the devil is you, Renton?" the voice boomed.

"Good Dmitry, can I introduce my partner today, Alex Brown from Mile-end police station." Renton motioned to Alex. Dmitry effervescent with his salutations towards Alex, invited her to sit,.

"Pleased to meet you, Alex, I am Dmitry Orlov," he shook her hand, the vice-like grip causing Alex to wince inside.

"Drinks!" the giant shouted, "What would you like," he said more softly, "your wish my command."

"Coffee." Alex said.

Renton, disappointed, he wanted one of those expensive spirits on the bar, "I'll have the same," he said looking at Alex. Dmitry picked up on it, ushered one of his minions over, and conveyed the order in Russian.

"What is this, Renton?" Dmitry said, "Year, maybe two, you have been leaving me alone, I told you I would take care of this place, turn it around, make it…" he searched for the word, "respectable" he laughed as he said it.

Renton went through what had happened over the last few days, showed them photos of Gormley, he confirmed that he knew Gormley and that Melissa had gone missing from her home in Cornwall and then what had become of her. Dmitry listened, taking a few long heaves on the cigar, bellowing more smoke, filling the space lit by the stained glass light.

When Renton had finished, Alex gauged his reaction; he had a good poker face, nothing. Flicking the build-up of ash into an ashtray to the right. "Hold my cigar." he was holding it down to the ashtray, to Alex's amazement, it moved. The ashtray was fixed to the back of a slender young woman, she couldn't be older than 20. Alex couldn't hide the shock and she wanted to do something, anything, she felt Renton's hand on her hand under the table, with a forceful squeeze. Dmitry caught Alex's look, he laughed.

"This is Slatka, my slave, don't be alarmed sergeant Brown, Slatka is a submissive concubine that chooses to be in my service as a slave, she has been for a few years now."

"She can't be older than 20." Alex retorted.

Dmitry looked at Renton. He wasn't happy with the judging gaze of an uneducated stranger. Dmitry smiled and returned the gaze to Alex.

"Slatka is 24 years old, Romanian Jew, brought up in the slums of Bucharest. She has experienced unspeakable acts of cruelty and deprivation. She has been my slave since she was seventeen, sergeant Brown. It's the safest she has felt in years, if your wondering, I haven't once engaged in sexual intercourse with her, she won't allow it and I respect that. Her position in life is to serve and she can leave anytime."

Slatka's gaze was dead ahead, now on her knees, "Can't you, beautiful Krasivaya?" she looked at Dmitry and her features softened into a smile, it was genuine.

He leaned forward, clasping both his hands, "So, what do you want from me?" looking at Alex, but the question directed to Renton.

"What can you tell us?" Renton said, he left it hanging.

Dmitry shrugged, "Your story is quite horrible, yet I don't see how I can be of service to you. I know this Gormley, just a guy with a watersports fetish that comes and goes, I don't think he buys anything while he is here. I wouldn't concern myself with this man, as for the girl that was taken," he looked around the room, "she has never been here. I don't even know where Cornwall is." he chuckled.

Dmitry looked at Alex, "What do wish to ask sergeant? You have a question written across your face, tell me?" he asked.

Alex didn't want to ask, but she thought why not. "What goes on here?" she sat back in preparation for the reply.

Orlov looked about the room, "This is a place of escape, sergeant. People come to express their desires, their perversions, a release if you will," he took the cigar from Slatka, took a few heaves to get the end going again, inhaled deeply and blew off the smoke.

"You see sergeant; we live in a desensitised world. Sex twenty years ago consisted of two people fucking and it was all over before the heart reached a palpable level. Now you can have five women or men a night, at the touch of a button, you can have sex with a complete stranger, no strings. You can come to a place like this," his hand gesticulated to the room "and exercise your heart's desires. If you want a fat girl, we can provide it, if you want a twink, legal age of course..."

Renton leaned into Alex "Young men that look like boys."

"...we can provide it. If you want someone to shit in your mouth, we can cater for that, too. As for the marital home, anal sex is de rigueur these days, while most husbands farm their wives out to a hotel room with a stranger that the husband will have met online and watch them fuck each other. The Fifty Shades of Grey is child's-play to what goes on in our cities around the western world. Let me ask you a question, Alex." It was the first time he had used her first name, "What is your fantasy, what makes you wet?" Alex flushed, even Renton felt embarrassed.

"That's for me to know and for my husband to discover." she replied, which then followed by a haughty laugh from Dmitry.

"How very English you are sergeant." He slapped Renton on the shoulder, "I like this lady, Officer Davis; you can bring her again, she's a feisty one."

Alex gathered up some papers, pulled a photo of Tasha and handed it to Orlov.

"Tut tut tut," Orlov said. He took the picture, "Now that's a face I haven't seen in a long time, she's much older, but I know this girl." Dmitry said, both Alex and Renton exchanged looks.

Alex asked, "What do you know about her, we can't find her."

Dmitry looked at both Alex and Renton; "You need to speak to the Zookeeper, he knows this lady."

Renton looked at the picture, "What's the Zookeeper and Tasha got in common?"

"This girl is called Tracey Stubbs, not Tasha, one of the best hookers on the circuit, or was." he mused. "She dropped off the scene about two or three years ago, high-class fuck machine, I know her address if you want it." Dmitry said.

Alex and Renton couldn't believe their luck; they looked at each other. He shouted at one of the guards; he walked off, "Gregory will be back in a minute."

Renton looked at Orlov, "Where will we find the Zookeeper?"

Orlov laughed, he couldn't stop, "You're fucking kidding me he gasped. "You don't know?" he asked, he banged the table with his hands, laughing.

Renton was looking none the wiser, "I don't know,"

Orlov laughed again "Damien Platford" Orlov said.

Renton knew the name, a real predatory sex offender, jailed for life a few years back.

"This is too funny." Dmitry said, "Platford is the Zookeeper."

"He just couldn't keep it in his trousers, a gifted businessman yet raping young girls while they slept was a thirst he could not slake. Personally, I would have cut his throat. Your judicial system set him up in a prison cell, DVD's and end to end masturbating material to serve out his sentence, he will be out in ten years, soiling the minds of young girls yet to be born right now, your system is as worse as the criminals themselves."

Renton's blood drained from his face, "I don't believe it." he said, he searched the table surface for answers.

"You won't find answers on the table, Officer Davis."

Renton looked up, "How do you know this?" he asked.

Dmitry flicked more ash off the shrinking cigar, "I have most of his business now, both the Zookeeper and I go way back, him getting arrested was let's just say, a convenience for my business."

Gregory returned, passed a small written note to Dmitry, he looked at it, went to pass it to Renton, as Renton reached out for it, Dmitry retracted, "This comes with the usual caveats Officer Davis." Alex had no idea what that meant.

Renton consented and agreed, Orlov passed the note. It was the Whetstone, North London address.

"Sergeant Brown," Orlov said, Alex looked at him, "if you and your husband would like to come to one of our evenings, please." He passed her his business card, "As my guest, sample some of the pleasures that my club can offer."

Alex smiled, her phone vibrating gently in her pocket, she pulled it out, Ricky had texted her, she's in the wind boss, nothing.

Alex typed no dramas, we have an address, get a gun team on standby, we're going to North London, wait out for the address.

They made their farewells and left the club, neither of them speaking, once they got out to the street, Alex grabbed his arm, "What caveats, Orlov demanded caveats, on what?" she asked.

Renton stopped, turned to her, "The caveat that he wants is for me to turn a blind eye to the to-ings and fro-ings of the club, drugs and questionable kinks of some of the clientele, things like that." Renton pulled out his phone, launched his satnav app, plumbed in the address, "Look, he trades information like any other major pin in the city, we know some of the things he does goes on, this way we retain an element of control. He has given us a massive lead, “Can we get her record, if she's known to him," Renton indicated to the club with his thumb, "Then she's known to us."

Alex was calling on her phone, "I am already on it," The phone answered. Ricky's voice boomed on the other end. "Rick, Tasha is a false name, plumb in," She looked at the note. "Tracey Stubbs; the address is..." After giving the address, they made their way back to the car, the journey from central London to Tracey's house was going to take at least an hour. It would be late when they got there.

Alex was feeling hunger pangs; she realized she hadn't eaten since leaving the house that morning and she knew tonight was going to be a late one.

She opened the glove compartment, nothing.

"Hungry?" Renton asked.

"Yeah" Alex replied, suddenly feeling cranky.

"We can swing by a drive-in en route." He suggested.

Alex agreed, she wanted a Kentucky Fried Chicken, always on a late one, it was the skin she liked, "I would have a bucket of skin from KFC" she said, Renton smiled and pulled away.

Whetstone was the destination.

20

Tracey was pacing in the lounge. The 1950's semi-detached house on Sweets Way hid behind the facade of drabness and rambling weeds. It oozed the color beige and mediocre, ideal for the safe homc Tracey sometimes needed.

Her past often caught up with her. This was her safe, default position to go to, no mortgage and no bother. It would be the last place anyone would think, being the bolt hole for the call girl from the city to go to.

Nervously chewing all of her nails, waiting for Broc. Everywhere she looked, reminded her that she needed to paint, repair, clean, update, only isolated her further, making her chew more quickly.

Where was Broc she thought.

The sun had gone down and she realized that she hadn't eaten all day and that the reality of her situation was all apparent. In the space of twelve hours, the life she had, the experience she enjoyed for the last few years was probably over. She struggled to keep control of the steam train of negativity, old emotional habits rearing their ugly heads to haunt her.

What next Tracey thought, getting back in the game was out of the question, she enjoyed the legit life, maybe, when the dust settles, everything will be ok and she could find an office job somewhere in North London.

Damn, no milk she thought. The front room bathed suddenly in the headlights of a car.

Broc she thought, realising that the house was in the dark, she ran round switching the lamps and lights on, in an attempt to make the building more homely, Tracey giggled to herself, it'll need a bit more than lights to make this shit hole more homely.

The door knocked, she quivered, snapped round to look at the door. Not thirty-seconds ago, the house, flooded with the cool xenon lights from her master's car, why did the knocking make her jump.

Broc had a key, Tracey licked her lips, her mouth instantly drying, her intuition maybe, she was still nervous.

She went to the door, opened it cautiously and peered, out. The frame wasn't Broc's,Tracey instantly alarmed and panicked, she had no time, the door was smashed open, her foot making a feeble attempt to stop the door from opening. The sharp corner of the PVCP frame gouged a wedge into the top of Tracey's foot causing blood to burst out of the foot. She cried out in pain, as she scrambled at the door, trying to close it.

She was no match for the eighteen stone muscle man. Tracey stumbled backward, the momentum of the giant of a man lurching into the house, her foot in agony but barely registering. Her fight or flight response was kicking in, her brain quick to realize that fighting was futile, she needed to exit and quickly.

The man preempted her, lurched forward again and grabbed her as though she was a Barbie doll, being tossed about by a cruel big brother. He grabbed her throat and squeezed, the fingers almost encircling the whole throat and neck. Tracey gasped instantly for air, her palour had gone blue as she sucked for oxygen, there was nothing, he pulled her head up. Tracey got a whiff of the man's fetid hot breath, the smell of fish, booze and cigarettes, he smashed his colossal fist into her nose. Tracey experienced a bang to the head followed by a white light, a flash. No pain, just nothing, she was out cold.

It was a good few minutes until Tracey awoke on the bed upstairs. She was cold, breathing through her nose was labored, she remembered and then the pain slipped into the thought process, as she relived the horrific few seconds not more than ten minutes earlier.

Tracey, in the low light of the hallway, the full-length mirror in the bedroom, she saw herself, hogtied, naked and face down, her legs bent upward, with the ankles securely fastened to the wrists. She then felt the plastic electrical ties digging in, she tried to struggle but knew from experience that breaking free was impossible, ''Calm down, calm down, breathe.'' She said to herself.

Her wrists and ankles becoming painful, taking over the pain from the face. She could make out the outline of her face, bloodied, her nose at an odd angle, broken, she couldn't breathe from her nose and the taste of blood in the back of throat was nauseating.

Tracey was confused. She could hear the voices downstairs, or in the hallway, it wasn't obvious enough. What the fuck was going on?

The voices were Chinese and talking fast, she made out her name mentioned a few times and Broc's, but nothing else registered. Tracey shook the stress away from her thoughts, to try a dial into what was going on. She did everything that Broc had asked, why was she now lying face down, hogtied up in the bedroom, and strangers in the house that meant to harm her.

Tracey heard the footfall of a man, not the sound of the same man that had forced their way into her space. The figure filled the doorway, blocking the light, but she knew who that was, she would recognize the frame of her master in any situation. Tracy's muscles relaxed, like liquid, her limbs stopped pressing against her bonds, she suddenly felt at ease.

Broc entered the room, ''Fucking savages,'' he said, he pulled out his Leatherman tool, opened the knife and sat next to Tracey on the bed.

Tracey began to sob, she felt the coolness of the blade slide in between the rigid plastic and her skin and suddenly pop apart, instantly relieving the soreness in the joints. As soon as Tracey was free, she scampered up and onto Broc's lap, like a scared chastised child, she curled up in his arms and sobbed her heart out.

Broc soothed her "Sshh, kitten, I am here, what the devil have they done to you?" he asked. He gently brought her face up to his, her face bloodied and wet from the tears. Her nose badly broken, Broc felt rage rise inside him but knew there was nothing he could do to appease the Triads. He kissed her forehead and gently rocked her.

"I told them nothing master," she said, her bottom lip quivering, looking into his eyes. She trusted Broc with all her heart. Hadn't seen him for at least two years she thought, but his sturdy frame and the distinctive smell of his cologne just made her warm inside and flushing between her legs.

Tracey was a fighter, and she was a great ally to have. But today, the Triads needed to minimize the damage caused to their operation, and she had to go.

"Did I do ok, daddy, are you pleased with me?" she asked desperately, her voice cracking.

Broc smiled down "Yes kitten, you did the best, you made me proud, my love." he soothed.

Caressing her back, Tracey didn't feel the tiny pinprick of the customized injection system that Broc used to render his victims unconscious.

Tracey sobbed herself calm, she was searching for the reasons of what was happening to her and then it started.

Her throat became scratchy, it felt tight, her body's responses kicking in, coughing, breathing quicker, heart rate increasing. Tracey's body was in its fight mode, physiologically, it was trying to rid the system of the agent Broc had introduced to her surreptitiously. The potassium was causing her heart to slow and the paralyzing agent had started adjusting the calcium channel blockers in her cells. Tracey's heart was now pounding harder, the electrical system in the heart trying miserably to override the potassium now fully absorbed into the heart tissues, the sinoatrial node and the Purkinje fibers losing the battle. The beat began to slow.

Tracey looked up to Broc, eyes like deep dark lagoons, she knew she was now dying, the sense of impending doom washed over her like a crashing wave. Her breathing was rapidly becoming shallow as the body tried to take more oxygen in and rid the buildup of carbon dioxide in the tissues, soon the paralyzing agent would fully kick in, it would be a matter of minutes before her heart stopped and Tracey would be gone forever.

"Why Dale?" she asked.

Broc looked down. She never really used his name. He gripped her tighter, he felt his eyes well up, it was an unusual sensation for him, he never really cried.

"I have done everything you have asked of me and more, and this is what happens?"

Broc, his mouth dry, he was genuinely upset by this "It's not your fault, kitten." he soothed, "I have my paymasters to answer to, they need to close the loops, I insisted that I do this to you and not them, be thankful it's not their way."

It was a feeble attempt at justifying the cowardly act Broc was doing.

She sobbed some more, her body feeling heavier and heavier as the drugs finally started winning the battle. She was a fighter Broc thought and a terrible waste, she was a good girl and this was how he paid her.

Tracey tried to speak, nothing came out, her masseter muscle under her cheeks started fluttering, it was seconds away, Broc slowly raised his hand, and felt her neck for a pulse. It was very thready, quick and not very strong. It suddenly disappeared, he reached down and gently kissed her forehead, "Goodbye my kitten, my place in hell is assured, thank you for everything you have done for me."

A long groan emitted from her mouth. People confuse this with a sign of life. Broc who had been around many deaths in the hospital knew this was the lungs expelling the final breaths called agonal. Tracey was gone.

He laid her on the bed, the big Chinese man walked in, swaying on his fat legs like an awkward calf, which had just been born. Following him was a slight man, impeccably dressed, "Have you finished it?" he asked. His English perfect, and well educated.

"Yes," Broc answered, he caught the fat man looking at Tracey's naked body, even in death, her figure was stunning.

Broc reached down and covered her; the fat man looked at Broc, Broc knew what he was thinking. ''Touch her and I will kill you'' he said to the fat man, the fat man glanced at Ng, Ng barked some fast Chinese at him and he waddled out of the room, looking appropriately chastised.

''The police are coming.'' Ng said, looking out of the window. He shouted in Chinese and all the lights in the house went out, plunging the house into darkness. Ng's face, illuminated by the light coming in from the bedroom window.

''You're compromised Dale, we need to get you out of the country, set you up in the South of France, something like that.'' he said, still looking out of the window.

"I am not comfortable with that. I told you, once compromised, I should stop. You agreed.'' Broc approached the window, he looked up the street, "That's what I told you, but that's not what my bosses want. They see you a bit of a cash cow. They need to you to carry on supplying the organ chain.'' Ng calmly moved to one side of the window, pushing Broc to the other side. ''They are here.'' Ng said.

Broc peered around the window and saw two lines of armed men running up the road, away from the house they were in.

Broc, feeling alarmed, yet there was a comedy about what he was seeing.

Ng still looking out the window, ''My contact at a sex club in town informed me that the police were sniffing around and had asked for this address. I got our friend Jamal to quickly swap all the details of the houses over, this home, is number 13, the house they're going to in 31, just a simple misdirection, like the hands of a magician.''

Broc stood back, ''That's genius.'' he said.

Ng smiled, ''I know and that genius wants to keep working with you.''

A group of armed men, in two files, entered the front garden of 31 Sweets Way, the left file peeled off and went to the rear of the property, while the right file approached the front door. Broc was gripped with fascination, watching from the safety of the house up the street.

There was suddenly a loud percussion thud, flashing and banging coming from the house, then the file of armed police entered the property, the street suddenly lit up. Every car seemed to be a police car on the street, with people milling around in the middle of the road, with police telling people to go back into their houses.

Ng checked his watch, "Time for you to go, my friend."

Broc turned to him, and moved away from the window "Where?"

Ng barked in Chinese to the fat man, he came in and picked up Tracey's limp, lifeless body. Her limbs hung like a rag doll, her hair obscuring her beauty, Broc felt a pang of shame.

The fat man hesitated, looked an Ng, then walked out of the room.

"She will not be defiled, Dale." Ng said "You have my word."

He took his arm and led him to the back of the room, away from the door and the window. The blue of the flashing lights dancing across the freaky wallpaper of the room. "I have to ask you now. I need to know if you're still with us, Dale? If you are not, then we can't have you as an unclosed loop...unnerstand?" The only tell if you didn't know Ng was Chinese, mispronouncing 'understand'. Broc knew what he meant, that he wouldn't leave this building alive if he decided to go. He wanted to, but knew this was not the right time.

"Where are we going?" Broc asked.

"I want you to follow Chen." Ng said, "Go through the attic space to the end of the street. The last house, there is an alleyway, at the end of the alleyway is a car waiting for you." Ng grasped both shoulders of Broc, "Dale, we will protect you, have faith, my friend."

Broc had to rely on Ng and he knew it was his only choice, he nodded, "How do we get to the other end of the street without being seen?" Broc asked.

Ng nodded to Chen, "Chen will show you. There are no fire walls between this house and the end of the street, what barriers there were have been removed."

Ng smiled, "Health and safety didn't exist eighty years ago when this street was built. Most of the attic spaces have no firewall."

Broc mused, "That was an educated guess Ng."

Ng smiled back, "More luck, Dale, sometimes fortune favors the brave. Now go." He gently pushed Broc in the direction of the ladder. Broc turned and followed Chen who was waiting at the bottom of the ladder.

As Broc entered the landing, he saw Tracey's body slumped in the bathtub. He thought fondly of her and the fun that he had had, the thought was gone as he ascended the ladder to the black square in the ceiling.

Broc heard Ng say "Instructions will be with the driver, you leave tonight Dale, see you very soon."

As Broc entered the attic, he heard Chen speaking in fast Cantonese on his phone. He peered through the dusty blackness that was punctuated with torches illuminating the path to the other house. The distance was about seventy meters. He followed Chen, his frame shielding the harsh white light of the torches.

When they reached the end, a ladder was poking up from the floor below. Chen motioned with his sausage-like fingers to Broc. He paused, looked at Chen, sweating, Broc considered that Chen wouldn't make old bones and he didn't want to tell him either.

He swung around the ladder and rapidly made it to the bottom. He recognized the voice, this was the guy Ng was speaking to. Equally as well turned out as Ng, he guided Broc to the stairs and motioned Broc to the go down them, he complied, descended the stairs and turned to go to the kitchen at the rear of the house.

He noticed the family of the house sat motionless in the dining room. It took a few seconds to realize that the family had been slain.

Mother and two teenage girls with their throats cut, the father severely beaten but still alive, what looked like a bomb was being strapped to him.

Blood was running from the table and sloshing onto the floor causing spatter marks on the mauve colored walls.

Broc closed his eyes tightly, did I just see that he thought, there was another well dressed Chinese man in the kitchen "What's happened here?" Broc asked, the man just grabbed Broc's arm and guided him through the back door and motioned him to the end of the garden.

Broc stumbled out of the kitchen, missing the step, he glanced through the dining room window and instantly began to throw up. Purging from Broc's body, the heinous image of an innocent family murdered for his exit was all too much. The man at the end of the garden rushed over, grabbed Broc, spoke in Chinese to the man in the kitchen, he closed the door. Broc felt almost drunk with panic, the man struggling to keep Broc on his feet. He got him to the end of the garden, the car about ten metres away from the gate. "GO!" said the Chinese man, "GO!" motioning to the car. Broc stumbled, vomited again, his chyme dripping from the bushes as he passed, he got to the car and dived in, the door instantly shut behind him. Seconds later the engine gunned, and the car was moving.

Broc slumped in the back seat. He glanced back, the image of Tracey, then the family. My God, he thought, what have I done?

"GET DOWN!" was the voice shouting from the front, "Keep your head down, there's police everywhere."

21

It was an early evening at the farmhouse. Carmen was used to dealing with the couriers. She didn't fully appreciate what went on in the barn. She had never set foot in the facility that Broc had set up, nor did she ever want too!

Simon Baldwin ran a small operation out of Weymouth. His haulage and courier company, like most small business, struggled for position in the marketplace due to the more prominent corporate players. Broc knew this.

Hacking into the company accounts, he knew that the company fought to meet the VAT payments and that the Inland Revenue was always chasing the corporate dividend tax return. As predicted, Baldwin could never meet the deadlines.

Along came Broc, aka Kevin Saunders, he was a Londoner living in Dorset with cash to spare. The cost of taking some packages to East London was tripled, with a cash payment of clearing the company debts and to ask no questions.

All Baldwin had to do was turn up when called and then take the packages to different locations, then drop the waste meat at a food disposal plant in the Tilbury Docks.

Don't stop and then return home a different direction from when you went. The latter was seeming odd to Baldwin, but he always complied.

His wife who ran the company books, on the other hand, wanted to know where the £20,000 had come from and how her husband could afford a brand new truck. She didn't want to be part of the seedy arrangement and nothing could go well from this Si, she would say. But the debt was paid and the lean on the house was gone. Coercion always had a price and the price was convenience to the truth.

Simon was a tall, proud Dorset man. His hip gave him *jip* as he walked, causing a change in his gait. Although his doctor said that he ought to lose the 30 kgs of weight and stop eating junk.

Si was at a time in his life where the drudgery of just surviving was becoming too much. Things just hadn't turned out how they should have.

Eating a footlong sub, the second that day, he told Calum, his laborer "This might kill me and if it does, don't bother calling the ambulance, just leave me be."

Simon had worked hard all his life, yet he never caught a break. When Kevin Saunders had come into his life waving the cash about, it was difficult to turn the money down. When the philanthropist then said that he would pay three times the going rate and didn't quibble at the quotation, this was the break that he needed.

What he didn't understand, the cash offer he was offered was the exact amount the HMRC was going to require to keep the wolves from the door.

He pulled into the drive the tires crunching the thick pile of gravel. He manoeuvred the truck around the back of the farmhouse, the headlights bathing the red brick and the flint-stone glistening in the white light. They both hoped that Mrs. Saunders was going to make an appearance. She was good value and one for the bank.

Carmen always played up to the boys when they came. They were a good laugh. Grassroots people that she understood. She could dispel the pretence with the working class and be normal, it was a relief.

Si pulled the truck up and saw the packages. There was no waste meat. Good job too, Si thought as this stuff always stank the truck out. He didn't really know what they were and with the smell, he didn't want to either.

He loaded the packages carefully. They felt solid. He sometimes wondered what was in them, but the price

Saunders was paying, it wasn't worth his while to ask, it couldn't be legal though.

He walked around the truck, hoping to catch a glimpse of the lady of the house, she wasn't anywhere to be seen. Lights in the house shone through the windows, casting wild shadows around the courtyard.

Si pondered if he should knock on the door, catch a glimpse of her, stating the obvious and telling her that they were here for a pickup.

She's not stupid he thought to himself. He got into the truck, it dipping violently to the right as he got in making the suspension creak.

"She not there?" Calum asked with a strong Dorset accent.

Si gunned the engine and engaged first gear "She's in, not up for us pair though, best we make a move, it's a bit of a trek to London, you better have forty winks, you'll be driving soon."

The truck wound its way through the driveway, down the drive and out onto the main road, three hours later, they were approaching the warehouse that Si sometimes delivered to.

The gate guard wasn't the usual uniformed jobs-worth, nonchalant to their very existence.

The Chinese man manning the gate didn't speak that much English which Si thought was odd. The Chinese man waved them through. Si glanced at Calum. Always riding shotgun with Si, his primary backup driver. He was a veteran traveler too for this particular job. He said nothing.

He was a young man with an even younger family. Born on the wrong side of the tracks in Portland, Dorset. Si gave him a chance. It paid off.

Not a shirker and up for any job that was thrown at him, he turned out to an excellent young man. He had really turned his life around. Si was kind of proud of him, but he never told him, maybe he should he thought.

The truck bounced over the sleeping policemen, another Chinese man was waiting on the corner, Si stopped and asked why he was there, he just gesticulated in reply to get the truck moving. The facility was eerily quiet.

"This is weird mate." Calum said.

At the end of the road, there were three cars. A group of Chinese men was smoking and chatting between the vehicles. They saw the truck approach, in unison, extinguished their smokes and dispersed to their respective cars.

Si was waved down by a sharply dressed Chinese man. Si stopped, the air brakes hissing in protest.

"OUT!" said the man. Si again glanced at Calum, Si opened the door and swung out. "YOU TWO, OUT!" the Chinese man was pointing at Calum.

Si turned and said "Do as he says, mate, I think this might be the organ grinder if you know what I mean, just probably a paperwork thing."

These weren't police, which was the primary concern for Si. He wasn't prepared to protect Saunders if it was. He would take a deal whatever they asked, but these guys didn't feel right.

Calum wandered around the cab of the truck, shrugging his shoulders at Si.

The Chinese man tapped Si on the shoulder. He looked, "Have you got the packages?" he asked in perfect English.

Si concurred he felt intimidated, "Everything is in the back, as requested, is Kevin here?" he finished.

"No, he is not." the man reached into his pocket, pulled out a pistol. While still looking at Simon, the gun aimed at Calum reported. The top slide ejecting the spent case, Si watched it fly through the air, tumbling gracefully, the light catching the edges, his eyes then following the flash and the dull blat coming from the muzzle of the pistol.

He didn't hear the flapping of wings from the pigeons minding their own business in the rafters of the warehouse. Then to Calum, the bullet, smashing through the bridge of his nose, and the back of his head exploding against the paintwork of the truck and the metallic clank as the shot found it's home in the bodywork of the lorry. Callum's legs buckled. There was no cry. This surreal and traumatic moment instantly etched in Simon's memory.

Callum buckled like liquid, slumping to the floor, both his eyes ghastly bulging with the pressure just exerted in his head, his tongue hanging loosely from the corner of his mouth. Callum, in an instant, was dead.

Simon didn't think about himself at this point, while starring, he noticed the hollow clatter of the spent shell bouncing off the concrete floor to his right. He was thinking about Callum's family and everything that Calum was hoping for as a man in life, in a nanosecond, gone.

Simon turned to look at the Chinese man, who was still looking at Simon, he felt nauseous.

"WHAT THE FUCKING HELL?" Simon retorted. He repeated the statement. He wanted to lunge at the Chinese man, but Simon's amygdala in his brain made him freeze. The part of the brain that forms the limbic system responsible for emotions and fears, the oldest evolved part of the brain that controls the survival instinct of the human genome. In a perverse thought process, Simon's brain was telling him not to do anything, as this might save your life, but in reality, Simon was seconds away from death and his mind didn't want him to die trying, he was going to die where he stood.

The Chinese man swung the barrel of the 5.7mm bottlenecked QSZ-92 Chinese military standard issue subsonic, high-velocity pistol at Simon and blue smoke twirled out of the end, the smell of spent carbon from the gunshot filled his nose.

"Mr. Baldwin, I will only ask you this question once, have you kept our relationship and particulars quiet?"

Simon stared down the barrel. It wasn't like Reservoir Dogs or Pulp Fiction. It was real. He stammered. "Yes, I have told no one, even my wife doesn't know what we do."

The pistol flashed. Simon didn't hear anything.

The smooth ball round spun out of the barrel and buried itself in the front of Simon's forehead. The bullet, skilfully aimed, traveled through the frontal cortex, in a downward trajectory. The bullet ripped through the amygdala, then the pituitary gland, through the pons and medulla oblongata, severing the spinal cord from its home. The wake of the subsonic round traveled fast enough to drag through the parts of Simon Baldwin's brain out the cerebellum through the skull with a hole the size of a fist, spattering the floor behind him with a sickening sound.

Simon crumpled to the floor like shoes falling from the loft.

His life didn't pass before him. He didn't get the chance to say goodbye mentally to anyone. He left on the terms that he hoped for, albeit traumatic. It was quick. Baldwin was dead, nothing but empty blackness. His legs were twitching, making a scraping sound on the concrete as the nervous system struggled with the absence of action and thought. His bladder voided, darkening the groin to the amusement of the spectators. His blood slowly spread across the dusty grey concrete floor, finally meeting Callum's already clotting gelatinous blood pool that had stopped about a metre from Callum's body.

Ng pocketed the pistol in the shoulder holster. Shouted in Chinese. The men sprung into action.

Within 30 minutes, the execution of the Simon Baldwin and Calum would be cleared away with absolutely no trace.

Ng, always respectful of the notion of family and would send the bodies home from where they came, he respected family, it was the cornerstone of life.

Life to Ng was cheap. He felt nothing, nor any consequence for what lives these people had. His heart cold and only for the cause. The family that he served. No doubt one day he would meet the same fate as the many souls he had executed, mostly by his own hands.

When that day came, he would show no remorse, no fear for he welcomed death, as death was part of his journey.

He got in the back of his 1990 rusty Mercedes.

Not one for drawing attention to anyone. The car gunned and left the warehouse. Dialing the phone, the car headed to Sweets Way in North London to rendezvous with his protege and deal with the loose ends.

This night will soon be over.

22

Graham wandered into the living room. He had just buttered his favourite dessert, an iced bun, with real butter.

Mavis, his wife, looked up from the TV Times crossword, Holby City playing on the telly, "Want some iced bun with your butter color sergeant?" she said.

Her tortoiseshell glasses perched perilously on the edge of her nose. Graham, a stick-thin giant of a man. A proud member of the 1st Battalion, The Grenadier Guards, had served countless tours of Northern Ireland, Bosnia, the first Gulf War and attached to the Scots Guards during the Falklands campaign. His culinary weakness was always an iced bun. If she was so critical, why always buy them he thought,

"I buy them because I love you." she said, the comment made him stop in his tracks, he smirked to himself and carried on walking.

Before Graham sat, he peered through the curtain, just checking the street. "Seems quiet on the street mave, is there anything on, like the footie?"

They had lived in Sweets Way since Graham had left the army in the mid-'90's, the house they lived in was a government acquisition strategy to make more money and sell 30% of the married quarters in the UK. They liked where they lived, Graham's distinguished service was ending and the people around them were like-minded either serving or ex-serving members of the army.

Fast forward 20 years, everyone had all but gone, sold and gone home, even their children had flown the coop. With a supermarket, police station, doctors surgery, pub and decent Indian restaurant all within a three-minute walk as well as a tube station, with no mortgage, why move?

She flicked through the magazine as he sat.

Picked up the remote and said "Nope there isn't" he said.

"I was checking," she chided.

"I don't know why you bother with that rag anymore."he wagged the remote control at her. "We have progressed, you should get with the times."

Charlie team was the primary entry team through the front, delta to the rear. Once Delta was in position, the three squelches on the comms set showed call signs were ready to move.

Tac team 5, experienced, ex-infantry turned coppers and moving to the firearms team.

A burly ex-Royal Anglian, Norfolk boy who was the team leader screamed 'BREACH BREACH BREACH!' Breacher guys in each team on the monkey spanners smashed the locks on the front and back door of the Bramley's house, which followed two cylindrical grenades called 9-bangers. In one-second the house was bathed in brilliant white light following nine sonic bangs. Both Graham and Mavis, stunned.

Sound of boots entering the house took Graham back to West Belfast. He grabbed his love "Get down darling, just get down." Mavis was hysterical but hung onto the calmness go her husband.

"ARMED POLICE, EVERYONE GET DOWN!"

"ROOM CLEAR!"

"ROOM CLEAR!"

Graham heard them systematically clearing the rooms. Then the front room door violently swung open.

"STAY DOWN STAY DOWN!" the first man screamed, staring down the sights of an MP5 Heckler and Koch submachine gun.

Graham counted six pairs of magnum assault boots. He didn't look up. He didn't want one of those boots to meet his face.

"HANDS BEHIND YOUR BACK!" was the next order.

The room filled with pungent smoke, it took Graham back to thunder flashes and grenades as a young soldier, he felt his heart pounding. His urge to get up was screaming at him but knew that it was fruitless. He noticed Mavis was sobbing.

"Darling, sshh, don't fret love, this will be ok, listen to my voice, this is a mistake, we will get to the bottom of this."

"Get them up."

Graham felt a hand grab his armpits. He heard Mavis cry out.

"Careful you fucking oaf's!" he screamed.

"Gently, gently guys," the voice of a female slowed the pace down.

Alex came into view, "I am sergeant Alex Brown" she flashed him her warrant card, "This is Renton Davis and Ricky Lambert, can I ask who you are?"

"Graham and Mavis Bramley," he smiled. "Not sure what we have done to deserve this."

Alex looked around the front room, military paraphernalia everywhere, the hallway adorned with platoon and battalion photos.

"Who did you serve with Graham?" Alex asked.

He stiffened and

stood to attention, "Grenadiers, 1st Battalion, 29 glorious years."

"Wow." Alex replied. "I am ex QARANC and military police."

Graham laughed, "You had my respect at being a military nurse, why did you throw that away and join the monkey's?" Monkeys was a nickname given to the military police.

Alex warmed by the man's attitude. "Uncuff these good people" Alex said to the sergeant waiting by the door, she went up to Mavis and apologetically rubbed her back.

"Ma-am."

The copper walked around the couple, pulled his knife out, "Tell me, why were you called monkeys? I never knew the reason why." Their bonds quickly snapping free, Graham soothing his wrists.

Ricky piped up, looking at the painting of a Victorian Trooping the Colour on the wall.

"The only story that is unsubstantiated was during the Napoleonic wars, a French supply vessel shipwrecked off the coast of Hartlepool. The only occupant was a monkey wearing a red hat." Ricky wandered around the room scanning. "The local provost Marshall hung the poor blighter, as the locals of Hartlepool were convinced that the monkey was a spy." Just stopping at the door, "In I think 1877, the uniform adopted a red cap, similar to the monkey that was hung, although not connected, the military provost or police then became known as...monkeys."

"Gosh, don't you love military history." Graham said.

"ENOUGH, for goodness sake, enough." Mavis slumped onto the couch. "Graham, they have destroyed our house, can you not think of something other than the bloody army?"

Alex got to the point, "Mr. And Mrs. Bramley, we are looking for a woman, called Tracey Stubbs, she is addressed here."

"I've never heard of her." Graham said emphatically.

Alex produced a picture, "She's familiar, but I don't know her." Graham went to his wife, sat next to her and took her hand, she was trembling and cold.

"She is registered as living at this address, you are not on the deeds, we checked with the land Registry."Alex said, she produced the documents.

Graham scanned the docs, "This is a mistake, we have lived here for more than twenty years, we paid the mortgage off 15 years ago sergeant, I have the deed to the property in my bureau." He got up, skirted around the bodies loitering in the room, he noticed the front door, and the back door, there was a terrible draft. "You'll fix my doors right?" he said.

Graham pulled the lid down and searched. Alex caught up with him and was watching what he was doing, one of the armed policemen stood guarding in the hallway.

"There it is." A neatly folded document, bleached in a yellow tone, wrapped in a blue silk string. Graham undid the tie and opened it.

Alex took it from him and was satisfied that they were indeed at the wrong house.

"Shit!" Alex said as she read it.

Graham watched her, chewing the inside of his cheek, "You'll fix our doors won't you?' he repeated.

Alex looked up, produced the photo again, "You have definitely not seen this woman before?" Graham looked at it closely.

He walked out of the front door, looked at the picture again. Alex followed him. Graham was looking up the street. He started laughing.

"What's so funny?" Alex asked.

"I do know this girl, not one for forgetting a pretty face. I don't see her that often, maybe once a month if I am lucky, you see my wife thinks I am the world's worse curtain twitcher."

"And?" Alex said.

"Sergeant, you're at the wrong house, our house is number 31. You need to go up the street." He pointed and then showed Alex the photo, "this girl you call Tracey Stubbs, lives in 13 Sweets Way."

Alex followed his finger, to the house on the bend, all but one light off, the bathroom light blazing.

"Mother fucker." Alex said under her breath.

Graham stopped laughing, "You'll fix my doors right?"

Alex pulled her phone out, found Frank's number, hit call. The phone dialed.

"What a fucking cluster fuck, speak to me Brown," was the first thing Alex got.

"I think it's the wrong house boss," she replied.

"Your fucking out of think's, Alex. I am inbound to clean this shit storm up, I can't tell you the giant shit my boss just took on my face, I warned you." the line went dead.

Alex drew a deep breath and held it. This was going to be uncomfortable. Renton came out.

"Mr Bramley just gave me the good news, he seems genuinely happy about that, the intelligence was solid."

"It doesn't matter that its solid, Renton. If it's wrong, we have to hold our hands up, there is no chance of getting an updated warrant until the morning and that's if they give us one. We are going to have to sit on the house."

They both stared up the street, the light in the bathroom was so temptingly close. There was a screech of tires, they both turned and saw Frank stomping up the road.

"GET THESE CARS OUT OF MY SIGHT!" he bellowed.

"This is on me." Renton said.

"Thanks, but Frank's gonna tear me a new arse anyway." Alex said.

"YOU TWO!" Frank screamed, as he approached the driveway.

"I think you are in the shit proper," the voice behind them said, it was Graham. "Is he the one I need to speak to about my doors?"

Alex smirked, she walked towards Frank, stepping in line with Renton.

"Speak to me." Frank said.

Renton pulled the note out that Dmitry had given to them, and Alex produced the paperwork of the deeds and Land Registry details.

"The intelligence stacks up, we hit the right house according to the documentation, but Mr. Bramley," Alex indicated to the grinning man on the doorstep, with the front door smashed to pieces. "Says that this person lives in number 13, not 31." Alex motioned to the house on the bend, the house that only had the bathroom light on.

"He is positive that he identifies this woman that lives in that house, then how does a government agency like the Land Registry get this wrong?" Frank asked, he pulled his phone out.

"Get hold of the Land Registry, when you have them, patch me through, I need to speak to them urgently." He hung up.

"Is there eyes on the house?"Frank asked.

Ricky had appeared, "Yes boss, two teams, front and back, covert.".

"Covert." Frank laughed, "You're kidding right, have you seen this circus?" He motioned to the build-up of press at the cordon, and the residents of Sweets Way, a cultural mix of many different races and sexual orientations, typical of a London street.

Frank's phone rang, he turned to speak on the phone, Alex, Renton, and Ricky chatted amongst themselves.

Ricky turned to Graham, "Mr. Bramley, we might have smashed your doors in, but we did nothing to your water supply.".

Graham got the hint,"Teas all round." He turned and grappled his way into the house, stumbling over his destroyed front door.

A few minutes later Frank returned.

"Right, the land registry have had a breach, about four hours ago, they were hacked, they couldn't identify what had happened, until I spoke to their IT guy. He confirmed that the details were changed remotely, both 13 and 31 Sweets Way were swapped in a deliberate attempt to throw us off." Frank pocketed his phone, "The good news is, none of you is going to lose your jobs tonight, I will, however, point out that it's still early." He thrust his hands into his coat pockets and looked up the street.

Alex looked at her colleagues, "This gives us the green light to hit the house, boss?"she said.

"It doesn't. The boss wants us to do this right, we have to wait until the magistrate and the CPS green light us, the earliest will be eight in the morning. Give these guys the good news. They ain't going anywhere tonight if she attempts to leave the premises, pinch her."

Frank didn't wait for an argument he knew he would get from Alex. He walked down the garden path, opened the gate.

"Alex, I expect you not to hit the house until I give you the green light, I don't care what manifests itself through the evening, even if the scopes pick out the reincarnated body of

Pablo Escobar, I will personally issue you with your P45 if you disobey my orders."

Alex knew he meant it. The wrong house was a calamity, a PR nightmare. The risk was, this girl is a no-one and not connected to the investigation whatsoever. Hitting 31 followed by 13 with nothing to show for it will result in both Renton and Alex having an interview without coffee with the top brass. Not to mention the bad press that will follow.

"Milk, sugar."Alex turned, Mavis was on the doorstep, Alex suddenly realized that the smell of bacon was drifting out the house like a tractor beam, she was so hungry.

"Is that bacon I can smell, Mrs. Bramley?" Alex asked.

"Of course, I've practically stuck a whole pig on the hob, your boys are troughing through the lot, you better get your skates on you three, we have ketchup and brown sauce."

"Egg banjos as well?"Alex asked.

Mavis, strummed a pretend guitar in her hands "Course sergeant, would you expect anything less from an army wife?"

She turned away and lumbered through the mess of the front door.

Alex shook her head.

"We turned their life upside down and 60 minutes later, they're cooking everyone in the gun teams bacon sandwiches." Renton said,

"What's an egg banjo?" he also asked.

Alex pulled her phone out, checked the time. She had time to get home, catch some sleep. This scene will wait until they breach the right house in the morning. She made her excuses and told both Ricky and Renton to exit and do the same.

"Not while there's an egg banjo of the go sarge." Ricky said.

"What's an egg banjo?" was all Alex heard again as she walked away.

23

The ringing phone in Alex's bedroom seemed to come from the depths of her dream. She was answering the phone in her head, but the phone wouldn't stop ringing.

"Alex, your phone," the voice drew her out of the deep slumber of a blissful night's sleep.

She arrived home earlier that evening to a delicious home-cooked meal, a sense of normality to the chaos and perversions of the day.

Spaghetti Bolognese and a couple of glasses of house red. Simon had regaled her of his exciting day looking for food standard issues.

It was so exciting to hear him speak so animated. Simon knew not to ask about Alex's day, nor did he ever want to hear. He heard enough, when Alex slept, her dreams were so violent and vivid, she would often wake screaming. When she could, she would tell him, but never in the throws of a case.

They turned in early, bypassing the lounge and the telly. Went straight up to bed and both promptly fell asleep with the lights on, each with their current read resting on each other's chests.

The clock was saying it was 5AM, Alex took a few seconds to adjust and hit the green light on the phone, she heard the voice on the other end but couldn't make it out. She felt Si's warm hand gently touch the small of her back. It felt good, reassuringly, he held it there.

"Hold on, wait a minute." Alex rubbed her face and cleared the tangled hair away, looked at the phone and saw Ricky's name on the screen.

"Frank got the magistrate to sign a new warrant?" she asked.

"Neggers," Ricky said, Alex loved the army jargon whenever she and he spoke, "I just had a call from Renton, he got a call from Orlov, he's going over there now. Apparently, they do have a mole that works for the Triads, he gave the wrong address. They have the guy. I am going to meet with Renton at the location, just phoning if you want in boss."

"No, I'll see you at the house in a couple of hours, be careful Ricky."

"Roger that." he said.

The line went dead.

She put her phone down, 5.03AM the clock said, she needed to be up in less than an hour. She swung her legs up and curled into Simons chest, falling almost instantly asleep.

Renton pulled up at the Gunwharf lockup near Camden Lock. It was a series of lockups, mainly one man bands and second-hand furniture shops that made up the row of retailers by the canal under the busy railway arches.

The canal that came from the north of England and fed into the capitol. Dilapidated, it had a bad vibe. Nothing but wrongness came from a place like this, especially at this godforsaken hour.

As Renton got out of the car, he squinted as another vehicle approached and pulled in behind him. Ricky got out.

"I just spoke with Alex, she said go careful and she will see us in the morning."

"Good." Renton said. They walked down the uneven path, the tarmac so rotten, you had to be careful one didn't trip over. At a lockup a out two thirds of the way down, they walked through a group of high-end Mercedes and a Range Rovers. All black with blacked out windows. A meat-head of a guy was standing by a door. He instinctively reached into his jacket pocket, no doubt a 9mm Kashtan submachine gun.

Renton already had his warrant card out. Reaching into his pocket now would undoubtedly sign their death warrants. "I am here to see Orlov, Officer Davies and Lambert, police, he's expecting us," he put his arm around Ricky.

The meathead's face softened, his hand came out of his jacket pocket and banged the door and a small hatch opened, the guy's twin was on the other side, they spoke.

A grating of bolts and locks and the wriggly tin reinforced door opened.

Inside was a gloomy smoke-filled room. The premises doubled as a servicing bay for car servicing and probably was for the Russian hoods that worked London. But behind the facade, the place was used for Orlov to meat out punishments, retributions, settle scores and interrogate his enemies. The room stank of sweat, cigarettes, engine oil tinged with the sweetness of Swarfega and… Pain.

At the end of the room, was a cage, with a single 50-watt bulb shining, blue cigarette smoke hung in the air.

Hanging upside down was a naked Chinese man, covered in tattoos, weirdly none on the arms or legs, for a triad, he should be covered Ricky thought. He noticed that the man had electrical crocodile clips attached to his nipples and testicles, wired up to a car battery. Water from the top, running continuously over his body. His abdomen violently going in and out, the man appeared in a lot of pain. He was still managing to scream with a whole tennis ball jammed in his mouth.

Both Renton and Ricky stepped in. "AHHH, OFFICERS, finally, you have arrived," gushed the shirtless Russian.

“I found my snake, mat ublyudki." Orlov spat on the man. "He works for the Triads, one of Ng's pieces of der'mo."

He saw that Ricky was struggling with the image. "Your friend doesn't agree with our methods Officer Davies." Renton looked at Ricky. He clocked the use of our methods which wasn't true, "This is Ricky Lambert, Dmitry, Alex's partner."

Dmitry went to shake his hand, realized that his hands covered in blood. “Forgive my ignorance Officer Lambert," rolling the first syllable. He pulled a rag from his back pocket and cleaned his hands. The long pause while he stared at Ricky, gauging him, getting the measure of him.

"I take it from your revulsion, you prefer the rule of law rather than the prehistoric measures I prefer Officer Lambert?"

"I do," he said, "You can't rely on any confession under these kinds of conditions." Ricky said.

Dmitry nodded his head and walked around the Chinese man's body, out of nowhere Orlov punched the man hard in the kidneys, a dull thud as the large fist met the small frame of the Chinese man. "Light this piece of shit up again."

The crackle of the electricity made the battery spark and the man contorted horribly, almost going into a fetal position, all his muscles violently spasming, he drooled uncontrollably from his mouth, the ball dropping out and bouncing away, eyelids closed so tight almost bursting his eyes.

The spasming stopped.

"This man is called Xian. Hired at my club as a barman, a university graduate. From Oxford no less, business, top of his class like most of his yellow friends. But digging deeper, he has been part of the Sun Ye On Triad organization since he was born, he even was financed through Oxford by Ng's corporation based in Hong Kong. Notice the tattoo's, the second generation Eurasian triad, opting only to have the family tattooing done in a less conspicuous place on the body, no arms and legs. This man fed the Ng organization the details of our conversation yesterday. Whatever took place after that is anyone's guess, but you ended up in the wrong place jeopardizing my relationship with you, Officer Davis, that cannot go unpunished."

"Hand him over to us." Ricky said. "We will make sure that he is charged and appropriately punished."

Orlov spoke in fast Russian. Men from the darkest corner of the room appeared and lowered the Chinese man. Dmitry pulled out a knife and started to sharpen it on a grinding stone. Sparks flew wildly in a downward cascade, bouncing off the Russian's Saville Row hand stitched black leather boots.

Ricky and Renton exchanged looks, Ricky felt Renton squeeze his hand, he looked at Renton and caught his head shaking very minutely. Ricky knew they were on dangerous ground. Any false move, they would end up in the same hole as this Chinese man.

"Unfortunately Officer Lambert, I cannot do that." He checked the sharpness of the blade on his thumb and went back to the stone. "I am the only one that can settle this score. I have personally been aggrieved by this pizda, I take it you won't get in my way?" he glanced at his men, "I would hate for anything to happen to you as well."

He turned and walked to the Chinese man, he spoke to him in Chinese, the man spat on Orlov's boots.

Dmitry started grabbing at the man's skin, looking for a decent purchase.

"You see, snakes shed their skin, this called how you say… ecdysis, it allows the snake to rid themselves of the parasites that may have embedded themselves in their skin, the metaphor can't be more apt here." He smiled at the two policemen, watching.

Orlov managed a decent purchase on the thin Chinese man, and with the knife, as sharp a surgeon's blade sliced the flank off the man. The man screamed in agony as blood hosed from the wound, splashing onto the floor. Between the fascia, under the skin and muscle now exposed, Dmitry pushed the blade into the tissue and in a slicing motion, sliced the skin from the whole abdomen away, the man now racking and shaking uncontrollably. Orlov was skinning the man alive.

"In my town, this what happens to snake pizda like this motherfucker." His accent was becoming thicker, more sinister. Within minutes, the Chinese man had his whole thorax and abdomen stripped of skin and was begging to be killed.

Orlov had had enough, he spoke in Russian and two men came forward with their long knives and started slicing the skin off the man's body.

Orlov walked up to Ricky and Renton, wiping his hands on the bloodied rag, blood all down his chest and bulging gut.

He turned and spoke in Russian again, "da Kapitan" was the reply.

He noticed how uncomfortable the two police officers were. He laughed haughtily, "You English with your sensibilities. This guy is scumbag. His death warrant was signed the moment he took a job in my organization, he knew it."

Ricky was the first to speak, "It doesn't make it right, sir," he said, "Why don't you just kill him and be done with it?"

"He would have done worse, believe me," the big Russian said.

The shrieking was distracting, sickening, they could hear the men grunting as they sliced through the tissues and the noise the skin made when it slapped onto the cold concrete surface.

''Anyway, this isn't for his benefit."

"How come?" Ricky said, unable to take his eyes off the laboring men.

Orlov turned to look as well. He barked some orders at the men, they stopped and acknowledged and then returned to their sickening work. Blood was running like a broken drain onto the surface, the pool getting bigger. The carcass of the man resembled a slender carcass of a slaughtered sheep. Sinewy, muscular, not an ounce of fat. It wasn't until the eyes went to the end of the body and the bloodied swollen face of the Chinese man made even the hardened of the stomach such as Renton tighten with nausea, what made the sight worse, the eyes blinked, as though the man had given up, he made no more sounds, only muted grunting sounds as the blades carried on slicing through the skin. Patiently waiting for the impending death that would be most welcome.

"The benefit of this my friend is to tell the mat ublyudki and his paymasters that actions have consequences, this Ng needs to know what happened to his pizda...Skinned alive."

He threw the rag to another man sitting oddly in a deck chair reading Hello magazine, with a roll-up cigarette emitting an unbelievable plume of smoke.

"The reason why I brought you, good men, wasn't to see me carve this piece of shit up. He gave me some information that I think you might like," he laughed loudly, echoing around the cavernous room.

They walked to the corner of the room.

"He took a while to break, but when he did, he sang like a...how you say?" he looked at them both and punched Renton in the chest, "like a canary." Clicking his fingers, his teeth a brilliant white, the molars at the back as one would expect, gold.

Ricky, his sensibilities compromised, but still very curious about what the Russian knew. "His employment in my organisation was purely coincidental, it just happens that a name came up that was on his radar and he acted on it."

"That name being Tracey Stubbs," Renton said.

"No shit Sherlock." Orlov said in a funny cockney accent.

"She was looking after this food processing plant, that's all he knew about her, what he did say though, was that the Triads have been in the illegal organ donation business for years." This didn't come as any surprise to either Renton or Ricky.

Orlov pulled out a cigarette and lit it. The smell was unpleasant, old mahorka tobacco. Strong cheap Russian smokes that probably came out of an oil refinery. He drew deep and long, finally letting go, two jets of smoke came out of each nostril like a dragon.

"Who was she running from?" Ricky asked.

Orlov shrugged his shoulders as well as his face, "Who knows, maybe from you." He laughed. "What the Chinese man did say, she has been terminated."

Renton pulled a face, "What do you mean? You mean killed?"

"Da, if you haven't got her, then she is mertviy."

Ricky frowned, Orlov caught it, "Dead, young man, it means dead.' He translated.

"What about him?" Ricky asked, motioning to the doomed man.

"His luck has run out, my friend. Go save the world. I will clean this shit up." He turned laughing and coughing.

Both Renton and Ricky went to leave, "How can she be dead if we know that she is in the house?" Renton asked.

"I'm not fucking policeman here, you go do your fucking shit, and I will do mine."

He turned and laughed, the room filled with laughter, the Russian loving every second of their torture flicking his cigarette and bouncing off the hanging man.

Ricky pulled his phone out, it answered. "Confirm you have eyes on the pax inside the house?"

The voice on the other end affirmed, "Roger, she hasn't moved from the bathroom, still a decent heat signature, she just lying in the bath by the look of it."

Ricky hung up. Looked at Renton, It's nearly 6 AM, who sits in a warm bath in a house where no one else is in for almost 12 hours?"

"Fuck…A dead one." Renton said. They both ran to their cars, Ricky dialling Alex, "Sarge, get up, we are going to the house, we think Stubbs is already dead."

24

Charlie and delta gun team had been briefed by Renton en-route to the police cordon of Sweets Way. With the strong suspicion of harm to Tracey Stubbs, the need for a warrant had expired. In the pursuit to prevent any further injury, the teams formed up at the house.

They entered the same way as they had at the Bramley's, Delta at the back and Charlie through the front.

Charlie's frontman cleared the hallway, the decision to go upstairs, issued and the team pepper potted their way to the top of the landing.

As the team reached the top stair, the air was dense and moist, as though it was a sauna. The third man from Charlie started to retch uncontrollably. The stench coming from the bathroom was palpable.

"What's that smell?" he struggled to say between urges over the radio.

"Proceed with caution, Danny clear the room with the light on." was the order.

The four-man group on the landing readied themselves.

Light spilled from under the door, with dripping water, no movement was detected on the other side. Optics outside,

"Still no change from the bathroom."

The third man steadied himself to kick the door in, Danny waiting, he counted, the size nine boots splintered the thin-framed door to pieces and swung open. Instantly being engulfed with a foul odorous cloud of steam.

The fetid fumes were immediately making the men on the landing vomit.

"GAS GAS GAS!" shouted Danny over the radio.

All call-signs in the tac team squatted and donned their gas masks. The smell still managing to permeate the filters of the respirators.

The cloud of steam cleared, Danny, the first man in, wasn't prepared physically, mentally or emotionally for what he encountered.

The water was hot, a creamy foaming mixture of water and human fat. Steaming hot, just below 90 degrees, the hot tap still on a slow stream. Tracey in the bathtub, her face contorted hideously, like the mask of a clown, her tongue lolling to one side and her head bobbing rhythmically with the movement of the bath water.

"What the fuck?" Danny said under his breath. It took a couple more seconds to realize that an electrical cord was trailing out if the bath, Danny gingerly moved around the tub, conscious to not touch anything near the bath.

He grappled for the pressel of his radio.

"All callsigns, Danny, no one move in the house, the bathroom is rigged to the mains, wait out."

He touched the electrical cable, his tactical gloves insulating him from the power source, gave it a gentle tug, and it came away from the bathtub. The end was a toaster.

"What the hell?" Danny said, over and over again.

"I think we need the fire service here," he said.

"Talk to me Danny, over," the sound drowned out with the armed team vomiting all over the landing and stairs.

Ricky and Renton had arrived just moments after the teams had entered the property.

Ricky had updated Alex to what happened with Orlov. Renton had been updating Frank. They were both on their way.

Frank had agreed that to conserve life trumped any need for a magistrates signature on a bit of paper.

"What happened with Orlov?" Frank asked, "On second thoughts, I don't want to know."

Renton didn't want to impart what he and Ricky had seen, being an accomplice to a brutal murder for the greater good was still a brutal murder. Holders of the Queen's warrant doesn't give them the right to choose who's immune from prosecution.

Police discretion Renton thought when he was in training will not stretch to murder. It wasn't the worst thing that he had witnessed in the past. He knew it was possibly the worst thing that Ricky had seen as a police officer. He made a mental note to manage Ricky through it.

Both cars screech to halt. The armed police officer manning the cordon recognized who they were and recorded their names on the clipboard.

Alex or Frank still hadn't arrived at the scene.

Up the road, they saw the teams lining up, then smash of the doors simultaneously caving in, the shouting of the guys systematically clearing the rooms. When they heard Danny on the radio, they raced up to the house.

A small thin man that looked out of place wearing the tactical gear of the police was standing in the doorway.

"Stand down guys. House isn't cleared," in the broadest northern accent.

"We need to get in" Renton shouted, "This is our case mate."

The guy clicked his radio and spoke to one of the team leaders in the house. "Roger that Gaz, send them up, make sure they got empty stomachs or bring a bag to puke in."

The small man waved them through. They entered the house. The stink was overpowering. They caught sight of the big Norfolk boy waiting at the top of the stairs.

"'ere boys, not to bootiful up 'ere." His Norfolk accent very strong.

Both Ricky and Renton climbed the stairs, Renton struggling with the smell, it clung to the back of the throat like his nan's boiled ham, the smell took him back to being forced fed boiled tripe.

"Funky up here Renton." Ricky said his forearm was covering his face, desperately trying to hide the smell. They made it to the landing and entered the bathroom, Tracey dead. Boiled in the bath.

One of the armed guys came to the doorway, "The fuse box has been messed with, they turned the bath into a giant fuckin kettle, sick cunts!" he walked off.

"You poor girl." Ricky said. He felt a genuine heartfelt sadness. The day before, he had met Tracey, or Tasha as he knew, he followed her across London on the CCTV and now, 12 hours later, she'd been defiled in a way that was just too much.

He wanted to sit, but there was nowhere to sit, the walls, floor, ceiling and windows slippery and coated with the dissolved fat tissue from Tracey's cooked body.

His mind went back to Camden and the lockup with Orlov and Xia, the skinning alive and his brutal murder. It came without warning, his body purging his emotions of revulsion, shame, and sadness, as a tidal wave, Ricky's body bucked and threw the contents of his stomach onto the floor in the bathroom.

Renton patted Ricky's back. He felt the same sense of failure.

Both Ricky and Renton were outside, drinking tea from the polystyrene cups provided by the catering vehicle at the crime scene when Alex arrived.

The SOCO's and forensics had already begun the grim task of processing Tracey's house. People clad in white paper suits, the hoods up and face masks on coming and going with metal suitcases and camera equipment.

Alex, dressed in the same clothes as the day before, apart from the tight black Barbour Polarquilt parka, the belt pulled tight, giving her an hourglass figure and light make-up applied.

Always a chance at this stage to be thrust in front of the media. She made that mistake only once.

"Ok you pair of mincers, sitrep me," she said.

Both Ricky and Renton apparently tired from the events of the night told her everything.

"Anything in the house?" she asked.

She told them both to go home and get their heads sorted. She went to the house, the door, monitored by a blue paper suit cladded man with a clipboard.

"Name?" Alex flashed the warrant card, "Sergeant Brown."

He looked closely at the card. Satisfied, he put the board down.

"You put the blue suit on sergeant, you need to wear a face mask in the house as it's a biohazard." He fretted around the big plastic box, he glanced over to her.

"You can put your coat and stuff in that bag, and put it in that big storage box, would you like Tinc Benz?" Alex started unzipping her coat, the precious heat escaping the cocoon of her coat.

"What's Tinc Benz?" she asked.

"Friars Balsam, pongs proper in there sarge, mask the smell, drop a bit onto your mask, it'll hide it." He approached her and dabbed a sticky bottle on her mask.

Alex put the mask on, "Smells like my grandmother," she curtly said.

"You'll be thankful, it's proper grim." The man repeated the word proper as if to emphasize that it was horrible and smelly.

Alex wasn't going to take any chances. She had arrived on many mass killings in Iraq and Afghanistan, seeing grotesque scenes of utter brutality weren't going to phase her, yet the run-down that Ricky and Renton had given her upped the unthinkable threshold in Alex's mind.

Alex entered the house. A damp pungent smell was overpowering the scent of the Tinc Benz. James Dugal, the forensic pathologist, was coming down the stairs.

"I thought I heard your voice, Alex." he laughed.

"I see you have taken the lightweights choice and used a bit of Friars Balsam on your mask." He pointed up the stairs, "Fascinating crime scene, Alex. I mean, off the hook fascinating, even better than the Troll crime scene last year, don't touch anything though." He started going back up the stairs. "Watch out for the piles of spew, your crew have been chucking up everywhere, made a right mess of the scene."

His tone was chipper. It seemed to Alex that he was genuinely excited by the event in the house.

Alex climbed the stairs, the suit making chaffing noises as she ascended the stairs. As she reached the landing, a rubberized tarpaulin had been stretched out, and another tarp of equal size stretched over what was evidently a body.

Cautiously, Alex made it to the landing, deliberately placing her feet on the white footstep stickers that were all over the landing, clear areas to put one's foot in the crime scene.

James was crouched, "Are you ready? Brace yourself, Alex," he said.

He carefully removed the tarp covering the body, she placed her hand on the balustrade to steady herself, it felt slimy under her hand.

Only Tracey's shell of a body was there. Her face grimacing, eyes missing, her features were still of the girl she saw the previous day, less than 24 hours ago. She seemed to have been deflated, as the tarp pulled back, the rest of Tracey's body was absent. Her spine was trailing from the entrails of her ruined lungs, stomach and liver with the ends of the spinal cord protruding further still beyond the simmered body like a ghoulish tail.

"What the fuck?" Alex said. Her stomach was instantly churning.

"I know, right." James said, poking the tissues with a wood spatula. "She wasn't boiled, whoever did this, purposely tinkered with the fuse box, the water was kept at a constant 185 degrees Fahrenheit, the hot tap on all the time, the overflow going down the overflow pipe in the tub." James got up and walked to the step ladder in the corner that led to the fuse box. He climbed halfway up the creaking ladder, not looking at Alex, Alex still fixated on Tracey's body.

"The water temperature would have destroyed all the connective tissue, muscles and ligaments in the body. Her fat content would seep out of every pore. Taking the contents of her body with it. I wouldn't look at the bath, it's a human casserole."

He turned, his knee raised to steady himself, "When we pulled her out, she came out like a slow cooked roasted chicken in the slow cooker, most of her stayed behind."

Alex shook her head "I get the picture."

"How long has she been in here?" she asked.

"You won't like this bit, Alex." James climbed down the ladder, it creaked under his small frame, walked into the main bedroom, "When they fiddled with the fuse box, caused a momentary break in the electrical supply, causing the alarm clock that's mains fed to short circuit'. Alex followed him into the bedroom.

"What does that mean?" she asked.

"Roughly after you breached the Bramley's house last night, about twenty past seven, yes?" James asked.

'That's about right." Alex replied.

He pointed to the clock on the bed stand. It was blinking 7:28 PM.

"Shit!"

She walked to the window, stopped just short of touching the windowsill and glass, "They were watching us." she said, looking down the street. Mr. Bramley was out talking to one of the neighbors, she could see right down the road.

Alex turned, "Necky fuckers," she said. "But hang on," Alex said. "The street was cordoned off, it was on total lockdown, where did they go?" she inquired.

Both sets of eyes slowly went to the ceiling. "Has the attic been checked?" Alex asked.

"I wasn't going to process the attic space." James replied still looking up at the ceiling.

Alex fumbled in her paper suit. Pulled out a radio. "All callsigns, this is sergeant Brown, stand to stand to, commanders to my location in the house now, OUT!"

No reply was required, Alex heard the doors of vans slide open, the metallic action of guns and carbines being drawn, the unmistakable commands of the team commanders ordering their teams about. Then the boots on the stairs.

Charlie team commander loomed into the room expecting a fight. The rest of the guys hung back, avoiding the corpse on the landing.

"Sup sarge?" he boomed reaching for his mic pressel, "Standby," he said into it.

"Just a thought, have you cleared the attic?" Alex asked.

He looked up, glanced over his shoulder, the fuck-up potentially spreading across his face. Reached for the pressel again.

"Delta, have you guys cleared the attic, over." Static squelched through the multiple handsets now on the landing of the house.

"This is Delta, neggers, thought you were on task to clear, over," was the reply.

"Are you fucking kidding me?" Alex said, her calmness simmering slightly, the house wasn't cleared sufficiently for unarmed agencies to be processing the scene. She knew the team commander knew this and was expecting the chat without coffee on return to base.

The team commander blew air out, making his face look like he was wearing a gum shield.

"Sorry Alex, we are on it now."

With a whir of activity, armed police officers readied themselves to breach the loft.

A little voice could just be heard, "Watch the body." James was already panicking that the crime scene, now ruined.

After a quick set of orders, the team breached the loft space, in thirty-seconds, the loft was cleared. When the radio screamed clear, Alex went up the ladder followed by James.

Alex was greeted by the second in command.

"Looks like they made their escape down all the houses on the street, there's evidence that they went through the final house on the road, we are about to blow the hatch and go through the house as soon a Delta is positioned.

Ricky appeared in the hatch space of Tracey's house, "Sarge, I have an aerial photo of the street, there is a path that leads to the road that runs parallel. He gave Alex the tablet.

"I thought I told you to go home," she said. He leaned in ignoring the comment, used his fingers to zoom in on the path, a little obscured by foliage. The path nonetheless, led from the house on the end of the street. The sort of path the kids take to school.

“Shit!” Alex muttered under her breath. A small part of her wanted to find the perpetrators still in the attic.

The radio crackled and the team breached the house. Seconds felt like hours. Then the radio crackled again. "PARAMEDIC to this location NOW!"

Both Alex, James and Ricky looked at each other, instead of going a long way round, Alex just legged it. Down the duckboards through the attic spaces down the street. She heard the other two behind her.

She arrived at the hatch at the end of the street, the dusty space scratching at the back of Alex’s throat. A police officer made way, she descended the ladder and went to race down the stairs. She was stopped.

Charlie team commander was coming up the stairs.

"Sarge, stop, quick sitrep."

He was breathing heavy, face wet with sweat. "House is clear, three bodies, two of ‘em are children, there is one male pax sat at the dinner table wearing an IED, he’s injured, we need to clear the street RIGHT NOW!."

25

Broc sat, staring out of the window. The lear jet had just taxied and taken off from London City Airport. The graphic on the flat screen showed a red line, arching gracefully to Perpignan airport in the South of France.

Bundled into the car after watching Tracey die and driven to the city airport. He climbed into a Chinese jet with diplomatic privileges, no credentials were asked for. Now he was heading to the south of France.

A million thoughts were racing through his head, Carmen, Lucy, the house, the hospital, his patients.

There seemed to be a finality to what had just happened. The past was finally catching up with him. There were so many lives he had taken for his own gain. It wasn't guilt or shame. Just a sense that a large part of his life had now changed, which wasn't part of his doing.

He knew better than to fight against it. The moment he got into bed with Ng, he knew he was cooked. The one thing that Broc felt a small element of relief was that the Triads wouldn't go to these lengths to hide him just to be killed, thrown in the Thames and at some point, your body turning up near Tilbury. That wouldn't even make a splash in the local news, let alone the nationals and that would have been a more prudent solution for the Triads. There must be a Plan B for him, apparently not yet at the end of my resources Broc thought.

A weird sense hit him. He realized the aircraft he was in was flying directly over Kings Stag and leaving UK airspace at the mouth of Weymouth port. Carmen, he thought again.

A brunette stewardess appeared, carrying a silver tray. On it was a drink and an envelope.

The heavily French-accented woman placed the glass on the side table, poured a ⅓ of the Fevertree tonic into the glass while looking at him in the eye with a gentle smile on her face, the fizzy effervescence bubbling for a second, she gave him the envelope.

"Compliments of Mr. Ng." she said, She straightened. "If you need anything, Mr Broc, I shall be at the back, press this button' she tenderly stroked the button on the side of Broc's chair. He smiled and nodded.

The paper, expensive, at least 110gsm, off-white, his name written in thick blue fountain pen ink.

He opened it.

Inside was a set of instructions that was to set out Broc's position in the organization. Rapid growth, most of the transplants will be routed through a villa in Collioure, a small picturesque fishing village near the Spanish border.

He would no longer be involved in the kidnapping, not a bad thing he thought, the part he dislikes the most.

A state of the art facility waited for him of which two to three victims will be provided per week.

Broc felt excited. The vivisection was the easiest part for him. No longer did he need to prepare and locate victims, nor the effort of kidnapping the subject. He would be living in a luxury appointed villa, Mediterranean sea views and all the specimens he could wish for.

Carmen, Tracey, the house, the hospital and his life paled into insignificance now. Plan B for Broc was going to work out better than what he was doing living in Plan A. Two. He could do more.

He hit the recline button. The silent motor kicked in. Within minutes, Broc was sound asleep.

26

"Cluster fuck." Frank said, "That's what this fucking mess is."

The team were sat in the squad room while Alex pinned her ears back to receive the bollocking of the century.

"Why wasn't the attic checked when the teams went in, I mean, Jesus. You clear a house, you fucking clear it top to bottom," he spat, holding his palms out, saliva stuck to the underside of Frank's mustache.

The gun team commanders shifting uneasily on their feet holding their helmets like they were ghosts holding their heads, there was a metaphor there somewhere Alex thought. The phone was incessantly ringing.

"Pull the fucking phone out of the wall, I can't hear myself think!" Frank screamed at the office assistant on the other side of the glass wall.

'Sergeant Brown, task your teams and get your arse in my office with a decent plan forward, ear defenders will be a good idea, understand?" He said.

Alex nodded curtly.

"Now fuck off," he waved his hand. The two team commanders went to leave.

"Wait, I haven't started reaming your arses out yet, stand fucking still." Frank barked, they stopped, stiffened and waited for in-coming.

Alex wasn't bothered, it was a monumental cluster fuck, a swiss-cheese situation she thought.

Having spent hours upon hours understanding human factors and how humans are destined to screw up. When you have swiss-cheese and all the holes line up, your subject matter falls through the holes creating the screw up.

The first hole, in this case, was not checking the address properly, the rest, well, that was yesterday and this morning and the facts spoke for themselves.

The bollocking from Frank was for the suits that had turned up 15 minutes earlier to vent their frustrations on. The only reason why they had turned up was that the Met was being slated in the online press.

Gone was the ability to control events after they happened, as the press machine had to wait for their words to be printed, often being widely inaccurate because the events had evolved before journalist could change it.

Now everyone with a smartphone was a broadcaster. Record and film any given situation, then post live to any of the dozen social media sites. If the story was interesting, funny, or relevant, millions can see, comment and judge without the proper understanding of how their options can be interpreted. That's why Alex didn't care. A crime had been committed, the apologies will be accepted, and the world will carry on spinning and spinning for the next story.

The family in 59 Sweets Way possibly unavoidable, but that thought process would have to wait for the dogmatic detective. She called a board meeting.

"Right, pin your ears back, this is what we have in summary to those that have just pitched up. We are time critical, chaps. We need to get ahead of what's happening, and try and stem the mission creep that's happening."

The team assembled quickly. Most in the room had been on murder hunts and knew time was critical. The phone was disconnected and every eye in the room was facing the team leader. Alex was armed with colorful marker pens and a roll of tape.

Alex ran through what she, Ricky and Renton knew. Heads shaking, groans when the body of Tracey flashed up on the projector. Then the Pattison family at number 59. The images of the children and the mother slain, throats cut. The mother's head almost decapitated, the father, in hospital after a brutal beating with a bomb being strapped to him.

The army guy from bomb disposal piped up.

"The IED was sophisticated, Chinese in origin, the component though Israeli, which is new to me, contradicted it being Chinese government."

"How come?" was a voice from the back.

Irritated by the interruption. He went on, "Chinese government either use Russian or American devices. Israeli is so left field that it could come from the black market, you know, terrorist connections, the detonator failed about two hours earlier, it was set to go off in the early hours. Big enough to devastate two or three houses, and destroy any evidence, we are very fortunate," he said.

"Any thoughts on what we are dealing with guys, anything?" Alex said.

The room filled with silence. Phones were ringing, mobiles vibrating in the background.

Amanda, a junior office secretary, was shuffling some paper as she left the copier room, she stopped looked at the board and went to walk off, "Illegal organ transplant operation," she said under her breath.

Alex turned and looked at her. Scorn must have been across Alex's face as Amanda recoiled, she apologized, she knew her place and felt she overstepped the mark.

"What did you say?" Alex turned and put her hands on her hips. "What's your name?"

"Amanda, I am one of the office administrators, very sorry," she said, she went to scurry off.

"Stop, what did you say?" Alex repeated, in a tone that didn't need repeating, she sensed the fear in Amanda.

"I saw a programme on the telly the other day, about the illegal organ donation market in India, parents selling their children's organs for money," Amanda said. She felt the eyes of the entire room on her, she felt sweat on her top lip, her dad was always telling her to speak up, "Seems obvious to me," she shrugged.

"Amanda, thank-you." Alex said. Amanda smiled, she felt good, she went to walk off. "Amanda," she turned, "don't be afraid to speak up again, this is a great help." Alex said. Amanda smiled, turned on her feet feeling lighter then they did two minutes earlier.

Alex brought the room back to the whiteboard with pictures, post-it notes and different marker pen colors. She wrote in large letters, the nucleus of a mind map, ILLEGAL ORGAN TRANSPLANT.

"There's a link here, it's all we have at this juncture, find it," she said circling the comment.

"This has to be organized." another voice came from the side.

Alex turned, "Who was that?"

A well-dressed twenty-something named Spence raised his hand.

Alex rolled her hand like it was game of charades, "keep going Spence." she said.

"It's well polished, I mean, packaged meat in a supermarket polystyrene tray, a woman killed hideously. A family murdered, it wasn't even in self-defense. The family killed in number 59 just needed roughing up and silencing, but to be murdered this way, then to booby trap the father, this is a well-oiled outfit. Professional. I wouldn't go so far to say its military though."

"Why do you say that mate?" Ricky asked.

"Soldiers don't murder people like this. Sick, twisted..." he searched for another word "abhorrent to even think this way."

Alex was writing the points on the board.

Renton piped up, "Orlov mentioned something about an organ blackmarket, looking at this now, I see there's legs in it."

Alex looked at Ricky "We need a meeting with the Zookeeper, set that up with Portland nick. I want the rest of you to eat, breathe, think this case. There's a link here. We find the link. We get the leverage we need to solve, it's that simple."

There was moving of bodies and the immediate commencement of chatter.

"WE'RE LOOKING LIKE MUGS FOLKS. LET'S CHANGE THIS!" Alex was trying to speak above the clatter of chairs and voices. Some smiles "And people, try not to watch the news tonight, not our finest hour," she said more softly, there was muffled laughter.

Alex turned and looked through the glass of Frank's office, he clocked her and waved her over, he was still with the head-shed of the division and the team commanders were looking a little more red-faced than before.

"Sarge," Alex turned. Ricky came up to her.

"You ok?" she asked. She could see that he wasn't.

"Yeah, I think so, it has been a tough day, I don't know what to do about Dmitry." Alex held up her hand.

"Listen, we'll deal with him when this is over, he's given us some nuggets, let's run with this and talk of it when we have a result," she said.

There was a silent pause, "Anything else, boi?" Alex said.

"Yeah, well, I dunno really gov," he said.

"Spit it out." She tapped the board, "Points mean prizes, you know that it might be irrelevant, might not."

"Ok, I have been keeping my ear to the ground with serious crime on the nationwide database since yesterday. It's probably nothing gov, but a courier van was discovered in the early hours this morning with the occupants of the van executed. They were left hanging upside down from the inside of the van, decapitated."

Alex pushed her jaw out, "Where?" she asked.

Ricky pranced off to his desk. He pranced back, "erm."

He clicked with his tongue, "erm, Dorset, Weymouth, Dorset police had attended, they're processing the scene right now."

"OK, call them, get some INT on it and get back to me."

Alex went to walk off. She turned, "Weymouth, that's right next to Portland, where the Zookeeper is being held."

"Yeah, kill two birds?" Ricky said.

"Cool, I am going to get my arse kicked right now, Ricky. Nice knowing you." Alex said.

Ricky clenched his fist and tapped his heart, "Peace out, sarge."

27

The appointment with the Zookeeper came through and because of prison bureaucracy, Alex couldn't get a time earlier than two days after the Sweets Way debacle.

Both Alex and Renton decided to drive rather than take the train. No one from Dorset plod was prepared to pick them up from Weymouth and drive them the three miles to Portland. Driving themselves would just be easier.

Alex and Renton made idle chitchat on the way, Alex desperate to quiz him about what had happened with Orlov, something isn't being said she thought. He just skirted his way around the questioning and then changed the subject. They stopped at Fleet services, sat at the same picnic table Broc had been at almost a week earlier, with the van Lucy was in, not twenty feet from where they ate M&S sandwiches and supped a poorly made cappuccino.

Passing Stonehenge, "It's amazing how long that place has been there." Renton said as they reached the stone circle.

Alex, busy on her phone, checking emails looked up. "I was based here, over the brow of the hill." She motioned with her head, past the Henge. "Larkhill, home of the Artillery, bleak in the winter. Actually, bleak at any time of year." They passed a World Heritage site sign, both of their heads swinging left reading the sign.

"Bit of a disappointment really." Alex said.

"What do you mean?" Renton replied.

"What you see is what you get, people flock from all around the world and that's all there is."

Renton chuckled "What do you expect, a rollercoaster?"

Alex's phone rang, it was Ricky.

"I expect a decent restaurant at least, pie and chips just don't cut it for me." Alex said as she answered the call.

"Pie and chips to celebrate." Ricky said on the other end.

"Make me smile Ricky. You got something right?" Alex asked.

"Yep, I got two things. We think we have found a link you wanted."

Alex could hear paper shuffling, she sat up and dialled in.

"It's a tenuous link and we are looking into it further, but we think there's a blood sampling trend." Ricky sounded hesitant.

"Ok, can you expand a little for me?" Alex said watching the rolling hills speed past.

"There's some girls have gone missing that have all been included on a database called HAEMOmatch, it's an information gathering software package designed by surgeons at St Georges," Ricky took a slurp from a drink.

"This package has turned the transplant registry on its head, saved thousands of lives, instead of the clinicians going to the marketplace and advertising that they have a patient that needs a heart or kidney, the software does it the other way round."

Ricky left a pause, he knew Alex would be slow to get it, she never got it the first time round, her brain, amazing, worked in a different beat to Ricky's.

"I don't know what you mean," she finally said, brain desperate to compute the information Ricky had said.

"Ok, you have a car accident right now and you are

dead at the scene. When you go to the hospital, your blood is taken and then all the blood machines in Europe, Australia and New Zealand from what I can work out are linked. Your parameters are uploaded and if you have a match, that clinician or hospital is pinged," another slurp.

"Hey presto, you have a donor, from what the person on the phone told me about the software, it's saved thousands of lives." Ricky left another pause.

"Who's the person we need to see?" Alex asked.

"On it already, we are seeing the professor of surgery at St Georges, erm..." More shuffling. "Professor Krantz, tomorrow at 9 AM sarge, so you can't have a jolly with sweet-cheeks in Weymouth, you need to be back pronto."

"Have you ever been to Weymouth, Ricky? It's like Streatham with a seafront, proper shit hole, Heroin in Weymouth is the cheapest in the whole of Europe apparently." Alex said.

"Cheap henry sounds lovely, you and Renton could proper tear it up." Ricky said.

"Ping me the details." Alex said, she waited, nothing came. "And the second thing," she said.

"Oh shit, yeah, Mr. Patterson is awake, from number 59. He's doing an e-fit on one of the intruders. He positively identified a chap called Mr. Tao Ng, a known Triad muscle man. The guy is a proper badass, sword waving lunatic type of dude, Oxford-educated in economics and business. Bit odd though."

"Triads aren't odd in London these days, it's normally a Russian affair but strayed a bit from Manchester maybe?" Alex asked.

"He's strayed a little further than Manchester. This guy is the enforcer and money man for the Sun ye On Triad's, white collar gang running legit businesses in Asia. Their HQ is in Hong Kong, for him to positively identified at number 59 Sweets Way has drawn attention from Interpol."

"Fuck. Alex said.

"They want a chat with you, fairly heavy shit, sarge."

"Who's the contact at Interpol?" Alex asked.

Renton turned his head towards Alex, confused, she looked at him and raised her eyebrows.

"Some guy called Simon Broadstone, from what I have gleaned about him, he's a bit of a spook, I told him you are unavailable until tomorrow, reluctantly, he said he would call tomorrow."

"Ok, we aren't far now, I'll call as soon as we hit the road again." Alex said. The line went dead.

After another couple of hours, Renton had arrived at the prison. Built of grey unattractive Portland stone, the jail housed some of Britain's worst sex offenders and pedophiles.

The usual high security checks were done. The building painted in white and black, the corridor smelt of bleach and the sweat of men. The smell took Alex back to the male accommodation blocks in the army. A noisy, unfriendly place to be, especially for women.

As Alex and Renton walked through the social block, prisoners leered and watched as they walked through.

"SHOW US YOUR CUNT!" was screamed, followed by a chastising by one of the screws.

They arrived at a metal door. Waiting was a prison officer with a clipboard. No salutations, official to the detail.

"Ok, The prisoner has been in solitary for more the two years, his access to the outside world is very limited," the portly man looked over the clipboard judging.

The pause signalled that the two police officers understood the hidden meaning.

"Just sign the log and I'll let you in," his brusk Dorset accent rolling off the tongue, big red cheeks wobbling as he spoke.

Renton signed, his tongue licking the bottom of his lips. Alex forgot to ask if he was nervous. She thought to herself that she wouldn't like to see any of the slags she had put away, some of which were probably in this nick.

Alex took the clipboard, scanned for her printed name and signed.

"Right, inside there will be one of me officers, he's in there now, there's a black rubberized strip that borders the room about waist height, say two inches in width. You can't miss it if he kicks off and things get ugly, hit that and me and my mates will be in to settle things down if you see what I mean."

The man pulled an enormous bunch of keys from his pocket, without flicking through the keys like one would, he selected the right key first time, inserted it into the lock and turned, the bolt giving a satisfying clunk as the lock opened.

Renton grabbed Alex's arm, "Go carefully in there, the guy's middle name is Machiavellian, don't get reeled in."

Alex nodded

"Right, in ya go." The guard simply stated.

The room was brightly lit, from white fluorescent tubing in the ceiling, protected by reinforced perspex, the thick frosted window allowing the sun's rays to bathe the prisoner, sat at the table that was bolted to the floor in an amber glow.

Sat in the chair, was a skinny man, gaunt features, Adam's apple that bobbed up and down like a fishing float in a choppy pond, soft downy hair protruded from the chin and sides of the face, the bushiest eyebrows that Alex felt the urge to pluck. This was the fearful Zookeeper Alex had come to know, not the person she thought he would look like.

"Whatcha gorgeous." Platford said. The denim of the prison uniform not unattractive on his thin frame, though he was still handcuffed.

Alex turned to the guard "Can you remove the cuffs?"

"Sorry Ma'am, the prisoner is a type one offender, has to be secured at all times." The guard not taking his eyes off the window on the other side of the room.

"He's a one hey, 'bin tryin to get him to smile."

Platford pulled a face looking at the guard. "Fuck all" he laughed.

"So, what's your name beautiful?" Platford said to Alex as she sat in the secured chairs.

"My name is sergeant Brown, this is..."

"I know who the filthy pig-cunt you brought wid ya is," he held Alex's stare, then slowly moved his head to Renton. Looking at Platford, Renton smiled.

"I should wipe that fucking smile of your boat race pig, fuckin' gall of it turnin up at my nick, you got more front than fuckin' Brighton." His cockney accent out of place in the depths of Dorset.

"I bet you're a bit surprised I am the Zookeeper, I kept that all this time," he said goading.

"Sergeant Davis is on my team as one of the investigating officers. I would appreciate if you addressed him accordingly." Alex said, "I am aware that he was the arresting officer in your case and I appreciate that this may be awkward for you, but I need you to show some respect."

Platford laughed, haughty, "Respect, if he were on fire, I wouldn't waste my piss to put 'im out," he retorted.

"You were convicted of the rape of underage girls, grooming them from social media, kidnap, not only ruining them mentally, you ruined them physically. Personal accounts and video evidence, the sentencing judge said..." Alex looked for the sentencing report. "...she said you were the most heinous animal she had had the misfortune to cast eyes on. The silver lining is that I get to send you to prison for a very long time." Alex read.

Renton smiled again. "You should be in here for the remainder of you naturals, no place on the streets for a nonce'," Alex shot Renton a glance.

"Fuckin' naturals, I'll be out in uncle Ben," Platford said, "you got a daughter pig, I will be all over her like a tramp on a bag of chips."

"Over my dead body, ten years." Renton added.

"Not helpful." Alex said.

Patterson turned to Alex, ignoring her interjection, "You darlin, your different, I could lower my standards and…" he licked his lips, looked her up and down 'I would wear my cock down to a nubbin on you, you're a bit of ocean pearl.'

Alex shuddered inside, desperate to not let the man in, hanging on to what Renton had told her.

"Can you show me your thrupenny bits" Platford said, smiling deviantly, "C'mon, show me your tits girl, give us a Midnight Express Tommy Tank."

Alex remembered the film. The award scene of the incarcerated boyfriend masturbating to his girlfriends breast, difficult to watch, even more difficult to think about it now. She ignored him, opened the Manila folder and laid out the photos of the house at Sweets Way, the slain family and the meat processing plant. Platford was curiously scanning the images.

He slapped the table "Is this my a Silence of the Lambs moment?" he asked, smiling, his teeth yellowed and crooked, Alex could smell his fetid breath.

"That's a bit a stretch, but if you like." Alex said, she smiled.

"Has anyone said you have a lovely smile?" he clasped his hand under his chin, gazing at Alex.

Alex went along, "Yes, my mum and my friends," she said. "You missed your husband" Platford commented, indicating to her wedding ring. Alex kicked herself. She should have removed it.

"I can see you guys fucking right now, so middle class, so regular, another level of vanilla, tell me what he does to you," he asked.

"Can you focus on the pictures" Alex tapping the photos, she turned the photo of Tracey. He remembered, his eyes narrowed, it was a tell, he tried to hide it.

"You know her," Alex asked.

"I might," he said, he sat back, hands under the table, thinking this could be currency.

"Who is she, what do you know about her?" Alex asked.

Platford clicked, "tut tut Sergeant, this comes with caveats," still leaning back in the chair. "Information is everything, gives me meaning in a place like this, I mean if the slags in there know I am talking to the old bill," he looked around the room "It'll have consequences, you feel me."

"You selectively keep yourself in solitary." Renton sneered.

"It talks." Platford shouted. He looked at Alex, "You see. You literally can't trust anyone, in 'ere or out there," Turning his gaze to Renton.

"Ow is it I am in 'ere and your still out there?" Platford demanded.

"You're in here has got nothing to do with me Platford, you have brought this on yourself." Renton expressed.

"And like a righteous copper, yet you ain't so fuckin meritorious are ya, OFFICER fuckin Davis?" Overemphasizing the word officer. He leaned forward, hands still under the table. "I mean, bit more than the big toe you dipped in the water of enchantment was it."

Alex shifted in her seat, Renton clocked it.

"Again, we came to see you."

Renton held up the picture, "You know her, tell us about her."

"I want a better cell, better food, a bit of Franky Vaughan maybe once a week and access to the phone," he smiled, "these are my demands for my information." He sat back beamed.

"That's not how this is going to work Mr. Platford," Alex said, "You see, this lady was brutally murdered by someone we believe you know and that's the information that we require." Alex looked at the guard standing by the door, still looking at the window.

She leaned forward, so did Platford, enjoying the connection, he felt a tightening in his groin, grinning, he let Alex speak.

"We can speak with the governor, see what he can do for you."

"He fuckin 'ates me, that's why I stay in solitary, keeps me away from the lunatics on the wing that always want to give me a kicking," Platford expressed.

"After being on the wing, I hope your arse looks like a broken cat flap, Platford." Renton said.

"OH DO YOU NOW, OFFICER DAVIS?" his whole body rigid with anger, screamed, "TAKE THESE CUFFS OFF ME AND WE'LL SEE WHO THE GEEZER IS!" he shouted at the guard.

"Prisoner Platford, wind your neck in and shut up," The guard said.

"Focus on me," Alex said calmly, Platford was shaking, "Ignore sergeant Davis, you guys have beef, I get that, but we are here for this poor girl." Alex tapping the picture of Tracey.

"She ain't no lady," Platford said, his chin wet with spit, still angry.

A glimmer of hope. "Tell me," Alex said.

"She a goer, proper slut. I mean, she would do anything for a deep sea." Platford said, slowly coming down.

"Deep sea?" Alex enquired.

"Deep sea Diver, Fiver, she'd fuck, anyone, even that cunt for a fiver," Indicating to Renton. "Good girl though, clever, switched on, knew what was happening. I knew one day she would wind up brown bread. Mixed with some nasty bastards, you know," he smiled, "Nastier than me, snuff, kids, animals, whatever. She would have her finger in the pie, I told 'er a few times to keep low and disappear. But she wouldn't, always turned up at my events. Very greedy girl." His stare was distant, searching his memories.

"Greedy, what do you mean, for money, what?" Alex asked.

"Greedy for money. No, a cock-whore and liked the pain as well, she would be known as a cum-dumpster, so she would always come to my greedy girl nights at the club, the center of attention, tied up and used by the men in the room."

Alex leaned back, "Do women like that?" asking confused. It brought Platford back, he laughed.

"What do you mean do women like that?"

"I can't imagine women liking that, from a woman's perspective," Alex said.

"Well, you ain't from my world sergeant Brown, the girls weren't forced, they came because they liked it, I mean, why do people like being tied up and beaten to a pulp for sexual gratification, I blame the parents, personally," He laughed. "Everyone that attended my clubs were there of their own volition, the rules were no coercion, let me tell you, there were more girls there than you think and from all walks of life."

Alex could feel Renton shifted in his seat this time.

"What about you?" Alex said.

"Me, I am a dominant man, I like tying women up, consensually, of course, bit of slap and fun, that's about it really, my downfall is I like underage girls, it's not something that I can control, it's a sickness…apparently."

"And the girls you raped?" Alex said, pushing him.

"HAHA, I see what you did sergeant Brown, the girls I had sex with was consensual, it was the detail of the law that deemed it inappropriate. Anyway, the youngest was fifteen. She looked like she was twenty five."

"That's no excuse or reason to do the things you have done." Alex said, knowing at any time she might lose him

"Do you think the average fifteen year old isn't sexually active, most had done things before their fifteenth birthday that were unimaginable twenty years ago." He claimed. Alex thought of her own daughter, now at university.

She brought Platford back to the task at hand. "I'll get you some Franky Vaughan if you tell me." Alex said.

"Kidding right, don't fuck wid me sergeant, you get me some porn, I'll sing like a canary."

"I'll see what I can do."

"The ting about you lot and I mean, your opinion of normal is not my opinion of normal, another man's perversion is another man's normality, right?" he said.

"I am not sure I agree with you." Alex replied, "So tell me." she stated.

"She used to knock about wid a girl called Tracey Burgess, a northern prozzy, came in on the train to Kings Cross." Platford leaned back. Renton nudged Alex's leg under the table, she nodded and took it to mean that Renton knew this girl.

"She was a corker man, another one that I snapped up and used for the clubs. Another proper greedy girl, I knew she was only fifteen but she had been around the world in a very short time if you see what I mean. They used to three-way a guy called the butcher boy most Saturdays, big nasty cunt of a bloke, professional like."

Both Alex and Renton leaned in, engaged, some progress.

"What do you mean, professional, can you remember if you saw him again?" Alex enquired.

"Not really, he used to be hooded, always kept himself to himself, would either wear a latex hood or a gas mask. Always bare-chested, jeans or leather trousers, he had no tattoos before you ask, posh as you like though." Platford said.

"Where would we find this Tracey Burgess?" Alex asked.

"She has a rap sheet longer than the northern line, I dunno where she lived, just turned up whenever I asked her to. You find her, you'll find the butcher boy."

"There's another ting you guys can do, there's a website, paid service, I set it up." Platford declared.

Alex flipped her notebook to another page, "What's the URL?" she asked.

"Whips and kinks dot com all one word," he said.

"Is this site still up and running as you're in here?" Alex said.

"Hope so, it's a paid service, I get paid nearly fifty K a month from its users and have a virtual assistant that looks after the running, kinda runs itself."

Alex glared at him "HOW MUCH?!" she said.

"Fifty grand normally goes into my offshore account, only tellin you soppy fucks because you can't do a ting about it, offshore init."

"How many people use it?" Alex still in shock.

"Dunno, hundreds of thousands, probably in the millions now, like I said, another man's normality is another man's perversion, your next door neighbor is prolly on it, bit like that Facebook shit, but for people that like that sort of lifestyle."

"Bloody hell." Alex exclaimed, "Have you heard of it?" She asked Renton, she saw his face, "Better not answer that sergeant," She said.

"Course 'es on it, proper deviant aren't you officer?" Platford accused.

"The site connects people with their different kinks. There's club contacts, an event page, a library of learning, plus a video portal so people can post their videos to the site, fully encrypted and protects the users." Platford said.

"How long has the site been going?" Alex writing everything down.

"Dunno, started as an event page for one of my clubs in London, snowballed really, I have no control of the people that join it, I can't view that kind of data here, they won't let me," he sniggered.

"Can you give me your passwords so I can look at them?" Alex asked.

"You have three hopes." he said.

"What do you mean three hopes?"

Platford laughed, "Bob Hope, Envelope and no fuckin hope. You'd 'ave to see me swing from the gallows before I let you 'ave that."

Alex thought that Ricky could probably access the site anyway, she wasn't going to push him, if she had to, she would organize a return trip to try and glean the information.

"Ok, Mr. Platford, you have been very helpful." Alex said.

Platford interrupted her. "No I haven't, that's what you tell everyone and what about my Franky Vaughan?" he demanded.

Alex looked at the guard, "Porn is forbidden in prison, Mr. Platford, there is no way that I can swing that for you, I will..." Alex was interrupted.

"YOU FUCKIN SLAG!" Platford screamed, "YOU'RE GOING BACK ON YOUR WORD AND YOU AIN'T EVEN LEFT THE FUCKIN ROOM!"

"I suggest you calm down." Renton said.

Platford shook, staring at Renton, clenching his teeth, the mandible flexing as he clenched, he then groaned again, Alex suddenly realized what he was doing, he had ejaculated under the table and it was too late to stop him. Platford's hands came from under the table, "'ere, 'ave some of my Bob Monk." Platford flicked his cuffed hands, and a trail of viscous fluid flicked across Renton's face. It took all of a nanosecond to realize what had happened, the warm gummy off-white liquid trailed off his top lip and dangled like a demolition ball from his chin.

"What the fuck?" Renton screamed with the look of disgust.

The guard sprang into action, "Prisoner, STAND-UP!" the guard maneuvered himself between the chair and the table and grabbed Platford by his shoulders and wrestled him to the ground, his arm outstretched to the alarm strip on the wall.

"YOU LIED TO ME!" Platford s voice muffled under the guard shouting instructions. The door to the interview room burst open. Four well-equipped men entered the room.

The guard that had let them in to the room entered. "You guys, get against the wall." They immediately complied.

"YOU FUCKIN PROMISED, I WANT MY FRANKY VAUGHAN!" he screamed, spitting at the guards, wriggling like an alligator on the floor, "YOU'LL FUCKIN PAY FOR THIS TREACHERY!" he screamed again, as he was unceremoniously carried out the room. By the time the guards had got to him, he was now half naked.

The first guard turned, "Apologies for that, chaps," he said calmly in a thick Dorset accent. "I'll get one of the guys to escort you out." He turned and went to walk away. He stopped.

"What's this Franky Vaughan he was screaming?" He enquired.

Renton was wiping his chin on a paper handkerchief given to him by Alex. She was stifling a laugh.

"He wants some Franky Vaughan, porn, it's cockney slang for pornography staff." Renton said.

"Oh, I wondered what he was shouting about, anyway, do you need to see a medical professional about that?" He motioned to the handkerchief, "I mean, it counts as a sexual assault as well as an infection control issue."

Alex was chuckling "I think sergeant Davis will be fine," Trying to hold it together.

"Ok, suit yourself, it's a serious business this is..." He left it hanging for a second. "I'll fetch your escort." With that, he left.

Alex burst out laughing.

"It's not funny, Alex." Renton demanded.

"Not the first time you had jizz on your face, Renton."

The laughing became uncontrollable "You should have seen your face." The laughing growing to a belly laugh. After the last week, Renton's shoulders started twitching, then he just gave in and burst out laughing with Alex.

28

The morning sun was piercing the horizon of the deep blue Mediterranean Sea like spears arching through the air. Throwing its rays far across the valley overlooking the picturesque fishing village of Collioure. The morning shadows small and cute under the acres of vineyards. Sandwiched between the city of Perpignan and the southern Spanish border. The Mediterranean was still, like a mill pond, the picture was perfect.

The day was going to be a scorcher. Broc, sipping a freshly made espresso, the aroma intoxicatingly intense the taste sharp and stimulating.

The Med was one of Broc's favorite places. There was a rustic beauty. So pretty and inviting, the food truly out of this world with the fine wines to go with it.

The Languedoc-Roussillon region of France, nestled in the south-west of the country, famed for the Vin de Pays d'Oc and the refreshing Cremant de Limoux sparkling white wine. Served with the most delicate seafood the world has to offer, Broc had hit the jackpot.

The villa, vast and appointed with no expense spared. The opulence was unparalleled to Broc. He had been brought up wanting for nothing, but even this house set his high standards apart.

Was it his, or was he the guest of the house, maybe this was his prize for the work he had done. The pool just disappeared off to the deep blue of the vast sea in front of the house.

A terrace with loungers and an arbor that nestled sumptuous sofas that can be hidden with white chiffon curtains, billowing gently in the sea breeze. The inside filled with marble, granite and woodwork that had no imperfections and showed exquisite lines of incredible craftsmanship, each aspect of the room saw the sea.

From what Broc had counted, there were five bedrooms, a large kitchen diner that commanded the view of the Med. A small snug of a room that had a 50" LCD TV floating against a beautifully plastered white wall. Leather chairs were facing the screen. The villa screamed masculinity, as though someone had read Broc's mind to what was the perfect house.

The heavy footsteps broke the solitude. Irritated, he turned.

"Mr Broc, can you prease come wid me?" an average sized Chinese man, wearing white flannel trousers and a tulle shirt, his accent tinged with his mother tongue. His wrist accommodated the biggest watch Broc had ever seen. He wanted it.

"Sure, where are we going?"

"Mista Ng is in the study, downstair, he wud like to a speak wid you," his Chinese accent thick.

"I didn't realize Ng had come to the south of France" Broc slid off the bar stool, piqued to have his joyous moment interrupted.

The man walked quickly, a short gait that Broc struggled to keep up with. The gait made even odder because the head remained still as he walked, like a duck swimming on a pond.

They descended some stairs, walked through seven-foot double oak doors, flanked by two muscled men, interestingly not Chinese.

At the end of a long corridor, they stopped, the man knocked on the door, there was a buzz. With both hands, the man opened both double doors, "Mista Broc, sir," he said.

Broc walked in. Ng sat behind an enormous desk. Broc's question was answered, this wasn't going to be Broc's house, this was Ng's.

The opulent decor unmistakably Chinese, red onyx and ivory figurines with black ash furniture, the texture of the grain almost three dimensional, yet so smooth to touch, filled the room. Beautiful Chinese paintings on the walls as well as a Monet that looked weirdly out of place.

The room was filled with the scent of incense and jasmin, Ng was busy typing on his computer when Broc had arrived, he walked in, slid one of the chairs back and sat. Ng acknowledged his arrival, but carried on typing, a small curt smile curled at the edge of his lips before he started gently lipreading what he was typing. Broc enjoyed the hand carvings of the black ash table that seemed to dwarf Ng. Red leather inlaid on the work surface stitched meticulously into the wood.

Ng finished, he leaned back in his chair, the leather chair beautifully creaking as it gently tipped backwards, hands on his lap.

Broc noticed the Chinese china tea set on the table, the steam gently tumbling upwards from the cup, the light catching the molecules of water in the steam, the source of the jasmine scent Broc thought.

"Is this your house?" Broc asked.

"Yes, it is." Ng said, studying Broc across the table.

"It's beautiful."

"Thank you. I have had it for many years, more a rabbit hole, I have sold it maybe twenty times over, it is owned I think by a dead frenchman from Carcassonne, the ownership dropping off many retail radars so the authorities can't trace me here in France".

Broc was jealous of the house.

"I think any police investigation linking me to this property would be very tenuous. This house is by definition, a safe house."

"I am guessing that I will be here for some time, namely the trouble you went through in getting me here?" Broc enquired still looking around the room.

"We're not sure at this time, Dale. We are a little concerned with the attention you are drawing from the police." Ng said, "Namely this woman." He leaned forward and swiveled the computer screen to face Broc. Alex Brown's photo was up on the screen.

"Who is this?" Broc Asked.

Ng turned the screen a half turn so they could both see it. "This is sergeant Alex Brown, Dale. She's the lead sergeant of a murder squad working out of the Mile End station. Her arrest record is impressive. Why she turned up at a meat processing plant that had a person closely connected to you working there is anyone's guess."

Broc felt a pang as Tracey's memory passed through at the thought.

"I did guess why and putting two and two together I think I came up with four."

He leaned back in the chair again.

"How you get rid of the corpses after you have done the deed is up to you, I did regularly think how you did it." Ng smiled. "For what it's worth, I think your process is much better than the rest of your peers." Ng said alluding to the rest of the surgeons dotted around the world.

Broc nodded "Clean, efficient and leaves no trail."

"Umm" Ng mused "that's an interesting notion, seeing that the UK has some of the tightest food standards, it was only going to be a matter of time before you were going to get caught." Ng took a sip of tea. "Our measures may have prevented that." He added with a smile.

"How do you think, MAY have? It's a bit presumptuous initiating your measures to protect me, this may have fizzled out." Broc declared.

Ng thought for a moment. "When you have someone dedicated to their job like this sergeant Brown, who is female, your days working in the UK are truly numbered."

"What is her being female got to do with this?" Broc asked.

"They're simply the stronger species, they're not emotionally driven like us lesser mortals, plus you have made an insult to the female gender by targeting them, she won't rest." Ng declared.

Broc mused, looking at the artwork, "So how long will you have me here, then?" he asked.

Ng forced air out of his mouth. "I don't know, maybe indefinitely, at least until we can get a handle on what the police are doing. We are not just talking about the local police. Interpol had a call, so we know that they are looking further afield. We know when they understand what they are looking at because at the moment they don't. But when they do, they will search every inch of Europe for you," Ng said.

Another sip of the tea. "If we can leave a digital trail to suggest that you are in South America we can maybe alter your features with plastic surgery."

Broc threw a glance at the notion, Ng saw it,

"I don't know, we need to look at our options."

"Ok," Broc crossed his legs, "So what do I do?" He asked, "Do I watch the sunrise and sunset each day until a decision is made?" He asked.

"This is a beautiful home, but it may as well be a six foot by six-foot jail cell, I'll go stir crazy living here."

"Well that's part of the protocol that we have put in place for you Broc, we anticipated this happening and you're too much of a commodity to discard." Ng said.

Broc clocked the use of the word commodity, not asset and the word discard. He knew only to well that once his material worth was spent, he would end up going through the mincer himself, he wasn't stupid.

Ng leaned, pressed a button on the table, his free hand extended out to indicate behind Broc. Broc turned and the wooden wall was sliding into the cavity, brilliant white light cascaded into the room, thick glass bordered the office and the room behind.

Broc stood and went to the glass. His head was peering around the wall as it retracting to see what it was. The room was an operating theatre, well appointed, top end equipment, tiled white walls, and a white marble floor.

In the center of the theatre was an operating table with a young naked woman tied to it, awake and trembling.

Ng had walked up and was standing next to Broc, equally as silent as the retracting wall. Broc had a tightening in his loins.

"Call it a gift." Ng said. "We kidnapped her from North Africa, in one of the refugee camps. Three hundred or so miles from here. No drugs and lucid."

"A gift?" Broc asked.

"Yes Dale, as a means of goodwill, you can do with her as you please, leave the body, it will be dealt with during the night."

Broc was fixated on the girl, like a gun dog waiting for their prey, Ng was watching, he smiled at Broc.

"Dale, we have perfected the storage of the human organs, we can keep a heart or liver for as long as eight months in storage, this was as a direct result of your invention with the transportation packaging," Ng said.

"What's that got to do with me?" Broc said, still looking at the girl and distant.

"Well, we don't need to supply the demand, we can become the demand if you see what I mean."

Broc stole himself away from the girl on the operating table.

"I still don't get what you mean, Ng." Broc said.

"We can store as many organs as we wish and then supply the market as it's needed using our new storage facilities in China, how many people can you harvest in any given week?" Ng asked.

He glanced over at the girl, looked back at Ng, "I can do one a day" He said.

"Ok, shall we call it five per week then?" Ng questioned.

"Are you serious?" Broc replied, visibly excited, "You'll get me five specimens a week?" He asked.

"Another reason to bring you here. We have an unlimited supply of bodies. We can take from the refugees coming across from Morocco, we intercept the boat and take the young from it. During the summer months, we can take our pick of young European girls on the holiday strips along the Spanish coast. We can bring them to you to do as you will, give us the organs, normal rates apply."

Ng lifted a small wooden flap on the wall. A combination keypad was on there. He punched in the numbers, "We chose your birthday so you can remember." Ng said with a smile.

Broc returned the smile, he wondered if Ng knew the codes to his basement in the barn.

There was a rush of air like a can of soda as the forced air environment pushed the build-up of air behind the door out. The smell of clean disinfected air instantly invigorating Broc.

Ng invited Broc to enter the room "Enjoy my friend." Ng said, "The glass is one way, you can't see out, but I will close the wall for your privacy."

Broc nodded and entered the room. Ng closed it immediately behind him. Broc heard the lock engage. The girl was trembling. She looked over. Her face said it all, wet with tears, she was petrified.

"Please, please." Her English was broken and pointless. The girl pleaded. She seemed to know her fate, now sobbing.

Broc walked up to the girl. She was stunning. Her body was perfect. She was small and petite, pert breasts, long slender legs, a swirl of soft dark downy hair attractively covered her abdomen leading to the promised land between her legs. A deep middle Eastern skin tone, flawless. She had been topless. The tan lines betrayed her provenance.

He caressed her foot, sliding his hands up the inside of her legs, to her vagina, she shivered as she tried to get away and whimpered as his hands invaded her femininity. He probed her. She was dry. His hand emerged, now flat, over her flat toned belly, over the xiphisternum, his hands squeezing her breasts, each breast getting a turn. Tears were rolling freely down her cheeks like a waterfall.

Broc's hands now round the girl's throat, he squeezed, he felt her choke, her larynx in her throat tugging desperately to gasp for air. He bent down and licked the salty tears of the girl while struggling for breath, her eyes wide and trying to take everything in, high on adrenaline, her fight or flight system in overdrive. The girls voice raspy. She pleaded "please."

Broc kissed her plump lips now a dusky blue as her body was running out of oxygen. Her breath smelt, it didn't matter. Fear oozed out of every one of her pores, Broc loved it, he let go of her throat, she instantly pinked up.

He stood and ripped his shirt open, the buttons bouncing off the walls and floor, and tossed to the corner of the room.

Next to the girl's head was a trolley of surgical instruments.

Blades, scissors, hammers, saws, cleavers and forceps. The surface was catching the light. Brand new instruments, freshly sterilized.

He toyed with some of them, picking them up and feeling their weight and quality. Broc's muscles bulged, he caught himself in the mirror of the glass.

The girl was hopelessly trying to see what he was doing. He noticed a stereo, he leaned over and pressed play. The opening cords of his favorite song "Jealous Guy" by Bryan Ferry chimed up. Ng knew how to treat a guest.

He looked down at the girl and grinned, he leaned in, with one of the cleavers in his hands, Broc dragged the blade over her cheek, feeling the sharp edge drag through the tissue, breaking the skin, blood oozing urgently from the cheek. So precise was the incision she didn't feel it, he whispered close to her ear, "This is a good day to die."

The girl screamed and bucked, Broc stood and smashed the cleaver through the girl's wrist, the hand dropping to the floor with a sickening thump. Arterial blood was spraying five feet across the room, spattering the virgin white tiles and marble floor crimson.

The girl now hysterical, fighting the bonds keeping her on the table, with the cleaver, he grabbed one of her breasts and hacked his way through laughing hysterically as he sliced. Blood spurting everywhere, the yellowy fat of the breast spilling out on her abdomen.

The other side of the glass, Ng was watching. The moment he saw Broc reach for the breast was all that Ng could stomach. A seasoned killer, this was even too much for him. The wall silently closed with the shadow of Broc's arm raising and hacking the young girl to pieces. An image Ng will never, ever unsee again.

29

Alex and Renton left the prison. The bright sunlight bleached their eyes. After the myriad of security checks leaving, finally breathing the fresh air on the outside was overwhelming.

Alex paused for a second to breathe in the fresh sea air. Renton clicked the car fob, the lights flashing in unison. He opened the door and checked to why Alex wasn't getting in the car. She stood there just breathing.

"Jesus, so good to be out." She said, she walked to the car "I can't imagine being in there for any length of time."

Renton smiled and got in the car.

He was putting his seatbelt on as Alex got in the car.

"You okay?" Alex asked as she got to the car and started putting her belt on.

"What do you mean?" he replied.

"You seem tad isolated, distant."

"I've just had spunk thrown in my face from the pedophile slag I had locked up," Renton exclaimed, "I am entitled to be a bit miffed."

Alex was looking at him "What was he saying about you dipping your toe in the pool of temptation." There was a pause, Renton had shut down and become instantly more withdrawn. Alex didn't want him to feel on his own here, if there was something to talk about, she was going to get it out of him.

"Listen, I get it, you work vice. All you guys are unsung heroes in the force, I couldn't do half the things you do.

People stay in vice for short periods of time. What are you," She looked out the window, "Fifteen years in or what? That's a bit weird, tell me, what's the draw."

Renton put the key in the ignition paused before turning the key. "Do you want to know why I work vice, Alex?"

He turned and looked at her. She nodded, palms of her hands uppermost "You have my confidence, Renton," she said.

"Because I feel I can do some good, on the backend of a shit childhood." He was struggling, his voice failing, Alex shifted in her seat to face him more.

"I went to boarding school and was repeatedly raped by my housemaster, Reverend Bedford, the priest of the school." He left it hanging, Alex felt utter sadness pour out of the strong, confident man sat next to her.

"He was known by the kids at the school as creamy arse Bedders." He wiped his nose, eyes filling with water. "When the police came for him, he resisted and was dragged off the premises, by the time they had him in the car, his cassock had come off and all the time he was naked underneath it while teaching."

He coughed to clear his throat, Alex had hit the pure emotion of the man. He continued.

"The kids were cheering as this was happening, I just remember watching in abject horror, a massive sense of shame. I told my father when I got home, he didn't believe me, told me to stop lying and man up."

Alex placed her hand on his and gently squeezed, she felt a tear roll down her cheek.

"Shit Renton, I had no idea, I would never have subjected you to that in there if had known."

"You weren't to know, Alex." He patted her hand with his free one.

"My dad was old bill too, senior. It was a right of passage that I followed my dad. When I was uniform, I would go to lots of domestics and be powerless to do anything. The children always suffering." He turned the key, the engine gunned to life. "Vice seemed to be the only choice for me back in the day." He fished in his pocket and pulled out some gum and offered Alex some, she shook her head. Renton popped two sticks in. "If I could do some good, it would be in vice finding and dealing with scum like creamy arse."

"That's what Platford has on you?" Alex asked.

"Yeah."

"Renton, what you have said is beyond hideous and you have my full support, but I am going to ask you now." She looked at him, engaged him. He looked back.

"If Platford becomes a material witness to our case and he takes the stand. We cannot afford for him to drop a bombshell on the case, you understand right, you must tell me now if there is something hiding in your closet."

"Off the record right?" Renton asked.

"Pinky promise," Alex said.

"He used to run big parties in the city, not always in London during the late 90's. These parties were well attended by the greater good of society, if you see what I mean." He chewed a coupled of times the car filling with the smell of spearmint.

"Jimmy Savile, Rolf Harris, you name it was there," Alex nodding, hanging in on every word.

"Do you remember a singer called Stephen Buffon?" Alex looked into the footwell for the answer.

"Yeah, kinda," She said.

"He was the lead singer of Lipstick Zombies, had a couple of hits, around the same time as the Human League, he was a dead ringer for Phil Oakley."

"I do remember," Alex said, "they had that song, gosh what was it?" she said, looking for the name in the vast data banks of memories in Alex's brain.

"Red T," Renton said.

'That's it, number one in the mid-eighties," Alex said.

"Well, Buffon was a regular at Platford's parties, turned out he was massively into kids. I caught him once, tried to bring a case against him, blocked by the CPS."

Alex shook her head in disbelief.

"Another time, I approach the CPS and was warned, if I pursue this case, my career would be over so against my better judgment I buried it."

"Then what?"

"About twelve years ago, a snuff film came across my desk, Buffon had a missing finger with a long scar here." He showed Alex the fleshy part of the thumb.

"His hand was around the throat of this child, a boy. I don't know the age but definitely under ten, he choked the child to death, then four or five men raped the corpse after. I told the CPS and was told the same thing again. You know these guys were connected to a higher power. High court judges, movers and shakers in government, they could do anything."

"What did you do?" Alex asked.

"I found him, walking his dog, it was the crack of dawn, Battersea Park, I used a cattle prod and got him in my trunk and drove him to Norfolk, made him dig his own grave. I blew his brains out with a pistol that I had confiscated from some random gangbanger that I had at a stop and search, then set the bastard on fire."

"Shit, and Platford knows." Alex mused.

"No, he thinks he knows something. Buffon had dropped off the face of the earth, Platford knew that I had had it in for him, he just put and two together. Nasties that disappear in this world are dead because of drugs. If they haven't been discovered, it is a clear indication that they have been removed from the scene." Renton rubbed his face, feeling the weight lifted, but unsure of Alex's motives.

"Okay, so let's assume that he doesn't know anything. You had him locked up. I wasn't familiar with your case, a concrete conviction" she asked, searching the possible outcomes of the situation, her brain working lighting fast.

"Yeah, had video and recording of him boasting, he was banged to rights. Although, the fucker pleaded not guilty, his barrister's defense was about mitigating the punishment." Renton paused again. "In truth, he probably will be out in ten. Crime does pay." Renton said.

"We will see about that." Alex said pulling her phone out. She found Ricky's number hit dial.

It rang once "Yo stud." Ricky's voice said.

"Okay, we are done, can you do a couple of things for me?"

"Sure, shoot.".

"First, call that guy from Dorset CID, tell him we are on the way, looking at the satnav, we are only five miles away."

"Roger."

"Then next, I want you to go on a website, called whips and chains dot com and look for a profile of a person called the butcher boy, in fact, can you do a massive solid for me?"

"Course boss, spill."

"When you have found the profile, print everything in it and the people connected and then shut it down." Alex said.

Renton stared at her and smiled. She smiled back.

"Come again boss?" Ricky asked.

"Time to poke the bear with a shitty stick, shut the fucker down, let's see what Platford does," Alex said, she felt deliciously wicked.

"Ahhh," Ricky said, "on it, checking it out now," Alex heard a clatter of keyboard keys "Ohh one of those sites," He said. "Fairly sophisticated but I should have the whole site down in a jiffy. "I'll text you as soon as I have done it." The line went dead.

"Let's go," Alex said.

Renton engaged the gears and was away in seconds.

They didn't really speak on the short journey to Baldwin's Haulage yard. Both deep in thought.

As the car approached, the plethora of police cars, vans and Vauxhall Insignias indicating a heavy CID presence at the address.

A slim guy, engrossed in his phone was leaning against a red brick waist high wall, his legs crossed.

"This must be our guy," Alex said.

He looked up, acknowledged this must be the Sergeant Brown and her sidekick from the big smoke that DC Lambert had phoned about. He straightened.

Renton pulled in beside him, Alex had wound the window, "DS Knight?" she asked.

"Yes," he said, "Alex?"

As the car came to a stop, the door was already opening.

Alex got out as the handbrake was applied.

"Yes, nice to meet you, Steve." He was already familiar with her. She returned the curtsey.

"Has Mrs. Baldwin arrived?" Alex enquired.

"Yes, about 45 minutes ago, she's the lady in the office." His accent thickly west country. He indicated to the building behind him, a woman, plump and red-cheeked was wiping her nose, speaking to a couple of uniforms.

"What's the morning glory?" Renton asked as he walked around the car.

"Come again?" Steve asked.

Alex smiled at Renton, the East End boy coming out, she loved it.

"He asked what the story was." Alex said.

"Ah, cockney slang."

Alex thought that Steve was about to spring into the Dick Van Dyke performance of Chim Chimney Chim Chim Cheree like most people outside London do. Mainly Americans she thought. He didn't.

"And no, that wasn't cockney slang." Alex said with a smile that she didn't really mean. He got the message.

"Basically, the other day, Mrs. Baldwin arrived for work to find her husband's van parked in the middle of the parking lot, both driver and passenger doors wide open with the engine still running." Alex looked at the wall, SOCO and the forensics team still milling about.

"He was nowhere to be seen, so she opened the back and found this." He turned to a file on the wall. He passed it to Renton.

Either this was a misogynistic act because he had to pass it past Alex, or he was worried about Alex's constitution. She stared in amazement as she watched the transaction. Renton clocked it, smiled and passed the file to Alex without opening it.

She grabbed it, the face of DS Knight showed the misogyny. "I am a strong girl, sergeant" Losing the familiarity.

"I meant no offence" he replied, flushing in the face, feeling the overstepping of the mark. He nervously unbuttoned his single-breasted jacket on his off the peg suit, then buttoned it back up again.

Alex eased the awkwardness "Do you know Jack Mathers?"

"Yeah, I spoke with him earlier, said you was coming down, he sends his regards, told me about the Troll case you were on together, grim right?"

Alex opened the file nodding, the high definition images did nothing but show the brutality of the murder.

Both men were striped naked, hanging upsidedown, their body's were impaled on a wooden post, exiting from the anus. The legs hogtied to the post. The heads pushed on the post between their legs.

"Thought I had seen enough this week," She flicked through the other photos of the cadavers.

She showed Renton, "Fuck me," He said.

"Any pathology yet?" Alex asked still flicking.

"Yeah, this apparently is a classic Chinese Triad thing, thought you may be able to throw some light on this?" He asked.

"Nope, we deal in your standard murders with a smattering good old Russian cruelty, the Triad thing on my manor is a bit limited these days." Alex said, passing the file back.

"We know that they were killed before this happened to them." Knight said.

"How so?"

He opened the file, a close up of the head showed a single gunshot wound to the head.

"Executed." Renton said looking at the image.

"Why?" Was Alex's next question.

"We don't know, this is way off our patch, we feel the killing was done in London, so when you guys reached out, my boss saw this as a lead."

Knight shuffled the paper in the file, "What's your angle on this?" He asked, looking at Alex.

"Well, we have an ongoing investigation, did you see the news the other night about a botched police armed raid in north London?"

Knight nodded, "I don't think there's a copper in the country that doesn't know about it, the worst nightmare for anyone," He said.

"Yours truly, Steve." Alex said, she leaned against the wall. "That's our case, we feel that this may have a link, so we need the evidence. On the face of it, the evidence isn't connecting them." Alex's hands thrust deep into her coat.

"The job they were on was a regular gig with a farm from Kings Stag that's up the road from here, just north of Dorchester. They do jobs two or three times per month. The farm is owned by an ex-soldier, who now works for the Ministry of Defense a guy called...." He searched in his notebook, "Kevin Saunders, he wasn't there. His wife though, not bad on the eye was there. He is rarely at home apparently, travels internationally."

Alex frowned at the comment.

"What were they picking up?" Alex asked.

"Something to do with the MOD, she didn't know. Sloane ranger kind of girl, bit thin for me though."

"Really? Alex said, shaking her head.

"Loops closed there, the key is in your neck of the woods," Knight said.

"Umm, I need to chat with the lady of the house, can you introduce me?" Alex said.

She walked off, crunching onto the gravel of the yard. Knight followed in step behind her, shuffling his feet faster to get in front of Alex, she smiled, hands thrust deep in the pockets.

Entering the office, the usually tired furniture, stained coffee cups, a dog-eared wall planner and a key press with signs written everywhere reminding the drivers of the law, parking restrictions in and around London, Bristol, and Birmingham. The counter was bare wood with chunks missing, biro graffiti telling Alex how shit working at Baldwin's was and how the police were wankers.

Mrs. Baldwin looked up, her face wet with tears and exhaustion.

Knight introduced her. She went to get up.

"Don't get up." Alex said. She approached her and Alex got to her knees. She tenderly held her hands.

"Call me Kat," Mrs. Baldwin said, eyes welling up.

"Kat, You have my deepest condolences from myself, my team and the Metropolitan Police," squeezing Kat's hands as she spoke.

"Thank you," she said. "It's been a bit traumatic."

"I simply can't imagine what you're going through Kat, but we will get to the bottom of things and make sure those that are responsible, get their time at Her Majesty's."

Kat nodded and sobbed.

"Kat, can you tell me anything that your husband might have been involved in, the type of people he mixed socially with or did business with?" Alex asked, she knew getting to the point was best.

Alex looked up at the fresh faced constable. She was barely out of school. "Go bung the kettle on the constable, Gandhi's flip-flop and all that."

The constable looked confused.

Kat laughed, "I haven't heard that in a while, my Simon used to say it all the time."

Alex smiled at her, "I bet he used to say things like so parched, it's like my throats been cut," Instantly regretting the comment given the situation, but there was no need. Kat looked at Alex momentarily then burst out laughing, Alex joined "Really sorry about that comment," She said.

"Don't worry. It came from a good place, Sergeant."

Back to business. "Is there anything you can tell me?" Alex asked.

"I don't know really, Simon was doing the job for..." she searched the name "Saunders, over Kings Stag way, he offered work at an overinflated price, my Simon wasn't worried. He always told me to stop fretting, but sometimes when something is too good to be true," She wiped her nose again.

"What can you tell me about this Saunders chap?" Alex asked, always pushing.

"I never met him truth be told, Simon always conducted the business and clients, I ran the fleet and the drivers."

Kat went through the history of the business along with the woes and successes, who the staff was.

"I suppose we can't visit this farm?" Alex asked, directing this to Steve Knight.

"Not really, Alex, you would need a warrant, my gov would need to get the okay as well and he has formerly excluded the Saunders and their premises out of the investigation which would make that application difficult."

"On what grounds?" Renton asked. All eyes turned to him. He was perched on a table by the main door, looking moody and nonchalant.

Alex thought that if she were still in London, she would pop round and pay a visit. But when on someone else's manor, you play by the rules and show respect.

"This is my partner Kat, Renton Davis." Alex said.

Kat nodded.

"On the strength that the story checks out, there's no impropriety there, I have been there myself and spoke to Mrs. Saunders."

"Tough old bird," Kat said.

"She is that," Knight replied.

"Can you give the address that your husband was going to so we can check it out when we get back to London?" Alex asked.

Kat leaned to her desk "Sure."

Scrabbling around for something, she found it and pulled out a bright notebook. Flicking through the pages, she found the location to the warehousing complex that Simon's job was.

She tore the paper out and handed it to Alex.

"Thank you, Kat," Alex took the note.

"Just out of interest Kat, have you had any dealings with the Chinese?" Alex asked, pulling her phone out and then took a picture of the note.

"No, not that I was aware, I would know seeing that I planned the pickups and drop off's." She thought harder, "No definitely not, I would know."

"Okay Kat, we must go, I really appreciate your time."

"That's okay Alex," Kat said. She felt at ease in Alex's company. She had a good heart. She patted her hands. "Thank you for coming," She said.

Alex pulled out a business card and handed it to Kat.

"My card, if you think of anything, just let me know." Alex stood, knees creaking and looked down.

She felt her pain. The emptiness that death brings. It brought home the previous case and the loss of someone that wasn't close to her. That feeling of disappointment and sadness. It wasn't a good feeling.

With her coping strategies, she moved her mind back to the case, placed a hand on Kat's shoulder and squeezed. Kat looked up, "We will catch these people Kat, you have my word."

Kat tapped Alex's hand. "Thank you."

Alex pulled her phone out as they left the office. Knight following, Ricky had texted her.

The site offline, located the profile, loads of media connected to it, too much to print.

She hit reply. Cool, check this address out, maybe send some uniforms, this was the destination of the couriers.

Renton stood, opened the door, stepped out and waited for Alex to join him.

"What do you reckon?" he said.

Alex thrust her hands into her pockets and smiled at Knight as he walked out and faced the two officers. "Dunno, think we need to get back to London."

She offered her hand to Knight, "Great meeting you Steve, can you get your gov'ner to ping the reports over to my office, here's my card. We will do likewise as soon as I get back to the office."

"Yeah, no problem," He took her hand and shook, then shook Renton's.

"And can you give my best to Jack," He nodded.

Both Renton and Alex crunched through the gravely drive.

"How long back to London do you reckon?" Alex asked.

"Three or four hours maybe," He said.

"We should stop at a KFC, get a bucket of skin," Alex said as her phone began to ring.

Unknown number. Fighting the urge to ignore it, her thumb hesitating over the green accept icon, she hit it and put the phone on speaker.

"You fuckin whore, who the fuck do think you are?"

Alex stopped and grinned at Renton. "Mr. Platford, what do I owe for this call?"

"Bet you and soppy bollocks think you got one over on me, put my site back online, or things are gonna get a little fuckin chronic."

"First, can you please stop using foul language, second, I can't do anything to your site as I would need a warrant or a blessing of a judge and thirdly, Mr. Platford, having a phone while in prison is utterly forbidden."

"BITCH!" the line clicked dead.

Alex looked at Renton, "Well that must be some sort of record," She said.

Renton laughed, "Nothing like putting a cat amongst the pigeons."

Alex got to the car, got in and the phone started to ring again.

She hit receive.

"Mr Platford, have you got control of your senses?"

"What do you want?" Was all he said.

"You know what I want," Alex said, she put the phone back on speaker. Buckled into the seat belt and indicated to Renton to drive.

"There's a nonce bar in the east end, called Lolly's, spelled L.L.Y, not I.E.S. Full of nonces and deviant sex pests, you need to find a guy called Bromilow, as in Stephen Bromilow MP, he owns the joint. He's a top government MP, as in the Home Secretary. Etonian posh lad, like butter wouldn't melt, 'sept he's got a shitter like a smashed in window. He will know who your butcher boy is."

"Why couldn't you have said all this a few hours ago, instead of masturbating and throwing your semen at my colleague and generally being an around bell-end?" Alex asked.

"Umph" h

He grunted. "You know why its called Lolly's right?" ignoring the question.

"No I don't." Alex said, not really interested.

He carried on anyway. "Lolita, the film, nonces call their charges or Lost Girls Lolly's after Lolita the young girl violated by a family friend that comes to visit. Girls ruined by fucked up parents and predatory sex rings. The bar is called that. It's a smokescreen. The place is full of fiddlers. Right 'orrible cunts. It's a gift from me to you. You raid that place, it'll make the paedo ring up north seem like a Club 18 to 30 holiday camp, you're fuckin welcome by the way."

Renton nudged Alex. She looked, he nodded.

"That gimp your with, Davis. Ask 'im. He knows the place. He's bin there."

Alex still looking at Renton, "Sure I will pump him for more info, thank you."

"When's my site gonna be back up on the level."

"If your info checks out, I will reactivate it." Alex said.

The line went dead.

"There's is a place called Lolly's, I have been there, a bit of a dive in the East End."

"If its a known place for nonces, why is it still operating?" Alex asked.

"It isn't, the place is owed by Bromilow, it's a well known gay bar that's all." Renton turned the ignition, "You turn up at that place, you're going to find all sorts of people from all walks of life. From postmen to high court judges to members of Parliament, it's just a safe place for gays to meet, especially the closeted sort that the media would have a field day with. That place legally, is one of the safest places on earth, this Bromilow, I know him."

"Who is he, what's the deal?" Alex asked.

"You know, he's this articulate, dynamic career politician but his true self is a submissive."

"What do you mean?" Alex asked, looking at her phone.

"He's known as a cage submissive, or chastised," Renton said.

Alex had had enough learning to know what a caged submissive was. A text from Ricky said, confirmed hit on the blood results. There is defo a link, 27 missing including one reported missing over the weekend, call me ASAP.

"Definite hit on the blood, there's a link, get us back to London as soon as you can, stick the blue light on, don't spare the horses." She hit dial to Ricky.

Renton floored it.

30

Alex went straight to the office after the drive back. It took them over four hours to get there. The return journey was half that, being escorted through the three counties by traffic police to get them through the busy motorways. Alex thought that Ricky was astonishingly clever to get that organized. Something she didn't ask for, but he did it anyway.

It was early evening. Still had not eaten. After parking, she dispatched Renton to the local Chinese for takeaway.

She bolted up the stairs and into the office.

The office, deserted apart from a couple of officers, looking bedraggled and in various states of dress. As the day had worn on, top buttons became undone, blouses loosened. Emily was filling her already stained mug of coffee, tight pencil skirt, blouses undone with her bra slightly showing, barefoot. In the morning she was impeccably dressed. And now, she looked like she had just survived a mugging.

She acknowledged Alex and padded back to her desk. Good copper, Alex thought.

Ricky was busy at his desk, laptop and computer open, Frank hovering behind him on the desk pulled over.

Lights and images flickering on their faces. Ricky was working the internet to his fullest advantage.

At the last moment, Frank looked up and saw Alex. He looked tired.

"The wanderer returns," He said.

Ricky looked up, and then went straight back the screen and increased the typing speed. He didn't want to be disturbed.

Alex sat, flopped her booted feet on the table, the heels pushing against Frank's thigh.

"Good trip?" Frank asked.

"Yep, knackered though, what's the update?"

Ricky had filled Alex in, as much as she could retain. She stopped him halfway through the conversation on the phone, as Renton's average speed was a little over 100 miles per hour.

"Give us a sec, sarge," Ricky said.

"This boy's amazing." Frank said. "Done stuff on this interweb thing I didn't know that was possible."

"Renton's getting the scoff from the Chinese, I guessed that you guys would still be here, so I got extra," She said.

Ricky hit print and went to the printer. Both Alex and Frank sat in silence, both looking at the floor, deep in thought.

Renton arrived with the food. They didn't budge "Rubadubdub, thank you for my grub," Renton said rubbing his hands together.

The smell of the hot food snapped Alex out of her reverie, "That was quick," She said and got up, Ricky now busy at the whiteboard, sticking printouts of files and mugshots of people.

Alex grabbed a plate and shoveled some food onto it. Her stomach was now screaming how hungry it was, her hand slightly trembling at the sight of the food.

Frank had done the same, slumped into a chair, "Let's crack on Ricky, show 'em what we have been up to."

Alex chuckled, she knew that Frank would have sat and watched Ricky do everything, but was happy to take 50% of the glory. Emily and some of the other team leaders that resembled a refugee camp padded and shuffled over. Scraping chairs over the worn out carpet, too weary to talk the small stuff. Slurping coffee and the unmistakable smell of energy drinks, Chinese and now the smell of a pizza given a whirl by the dysfunctional air-con unit. Mixing the smell with the musk of bodies needing a wash. Alex loved these times, yet hated them at the same time. The level of anticipation and trepidation dampened by the sheer fatigue yet dedication of the team. The commitment of her squad was awe-inspiring, she loved each of them for it.

Ricky finished, not caring about the food, he was buzzing, Alex knew they had progressed at last. This case had to be fast paced with the evidence and nature of the of the crime. Maybe an arrest in the morning.

"Ok, guys, listen in," Ricky said. He stood at the board waiting patiently for the group to dial in.

"This is a sitrep to the what's going on. Alex, do you want to share your progress before I go into mine?"

Alex nodded, mouth full of food. She stood, looking almost hamster like as she grabbed her notes.

Finally finishing off the mouthful of noodles.

"Okay, Renton and I took a jaunt to deepest darkest Dorset, Portland to be exact and went to meet Damien Platford aka the Zookeeper, inmate number..." She checked her notebook and couldn't find the prisoner number.

"Okay, this nonce's number not relevant. His name was brought up when we went to see the Dmitry Orlov, the owner of Club Schwartz. It turns out Renton was the copper that had him jailed for crimes against humanity."

"He's a nonce?" Someone asked from the back.

Alex held up her hand to shield her eyes from the bright spots shining on her to see the back. "Yeah, he's a pedigree fiddler, the best place for him. An incident happened in the nick he was in," she looked at Renton.

"What happened?" another voice asked.

Still looking at Renton "Well, I am going to have to take the fifth on that one, when Renton gets over it, he will no doubt regale you with the events."

Renton stood and turned to the group. "Okay, he flicked his sperm in my face, not my finest hour." Renton said as the room stopped eating and drinking and stared.

"You let him masturbate in front of you?" A voice said.

Alex chipped in, "'Erm nope. He was doing it secretly while talking to us, like I said, a pedigree sex pest."

Alex turned to the whiteboard. She found what she was looking for. He mentioned this name, the Butcher Boy. "It's from a BDSM website that works in the same way as Facebook. The guy of significant interest to us has this profile and apparently, we need to go to a boozer called Lolly's, anyone know it?"

There was silence. "Okay, that's no dramas, we will try and pay the place a visit tomorrow evening."

The gruesome photos of the van containing the slaughtered bodies of Baldwin and Callum were tacked to the board.

"We also paid a visit to Baldwin's haulage yard. Ricky wisely kept his nose to the ground with the national serious crimes grid. This case popped up, a haulage company that had sent the owner to a London address, I think a warehouse." She looked at Ricky, "Did you check it out for me?"

Ricky stood, "Sure, sarge." He walked over to the boards.

"Okay, the van had been to On Target storage. It's a freight storage facility that's close to the London City Airport. A couple of armed uniforms have been and nothing out of the ordinary, I am working on the CCTV footage of their van as they entered London and then left."

"James, the pathologist, has definitely confirmed that Tracey Stubbs was killed before being placed in the bath and slow cooked. There was a toxicology report, James said it was a bit skewed. But there were definite traces of barbiturate, potassium, rocuronium and propofol if you look at this hand-out, any idea what these drugs do?" He walked around the group handing out the folders.

"The question the brass are keen to have answered is how we got the addresses on Sweets Way wrong."

Alex felt a pang of embarrassment connected to the whole debacle.

"The hacking was done at such a high level it was not really seen by any of our tech guys. Who ever hacked the system and managed to change every aspect of the addresses, was very clever, that's a priority for the cybercrime guys who will be here in the morning."

Ricky shuffled some papers that he was holding.

"The family murdered on Sweets Way seem to have been killed for no reason at all. The father should also not be with us. Luckily for us, the detonator didn't trigger and he survived the ordeal."

Ricky looked at the photo. "Although I suspect he wants to die right now."

"The upside of this is that Mr. Tao Ng, a known Triad mover and shaker was positively identified at the hospital along with a Caucasian male late forties, this is the e-fit." Ricky tacked it to the board. The resemblance of Broc was crystal.

"I also ran a traffic check on all planes leaving the City Airport. As Alex always says, there's no such thing as a coincidence."

Alex smiled and nodded, looking at the mounting evidence building on the board, plate still on her lap with food still on it.

"So, why did two Chinese diplomatic jets leave City Airport one hour between each other."

"Is this Ng in London still and if so can we send some armed teams to pinch him?" Frank asked.

Ricky pursed his lips, "I spoke to the CPS and they have said we need more evidence, as soon as this chopper's name was mentioned they closed up quicker than a bear trap."

"Weird," Alex said she looked at Renton. "Is this along the lines of what we were discussing?"

Renton nodded.

Frank shifted in his seat, Alex turned to him, some food caught in his mustache.

"Care to share?" Frank said.

"Renton and I were chatting about this club Lolly's, frequented by the scum of the earth posing as MP's, judges and barristers amongst its core members, but mainly a hang out for pre-release homosexuals from the closest in high profile jobs."

"So," Frank said.

"Well, as they are connected, getting anything official regarding searches and stuff is difficult," Alex extended her arm out to the board, "Case in point."

"I don't give monkeys, if these scrotes think they are above the law, then they're are mistaken, find a way to bring 'em in, even if that means you get your paws a little dirty." Frank said.

Alex looked at Renton and smiled.

"Okay, I've saved the best 'til last." Ricky said.

"I think we have found a significant link." He shuffled more papers and tacked them to the board, passed around another handout.

"Right, this clearly seems to be a high-end operation with a lot at stake, given the bodies stacking up in the morgue. So applying my own algorithm to the situation, I sent that out to the ether not really expecting anything back, and I did."

With a laser pointer, he pointed at the board showing a print out of a website. "This is HAEMOmatch. Anyone know what this is?"

"Yer," said a small voice from the back. "It's an organ donation database. I remember reading about it ages ago."

"Correct. Now, the old way was a protracted process, let's assume for argument's sake I need a new liver. In the past I would go on a register, ask if a match was found, clinicians would argue who took the clinical priority. With me so far?" Ricky asked. A universal nodding of the heads.

"Okay. What this software program does is turn the list on its head." He walked over to Frank. "Now let's say Frank is involved in a car accident and is brought into the hospital dead, but with his organs still viable for transplant, they have a name for this, called a beater. The first thing doctors do is a blood test on all admissions to hospital, and that's all admissions." He walked back to the board.

"Frank's blood screening automatically goes through the interface of HAEMOmatch and if there is anyone out there in Europe, Australia or New Zealand that requires organs, the lead clinician of that patient requiring the organs are notified, it's literally turned organ donation on its head," Ricky said.

"So how does that have a bearing on the case?" Renton asked.

"The software goes one step further. Anyone that goes to a GP surgery and had a routine investigation, the GP will automatically send the patient's blood off for screening, again, if that person's blood fits the parameters of a person needing an organ anywhere in the world, America is coming online in the next few weeks. The clinician gets notified," Ricky started putting up the mug shots of the girls that have gone missing.

"What's creeped me out here, every one of these girls aged between 17 and 25 years of age, has had a routine surgical procedure, a routine blood test taken and then roughly three to four weeks later, they have gone missing."

"Holy fuck!" Frank said, Alex leaned forward, her attention grabbed.

"How do they fit with what we know?" Alex asked.

"This is where it makes my blood run cold," Ricky said.

"Melissa Davies was the 26th."

"Melissa wasn't the last one?" Frank asked.

"No," Ricky went through his papers.

"A girl called Lucy Hodges from Colchester went missing last Saturday. Been put up as a misper. Boyfriend reported her, caused a bit of a commotion apparently."

"Do we know anyone there?" Alex asked.

"Yeah, we do. Simon Cuthbert."

"Cuffy?" Alex asked.

"Yeah, he's demobbed and works in the Colchester nick as CID Inspector," Ricky said.

Alex pulled her phone out, hit contacts, and flicked through. She found Cuffy's number hit dial. She got up and walked to the darkness of the corner of the office complex. The traffic was going about its usual business outside on the road, oblivious to the unfolding events in the office.

"Alex, blast from the past." Cuffy said,

"I know Alex," he said.

"Inspector, look at at you," she said.

He seemed embarrassed.

"This isn't a social call, mate," Alex said.

"I guessed that." He laughed.

"Talk to me about Lucy Hodges," There was a pause. The pause became a little awkward.

Then Cuffy spoke. "Why did you mention that name, Alex?"

"Her name popped up in an investigation," Alex guarding her information, testing the water.

"She was reported missing at the beginning of the week, actually dropped off the radar Saturday, out of character."

Another pause.

"I feel there's a but coming," Alex said.

"Just something telling me that this isn't a straightforward misper. More than out of character, passionate boyfriend. Everything is telling me that she's been pinched, but I have nothing concrete."

"You have something though, tell me," Alex said. She was aware that putting anything into Cuffy's head could hold things up, her probing forced him to think aseptically.

"Cars been left with wet weather gear in the car, she was on a night out. She should have gone to the car to get her coat and trainers, but they were still in the car," She could hear him walking.

"What's really odd though, the car was parked in a well-lit car park and an area covered by high definition CCTV cameras."

"Oh, have you got footage?" Alex asked.

"Well, there's a thing, the lamps were taken out and the CCTV cameras were all disabled from the carpark, along the slip road, down the main drag and out of town. Where the camera outage ended, looks to me like a…"

"…a route." Alex completed the sentence.

"Yeah."

"Tell me what you know Alex," Cuffy said.

She told him the whole story.

"Okay, well I'll cordon the area off immediately and get the SOCO's on it."

"Can we meet?" Alex said. "I have a meeting at the hospital tomorrow at 9 am, can we come up and take a butchers at what you have."

"Sure, I'll square it with my governor, I'll send you a location where to meet, just give me a time."

"Thanks, Cuffy" Alex said.

The line went dead. Alex starred out the window for a couple of seconds to compose her thoughts. She then walked back to the group who were brainstorming their ideas.

Ricky broke off. The group stopped talking.

Alex's phone vibrated, a text from Cuffy. She clicked it open, a location marker for her maps was blinking.

She noticed a text from Si. What time you home, worried about you, text me your plans.

She hit reply, fingers sped across the glass of the screen, I am not sure I will be home tonight, things have progressed, don't wait up babes, bonus if I am there in the morning, emoji love hearts. The message sent was instantly received and read. Dots…followed with a love heart.

"Guys, just spoke to a mate of ours," she indicated to Ricky.

"They have a girl missing, Lucy Hodges. DS Cuthbert feels that there is something wider occurring here."

She filled in the team and then urged them to go home and catch some sleep.

Frank was pulling his coat on. "I have known you for a long time Alex, what's your gut saying?"

"Shit, we are days away from the kidnapping, she's probably dead already, I dunno if I am honest, just very tired to think straight.

"Sarge, Gov," Ricky called.

They both turned, "We have to go, there's been a shooting at the hospital that's looking after Mr. Pattison from 59 Sweets Way."

Alex frowned, "What do mean a shooting?"

"He's dead and the armed uniforms looking after him, some woman disappeared as quickly she arrived."

"Let's go," Alex said to Renton.

"Stop" Frank said.

Alex half with her coat on turned to look at Frank. "Go home, you guys are running on empty, with a shooting at a hospital you won't have access to the scene. Go home people. We start fresh in the morning."

Alex was about to demonstrate, Frank held up his hand "It wasn't a request Alex, go home, get some rest. You and all of you will be no good to me if you don't sleep."

31

It was pointless for Alex to go to the hospital that evening she reflected. The deed was done. The local CID were all over it. They said they would fill her in the following day.

Apparently, there was security footage of the assailant entering the hospital and swiftly making it through all of the security checkpoints. They cleared the corridors and entered the secure ICU, located the target, three rounds, one to the head and one for each lung. Then dispatched the armed guards with a bullet to the head. Ten minutes after she entered the hospital, she was nonchalantly leaving on a motorbike with no plates. This was a video Alex was going to look forward to seeing.

She went home and got into bed in the early hours. She was cold and hungry. Si felt hot, swaddled in his eiderdown chrysalis. He stirred, his arm instinctively sliding around her waist and over her tummy, she felt safe for the first time that day and then it came. Involuntary, the tears flowed as Si squeezed, she tried to cover up the sobs, but Si, alarmed from his slumber, realized his wife was in trouble. He knew the drill.

Sitting up, switching the light on and then getting nothing but paralysis of the analysis was all that would be achieved at this time of night.

He drew her closer to his warm body. He inhaled the trademark smell of her hair as he buried his face into the back of her head, his warm breath caressing the nape of her neck.

Alex responded and contoured her cold naked body against the love of her life, finally drifting into a sweet, peaceful sleep.

The next thing Alex knew was the smell of Si's aftershave. Drakkar Noir, her favorite. It oozed the aroma of the eighties. She didn't care, then suddenly, fuck!

Alex sat up.

"What time is it?" she said.

Si was threading his cufflinks, he glanced at his watch, "Just gone seven, babes."

"Wow, why didn't you wake me?"

He sat on the bed. "Well, you came to bed at god knows what time, I thought you could do with the extra hour in bed."

Alex's hair was a mess, it covered her face. She grabbed his tie, "Take this off and come to bed, you know, your usual 30 seconds of joy you bring me," Laughing she kissed him, dragging him down.

"Babes, I would love to," He pulled the covers back exposing her naked body, he ran his eyes over her, he felt the twinge "But alas I can't."

Alex pulled a sad face, "How can you turn this down?" She grabbed his hand and placed it between her legs. She was wet, Si's twinge got more intense.

"Well it'll make me late for work and that's not the problem," Si said, keeping his hand where Alex wanted it, her hips gently pushing against his hand rubbing herself against Si's hand in preparation to receive his manhood.

"Who's Renton Davis?" .

She stopped. "Why?" Looking puzzled.

"He's downstairs eating a bowl of corn flakes and drinking your coffee."

Alex sat bolt upright, "What the fuck." In a whisper, "You let me do all that when you, you knew he was downstairs."

Si was laughing. "I enjoyed it," He said, "And I get to enjoy this all the way to work as well," He said appreciating the view.

"Your disgusting, Simon Brown."

"You home tonight?" He asked.

"I am not sure, babes." She said. "Things have moved on in the investigation."

Si knew not to ask, even though he was desperate to know.

"He's a nice guy," Si said.

"Renton, yeah, he's a top bloke, switched on." Alex swung her legs off the bed and padded and shuffled to the en-suite, "Kinda ruined my moment though. Tell him I will be down in a jiffy." Si heard the shower go on.

They chose to drive to St Bart's and avoid the battering commute across the city. The hospital was basking in the low sun of the autumnal sky. People busy arriving and leaving the building. A mixture of the old and the new.

A flagship NHS hospital that delivers unbelievable attention to the worst life can throw at someone. As Renton and Alex entered the building, the smell was familiar to Alex.

She left nursing and working in the operating theatres after seeing how cruel life can be for some people. She often asked why so many good people succumb to the most heinous diseases and are so accepting. In her world, some of the most degenerative creatures go through life as though they are coated in Teflon.

The receptionist, an Afro-Caribbean girl, hair like an explosion of ambers and oranges, with the most amazing complexion greeted them with the biggest of smiles.

"Wow, your hair," Alex said. The girl's smile lowered. "I mean, it's beautiful." She said, surprised by her own outburst.

"Tanks." Her smile widened again, the Caribbean accent sweet and exotic.

"Can I help you guys?"

Renton leaned on the counter, "We're after Professor Krantz's office."

"Okay, you need to take the elevator to the turd floor, when you leave the lift, turn right and you will find the liver team offices down there, someone should be able to direct you."

"Gosh, thank you." Alex said.

They walked off, "Gosh," Renton said "A bit gushy weren't you," He said.

"Did you not see how stunning she was? Not every day you get to see beauty like that."

Renton looked back and checked her out. His face approved, Alex smiled.

"She was so checking me out as well," Renton said.

They entered the lift, Alex waved at the girl, she smiled and waved back. "She's a lesbian, Renton," Alex said.

"How do you know that," He said as the doors closed.

"She's wearing a necklace with two Venus symbols on it, her sexual preference."

She turned to Renton, "And for the record, yeah I would turn for her, she is totes off the hook gorge."

Renton laughed.

They entered the corridor, the doors either side with the names of the surgeons and physicians that work in the department. A hive of activity. People in scrubs, nursing uniforms, and suits.

Mr. Grately, Mr. Simmonds, Mr. Broc, Prof Krantz.

They stopped, Renton knocked.

"Enter" Came the voice from behind.

The door opened and in a large office, with a view of St Paul's Cathedral, sat a thin man, glasses perched at the end of his nose, typing furiously on the laptop, his tongue darting from left to right of the lower lip like the light on KIT in "Knight Rider."

They stood and waited, the professor sensed it and stopped typing. He looked up, then carried on typing.

"Sit," He said.

Both Alex and Renton sat and took in the office. The wall was adorned with certificates and photos. The professor shaking hands with a couple of Prime Ministers, Health secretaries. The pride of place was him with Margaret Thatcher and another with the former secretary to the United Nations Ban Ki-Moon.

"RIGHT!" the professor shouted and slammed the laptop lid and leaned back.

"What can I do for you officers?"

Alex was taken by surprise that he knew who they were.

"We are Sergeant Brown and..." The professor held up his hand.

"I know who you are, listen, I haven't got much time. I am in surgery in twenty minutes, my time as you can understand is not infinite, I don't like pleasantries or fluff, can you get to the point."

It wasn't delivered rudely. A sincere smile followed the comment, the man was genuinely a busy professional, but Alex had forgotten how rude yet decisive surgeons could be.

Alex had gone through the case with him.

"What's that got to do with my team?" Krantz asked.

Renton shifted in his seat, "There's a strong link to the missing girls and your software program HAEMOmatch."

"Rubbish, the system is concrete, it has these firewalls and security measures to maintain confidentiality to the patient," Krantz said.

He turned the screen of his desktop, HAEMOmatch, already loaded.

"Look, the program is very secure, it would never have passed through ethics if it wasn't. The NHS takes it's security very seriously. This program is monitored by our own IT team."

"What about internationally?" Renton asked.

"How do you mean, sir?" Krantz asked.

"I mean, your program is accessed by all the European countries, Australia and New Zealand with America going live in the next month or so."

"You forgot Canada and India. The software was rolled out to all the Commonwealth countries as we have reciprocal healthcare agreements in place. This extends to organ donation as well. Contractually this was easy. The Americans on the other hand, legally a completely different kettle of fish," Krantz said.

"But if you're suggesting that one of our commonwealth brethren have done something prohibited, I can assure you that we would have known about it," He said irritated.

"Just asking the question Professor," Renton said.

He held up his hand, "I know you have your job to do and without going through any particulars, this investigation has the hallmarks of someone very damaged and please call me Sam, this professor bollocks, drives me potty."

Alex and Renton smiled.

"Do you know of anyone that would fit the bill?" She asked seizing the moment.

"Sure, I work in a department full of surgeons, all Apex predators. If we weren't performing miracles on the operating table, most of us would be incarcerated. We are people that just did well at school and was given an outlet, we see the world differently. We live with stress everyday, stress of life and death. Coming to terms with the death of a patient is often the worse. We as surgeon's treat most of them successfully, it's the ones that die that are the ones we remember," He looked out of the window, pursed his lips "It's sometimes difficult."

"Who actually set the HAEMOmatch program up, how was it conceptualised?" Alex asked.

"Well, our rising star Dale Broc was the brainchild. Knew his father, both gifted surgeons, Broc will become a household name in the very near future. With this program, he will almost certainly be eligible for a Nobel," Krantz said.

The phone rang, then it cut off immediately, intercepted by the PA on the other side of the glass.

"Dale pushed it through. The Trust wasn't going to fund the design and implementation as we are financially bankrupt, so Broc paid for it himself, once the program was up and running he sold the program to the NHS Blood and Transplant organization."

Alex was writing in her notebook. "Has Mr. Broc got access to the program still."

"No, categorically no. Ethics insisted that the program was end to end and only accessible from this very building, there is no way that the program can be accessed," Krantz said.

Renton crossed his legs. "So, if the security of the program is as good as you say it is, what is your opinion about the 27 missing women that have all been run through your software program?" Deliberately using the word women and not girls, Alex clocked it, clever she thought.

Krantz shifted in his chair, pursed his lips and pushed his glasses onto his face. "Maybe a coincidence and it is not my system."

He leaned forward while Alex and Renton looked at each other, no such things as coincidences Alex had written in her notebook. Renton nodded slowly.

Krantz picked up the phone, "Helen, is Broc in today?" He was nodding, they could hear the muffled voice on the other end.

"Okay, can you find Squibb then, tell him that I want to speak to him urgently. I know he's not operating, kissing my arse in the toilets this morning, I am fully appraised of his whereabouts, unfortunately."

He put the receiver down. "Broc isn't in today, but one of his proteges is." He paused for a second. "Well I say protege, but that all abruptly ended a few years back now, he's on another training rotation, but he knows Broc, and he definitely knows the program as he was one of the guys that implemented it."

Two minutes later, there was a knock at the door, then it opened.

A small man, dressed in grey tweed, thick, expensive brogues, with a bow tie. Thick round-framed glasses snuggly fitted to the chubby round face, cheeks flushed. He had apparently run as soon as he got the call.

"Professor," Squibb said puffing.

"Squibb, you shouldn't have rushed old bean, I told Helena to tell you not to rush, you buffoon." He lied, Alex noticed.

"These people are from the metropolitan police," Krantz said.

"Oh," Squibb said.

"Don't worry, you're not being carted off, they want to talk to you about HAEMOmatch."

Alex offered her hand, "Alex and Renton." He looked at them suspiciously, slowly shaking their hands. "Your ranks?" he asked, his public schooling evident. Eton, Fettes or Marlborough, she thought cock.

"Oh, of course, silly me," Alex said. She flashed her warrant card, "Sergeant Brown and this is Sergeant Davis, murder squad, East End."

"Murder squad?" Squibb slumped in the chair behind the wall. "What's a murder squad got to do with HAEMOmatch?"

Krantz was putting his jacket on. "I have to go, people, feel free to use my office."

He skirted around the desk and shook the officer's hands. "Squibb, have we got the bloods back on Mrs. Meakin?"

"No professor, I was on my way to hematology when you called."

"When you're done here, get them to me in theatre sixteen, understood?"

"Professor," Squibb acknowledged with a curt nod.

Alex's phone pinged, it was a message from Ricky, footage of the assassination of Mr. Pattison from number 59 Sweets Way.

She hit reply. I will check it out later, just chatting with one of the surgeons, be about ten I guess.

"Can we circumvent the efficacious nature of Haemomatch?"

Alex looked at Renton, "Sure." She sat opposite Squibb.

Alex led from her intuition "What do you want to talk about?"

Squibb looked at Alex, "Tell me why you're here first," he said.

Alex and Renton looked at each other, then went through the investigation again, leaving nothing out.

Squibb put his hands on his face and leaned. He seemed tired, at the end of his rope.

"All I ever wanted to do was be a surgeon, but Broc put paid to that."

"Why?" Alex asked.

"There was a patient that died on the operating table a while ago now. My only saving grace was that the portal vein, dissected by Broc was too short to be anastomosed to the portal vein part of the new liver. I admit now because the case has passed and I cannot incriminate myself anymore.

But if the portal vein was at a decent length," he shuddered at the memory "I made a mistake taking the clamp off, that was imbecilic."

Renton asked what anastomosed meant. Squibb, piqued by the uneducated question and ruining his chain of thought.

"It simply means officer, the joining of two vessels together, in this case, allowing the liver to drain deoxygenated blood back into the venous system from the liver."

"Still kinda don't know what that means," Renton said.

"It isn't important." Squibb looked at Alex.

"The coroner judged that the patient would have died anyway as the portal vein wasn't dissected properly, I believe that Broc did this on purpose to drum me off the training rotation."

"Why would he do that?" Alex asked.

"He hated me. I know that I come across as a little annoying and a bit odd. My colleagues are not particularly fond of me. I am just over exuberant, and I challenge everything. 'Living the dream' as my mother says."

He plucked fluff from his suit. "You see, Broc just hated me from the moment he clapped eyes on me, I also heard the patient ask for Broc to kill him."

Alex wrote her notes. "You heard this?"

"Yes, I can't prove it though."

"Could you not make a case against him and whistleblow, isn't the NHS into that sort of thing these days to stamp out poor practices?" Alex asked.

"You would think so wouldn't you, but have you met Broc?"

"No, I haven't, what's the deal with him, is this not sour grapes on your part, no offense meant." Renton asked.

"None taken, that's another reason why I haven't come forward and unlikely to as well, because the professor would see me booted out of this hospital before he saw Broc given his marching orders. He's the Great Broc, everyone in my world knows who he is. The chosen one as he is sometimes referred to."

He pushed his spectacles against his pudgy face. "And before you ask, no he wouldn't have done that by accident."

"Can you get me a copy of the patient's notes?" Alex said.

"Of the patient that died, the one that took me through the coroners' court?"

"Sure, can you get them?" Alex asked.

"Definitely, I copied all of them. I have the whole file." Squibb said smugly.

"Really?" Renton said.

"Yes. There was no way I was going down for this. The moment after the incident, I felt that something was up. To protect myself I was compelled to copy them."

"Can you send them over by bike courier to my address." Alex dropped her file on the table. Some documents slid out, she fished in her pocket, pulled out her wallet and grabbed one of her business cards.

"I can do better than that," He looked at her card, pulled his phone out, pushed his glasses back on his face and typed into his phone. "I'll email them to you now."

Alex pulled her phone out and waited for the email to drop in.

"Thought you didn't know who Broc is?" Squibb said.

"We don't, we've never heard of the guy before meeting your boss."

Squibb sat forward, opened the folder on the corner of Krantz's desk, the e-fit of the man Mr. Pattison from 59 Sweets Way had described.

He tapped the image, "This is Dale Broc, sergeant."

Alex and Renton snapped forward and stared at the picture.

"Are you sure?" Renton asked, Alex was staring open-mouthed at the picture.

"Positive, that's Broc. He has a face you will never forget."

Squibb got up andlooked at the wall of photos behind Krantz's desk. After scanning some of the pictures, he found what he was looking for.

"There you are," Squibb said as he pulled the framed photo off the wall. He turned and handed the picture to Alex. The image was of Pressor Krantz, a couple of other influential people, but stood right next to him was the unmistakable face of the e-fit that Mr. Pattison had described.

"Holy fuck!" Renton said over Alex's shoulder. Alex looked around then back to the picture.

"Mr Squibb, I think you ought to come with us, I think in light of what you have told us and the events over the last couple of days, you need to be in protective custody."

"What?" Squibb sat in the chair. He was putting all the pieces to the jigsaw, his own experiences, the case that Alex had told him about, Broc was a killer.

While they were all sat in silence, Alex's phone bleeped. The email from Squibb had bounced in. She redirected it straight to Ricky, take a look at this file from a surgeon that has some info, we need to arrange protective custody for him.

"Protective custody?" Squibb said. "How exciting, I need to finish my rounds though."

"Erm, I think it would be prudent that you come with us right now Mr. Squibb, your rounds are done."

He got the tone of the urgency, paused, thought of his options and then agreed to go with them.

They left the office, Alex dialed Ricky. He answered.

"Wadup masser?"

"Get me a uniformed car to meet us at the main entrance to St Bart's. No fucking about, blue light them here NOW!"

"No dramas, roger out." The line went dead.

"Lets go and don't look back Mr. Squibb."

Sandwiched between Renton and Alex, they walked hurriedly to the elevator. Alex was choosing the stairs opposite.

Professor Krantz came round the corner.

"Are your done, Squibb?"

Alex held up her hand, "Can you get out of our way Professor, Squibb is in custody and please do not talk to him." Squibb felt the tightening of Renton's hand on his arm.

"You can't just take a member of my staff, Sergeant," He said, hands on his hips.

"You have my number professor, call me sometime this afternoon and I will discuss it with you."

They entered the stairwell and descended the stairs, Squibb keeping his head down, he was finding this all a bit embarrassing.

They entered the main foyer, a bit busier than earlier. Alex saw the police car pull up, the blue light flashing.

Leaving the building, one of the uniforms recognized Alex.

"Sarge," Opening the door, Alex bungled Squibb into the back seat.

"Get him to my nick. DC Lambert will meet you. Do not stop for anyone, you understand?"

Krantz was confused. He went to his office. He noticed the picture on the table removed from the wall.

He pulled out his phone. Found Broc's emergency number, hit dial.

It rang three times, "Professor, how the devil are you, why are you using my emergency phone number?"

"Dale, apologies, I didn't know what to do really."

"What's up?" Broc sensing the confusion in his boss's voice.

"I had the police here, asking all sorts of questions about HAEMOmatch, is there something you need to tell me, Dale?"

There was a pause, Broc thinking it through, he needed to get hold of Ng. Things were progressing in a fashion out of his control.

"They took Squibb, Dale, what has he done?"

"Apart from being an incompetent fartleberry," Broc said, "Have they arrested him?"

"I don't know, the officer said that he is being taken away into custody, she didn't say arrest, Dale."

"Who was the officer?" Broc asked.

"It was a female police Sergeant, pretty thing, but the kind you don't want to mess with called Alex Brown, she came with another officer called Davis."

"SHIT! SHIT! SHIT!" Broc screamed down the phone.

"What's going on Dale?"

"Shut up, Krantz, you blithering idiot!"

"I beg your pardon Dale, don't you ever speak to me like the.."

The phone line clicked dead.

"Broc, hello, hello?" Krantz looked at his phone and held it to his ear again, "Hello, Dale."

Broc was gone.

32

The journey to Colchester was seamless. Apart from a hold up near Chelmsford. It didn't matter though. Both Alex and Renton's minds were racing. When Alex finally caught the scent of her prey, nothing else mattered.

Alex had filled Ricky in while on the road. He was searching the closet that was going to be filled with skeletons. "I want every stone, everything of this guy's life looked at and documented and ready for the team tonight. Put the whole team onto Dale Broc." She knew that Ricky wouldn't leave anything, his attention to detail was incredible.

"Have you seen the video of the attack in the hospital, yet boss?" Ricky had asked.

In the melee to get Squibb out of the hospital and then get on the road to meet Cuffy in Colchester, she had forgotten about Mr. Pattison from number 59 and the attack on him.

She clicked the link that Ricky has sent. The HD CCTV footage rendered and was edited. Ricky had cut and pasted the video, so there was an unabridged version of the assailant.

She arrived on a moped. Parked it at the main entrance of the hospital. The big box on the back of the bike gave the impression that she was delivering food.

Not an unusual sight in an NHS hospital, in the early hours. Either staff were working the night shift or patients fed up with the seventy pence daily food budget and ordering in a slice of heaven.

The person was clearly a woman. Slender, fit and agile. She donned a baseball cap, ponytail through the hole in the baseball cap. She wandered into the building with purpose. Bolted up the stairs like they were nothing.

At the top of the stairs, she turned left without looking. Walked the 250 meters to the door to ICU. She pulled out a security card and swiped. It failed then she did it again, and the entrance to the unit slid apart. Alex was confused. She knew precisely where she was going and she had a security card.

The next image was her walking into the unit. To the side room where Mr. Pattison was and opened the door. The next camera angle was Pattison in bed watching the TV, remote in his hand. He looked up and acknowledged the girl in the room. She threw the pizza on to a side table and drew out a pistol and adopted a well-versed firing stance.

"Wow, this chick's got a Maxim 9, she knows her guns," Alex said, Renton, trying to look over and still keep an eye on the road.

Alex watched the top-slide of the pistol snapback three times ejecting the spent jacket. She dialed the video back, watched Mr. Pattison in horror realize that he has come to the end of his rope. He jolted once, then twice. Dark patches started spreading like a grass fire across his chest. The third shot snapped his head back with his arms flying outwards. Alex hit pause. With her fingers, she spread them to zoom in. The round entered the space between nose and the upper lip. The trajectory of the round would have smashed through where both sides of the maxilla meet. Breaking off two triangular pieces of bone causing them to tumble through Mr. Pattison's face, and into the cerebral space. Destroying the connection of the pons and medulla oblongata, efficiently severing the brain stem from Pattison's brain. Killing him instantly.

Alex hit play.

The assailant turns, stops, and looks at the camera. She smiles with a wink and leaves.

The Maxim 9, a specialty pistol with an inbuilt silencer and using subsonic ammunition. With all the noise of the ICU, no one would have heard the report of the pistol, making nothing more than a fizz of air, like a tire pressure gauge on a car.

People in the communal space in the ICU going about their business while the assassin carried out her work, soon the life support monitoring alarms would alert them.

The corridor to the entrance of ICU, the two armed officers that should have been at Pattison's door at all times wandered nonchalantly down, looking at each other's phones.

The girl passes them. They say something probably hello. They pass, she stops at the other CCTV camera, smiles. Pulls out the Maxim 9, turns. Each officer gets two rounds in the head both dropping like liquid on the floor. Blood was spreading like a broken washing machine across the melamine floor.

The girl follows her path back. Leaving the now chaos in the ICU. Dons her helmet, gets back on the moped and drives off as if nothing had happened.

"Jesus," Alex said.

She called Ricky. "Just seen the vid."

"I know, what the fuck, before you ask. Nothing on facials or anything Interpol have. I lost her on Liverpool Lime Street, just disappeared, sarge."

"Chinese, clearly Triad, maybe she was brought in specially," Alex said.

"That's the obvious answer." Ricky said. "Oh by the way, that Simon Broadstone called again, said that it's becoming matter of urgency that he speaks with you."

"Simon who?"

"Forget it. I will make you call him tonight," Ricky said.

"We are near Colchester. I will call when we are done unless you have anything happen of significance."

"No drama, boss."

"Make sure Mr. Squibb is looked after."

Ricky laughed. "I have the Rupert in a cell, locked up. He seems comfortable there. He's a bit spooked."

"Not surprised." Alex said.

The line went dead.

They arrived in Colchester, Alex had only been here a few times while in the army.

The satnav took them down the high street, forking right down Queens Street. Down the hill and turning onto Osbourne Street. Renton switched the Satnav off as he clocked the heavy police presence along with the familiar forensics vehicles. People clad in white and blue paper suits milling around. The mine taped blocking the road was guarded by a young constable.

"Can I help?" He said in a high pitched Essex voice.

"Yeah, sure." Renton flashed his warrant card to him. "Sergeant Davis and Brown to see DI Cuthbert, he's expecting us."

"Roger that sarge, he's already been on the blower to remind me, just park your car over there and sign in. You need to don the gimp suits to be at the crime scene."

"No sweat constable."

Renton parked the car. Alex was out, greeted by a forensic coordinator armed with a clipboard, she signed in and started climbing into the suits as Cuthbert appeared.

"Well bugger me." Alex looked up and smiled, half stopping from putting the suit on. "You ain't changed, Alex." Cuthbert was outstretching his hand to shake Alex's. An awkward encounter, do they kiss or just shake. Alex chose to do both.

"You've put on a bit of timber Cuffy. You look well too," She asked.

She noticed Renton was waiting, "Married life agreeing with you." Cuthbert smiled and nodded.

"Oh, sorry, Cuffy, Renton Davis, East End vice; Renton, this is Detective Inspector Simon Cuthbert."

The pleasantries over, they walked to the car park, Lucy's car opened with stickers, numbers and tape all over it.

"We've found nothing, Alex. The car park is clean. The cameras have nothing."

Alex slowly spun around, looking at the walls, the buildings. "Anything in those businesses, have they been checked for any security camera footage."

"Yep, everyone, all closed, obviously given the hour, but nothing was filming in this direction." Cuffy said.

Cuffy indicated to beyond the railings behind Lucy's car "The taxi rank that was busy at that time of night said they saw nothing out of the ordinary."

"No dash cam video from the cars?" Renton asked.

"Nope, all been interviewed that was there that time of night. Everyone that we have approached has been incredibly helpful," Cuffy said.

"There's some homeless people over there, are they here all the time?" Alex asked, "Have they been interviewed?"

"I can't confirm that Alex, wait out." He wandered to the uniformed police sergeant standing by one of the vans chatting to one of the forensics. Alex watched them chat then Cuffy came back.

"They weren't here at the time. A patrol car had moved them along just after nine thirty that evening. When the rain started, the tramps generally congregate either at the Salvation Army that's opposite the nick, or the church on Trinity Walk."

Alex walked to the car. She studied it. Renton joined her.

"Why did she need the blood test?" Alex asked.

Renton put his hands on his hips, squinting, the late morning sun strong and piercing for an autumnal day. "She was about to start work at the local NHS hospital. It was a standard occupational health policy," He said.

They heard a commotion by the stairs. A constable was moving a female homeless person along.

"What's happening?" Alex asked Cuffy.

"That's Deirdre, a regular. Always under the stairs, she's not long for this world, bounces in and out of A&E like a yo-yo. Lives on anything that she can get her hands on including antifreeze."

"What's she saying?" Alex asked.

The three of them turned and watched the constable struggle with her. She wasn't going to climb the stairs and disappear. Alex was intuned with her intuition, she felt a compulsion to speak her. She wandered over.

"Steady constable." He stopped jostling.

"Hello Deidre, are you okay honey?" Alex grabbed the gnarled hands, filthy. Alex ignored it. She smelt of stale urine and filth. It didn't matter though.

"Purple van." Her voice raspy, the smell of cider on her breath.

"Constable," Alex gave him a ten-pound note. "Make yourself useful, wander over to the burger bar over there and get me the biggest burger and large fries, you like coffee or tea Deirdre?" Alex asked.

"Cider," she said.

"Get her a sweet tea, a large one." The constable looked at the tenner, looked at Alex and decided this wasn't a fight he was going to win. He nodded and walked away.

Deirdre sat on the lowest step. She pulled Alex down. Renton walked over to Cuffy. They held back. They would only cramp Alex's style.

Still holding her hands, Alex asked, "Tell me about the purple van, lovely."

She went into some incoherent rants, Alex found it difficult to decipher the words. She reached into her Barbour jacket. Pulled out an image of Lucy.

She showed her. "Yes Yes Yes, over there, I saw her fall over there by the purple van." Voice getting raspier, she coughed.

Alex dialed in, Renton also.

"How did she fall, honey?" Alex asked tenderly.

"By the van." Deirdre said.

"Was there someone with her?"

Deirdre nodded.

Alex shuffled the photos she had, found the e-fit of Broc. She showed Deirdre. She grabbed it.

"Yes, Yes, he took her," She belted out tapping the image, "In the van, he carried her."

Alex swiveled on her heels while still squatting, squinting in the low sun.

Cuffy was looking a little coy. Alex stood.

"My bad" Cuffy said.

"You're here, you knew something had happened, I guess she's always crying wolf a little." Alex said.

"Just a bit." Cuffy said.

The constable returned. He stood like a spare part holding the food.

"She won't bite constable, give Deirdre the food."

"Yeah, sorry Sarge."

Deirdre grabbed the bag and started devouring the contents, dropping french fries on the floor like confetti as she ate. It didn't bother her, she scooped them up and added them to the cement mixer of a mouth.

"You're forgetting something, constable."

The constable stood for a moment, "Ah, sorry Sarge." He scrabbled about into his pocket and handed Alex some change.

"That's it?" Alex said.

The constable nodded.

Cuffy stood with his hands deep in his pockets. "You think she is a credible witness, Alex?"

"Her testimony along with another very credible witness is all we will need to pinch this Broc geezer. He's on very thin ice." Alex said.

"I need her in PC, Cuffy, can you deal with that?"

"Why, she's a vagrant, why do we need to spend the money on sticking her in protective custody?"

Alex pulled out her phone. She flicked through the screens and gave the phone to Cuffy, Renton hadn't seen the full video at this point, they shared the screen.

Cuffy hit play. Both Renton and Cuffy's eyebrows were dancing with what they were seeing.

"Is that a Maxim 9?" Cuffy asked.

"Looks like it." Alex said.

The video ended, Cuffy passed the phone back to Alex. "I'll speak to my governor, he might not be so keen. So that I know, what's the scope with you taking her to your nick until something more long-term is squared away?"

"Zero."

"That's a definite answer, Alex?" Cuffy asked.

"I have a surgeon locked up in one of our cells that's been on the wrong end of Broc. This woman is from this town. She needs to be around people she knows." Alex said.

"Fair point, Alex."

"Also, just because she's homeless doesn't make her less safe. If the truth be known, she is far more vulnerable because she is homeless."

A uniformed sergeant approached.

"Excuse me chaps. I have a gentleman at the mine tape asking about you Cuffy."

"Who is it?" Cuffy asked.

"A Harvey Prossor."

"That's the girl's boyfriend, the person that reported Lucy missing," He looked at Alex.

She shrugged. "Send him in."

"Roger that," The sergeant said and turned on his heels.

"I fucking told you that she was taken."

Alex turned to see a tall, thin guy. Physically strong and well groomed.

"Hi, Harvey, pleased to meet you, my name is Alex Brown." She headed him off at the pass with her arm extended.

He stopped abruptly and looked at the hand. Gingerly he took it.

"I told you lot that Lucy had been nabbed and you have done fuck all about it," Harvey said. He was shifting from one ball of his foot to another. He was tanked and pumped.

"Harvey, look at me." He ignored her. She said it again "Look at me."

He stole his hateful glance towards Cuffy.

"Harvey, sweetie, we're doing everything in our power to find your girlfriend."

His features softened, he wanted to cry. A combination of his age and his masculinity was preventing the tears from flowing. The chances are, there was every chance that Lucy was already dead. But this guy didn't need to know that just yet.

"Here's my card Harvey, plumb my number into your phone and send me a text, so I have your number, I'll keep you informed."

He nodded.

"Are you smashing the bong Harve, can I call you Harve?" She touched his hand and squeezed, he nodded, "What Lucy calls me."

"Not judging you son." She said, her voice gentle.

Ashamedly, he looked down and nodded. "It's the only thing I can do to get me through the day, keeps my mind elsewhere."

"Your mind isn't elsewhere, Harve. I need you. Lucy needs you to be firing on all cylinders, do me a solid."

He looked at her. "Stay off the weed okay. We can get you in touch with victim support and they can help you through the process, do you have family?"

"I have Lucy's parents. They're a bit of a mess tho." His Adam's apple bobbing as he spoke.

"Okay, lean on the family, no matter how shit they are, they will give you some comfort."

"Okay," He said.

"When I call you, whatever I will tell you on the other end of the phone, I need you to be crystal, you feel me?"

"I do Alex, thanks."

Alex, always looking at the emotions of people. She rubbed his back and led him to the railings by Lucy's car. She wanted him to be near her energy inside the car.

"Tell me about Lucy."

He looked at her, a bit confused "I've told the plod everything, Alex."

"Not the stuff they want to know, Harve." Using they to disassociate Alex from the police. She knew how to get the best and the worst from people by talking, gestures and triggers. It was a particular skill that was very rare in the police.

"Tell me about her, why do you love her, what is her favorite food, who's her favorite band, stuff like that." Alex said.

He pulled out a photo of her. She was gorgeous. Alex took it from her, "Gosh, she has a beautiful smile, you bagged a hottie there Harve, lucky devil you."

He laughed. "She has a wicked smile, makes me fall apart every time, she loves pasta, any kinda pasta. She'd 'ave it every day if she could, not my thing, a bit of a gym rat you see Alex, I think carbs are the devil." He smiled, Alex genuinely thought he was a very sincere young man. She could see what a beautiful woman such as Lucy would see in a guy like Harvey.

Beyond the facade of his Essex boy looks and attitude, was a kind soul, damaged by his parents as most kids are. Alex thought of her children again and wondered where she failed them, knowing that on some level, all parents do.

Harvey spoke openly and frankly about Lucy and her past, her loves and what she wanted in the future. He was undoubtedly invested in her future as much as she was to his.

Alex ignored her phone vibrating in her pocket. After about ten minutes, both Alex and Harvey were friends. All he needed was a shoulder to offload on. He hadn't been given that option from the Colchester nick. Left horribly isolated and at the mercy of his demons. He found solace in the bong. Augmenting the paranoia, verging on the psychosis. The one thing this nick didn't want was for Harvey to go postal in the town center or be found swinging from the balustrade at home.

Alex didn't blame the police for his neglect. They are a stretched service like every other. If Alex made a difference here, in this infinitesimally small amount of time by comparison, then some good had been done.

"Go back home, wait by the phone, don't forget to text me, Harve." Alex motioned to a police constable.

"Make sure you see him home." The constable nodded. "Harve, that photo you have of Lucy, can I keep it for now?" Alex asked.

He stopped and pulled it out of his back pocket,"You can keep it, I have this on my computer."

Alex pulled her phone out. Five missed calls from Ricky and a text.

Renton walked over, "Ricky's bin on the blower."

"I see." She waved her phone at Renton, "What's the sitrep?"

"Broc's house is empty Alex, they breached it an hour ago, the place apparently rigged to an incendiary device, didn't go off," Renton said.

Alex held the phone to her ear. She was nodding.

Renton stopped speaking when Alex held her hand up, "Ricky, been a bit tied up, Renton has just filled me in about Broc's house."

"Yeah, the incendiary charge didn't go off, the reason being it was rigged to a complex detonator that had its own modem."

"What does that mean?" Alex asked.

"Well, the device was a mobile device in its own right, the circularity was very complex, like beyond your average jihadi bomb builder type of skills, like the device was plumbed into an app."

"Triggered from a smartphone?" Alex asked.

"Exactly sarge, the trigger is the phone that connected to the app, clever stuff. He's not your average slag sarge."

Alex looked at the floor, searching for questions "Any more on the shooter?"

"Zilch," Ricky said. "I have accessed every database, including hacking into Chinese intelligence, she's in the wind and off radar."

"Have we got enough to pinch Ng?"

"I'll ask the CPS sarge, probably if it was Joe Soap from Croydon on kiddie fiddler charge, but this guy looks a bit Teflon, I'll locate the twat first," Ricky said.

Cuffy came up, waited while Alex was on the phone. "Find him before the CPS get wind, maybe pinch him then ask the CPS."

"I feel you sister, loving your thoughts," Ricky said, "Give Cuffy my regards."

The line went dead.

"Ricky Lambert sends his regards." Alex said.

"Harvey alright?" Cuffy asked.

"Yeah, I think so, he's a bit pissed at not being listened to, and her of course," Alex said.

"I'll take that to the bank Alex, what's our move?" Cuffy asked.

"Well, we have to get back to London, and go to a bar that's frequented by the Jimmy Savile's of this world."

"They have bars in London for nonces?" Cuffy asked.

"No, I was joking, it's normal bar but it's where nonces congregate, it's a stretch really, it's a gay bar run by a high profile," Alex said.

"Same thing init," Cuffy said.

Renton chortled, "We are going on information provided by a snitch, it's not advertised as a paedo bar, we'll raid the place after and clap the lot in irons before the week is out."

"What's that." Alex walked past Lucy's mini, against the railing on the floor the men following her.

A small gully was directly under the railings that fed into a drain pipe. She called to the crime scene coordinator.

They came over.

"Have you processed this part of the scene yet?"

"No, we haven't, otherwise we would have told you."

Alex bent down, with the end of her pencil, she picked up what appears to be a yellow cap of some description.

"Ah, hello," said the forensic coordinator pulling out a plastic bag. Alex dropped it into the bag.

Renton peered into the bag. "What's that?"

"That my friend, is a bit of a smoking gun," Alex said.

Both Renton and Cuffy looked at Alex. It's a lid from a volatile anesthetic gas called Sevoflurane, bit odd don't you think to be in a random car park where a woman has been recently taken by a suspect that is a surgeon. I'll wager a month's salary that cap has the paw prints of the great Dale Broc all over it."

She looked at the coordinator, "Get that to the lab ASAP, that has to be processed immediately."

"I concur," She said with a frown as she looked closely at it.

Alex's phone rang. She pulled it out, Ricky.

"Speak to me," Alex said.

Alex could hear Ricky fumbling about, "Alex, I found Broc, get your arse back to my location, he's been a sneaky little shit."

33

Alex and Renton made their goodbyes. The usual "We must catch up properly," "Let's not make it so long again" Goodbyes were always the worst.

Alex and Simon were the most antisocial people they knew. They hated social occasions. Even weddings were off, sending a gift instead. Their friends knew only too well. Ricky wouldn't ask them to come round for the departmental pub crawls and payday curries. He would turn up, off spec with his family without asking around Christmas time knowing that Alex would never invite them in advance and if it was done, a text of cancellation was always inevitable.

It wasn't because they hated people. They were just so invested in their relationships. They hated sharing the little time they had. Plus an element of co-dependency coming from poor childhood emotional abuse.

She sent a text to Ricky, leaving now, as soon as we are 10m out, i'll ping you, get the coffee on emoji coffee pot, cup and saucer and love heart.

Alex reclined her chair, "Going to get some scratcher time Renton, wake me if you start bobbing for apples."

He pulled a face, "I never sleep driving."

"Whatever," Alex said.

The Mile End police station was situated on the corner of Wraxhall Road and Eric Street. A few minutes walk from the Mile End Tube Station. An old police station, built in the

Victorian times. It had many refits over the years. The current refit took passers-by from the Victorian era to the mid-80's. Notable occupants during its time included the Krays, only for drunk and disorderly and Jack the Hat for something similar.

For reasons less known, two Fenians, Richard O'Sullivan Burke and Joseph Casey, had been hidden in the Mile End Station, after intelligence reports that the prison they were being held in on remand was about to bombed to free them.

The bombing took place killing twelve innocent bystanders on Corporation Row and breached a hole in the twelve-foot prison wall. Both Fenians were then tried for treason. Other than that, over the centuries, the police station was unscathed in the turmoils of London life even escaping the Blitz by the Nazis.

The Mile End nick was about to make the news for entirely different kind of breakout.

Ji-Yeon now a dissident from the North Korean regime. In a previous life, Ji-Yeon was known as Changgok Hyuk.

An average sized man with a chiseled physique. A brutal supporter of the regime and steadfast in support to the Kim Dynasty.

A member of the infamous State Security Department that rule the DPRK with an iron fist. One thing that scuppered his career advancement was that Changgok Hyuk was born in the wrong body.

Confused with the emotions of gender dysphoria yet the support to his beloved leader. He felt he had to leave the DPRK.

He traveled to China and then ended up in Hong Kong. There he met Ng.

Ng, always seeing the positive for business in every situation paid for Changgok Hyuk's gender reassignment surgery.

After the operation, Hyuk became Ji-Yeon, after her aunt who was killed by South Korean National Intelligence Service drone strike on the family home.

Ng put Ji-Yeon to work as soon as she was able. Staying under the radar for many years as the authorities had no idea that a woman could be so capable of performing the acts that she did. Plus, being an effective unknown to the security services, which was why there were no photos or records in any official capacity. She was effectively, in the digital world, invisible.

At 1300 hrs. A van pulled up outside the police station. The occupant got out and got on the back of a big engined motorbike. The driver had left the van with the engine still running. Hidden in plain sight, no one batted an eyelid.

The incendiary device inside the van wasn't to destroy the police station. But to cause panic and diversion.

At 1304 hrs the detonator triggered igniting the oxidizing fuel. An explosion followed by a brilliant white fireball. White smoke was billowing upwards filling the expanse of the road between the buildings. The windows in the police station flexed inwards as the shockwave battered the building.

In the pandemonium that ensued, all the alarms triggered, emergency lighting and flashing lights added to the confusion.

Some casualties lay burning on the sidewalk outside the police station.

A police car that was parked out front, behind the van collaterally exploded and was burning ferociously.

The police station fire exits burst open, people running as drilled to their assembly points.

The fire brigade arrived, the Watch Commander knowing instantly what this was.

"PUT IT OUT!" screamed the Desk Sergeant.

He calmly went up to the fire, walked back. "I can't, it's an incendiary device, we have to let it burn out, there's nothing we can do."

"Block the roads at each end, evacuate all the buildings on the road, have you accounted for the staff in the building?"

The head counts were done, the desk sergeant confirmed. "Apart from the custody suit, there are twelve in there, with six prisoners and one guy in PC."

The watch commander looked at the manifest, "What's PC, that isn't connected to a Police Constable."

The desk sergeant took a look. "PC is protective custody. He's there for his own safety."

The watch commander nodded, "What we will do is prioritize the station, we will dowse it with water to stop the heat from building, when the other crews arrive, they will do the same to the surrounding buildings, are you in contact with the custody suit?"

The desk sergeant clicked his radio, "You ok back there?"

"Yes, all good, get it stopped, we are all in the main foyer, the prisoners are all ok, they have been fed and watered, so they are happy."

The barrier to the rear of the station slid open as Ji-Yeon approached on her black moped. She maneuvered the bike, so it was facing outwards to ready her escape.

She stepped off, took her helmet off like a shampoo commercial, pulled out a rifle bag and unzipped it. She removed an IMI Galil assault rifle with the 7.62mm high-velocity conversion, customized with a silencer.

She pulled her jacket off exposing an assault vest with ten, thirty round magazines of 7.62mm ammo, in the sides of the vest housed two Chinese CF98 9mm Parabellum pistols, each silenced.

She walked without a care to the door. As she approached, her earpiece 'clicked radios down.'

The steel door, cold and uninviting clicked, it opened slightly changing it to come in.

Ji-Yeon opened the door wide. Target one, gun already raised to her shoulder looking over the sights, double tap, dropped. The 7.62mm rounds splitting the body armor like brittle toffee putting two holes in the target fist sized.

Next target, double tap, down, another double tap, down.

The custody sergeant, ex-military knowing the report of a high-velocity weapon. Frantic on the radio. Nothing.

The black-clad figure entered the suit, flicked the gun to fully automatic. Three round burst was scything through the police officers like butter.

So much blood, it hung in the air like the morning spray of deodorant. Ji-Yeon clocked the desk sergeant, perfect English with a tinge of Korean, calm and almost eloquent, "Squibb, which cell?"

The sergeant looked at her. He started to shake.

Sergeant Daniels had spent twelve years in the police after 22 years in the Royal Engineers. With multiple operational tours under his belt coupled with the hard yards on the beat in the Met Police.

Running the desk in the custody suit for the last seven months had been the dream job. His wife and children flashed before him. The cold, thick silenced barrel attached to the CF98 pistol almost made a sound as it touched his sweaty forehead.

Ji-Yeon canted her head saw PAX PC in number one cell, straightened her head, smiled, teeth perfect, "Jug-eul sigan."

She leaned forward, the leather of her suit creaked, licked her lips, the smell of expensive perfume was filling Daniels nose, "That mean, time to die."

She operated the trigger. The topside smashed back in a satisfying mechanical action kicking out the empty case, clattering across the counter. The bullet exited the back of Daniels' head spraying the wall chart with the officer's brains, bone and blood. For a second, Daniels stood there, eyes bloodshot, slowly becoming cross eyed and sinking in their sockets, as his soul left his body, his meat vehicle slumped to the floor, smashing his chin on the table below.

Ji-Yeon pursed her lips, "Tut-tut."

She turned, another target, holstered the pistol, shouldered the rifle, three round burst. She stepped over the slumped bodies, their pooling blood between them.

An armed response copper appeared, his Mp5 in the shoulder, he didn't get a round-off.

Ji-Yeon stepped on the wall to the left, to the right and to the left gaining height as she went. She wrapped her legs around the copper's neck and twisted, his knees buckled, and slowly went to the ground like a wrestler. When Ji-Yeon's knees touched the ground with the copper choking in the grip, she drew her pistol again, two rounds, one for the neck.

She peered into the man's face, still alive his eyes darting and now having lost all motor function as the 9mm round severed the spinal cord, smiled, "You cheeky monkey."

The second round in the left temporal lobe. He will take at least five minutes to properly die she thought.

She stood, walked into the corridor of the cells, the prisoners banging on the doors begging to be let out.

A female officer was lying on the floor shaking, hands up covered in blood. "Please, please, I am pregnant."

Ji-Yeon crouched, "Congratulations," She looked at her name badge, "Officer Holmes, you married?"

The police officer nodded, sniveling. "I be sure to send your husband flowers." Ji-Yeon placed the pistol under her chin, fired one shot. Holmes' head snapped back. The position she was in, the force of the bullet snapped the cervical vertebrae as well as liquidizing her brain.

Ji-Yeon stood over her dead body, considered the unborn child she was so apparently with. Fired two rounds into Holmes abdomen, "No witnesses," She said smiling.

The communication flap to cell one, Ji-Yeon opened. Squibb was cowering in the corner of the cell crying.

He looked,"I'VE SAID NOTHING!" He screamed.

Ji-Yeon recognized his photo.

"You die in a special way, Mr. Squibb," Ji-Yeon said.

She reached into the assault vest, pulled out a grenade. Not your average fragmentation grenade. This grenade was labeled Smoke WP bursting type.

She pulled the pin, the fly-off lever flew across her face and bounced off the shiny tiled walls. She let it cook in her hand for three-seconds then dropped it into the cell. The five-second fuse popped, it started emitting smoke, the phosphorous met the oxygen in the air and ignited.

Ji-Yeon shut the flap and leaned against the wall. She put her earphones in, "The Pretender" from the Foo Fighters was playing. She waited and waited.

Grohl was crescendoing the song after the instrumental break. She opened the flap. White smoke billowed out. Squibb was rolling on the floor on fire, Ji-Yeon stood listening to Grohl screaming in her ears unable to hear the wailing of

Squibb as he burnt to death, air guitar being thrashed in her hands. His thrashing slowing, finally stopping. His charred body still burning but nothing.

She closed the flap, changed all the magazines on her weapons systems and walked out.

Nothing was in the yard, smoke from the front mixed with smoke in the back. She bagged the Galil, put her black leather jacket on, popped the helmet on. Climbed on to the bike, kicked up the stand and left the yard listening to Audioslave "Doesn't Remind Me." The gate sliding closed.

The whole task took her twelve minutes, the teams at the front oblivious to the carnage that had occurred around the back.

34

The police had closed both ends of Eric Street and the Eastside of Wraxhall Road to allow the fire brigade to contain the fire. The oxidizing agent wasn't showing any chance of abating. The plastic window frames slowly buckling on the building, the firemen trying hopelessly to keep the building cool.

Ricky had made it out of the building with his tablet and phone. The phones were dead, which was odd. There was a good signal where they were, usually.

Ricky went up to the duty Desk Sergeant, now acting as the incident control commander. He was busy directing his constables, dealing with the injured and the fatalities that littered the sidewalk caught in the initial blast of the van.

"Sarge" Ricky was trying to get his attention. "Sarge."

The desk sergeant clocked him. "You alright ,Ricky" He said.

"Yeah, bit weird, I have no phone signal."

"Not the time to discuss your love life Ricky, bit busy here mate."

"I get that sarge, trying to get my Gov on the blower, why would the signal be down?" Ricky said.

"No idea, we haven't even got radio signal, the constables on Eric Street say they have contact with HQ, but this street is dead. The watch commander said it's because of the fire, yes, send the ambulance crew to the top end of the street." Interrupted by a paramedic.

"Really, the fire?" Ricky wasn't convinced. "Can I go to the rear of the station, to the car park, I have another phone in my car."

"Take PC Stamm, don't go alone. The building is safe to the rear. It's just the front that we have to watch. Stamm, make sure this guy doesn't enter the building, if he does, double back to me and inform, okay."

Stamm nodded.

Both Ricky and Stamm headed towards the rear. They turned the corner, Ricky pulled his swipe card out. Swiped through the key coded entry system. The gate creaked, then the lubricated mechanism kicked in and drew the gate back.

Ricky headed for his car. Stamm had veered off, he stopped and saw what Stamm was looking at.

"Hold on there, mate." Ricky said. Stamm pulled his extendable baton out, flicked his wrist to extend the weapon.

Ricky walked over to him. "What's up?"

Stamm nodded to the door. "The security door is open."

Ricky didn't see any issue, "Probably hot in there. There's a massive fire outside in the front," Ricky said.

"Not sure there, I worked custody, that door has to remain closed at all times, no excuses and I know Sergeant Daniels, ex-army, nutter. You kinda do as your told."

"Ok," Ricky said. He walked up the steps, along, the walkway and opened the door. Target one's feet were the first thing Ricky saw.

"Fuck, get the medics NOW!" Ricky shouted.

Ricky turned, Stamm was frozen, "NOW!"

Ricky entered the small security corridor, felt the carotid, nothing, body still warm, three feet from target one was target two, same grouping in the chest, two rounds. Lying next to him was target three. All carotids were pulseless.

The door to the suit, ajar, target four's feet were being repeatedly battered by a door that was trying to close, pulseless.

Ricky stared at the chaotic scene in the suit. Clotted blood on the floor pooled around the bodies, blood spray and spatter all over the walls. The empty brass cases littered the floor like confetti trapped in the globules of blood. He counted twelve. He spotted an Mp5 on the floor. He ran to it, picked it up and pulled the magazine off, fully bombed up. He pulled the cocking lever back, no round in the chamber. "Fuck, they didn't get a chance to make ready."

He made the carbine ready, forward assisted the cocking lever, he felt instantly safer with a round up the spout. He took the safety off, put the gun in the shoulder at the ready and took the slack up on the trigger. It wouldn't have far to travel if he had to send rounds down the two-way range.

Crouched, old habits do die hard he thought. Eyes on stalks, barely giving time to blink. The adrenaline was coursing through his veins pouring sweat down his face. The taste of shampoo in his mouth from the sweat running down from his head.

He was looking for some movement while keeping a check on the doorways. The prisoners were banging on the doors.

He waited until support came. If the team that cleared this custody suit were still there, he needed his back to the wall to gain as much of an advantage as possible.

The door Ricky had come through swung open.

"FRIENDLY, FRIENDLY!" Ricky shouted.

"PUT THE GUN DOWN!" came the reply. He did and instantly lay on the floor. The team commander came through, "I recognize you as Ricky Lambert."

"On your feet, Ricky, sitrep me."

Ricky stood. He realized that he was soaked in sweat and some blood from the floor.

The team commander crouched on one knee, "Check the rooms, clear the suit, weapons free."

"What happened, Ricky?" He looked at Ricky's chest, Ricky looked down.

"Shit, no, I am not hit, I just laid on the ground there."

The commander followed his hand, the outline of his body on some blood spatter.

"I literally came in, the door was open, fuck." Ricky was trying to compose himself.

"Take a breath mate. They are all our friends. We mourn when we are clear." He got up, "Stay here. I will be back."

The voices from the recesses, rooms and offices repeated "CLEAR!" as every inch, checked for any insurgency.

Ricky saw the bench against the wall, he went and sat just staring at the carnage in the room.

What seemed like an eternity, people coming and going, going about their business.

"Ricky." He heard his name again "Ricky."

He snapped out the trance he was in. He saw Alex and Renton standing in front of him.

Alex crouched in front of him. She grabbed his hands. They were shaking. Sweat still pouring out of his body.

"Get me that bottle of water, Renton." Alex said. He spun and grabbed it from the table. He passed it to her.

She held it to his mouth, "Take a sip, Ricky."

He complied and took in a gulp.

"It's not Iraq, Ricky," her free hand cupped the side of his face.

"Look at me, Ricky, look at me."

He looked, and the tears tumbled out of his eyes. He drew in a breath as though it was his first drag of air in an hour and he sobbed, he cried so openly and honestly, his shoulders heaving up and down as his emotions wracked his core with the memories.

Alex turned to Renton. "Ricky was the QRF commander at Majar al Kabir near Basra. Where we lost six of our own, he was the first on the scene," She rubbed his head in her soft belly. "I followed up on the job. It took a while to get to them as the contact lasted for more than two hours."

Renton struggled to fathom the flashback. He saw some guys in the custody office.

He walked over. A TV monitor was playing the scene.

Renton walked in, "Guys can we play that back?"

They looked up, one of the guys stopped the play and hit replay.

They saw one loan gunner enter the custody suit and systematically slaughter everyone in the room.

The team commander from armed response, clearly ex-military.

"This chick knows her shit, she's got a good blaster and those pistols are off the hook."

Renton, not military minded at all. "What do you mean, gun's a gun, right?"

The creak of body armor and the scraping of feet with all eyes looking at him.

"Dude, look, she's got an IMI Galil, stub nose assault rifle, that's been suppressed, gold standard Israeli gat."

He held up a pencil with a spent bullet case inserted on the pencil.

"She has the 7.62 conversion which is very unusual, this gat is a destroyer, puts a hole in you like a tennis ball, hits bone if you're lucky it'll just smash through, if your unlucky, it'll track the bone and come out of some other part of the body. The pistols are Chinese CF98's, made with a polymer carbon body, virtually undetectable, but that's not the reason I suspect this bird is using them."

Renton watched the screen, police officers dropping like flies, "What would the reason be?" He asked.

"These pistols have a unique magazine delivery system, it is dual fed which means it won't ever jam, guns I would use if I couldn't grab a Sig Sauer."

One of the gunners high fived the commander, "Roger that boss, one of my favs."

"Also the gun has a small traveling trigger, meaning that the nanosecond it takes you to operate the trigger on a western pistol, she would already have two rounds on the way. You might like to call that a hair trigger." There was some sniggering.

"You mean pull the trigger?" Renton felt smug, trying to fit in.

The creak of body armor and the scraping of boots on the floor again, eyes boring into him.

"The only thing you pull sunshine, is your dick or a bird." He looked him up and down "Or a dude." He returned to the scene, "You operate a trigger." The commander said, heads in the group shaking.

Renton decided to keep his mouth shut.

"These guns are rare, not really seen them this side of the Great Wall," The commander added.

One of the guys on the seat watching the screen. "She's got skills, boss." With his finger, he was tracing the empties ejecting out the side of the rifle, "She's triple tapped her way in, then gone to auto, three round bursts."

"What do you mean skills?" Renton asked.

The watch commander raised his eyebrows. "To have this level of control in a close quarter combat environment, she's special forces or intelligence of the Asian variety. Anyone else would just stand and spray the room. The gunner coming out the corridor with the Mp5 would have slotted the bitch, she was on point with her skills, watch how she takes him down kill bill style or what."

They watched the armed officer come out of the cell corridor, about to fire. The assailant was vaulting the walls like Bruce Lee and taking him down.

When she pumped the second round into his head, "Wow, savage bitch."

"Why Asian?" Renton asked feeling decidedly out of his depth.

"Russians or Americans wouldn't do this. They would use a fuck off bomb or poison," The commander said.

"Or a gas." Another voice piped up.

"Either Chinese or Korean, she's got the bod of a Korean… Hot." Said another voice.

"What is she doing at this cell?" Said a voice in the group.

"Fuck!" Renton exclaimed. The group looked around. "He's my guy. I totally forgot he was in there. He's in our protective custody."

"WOW!" One voice said.

"Has she just bunged in a white phos grenade, blimey, she's waiting for it to finishing fizzing."

Renton left the room, ran around the counter, avoiding Daniels' slumped body. He went into the cell corridor. Cell one was open.

The charred remains of Squibb lying on the floor. His knees were drawn up to his chest, his hands reaching out to the sky with his fingers gnarled and grabbing at nothing. His face burnt off, with his teeth showing, eyes ruptured under the intense heat. Still smoking, his partially charred guts spilling the only liquid left in his body onto the floor. The green chyme was adding to the offensive smell in the room.

An armed officer walked in with a fire extinguisher, squirted foam at the charred remains. It sizzled. "Friend of yours?" He asked. He didn't wait for the answer, just turned and left.

"Fuck!" Stepping his feet.

Renton went back to Alex and filled her in. Ricky was in a better state than when Renton had left him twenty minutes earlier.

"Same girl from the hospital," Alex asked.

"Yeah, looks that way." Renton sat next to Ricky, the three of them on the bench looking at the carnage in front of them.

Renton nodded to the custody room, "There's a video of the woman entering the suit and slaughtering everyone in here. She was alone. The guys in the room reckon she's either Chinese or Korean. With her set of skills, possibly even intelligence."

"Really? Chinese national or even Korean, which I would be assuming that would be North, would create an international incident?" Alex said.

There was a pause. "This has Ng's name all over it. I want this cunt in my nick at the earliest opportunity." Alex said.

"Alex, I was trying to call you, they must have jammed the radio and mobile frequency." Ricky said staring into the abyss of the room.

"What about?" She said.

"This patient of Squibb, the notes you sent me."

"Yeah, what about them?" Alex said.

Alex was dialing her phone, "Hold on, matey."

Alex got up, "Cuffy, you heard the news?" Renton and Ricky could hear Cuffy on the other end.

"Okay, I would get her out of the nick and somewhere else, other than a police station, she would be a target, probably use one of the barracks with the airborne."

"Agreed."

"Okay, yeah, thanks Cuffy, speak in the next couple of hours."

Alex went and sat next to Ricky. "You was saying about the notes Squibb gave us."

Ricky scratched his head. He couldn't remember what happened to his tablet. He scanned his mental databanks.

"Yeah, when you guys were in Dorset, at Baldwin's Haulage, their last job was at a farm in a place called Kings Stag. Owned by a Kevin Saunders."

Alex looked at the floor, "Yeah, Dorset plod had been round," she said.

"They spoke to the wife, a lady called Carmen, I believe," Renton said.

"The patient notes are for a guy that died on Broc's operating table. He was called Kevin Saunders. Ex-military, Coldstream Guards."

Alex stopped and turned to look at Ricky, "Really. You don't say."

"I spoke to the regimental sergeant major of the first Battalion the Coldstream. He remembers Mr. Saunders. Joined the Coldstream guards to get away from the family. Father was a bully, all the usual stuff we all joined the army for, no such thing as coincidences right."

Alex slumped in the bench, leaned forward and put her head in her hands.

"I went on the DVLA website, plumbed in Saunders name and address. Give me your phone Alex," Ricky said.

Alex still with one hand on her face, reached into her jean's pocket and pulled out her phone.

Ricky punched in the passcode, Alex not surprised that he knew it.

Pulled up her email, the email from Ricky and clicked it. He opened the attachment titled photo.

A DVLA license came up, Kevin Saunders, Saunders Farm, Kings Stag, Dorset. The photo matched the e-fit of Broc. Alex stared at the image.

"Look at the date the license was issued, Sarge," Ricky said.

Alex looked, the license had been issued nine years earlier.

Alex did the math, "Nine fucking years!"

Renton leaned and looked at Alex. "He's been operating for nine years."

"There's something else, Sarge." Ricky said.

"What?"

"I ran facials with Broc's image for the photos we have. I struggled to find him, to be honest. Then it got me thinking about the two diplomatic jets leaving Dockland's Airport the other day. So I ran facials on everything, I got one hit."

He grabbed the phone again and then selected another image. In the wing mirror of the BMW that Broc had traveled in was one solitary image. Broc was looking over his shoulder heading to the plane.

"He got on the first aircraft, Sarge. I am guessing Ng got on the second. But we know that Ng is back in the country because facials got him in Chinatown this morning."

Alex was thinking fast, "Where did they go?"

"Well that's the issue, once they left UK airspace, we can't track them, diplomatic. It's illegal," Ricky said.

Alex canted her head at him and smiled.

"You really have a bad opinion of me don't you?" Ricky said.

"But you found a way, right?"

"Course I did." He sat back for a bit of a gloat.

"I painted the aircraft digitally, then ran it through the NATO radar tracking facility in Hendon, Italy and Spain. The triangulation of the aircraft took them to Perpignan airport," Ricky said.

"Perpignan," Alex thought. "That's the south of France, right?"

"Yeah." Ricky said.

"South of France is a big area," Renton said.

Alex smiled, she knew that wasn't it.

"Well, I did a bit of digging. There is a villa in a small fishing village called Collioure that was owned by the Triads. It was a property business that was liquidated ten or so years ago. The organization sold the business on. Looks like that it had been sold on multiple times."

"Who owns it now?" Alex asked.

"Well the villa nearest the airport is in Collioure, but that's owned by a Frenchman who lives in Carcassonne."

"Dead-end then?" Renton said.

"Oh for fuck sake Ricky, it's like pulling teeth." Alex said.

Ricky laughed, "You got me."

"A totes dead end, Renton. The man in question is dead, died about twenty years ago. The purchase was a front. I think Ng didn't get rid of any of the properties, maybe some, but not all. He still owns it. The money that the property requires comes from Hong Kong. Now call me a stick in the mud," He paused, "No racial slurs please."

"But the average Frenchman who died twenty years ago doesn't flow money from Hong Kong to fund the upkeep of the property that requires an awful lot of money, hook line and fucking sinker." Ricky said.

"So we can maybe assume that Broc is holed up in Ng's Villa," Alex said.

She pondered for a moment.

"Now it's time to ring that Interpol guy you keep reminding me about."

"Simon Broadstone."

"Yeah," Alex said.

The door to the custody suit opened, in walked Frank. "What the freakin fuck has happened to my fucking nick?" Frank screamed.

Alex looked up at Frank, exhaustion written all over her face.

"Right, you three, out, get in my car. We are grabbing a Ruby Murray and a debrief at my house." They all stood, seemed the best thing to happen that day Alex thought.

"Can I grab Chinese, I can't stand curries." Renton said.

Frank, Alex and Ricky surveyed the room and then looked at Renton.

He looked at the three of them, "Fish and chips will do."

"Okay, the chippy is on the same street as the Indian, let's go."

They filed out, Alex bringing up the rear. "I want Ng in custody by the end of the night boss, Ricky, while we are at

Frank's house, on his computer you find him when we have eaten, I want to go a get the scrote and take a run at him."

35

Dinner destroyed, Frank was filled-in. He had grabbed a couple of the other members of the team to cast an eye on the global picture of what was happening.

Ricky was frantically working Frank's family computer. "When did you buy this computer gov, I think it needs coal to keep it running it's that old," Ricky said.

He had tapped into the Met police software and was using the facial recognition and the vehicle number plate tracking software.

Ricky knew that Ng was in Chinatown on Lisle Street. A restaurant called the Black Dragon hailed from Hong Kong had been open there for nearly twenty years. The only restaurant on Lisle Street that was from that region in East Asia. It had to be the first place to look for Ng.

The next software that Ricky tapped into was the mobile network. The criminal underworld had wholly gone digital in the last ten years thinking that their systems were safe.

Landlines were, in essence, a no-no. But the authorities were as quick to catch up with the technology evolving in the criminals' favor. The software that Ricky was using was a tympanic resonance system installed in most of the cameras in and around the major cities in the UK.

With the right access, of which Ricky didn't have, the tympanic sensors isolated people talking and by using the vibration of the voice digitally through lip reading and muscular facial contouring the camera could transcribe almost 95% of the what the person was saying. The software goes one step further and the energy rebounding off surfaces such as plastic bins and windows can make this 100% accurate. The only thing that dampened this down was the rain.

"Are you kidding that the intelligence service uses this all the time?" Alex said.

"Yep, it's how most of the jihadis and drug dealers are caught. The authorities don't particularly like using this software as the means of arresting or taking down the perpetrators, so they will use other methods to secure the arrest. Follow or react to the information shared," Ricky said.

"Does this not scare you, Ricky?" Alex asked.

"Not really Sarge, I kind of like it, if you have nothing to hide, it's the price of living in the free world I guess," He said shrugging.

"So what are you doing now?" Alex asked, sipping a coke, she pulled up a chair. The talking behind them became distant as Alex dialed into what Ricky was doing. She loved watching him work the keys, the screen dancing in and out of other screens and video feeds. She had no idea what he was doing.

"I have triangulated the cameras on Lisle Street," Ricky said.

Tapping away, the cameras on Lisle Street pinged up, three different views. Apart from the hordes of tourists plowing through the pavements, it was difficult to pinpoint anything.

"How will you see him?" Alex asked.

"I won't. The software will." They were both looking and watching for something.

"Let me try something else." Ricky said.

He highlighted the large window of the swanky Black Dragon restaurant. "Let me see if there is a digital signature emitting from inside the restaurant."

"What does that mean?" Alex asked.

"Simple, if there is a camera on a WIFI network, it will give off a signature, which means I can access it."

He was typing furiously, his tongue in the corner of his mouth. A couple of seconds later, a small black screen came up and green dot-matrix style script started listing.

"Bingo!" Ricky said. The next image was the camera at the back of the Restaurant, just above the serving pass. The camera was adjustable.

"It's even got sound," Ricky said.

"Bloody hell!" Alex said.

The camera stopped panning, Ricky zoomed. A thin man matching Ng's description sat eating with another man who was very fat, face not accessed by the camera.

"Bosh, there he is, hold on, let me clean up the audio."

It crackled, then became sharp. The men spoke. One is eloquent English, Ng. The other was a heavy Russian accent. Ricky dialed into the software with the names, then targeted the audio.

Alex was curious, "What are you doing there?"

"Voices are like fingerprints, we have started storing audio that is used in all surveillance." Ricky was trying to concentrate.

"It means if the audio has been stored before in any police or intelligence surveillance, their names will come up." He stopped and looked at Alex, "Banged to rights, basically."

"Blimey," Alex said.

"You'll be on here too, Alex," Ricky said smiling. "In any investigation, if I were to plumb your name into the software, every surveillance, audio including interview times that are digitally recorded would be available."

"That's perturbing." Alex said pulling a face.

"Not every tom, dick, or harry can just access the audio. There are levels of security." Ricky said.

"Even so."

"We got a hit on one of the voices." Ricky said, acquiring the name of the signature.

"Well bugger me with a pitchfork," Ricky said.

"Who is it?"

"It's Dmitry Orlov, from that swingers club you and Renton went to."

"What the fuck is he doing there?" Alex was still unaware of the encounter both Ricky and Renton had with him.

"Can we turn up the sound?" Alex said.

"Sure."

Voices associated with the names, the transcriber on the computer screen was listing the conversation like some weird text messaging thread.

Ng: You didn't have to kill my associate.

Dmitry: He shouldn't have got involved with giving me the wrong information to the police, have you any idea what kind of challenge that could cause my operation.

Ng: That has nothing to do with me, he was under instruction to do as I told him to. You might need the police in this instance to help you out, but I need the police to disappear. They have compromised my entire operation in the UK and potentially Europe.

Dmitry: Why did you not call me first, I had time. I had those pair of pigs sat eating out of my hand, they would have waited ten more minutes.

Alex felt betrayed, but quickly got hold of her emotions. Orlov was no friend of hers. She had met him only once. At the behest of Renton, the information wasn't that brilliant she thought. Alex turned to the rear in the dining room "Guys, check this out. We are in Ng's restaurant. He's having dinner with our friend from Club Schwartz."

The conversation was cut short. Renton and Frank filed into the corner, all watching the screen of the computer.

Dmitry: Those pigs won't give you any shit anymore, I have something on them that will make them go away.

Ng: What would that be?

Dmitry reached into his pocket. Some men in the room stood up and reached into their pockets. Ng held up his hand while shoveling egg noodles into his mouth.

Dmitry: We are here as friends Mr. Ng, no fireworks tonight please, I have plans.

He laughed haughtily.

He pulled out his phone and clicked the screen.

"Can we zoom on to that screen?" Alex asked.

"I'll try, the image will probably be a but noisy," Ricky said.

Then the sound came. The unmistakable sound of the Chinese man being flayed alive. The sound of the man sickeningly begging for his life, bringing back to Ricky the events of that night. He instantly felt nauseous. His mouth went dry, his tongue searching for some moisture, there was none.

Alex sensed it, she touched his leg and gently squeezed and leaned in, "We get through this first," She said quietly.

Frank saw the touch and the whispering, he frowned, tried to put the numbers together, "Anything you need to tell me, Alex?" Frank said.

She looked up, "Not right now, after this is over."

Frank nodded, he knew it was a fire that he would need to put out and he would, for Alex and her team, do whatever he needed to do.

The image was too noisy to figure out.

Ng: This has no value to me, you think coming to my restaurant offering me an olive branch would make your actions go away. You Russians believe you can buy or muscle your way into any city in the world. You lack class.

Orlov laughed.

Dmitry: Everyone has a price and if the price is right, anyone can be bought.

Ng: That's a mistake you can ill afford to make sir.

Dmitry: How so?

Ng: You're on the police radar, your sexual preferences and practices are not good for my business.

Dmitry leaned forward, his girth pushing the table toward Ng while he was still eating. He stopped and looked at the fat man in disgust.

Ng: Do you mind.

Dmitry: Apologies, listen, Mr. Ng, how can we go forward in business?

Ng: You think the triads want a piece of your action, you're mistaken. We might take your business, but we don't want it. Why can't the world just have normal prostitution and normal sex. Why do we have to complicate it.

Dmitry: It's the way of the world. The world has evolved. The internet is the conduit to all the closet sinners out there.

The script was listing the conversation. The room was watching as the green dot matrix script pumped out line after line of evidence.

Ng: I can't have you leave here, you know that right.

Dmitry: What do you mean?

Ng: You made a mistake coming here, I find it insulting that you would think this was OK. I had that mole in your organization spying on you. It wasn't the first thing that he had told me. You had him in your employ for more than a year. Second to this, he was a nephew of mine.

Dmitry leaned back in his chair, the creaking audible in the CCTV camera suspended from the ceiling.

Dmitry: And what of it.

Ng: I have to tell my brother who entrusted me that precious child of his, who is now dead, who died in the most horrific way possible.

Alex was enjoying the eloquence of Ng's English.

At the front of the shop, the door opened. A woman dressed in black sassed their way into the into the restaurant.

Ng turned and nodded to the women.

Both hands reached behind her back, her front knee dropping to the ground. Heavy one stood and was pulling out a Makarov pistol. He was immediately halted by the report of three rounds to his chest. He flew into the back of his chair almost toppling over. The woman stood. She sassed with attitude, as though it was a catwalk. Struggling for breath with both hands frantically searching his chest for the holes that were causing positive pressure in the chest making it impossible to breathe, blood spreading across his white shirt like a forest fire.

She approached the table and pulled out a plastic bag and snapped it over the man's head and yanked on a drawstring. The man fell forward clawing at the plastic bag. He was doubly doomed.

The second heavy stood and uplifted the table out of the way. The woman sidestepped, jumped on a table and somersaulted over the second heavy. He stared as she vaulted over him, at the same time she snapped a black leather belt around his throat and her full weight pulled on the belt as she came to the ground behind him. Instantly, the pressure in the heavy's face made him go puce, eyes bulging. The woman bent forward dragging the 110Kg man off the floor pulling hard on the belt. Frantically scrambling at his throat as the oxygen-depleted in his body, his face getting bluer and bluer.

At the last minute, she released the belt. The heavy fell to the floor gasping violently for air. His body started to recover from the oxygen debt. The women pulled out her pistol and looked at Ng, he nodded. The heavy didn't even see the gun. He didn't even know what had hit him, as three rounds ripped into his brain, liquifying the cerebral matter to mush, dropping like liquid to the floor dead. In the ten seconds, it took Ji-Yeon to kill the two heavies, the restaurant cleared of Chinese diners. Their silence already assured. The kitchen staff entered the dining area and started removing the bodies.

Dmitry: Ublyudok Ng, what the fuck.

He went to stand and reached behind his rotund girth, his hand meeting the delicate hands of Ng's assassin. She pulled out the 9mm Beretta, clicked the eject button and the magazine dropped out. With her thumb, still watching Orlov, flicked the 15 rounds out. Each bouncing off the Russian's chest. When the last round was cleared, she pulled the top slide back and ejected the chambered round. She caught it and dropped into his drink. Snapped the magazine back and handed the pistol back to Orlov.

The woman slid into the chair next to Orlov without making a sound, she turned, so she was facing him, he was less graceful sitting, the chair scraped and the table rebounded on its legs.

She picked up his drink, held to the light, looking at the ejected round in the glass then took a sip, eyes all over Orlov.

The room at Frank's house was holding their breath.

"Did we just see that?" Alex said.

"I think so. We are duty-bound to intervene. People have been killed," Renton said.

"Chill your beans." Frank said.

Alex turned, surprised by his reply.

Renton glared at Alex.

"I know what you're thinking, Renton, but we have a good chance of collecting some major intel here, we have to let this play out."

The room fell silent again as though they were watching the hottest blockbuster movie.

Ng: Meet Ji-Yeon, I no longer need to get my hands dirty. She is my secret weapon. She genuinely loves killing. The North Korea's loss and very much my family's gain don't you think?

Dmitry was staring at her, pulling away feeling hopeless. She reached to his lap, he hesitated and closed his eyes. She smiled and gently squeezed his thigh.

Ng: You see, I have no reason to keep you. I don't want your business and you are free to go, but first, I want something from you.

Dmitry's features softened.

Dmitry: What can I offer you in return for my freedom.

Ng: You won't give it lightly, nonetheless, we are going to take it from you.

Ng motioned to some people out of camera shot. They came into view and pulled the table behind them out of the way. They grabbed the fat man and Orlov started to cry out.

Dmitry: What are you doing. .

He was laid out on one of the dining tables. His trousers and jockeys pulled down to his knees exposing his manhood.

Ji-Yeon smiled wickedly.

Dmitry: What you doing?

She grabbed his testicles and started massaging them. Looking at him, she reached behind her and pulled out what Dmitry thought was a weapon. He flinched and screamed. Then he felt it. The warm tingling of vibration on the end of his penis. Ji-Yeon was gently rubbing the end of his glans with a vibrator. She started gently masturbating.

He closed his eyes. Ng stepped up and pulled his eyelids open.

Ng: Look, you filthy Russian pig, look at her.

His legs started to thrash. The men were holding him down tighter.

His penis now stiffly erect, Ji-Yeon started rubbing him more vigorously, then it came. Semen spat out of the end of his penis like molten lava. He groaned as his body wracked with orgasmic ecstasy. His hormones and natural feeling taking over him in the five seconds it took to ejaculate. Dmitry sat up.

Dmitry: What the fuck did you do that for?

Ng walked round, Ji-Yeon handing him the vial. Ng held the glass jar with the seminal fluid inside to the light.

Ng: A bit of a disappointing yield Dmitry.

Dmitry: If you wanted me to fuck someone, you only had to ask.

Ng: The only person that getting fucked tonight is you, my friend.

Ng threw the vial to one of his men who then left the room.

Dmitry: What do you mean?

Ng: Call it insurance, you see. When I come calling, I Will require you to roll out the red carpet and also, 20% of your gross income.

Dmitry: What the fuck do You mean 20%, why would I give you 20% of my income?

Ng: Simply because I now have your DNA.

It dawned on Orlov what had just happened. He spun his legs off the table and looked at the floor.

Dmitry: BLYAD. Gripping the table with his hands and violently shaking his body against the table.

Ng: You don't comply with my demands. Then I will deposit your DNA in some poor girl or boy and watch the justice system take you down.

He patted him on the shoulder.

Ng: Remember 20%, of which my men will be around tomorrow and take the first increment for this month.

Dmitry: Tomorrow.

Ng: And try and fuck me, not only will I see you set up for a murder, I'll be sending Ji-Yeon to your loved ones and have them slaughtered in their sleep, ponimayu.

Dmitry: I understand.

Ng: My men will take you to wherever you would like to go Dmitry.

Dmitry: I have my own driver.

Ng: You mean you did.

Ng was already leaving.

Ng: He's dead as well and your car is gone.

Dmitry watched him leave, Ji-Yeon hung back, watching him. She winked and kissed the air at him, turned and filed out the door after her paymaster.

The room was silent. Within two minutes, Dmitry had left and diners started entering the restaurant. Nothing told them that two men were murdered and a third sexually assaulted in a way no would ever have imagined.

"Do we go in?" Ricky said, still staring at the screen.

"No," Alex said. There was a pause. "Our primary target is Broc. We have to get back to Dorset to this farm. We will find what we are looking for."

"What about these guys?" Frank asked.

"Renton has got Dmitry another day and I need to make a phone call," Alex said waving her phone above her head as she stood. She made her way to the patio doors and slid one of the doors to open. She stepped into the conservatory and pushed the door shut. Her phone was lighting up her face as she searched for the number.

"I have been chasing you all week sergeant Brown," Said the voice on the other end.

"Been a bit busy, why do you want to speak to me, Mr. Broadstone."

"Well, considering the late hour and what's happened at your nick today, I might ask you, why are you calling me?" Simon said.

His voice very English, white middle class, Waitrose customer type. It was a strong voice that had the typical military edge to it, he sounded a little tinny, in a car maybe thought Alex.

"I have just witnessed something that I feel I need to share with you."

"But you can't trust me," Simon said.

"That's about right." Alex replied, she sat in the cane furniture, it creaked to the extent that she stood again.

"Your investigation is leaving a lot of bodies around the place. Which is looking a little unexplained, not good for police business, I'll wager," He said.

"I am beginning to feel the heat from the head-shed," Alex said, looking into the darkness of the garden through the double glazing.

"I need to make headway and arrests, one arrest is not enough," she added.

"Mr. Gormley." Broadstone commented.

"Umm, yes. You're informed."

"More than you know," Broadstone said. "Speak to me," Broadstone added.

"I have just seen Ng and Orlov meet."

There was a paused.

"How did that end up?" He asked.

"Your pause told me that you think something happened. It did. Two of Orlov's heavies got slotted. Orlov, well, not sure what happened there, but he walked away. He's going to owe Ng big time.

What's the deal with Ng, you must know something," Alex said.

"I do, the number you've called me on is a secure line. For you to trust me, Alex, I am going throw you a couple of bones."

"I am listening," Alex said.

"Ng works for British intelligence, has for many years. We met in Oxford when he was a student. His connections to the Chinese government has given us both strategic and corporate edges in our favor. You could say at this juncture, he's protected."

"Bullshit."

"I beg your pardon," Broadstone asked.

"I just watched that piece of shit kill two men, sexually assault another man. My police station had his name all over it and second to that, the fucker is implicated in a serious crime committed in this country. I want him in irons and standing trial."

"Not going to happen, Alex," He said flatly.

There was a pause.

"So this guy works for British intelligence." Simon cut her off.

"Government, not intelligence."

"Don't take me for a mug Mr. Broadstone, governments come and go, he left Oxford years ago. If you recruited him then, then he works for intelligence."

Broadstone was silent.

Alex knew she wouldn't be able to go against the establishment.

"So, let me rephrase for the sake of your intentions. Ng works for the establishment as a spy, delivering you guys defense documents and corporate espionage." Alex deliberately using clandestine words to steer the conversation. Broadstone smiled, he clocked it.

"You know about his Triad connections?" Alex asked.

"Yes we do," he said.

"And do you know of his connection to a Dale Broc?"

There was a pause.

"Okay, listen Alex. I am going to throw you another bone."

"Do you know of his connection to Dale Broc, simple yes or no?" She pushed.

"We do, but not the full extent until we tapped into your investigation."

Another pause.

"I'm kinda pissed, Mr. Broadstone."

"Why is that?" He asked.

"Well, that an intelligence agency has tapped into my investigation, that you know that one of your known criminals, that takes the piss out of its paymasters and uses his connections to get a fugitive out of the country by foreign diplomatic means. Namely, because the fugitive is a suspected serial killer that feeds a black market in human organs. Then puts his victims through a meat mincer to hide his tracks and you just asked me why I was pissed?"

"I can see-" He was cut off.

"I don't think you do actually." Alex was raging. "At what point when you were at boarding school, which forgive me if that assumption is incorrect, did you think that you would handle a psychopath who looks after an even bigger psychopath in the name of the Crown, in maths or English or when the housemaster was bumming the shit out of you."

She left it hanging.

Broadstone smiled.

"Have you lost your mind?" She added.

"I can see how this all looks," Broadstone said. "But we genuinely didn't know about Broc, we knew of him, but not to the extent he was operating."

"So why can't we lift the whole lot of them, we have the evidence?" Alex inquired.

"Ng is off limits for many reasons I cannot go into. These reasons are not self-serving. What we can do is remove Ng and his organization for the UK."

"I don't believe you." Alex said.

"What do you mean?"

"Are you Harry Potter or something, you think you can wave your magic fucking wand and this all goes away?"

"I don't get you?" Broadstone said.

"Innocent women have been killed for the most heinous of reasons, and you think that taking Ng away is good enough for me?" Alex said, she was feeling the anger bubble inside her.

"We can hand you Broc. I'll get Ng to hand him over to me or at least get his whereabouts."

"That's a start I guess," Alex said.

"Another bone Alex," Broadstone said.

"I am listening."

"Platford pointed you in the direction of the butcher boy."

"That's right," She said, thinking how did he know.

"It's the wrong guy."

"Oh'" Alex said.

"The name is nuanced. You need to find to the butchers boy. Now, the butcher boy owns Lolly's nightclub and is a well-known politician. He knows Broc very well."

Alex thought for a moment. Butchers boy and butcher boy, "What's the correlation?" She asked.

"Drop the S, you have the master, add the S and you have the student. If you want to know where Broc came from, he's your man."

"Is he a nonce?" Alex asked.

"God no. He is into twink's, but of legal age and very submissive. He's Stephen Bromilow."

Alex searched her databanks in her head, the guy that the Zookeeper was talking about. What was a twink and she came up with the Home Secretary.

There was a pause. Simon filled the gap. "Yeah, the Home Secretary. He's expecting your call." Alex phone pinged. Withheld number. "You?" she asked.

"Yes, it's his number, he's a lovely guy, very eccentric and as I said, owns Lolly's."

"That's where nonces hang out though?" Alex asked.

"I think you will find that nonces hang out everywhere. If there are child abusers there, they won't be doing anything illegal, it's a gay bar."

"Thanks," Alex said softly. She paused, "I thought you were Interpol," She asked.

"I am, but I also work for the government."

"You mean intelligence" Alex said probing.

"If that's what you want to call it." Another pause.

"I threw you those bones because I want something in return."

"I'm listening," Alex said.

"There's a lot of corruption in the healthcare system globally. You have experience in the clinical world, military and now a seasoned detective in the Met Police. I have watched your progress through this investigation. I want to offer you a job."

"Doing what?" Alex was looking through the window, her team crowded around the computer.

"I want you to run out of London, your own team, great budget. Chasing healthcare related crime throughout Europe."

"I can't imagine anything that would warrant an international police unit that would chase healthcare related crime, seems lame."

Simon laughed. "You'd be surprised. Venture capitalist are running most healthcare infrastructures into the ground. Anyone gets close to it, they disappear. We are also dealing with a lot of cybercrime that relates to healthcare.Rouge scientists and dysfunctioning pharmaceutical companies. You read the book Coma right?”

Pause.

"I’ll give you three strikes off the crease, Alex."

"What do you mean?" she asked.

"I will ask you only two more times. Then you won’t hear from me again," He said.

"Okay, let me think about it."

"Sure." The line went dead.

Alex went back to the room. Everyone looked around.

"Ricky, find me everything you have on Simon Broadstone. Don't leave anything unturned."

"Sure Sarge, on it."

"Renton, grab your coat."

"Where are we going?" He asked.

"Dorset, we are going to Dorset."

36

The journey to the south-west was like deja vu. Apart from it being dark. The motorway echoed eerie shadows between the amber glow of the street lamps. Intermittent to total darkness with long stretches of highway with no lights. The headlights of the oncoming traffic giving Alex a headache causing her to squint as her eyes struggled to adjust to the constant change in light. She felt dirty, tired and utterly traumatized from the last week.

And it wasn't over.

They briefly talked about what they might find down in Kings Stag. She slept on and off while listening to a cheesy 80's party mix on Renton's phone, taking Alex back to more innocent times. Leg warmers, Relax and Simon Le Bon.

She glanced over to Renton, the light almost strobing as cars past, making the bags under his eyes darker.

Her phone vibrated. She reached for it. It was Ricky,

"Okay sarge, your Simon Broadstone has minerals of the concrete variety."

"What do you mean?" Alex placed the phone on loudspeaker.

"Well, educated at Oxford, in Corpus Christi College which was the same as Ng before you ask." Alex wasn't going to ask, smiled at the comment.

"After graduating, they went their separate ways. From the looks of it, not to meet again until much later."

"Broadstone then became a second lieutenant of the first battalion The Grenadiers Guards after receiving the Sword of Honor at Sandhurst, top of his class."

Alex looked at Renton, she nodded, he had to have respect.

"After that, he deployed to South Armagh where he met a member of the FRU. He transferred on a temporary secondment to 14 Intelligence."

"That's hardcore," Alex said.

"Who are they?" asked Renton.

"Infantry soldiers and officers that pass the eight-week selection process run by the special forces. They infiltrate paramilitary organizations in Northern Ireland. It's pretty badass." Alex said.

"Yeah, I know right. He excelled so much so that his army records stated that he was invited to attend the sickners of the SAS selection in Hereford of which he walked through."

"After that, he was in Tora Bora post nine eleven, the Battle of Qala-i-Jangi prison in Afghanistan. Picked up the Military Cross in Sagin attached to the Parachute Regiment.

"I fucking hate him already, his kill count is way past 100," Ricky said, Alex chuckled.

"From there he changed his combat gear to a suit, but still in a clandestine role. The trail goes slightly cold. Couple of pop-ups at the Queen's garden party, a fracas in Paris with some jihadis, nothing of note though."

"Anything to do with Interpol?" Alex asked.

"There's no reference, why?"

"He is supposed to be from Interpol, so why is a spook getting involved in police business?" Renton asked.

Alex knew, he was muscling the heat away from his Chinese asset. She couldn't fault him for that. But allowing Ng to get away without facing charges was rankling her morals.

"Anything on the farm?" Alex asked.

"Frank told Dorset plod, he thought they needed to be in the loop." Alex tutted. "Considering what's happened over the last couple of days, if shit gets real, you're going to need some cannon's to back you up."

"Are they there now?" Alex asked.

"Roger that sarge, they have the farm under surveillance, I'll ping you some drone footage."

"Any sign of Broc?" She asked.

"Neggers, the house only has the one occupant in there, they have confirmed that it's a female tango," Ricky said.

Alex opened the phone and clicked on the video link that Ricky had sent. The drone shot, taken high up, then it swooped down, around the house, looking into the windows.

The drone then flicked into infra-red and panned around the house again. The only primary heat signature was coming from the home. The barn was glowing hot too.

"What's with the barn?" Alex asked.

"Wait out Sarge" there was a pause, Alex could hear Ricky tapping away, then he was speaking to someone else. Probably the boots on the ground.

"Yeah, Alex, just spoke with the team commander on the ground, the heat signature is either manure as it's a barn giving off a heat signature, or there's a generator of some description, they can't be sure without compromising their position."

"Okay, we will take a look when we get there."

"How far you out?" Ricky asked.

Alex looked at Renton, he was searching for road signs and realized that the satnav was on.

"We're twenty minutes or so out, just passing through a town called Shaftesbury I think, heading towards an HMP Prison called Guys Marsh," Renton said.

"Awesome, ping me when you arrive, I'm gonna tell the team commander on the ground your locstat, his name is Tray by the way."

Both Alex and Renton silently mouthed the name Tray to each other.

"'Has the warrant been issued?"

"Yeah, the Dorset guys are in possession of it, you have a copy pinged to your inbox." Ricky said.

Alex checked, another unread from Ricky, she opened.

"Got it." She made sure it had the house, personal possessions and any surrounding structures or dwellings in the name on the deeds. Which was Kevin Saunders.

“He just said as soon as you pull off the main road and head into the village, there is an unmarked car in the lay-by, pull in and make yourself known to the detective there. I think it’s Steve Knight. They will then close all four approach roads into the village and you will be tactically followed to the property."

"Roger that Ricky, I’ll ping you as soon as we get there."

The line went dead. Alex went to pocket her phone, it pinged. Si…

I take you're out for the remainder of the night, let me know you're alright so I can fucking sleep the text read.

Alex smiled. She felt his love, it made her feel warm and wanted.

She hit reply, babes, go to sleep, I am safe, heading to close this case tonight I hope. I will see you at some time tomorrow. Meet on the sofa for cuddles and wine? Emojis. Dots, he was waiting for the reply.

It’s a date, be safe my love, love you!

Alex felt suddenly on her own. Missing her man and her bed, where it was always safe.

"You okay?" Renton asked.

She snapped out of her isolation, "Yeah, yeah, 'lovin it".

She waved her phone, "Si, wondering what I was up to."

"Ahh, checking up," Renton said.

"No, just concerned, Renton. He doesn’t like me being out on jobs. He senses the danger I think."

"You think we’re in danger? Renton asked.

"I dunno mate, a lot has happened over the last couple of days. Something things you wouldn’t think was possible. I don’t want to take any chances."

"Amen to that.” He said.

They were ten minutes out, the tension in the car, rising.

37

Renton pulled the car into the lay-by, the tires scrunching the loose stones, lights off.

There was a pause, then the interior light of the front car came on. Knight stepped out. He was wearing the same clothes that he was wearing yesterday, everything about him was a bit more tired.

The view of the village skyline, some lights on, looked almost like a picture box. It was so quiet. You could understand the draw from the big city. Alex suddenly felt that she wanted to live here.

Knight made his way to the rear door and opened it. Alex shifted and watched him get in.

"Alex, hi," He said, nodded to the rearview mirror as Renton watched him climb into view, the car rocking on its springs.

"Steve, you well?" Alex asked, she noted he wasn't as sharp looking. Bit of a five o'clock shadow and probably down to the enormous bollocking he had received today.

"Yeah, sure, bit embarrassed that you guys are back here. I've looked at the evidence and can you accept my apologies?"

Alex was taken aback, she glanced quickly at Renton, still eyeing him up through the mirror. "Don't worry about it mate. We all make mistakes. You weren't to know."

He shrugged and pulled his radio out. It squelched. "Go ahead.

"I am in the car, heading to the farm now."

"Roger that. All callsigns, this is zero. Car approaching the farm is the target vehicle. Close the approaches and the inner cordon teams standby for my command to move."

All the radios squelched.

"Okay Alex, let's do this."

Renton engaged the gears and drove normally, just under the speed limit.

"Just past the garage which is coming up on your right... now, indicate left."

Renton did, he didn't need to be told to turn.

The car entered the lane.

"Slow down mate, just to the right is a bridge, that's the entrance to the farm now." Renton clocked it, indicated and turned.

They noticed a heavily armed police officer, squatting by the wall, looking over the sights of his .50 Barrett sniper rifle.

Steve saw that the two in the front had clocked him, "We saw what happened in London, we aren't taking any chances."

Alex smiled, she looked at Knight in the back, "Targets will fall when hit." she said.

"Exactly." Knight replied.

They pulled up at the front of the house, soft sidelights on in the front room, the smell of a wood fire filling their noses. Alex was the first to get out.

"Do you want me to go first?" Knight said "She kinda knows me."

"I don't think so," Alex said. "We don't need any cooperation, people are being arrested tonight, we go in hard." She said as she tailed off towards the door.

They climbed the three steps to the double wooden doors, Alex knocking hard.

There was a sound behind the door. Steve reached his hand to the rear. "You carrying?" Renton asked.

"Yeah," He looked at the two of them "Like I said."

The bolts on the door slid, squeaked, then the deadbolt went, the door cracked open, the smell of sandalwood and clary sage filling their noses, Tonight's the night by Rod Stewart softly being played in the background.

A fresh-faced attractive woman peered at them in surprise.

"You're fucking kidding me?" Renton said, he pushed past Alex and forced the door open.

"What the fuck?" She squealed, then she realized she knew the towering police officer who stood over her.

"Well Tracey Burgess, as I live and breathe," Renton said.

Both Alex and Steve followed him in, eyes searching the available spaces and beyond.

"You know each other?" Alex said still searching the shadows for her prey.

"Sure do, don't I Tracey?" Hands on his hips, bearing down at the small framed women. "Tracey Burgess, a tom from my past."

She looked spooked.

"What are you doing here?" She said

"You told me your name was Carmen Saunders," Steve said, pulling his notebook out.

"It is," she replied.

"No, it isn't." Renton said. "Last time I saw you, you were being shaken down in Euston station nick for soliciting at the railway station."

"You bailed me out," She said with a smile. "I changed my name to Carmen when I married my beau, Kevin."

Alex wandered off, "Where is your..." She stopped and turned "Beau?."

"He's away, works for the military."

"When's he back?" Renton asked.

"He never goes for more than a week at a time, have you got a warrant to be here?" she asked.

"We do, we need to speak with your husband as soon as..."

"Like I said, he isn't here and hasn't been here for a couple of days now...I asked if you have a warrant."

Alex went into the front room, "We do, to search the entire property, which is another reason why we need to speak to your husband."

The room was furnished immaculately. No expense was spared with the decor or the furniture.

Alex wandered to the coffee table at the rear of a sumptuous five seater sofa, the kind of couch you wouldn't find in a business park next to a DIY store.

They followed in.

Alex picked up a wedding photo of Carmen and Kevin.

"Is this your husband?" Alex asked.

"You have the warrant, you tell me?" Carmen chided.

Renton grabbed her by the hair, dragged her over to the picture. Alex was shocked, she went with it and showed the picture inches away from her face.

"Course it is," She said wincing, Renton let her go.

"Still a smooth bastard Renton," She said.

"You know that Kevin isn't his real name Carmen or whatever your name is."

"For the right price, you can call me whatever you like honey," She said seductively "Like before," There was a pause. Humor wasn't going to work.

"I know he changed it too, wanted to get away from the London scene."

"Is that what he told you?" Alex asked.

Carmen walked around the sofa, took a seat and buried her face in her hands, she looked up at Alex and smiled tenderly.

Alex walked the other way round and sat next to her.

"What's the deal here?" Alex said looking around.

"What do you mean?" Carmen replied.

"This house, the name change, what's the goal here, I have a feeling you know what we are here for. It's all a convenient truth right?" Alex said, bearing into Carmen's soul.

"I guessed this day would come."

She pulled a tissue from the ornate tissue box. She wiped her nose.

"Have you ever met him?" Carmen asked.

"Nope, we haven't." Alex replied, trying to gauge Carmen.

"He is very persuasive and for the record, I do love him."

"What do you do here?" Renton asked.

"He gave me a ticket out of the game, I took it with both hands, I don't know what he does here, my job is to look after the house and make him happy when he comes home. It's a front I know that, but it's not the life I had."

"How long has he been away?" Alex asked.

"He left the other day, in a rush. Said he was off to London. I haven't heard from him since."

Steve had left the house to speak with the gun teams outside.

"I can get him on his emergency phone, maybe you can speak with him," She said.

Alex thought fast. He's going to get to know very soon that the police are at the house.

"Okay, get him on the phone." Alex said.

She got up and went to the kitchen. Alex nodded to Renton, "Keep your eyes her," She said softly, Renton nodded and moved himself to get a better view.

"How do you know her?" Alex asked as she pulled her phone out, no messages from Ricky.

"She was a dollymop working my manor. She was high class though."

"Under the Zookeeper?" Alex asked.

"Yeah, definitely."

"Has she got priors?"

"Yeah, I've had her on a couple of charges." Renton saw that Alex was tapping into her phone.

"Tracey Burgess is her name, full name that is. I couldn't tell you her address."

"Cheers."

Get everything on a tom called Tracey Burgess, Renton had arrested her a couple of times. She's married to Broc.

Dots, he was reading and replied - WTF.

"She's coming back," Renton said, as he walked around the large sofa and took a seat next to Alex.

Carmen walked in, holding the phone up, she was in a video conversation with someone. Alex's heart quickened. She was on the phone to Broc.

As Carmen walked in, both Renton and Alex were in conversation, pretending to ignore Carmen as she came in.

Carmen skirted around the sofa and stood in front of both of them. Held up a 9mm pistol, and fired.

Renton's head snapped back, brain, blood and bones slammed against the expensive upholstery of the sofa, he paused, then slumped face forward, hitting the ground with a sickening thump. His right leg kicking out as the involuntary nerves expended their contained energy.

Alex shifted in her seat back, holding up her hands. The pistol now pointed at Alex, smoke coming out of the barrel and side ejection port. She wanted to act but felt powerless.

Alex could hear the voice on the phone screaming "Shoot the fucking bitch." Broc was watching.

"Carmen, shoot that fucking whore."

"End of the road darling," Carmen said. She put the pistol under her chin, Alex jumped up to stop her. It was too late.The report of the gun came, the top slide flicking the spent casing out, the top of Carmen's head spattering the ceiling.

"NOOOOO!" shouted Broc.

The phone was tumbling out of her hand, Alex catching it, and letting her fall to the floor, arterial spray jetting across the room into the fireplace. Her legs jerking spasmodically with her hands coming up to her chin. The spark in her eye extinguishing as her heart stopped beating. The pool of blood spreading quickly across the floor.

In the commotion, Alex didn't hear the front and back doors being smashed in, with the tactical teams entering the property. The sound of boots and equipment coming into focus.

Alex raised the phone. She was looking directly at her prey. She felt nothing but contempt for him.

"You fucking bitch, look what you have done!" He said. He was puce with anger, stood up, screaming other obscenities that Alex chose not to hear.

There was a pause.

"Have you quite finished?" She asked.

"I haven't even started with you." He spat. Saliva hanging from his mouth.

"You're finished Broc, your whole operation is finished. We have Ng's operation, HAEMOmatch, everything. You're done."

"You have no idea what you have started Brown," He said.

Alex startled that he used her name.

"Yes, that's right," He looked closer into the screen. "I know everything about you, your boring middle-class life, your husband who works for the food standards agency. Your children at university, everything."

"I don't respond well to threats Broc. Typical bully, on the grand scheme of things, you're a nothing. You might be in the South of France sunning yourself, but trust me. It's a matter of time I see your ass in bracelets, preferably in the crosshairs of a rifle," Alex said.

Broc was equally as startled when she mentioned the south of France.

Broc held up a phone, "See this," he said.

The phone was held close to the camera.

"What is it?" Alex said.

"It's remote charge to the house your in. You have under a minute to get out."

It took a couple of seconds to realize what he had said, then she heard it. A low whine, a subtle alarm in the background. Police officers were milling about.

"GET OUT!" shouted Alex. The people in the living room stopped and stared at Alex.

"BOMB!" Was all they needed to hear.

The milling turned into urgency. The trained men darted for the exits. Alex started to move Renton's prostate body, one of the policemen saw her struggling. He stopped, vaulted the coffee table and sofa, and just picked him up over his shoulder.

"FOLLOW ME!" he shouted.

Alex was the last person to leave the house, then she heard it. The fizzing. As the valves holding the separated liquids positioned in the house cavity walls mixed.

"EVERYONE DOWN THE DRIVE!" Shouted the team commander. Like ants in the dark coming from different directions, people ran down the bridge. Then the spark came, the intense heat and the fireball that engulfed the house.

Alex stood on the road, under a cool blue moon, suddenly her face lit up, as she felt the intense heat from the house and the fire that devoured it.

She held up the phone, Broc still there.

"You made it out," He said. "Lucky you weren't sandwiched between the barn and the house."

Alex, thinking fast. The barn she thought. It didn't go up.

She held up the phone, "Fuck you, Broc." His face stony and expressionless as she hung up the line.

He stood in Ng's office in the villa, with his forearm, in a fit of rage, screamed and cleared and upturned the table. "FUCKING BITCH!" He screamed "FUCKING HANG UP ON ME!"

Alex turned to the team commander. "I just spoke to the target on the phone. He said that I was lucky that we weren't sandwiched between the barn and the house."

The team commander looked over her shoulder, looking at the house and the barn, the fire deepening the creases in his face, he frowned.

"The barn didn't go up at the same time," He said.

Alex turned and faced the property. "That's what I thought, Broc thinks the barn went up with the house. We need to get in that barn, NOW!"

38

The armed response team filed across the bridge fanned out and skirted the barn. Avoiding the house that was still blazing.

"When they breach, if clear I'll let you go through, Alex." The team commander said.

Alex was watching the men like ants skirt around the wooden structure, guns at the ready. She was eager to get inside.

"Once inside, can you tell your men hold back, they can't just go through kicking everything in."

The team commander looked down at Alex, partly insulted. Still looking at her, he pressed the Pressel on the radio.

"All call-signs, this is zero, once inside the barn, clear with caution and then hold back," He said softly.

Alex looked up. She smiled at the big guy "I know what you guys are like."

His radio crackled into life with the acknowledgments from the other teams.

"With caution means they won't go in like a bull in a china shop, they might have to blow the main door though as its locked, with reinforcements, so our initial assessment said."

There was a commotion from the road. A fire engine was trying to get into the lane.

"MOVE YOUR VEHICLES AND GET OUT OF MY WAY!" Shouted the fire chief.

The team commander turned, unnerved, ignored him.

"Fire brigade, think they trump everything."

The fire chief was on foot, storming up to the bridge, "WHOS IN CHARGE HERE!" He demanded.

Alex nodded to the tactical commander, he smiled and turned. "That would be me, chief."

"Move your men and vehicles," He demanded again.

"Can't do that treacle," He said.

"WHY NOT?" t

The chief, red with rage hands on his hips wanting a fight.

"I have an active scene in progress until we have squared the barn away, you're gonna have to let the house burn."

The chief walked to the bridge and stared at the house.

"Anyone in the house?" He asked, the noise of the fire making the chief shout.

"One fatality, suicide, other than that, I can't be sure at this point."

The chief sniffed the air "Oxidiser, this'll burn for hours."

"Can you guys start soaking the barn to protect my officers?" The tactical commander said.

The fire chief turned, nodded and walked off to his truck shouting orders. His fire officers were scurrying around opening doors and dragging ladders off the truck.

"BREACHING! BREACHING! BREACHING!" Came the call on the radio, then the report of a low percussion charge blowing the barn doors off. Followed by the shouting of the officers clearing the nooks and crannies of the barn.

There was a muffled voice speaking to the team commander "Roger that, on our way, OUT."

"Let's go Alex, the barn is clear."

Alex filed in behind the team commander, flanked by two other armed officers.

They got to the barn, the heat from the house fierce and searing. Water was cascading from the ceiling as the fire brigade had started dowsing the wooden barn.

Alex entered the barn, "So clean" she said.

"Sorry Alex," The commander said.

"It's a barn, locked up and it's so clean."

The team commander was stood in the middle, looking around.

"What's this for?" Alex asked standing at the metal pole sticking out of the ground nearly head height, with a digital combination keypad on.

She pulled out her phone, dialed Ricky.

"Yo," He said.

"I'm in the barn with the tac team. There's a combination lock on a stand-alone pole in the middle of the barn, which seems to be a bit odd."

Ricky thought for a moment, "Try date of births, hold on." Alex could hear Ricky assault the keys on his keyboard.

"Renton has all the details on his phone, I think." Ricky said.

Suddenly it hit Alex like a sledgehammer in the face Renton she thought.

"He's dead," She said, voice cracking with the emotion of the day.

The typing on the other end stopped "Come again, Alex."

"He's dead. Carmen shot him in the head."

"What the fuck?" Ricky said. There was a long pause. "You okay, were you there?"

"Yeah, she came into the room we were in and just pulled the gun and shot him. I think she was supposed to shoot me."

"How do you mean?" Ricky asked.

"She was on the phone to Broc at the time. He was telling her to shoot me, she just stuck the pistol in her mouth and blew her own brains out."

"Wow, Alex."

"Enough Ricky, we have to get to Lucy, she is here, I can feel it. We mourn Renton when the day is done."

"Okay, try Saunders DOB," He said, his voice failing miserably to hide his emotion.

She punched it in, the red light flashed. "Nope."

"Try Broc's DOB."

Alex punched it in and the green light flashed. There was a creak and a rumbling underfoot, "That's done something." Alex said looking around the barn.

The team commander almost fell as the concrete apron he was standing on started to sink, creating a ramp.

"BLOODY HELL!" He screamed.

"What's happening?" Ricky said.

"Hold on."

Alex hung the phone up, dialed into video calling, Ricky's fresh face came up, Alex smiled when she saw his familiar friendly face, hit the camera flip button on the screen.

She turned and walked to the ramp.

"Bloody hell, what's happening to the floor?" Ricky asked.

Alex walked down the ramp, the double doors opened. The keypad on the opposing wall was flashing green.

Inside was not just spotlessly clean. The familiar smell of detergent and air filtration filling Alex's senses, taking her back to her nursing days.

The team commander entered after her.

"This is a bit different," He said.

"This is the twilight zone," Alex said.

"You wouldn't expect to see this under a barn."

"Indeed," Alex said.

Alex instinctively turned left and walked the short passageway to another set of double doors. The air escaping was loud and cold. Typical air filtration of an operating complex. The team commander was grabbing her shoulder.

"Let us enter first, Alex."

"No," Alex said, "We've got this far, the chances of anyone being here alive is remote."

She pushed the doors open and entered an operating room. Anesthetic machine, operating table. The white tiled floor and walls bathed in a cool blue subdued light.

The unmistakable sound of a ventilator pushing air in and out of a patient. The back of an operating table at 75 degrees.

Alex's walk quickend, the sound of a ventilator meant that Lucy was still alive. She skipped to a half run followed by the team commander.

She circled the table and stopped suddenly. Hand to mouth, Alex recoiled in the barbarity with what she saw.

Lucy was serene, asleep, from the neck down her thorax to her abdomen was stripped of everything. She resembled the carcass of a Belfast sink. A rectangular hole of nothingness, just blood that had clotted in the the recesses of the abdomen.

Alex looked at the screen, blood pressure was low, but okay, pulse was determined by the ECMO, which was whirring at the foot of the operating table. Lucy's oxygen saturation was around 95%, again normal.

Alex got a grip of her emotions, "What the..." Alex heard as the team commander came into her peripheral vision.

"Get paramedics, I need an anesthetist here too, not just a pair of bread and butter stretcher bearers, get the chopper here pronto," Alex said.

The team commander was frozen, incapable of movement.

"MOVE!" Alex shouted.

The man shook himself out of the trance, spun and sprinted out the door shouting in his radio.

With the noise, Lucy stirred, her head lolling slowly left and right.

"Lucy" Alex said, "Lucy."

She opened her eyes, eyes dry and crusty. Alex grabbed a swab from the trolley and soaked it in water. She wiped her eyes.

Lucy was groggy and unable to speak.

Alex looked underneath, saw the epidural pump in her neck and the white milky substance dripping into her system via her hand. She reached and slowed the pump down to a lower dose. Alex's mind searching the very bottom of her data banks from a previous life as an ODP.

"Where is Broc?" Lucy asked. Voice horse and struggling.

Alex came back up and caressed her face. "He's not here Lucy," She said tenderly, "You're safe now."

"Your in a bit of a pickle." Alex said.

Her eyes darted down, then back to Alex, "You must be a detective." She tried to smile. "What is your name, you have lovely eyes?" Lucy said.

"Thank you, Lucy. My name is Alex. We have been working very hard to find you. I am glad we have."

"Thank you, Alex, it's been a bit of a weird time." Lucy began to cry, Alex couldn't stop herself either, the tears came down, relief for finding her, but knowing there was nothing that she could do to save her. Her time on this earth was going to be cut so brutally short.

"I wish I had found you sooner lovely." Alex cried.

"I am glad you have found me. I know what Broc has done to me."

"You do?" Alex said.

"Yes, he made me watch him, I have gone past being upset. I know I am going to die," She sniffed, felt disconnected.

"He made you watch him?" Alex asked, she gripped the sides of the table, her knuckles cracking with anger.

"Yes, my throat is so dry, Alex."

Alex looked around. She knew she couldn't give anything to Lucy. "We need to wait for the doctors to come, Lucy."

"I know, he has me connected to this machine that is doing everything that my bits were supposed to do."

She indicated to the device at her feet, "It's a bit big considering what he took out of me don't you think?" A smile curled Lucy's lips.

"It's a miraculous machine Lucy."

Voices were approaching, "IN HERE!" Came the voice.

A couple of paramedics and a woman in a orange flight suit came into the room changing the energy in the room.

"Doctor Liz Cranshaw, a gasman from Southampton," With a craze of long blonde hair and an orange flying suit.

"Sergeant Alex Brown."

"Call me Liz, Alex."

She came round almost knocking Alex off her feet. Alex stepped back. She kept stepping back until the wall hit her. The coolness of the wall so welcome. She slumped, her buttocks bouncing off the backs of her heels. Her head sank and she placed both hands on the back of her head, cocooning herself in her limbs, hiding from the reality of the week just past.

A voice was calling her back from the light she was bathing her emotions in "...Yo Alex."

She looked up. Eyes red and tired, she blinked to focus.

Liz was stood in front of her.

Alex stood, Liz helped her to her feet.

"Something you don't see every day," Liz said.

Alex nodded "She's victim number 27."

"Shittydeath," Liz said, "What's the story?"

Alex regaled her the summary of what had happened, Liz shocked and upset by the information that she heard, trying to fathom any sense to it.

"Surgeon, from London," Liz said.

"There's an unwritten law about surgeons," Liz said.

"All surgeons are cunts," Alex said.

Liz laughed "You know it."

"Theatre nurse and anesthetic ODP before I saw the light and got out."

"You saw the light and got out," Liz asked looking around.

"More like jumping out of the frying pan and into the fire."

Alex nodded to Lucy, "What' your plan?"

"I dunno, I can't take the ECMO with me, it's too large. I have been on the phone to St Mary's in London. They have a portable ECMO, but even if we manage to get her into a cardiothoracic theatre in Southampton, what do we do. She has no organs."

"How long can she stay on ECMO for?" Alex asked.

"In theory, indefinitely, although we run a significant risk of infection at the access points, this..." She motioned with her thumb "...Has never been done before."

"What did this guy do with the other 26 victims?"

Alex motion to the meat mincer, "They went through that."

"Sick fuck, without exception, all surgeons really are cunts," Liz said.

"Can I do anything for you Alex, you look like you have been through the mill yourself."

"No, thank you, Liz. Although I don't have a friend to take home, he was killed earlier in the night."

Liz pulled a face "Oh, you poor thing" She rubbed her arm.

Alex nodded and went to Lucy. Lucy looked up and smiled. "Gosh, never had so much attention."

Alex laughed.

"I met your man, Harvey." Lucy's eyes widened with a large grin.

"He's a keeper," Alex said.

"Isn't he." Lucy said agreeing "That's what I thought."

"He's ruffled some feathers for you," Alex said.

Alex turned to Liz who was now tending to the syringe drivers. "How long 'til you move?"

Liz stopped, she looked at her phone, "We are going to be at least three or four hours here before we think about moving, I have some senior guys coming in from Southampton for better advice."

"Can I make a call and get Lucy's boyfriend down here."

Liz shrugged "I don't think that's a bad idea, I would agree to that given the circumstances."

Alex nodded, "Lucy, I have to go, I am going to make a call and see if Harvey can come down."

Lucy sniveled and nodded her head. She mouthed the words thank you with tears coming from the corners of her eyes.

Alex stepped away while the medical teams worked on her. She found Cuthbert's number.

"Alex," He said picking up immediately.

"Can you get Harvey to my location ASAP?"

She pinged her location to his phone.

"Sure hold on," He paused looking at the message.

"It'll take us around three hours on a blue light, will you be there?"

"Neggars Cuffy, one of my guys was slotted on the job tonight, need to take him home."

"Not Ricky."

"No, Renton, you met him yesterday, took a round in the head," She said.

"Shit must have got real with you guys tonight then." Cuffy said.

"Pretty much, listen Cuffy, I need to fill you in about Lucy. She's alive of sorts..."

Alex explained the situation, Cuffy not quite understanding nor believing half of it.

"What do I tell him?" He asked.

Alex blew out, after the last week and all of the tribulations along with it, Alex usually so decisive and driven, knowing exactly what she wants in life, was for once stuck for words.

"I dunno Cuffy, just tell him that she is alive but expect the worst, I guess."

"Okay, take care of yourself, Alex, I'll be in touch as soon as we touch down in Dorset."

"Thanks, Cuffy."

The line went dead.

She scrolled and found Ricky.

"We've got her," She said.

"Alive?" Ricky asked.

She recounted the story for the second time. Ricky was having the same reaction as Cuffy.

"I've sent James down to pick Renton up," Ricky said. "Will you wait for him?"

"I think I will make my way back. I'll go straight home, Rick."

"No dramas boss, I'll stay at work until you make it back home safe, call me if you need me."

"Thanks Ricky, I don't know what I would have done without you on the team." Alex said.

"Get yourself home, boss. Otherwise, you will make me cry."

"Laters stud," Alex said. The line went dead.

Alex went to pocket her phone, but then she thought of Simon.

She scrolled again, found his number. Always sleeping with it under his pillow when Alex was on the job.

It rang six times, then Si answered. A little fumbling first. "Babes, I am here." Being such a late hour, Si knew that Alex needed him.

Alex sank to her knees again, she started sobbing, "Babes, speak to me" Simon said tenderly.

"I can't." She sobbed eyes streaming and unable to find any words other than noise.

"Baby, come home." He knew she had finished whatever she had to do.

She nodded, "I am on my way, gonna take a while though, I am in fucking Dorset," She said, voice cracking, her emotion trying to get the better of her.

"I'll be here waiting, warm hot chocolate, cheese toasties and a warm bed."

Alex laughed through the tears. He totally knew her.

39

39.

The drive to Southampton was sullen. Renton's funeral seven days later had been emotional for the whole team. Makes it even more upsetting when you see the man behind the job.

Wife, children, mother, father and friends. Bewildered and confused how someone can die while being so young.

Police officers are always in the line of fire, yet they play down their jobs to protect the people that love them.

That's what Alex felt anyhow.

The traffic was light. The sun low and strong in the autumnal light. The lush green of the trees turning vivid shades of orange and yellows.

Both Alex and Ricky had driven in almost total silence. The radio, oblivious, filled the silence. Alex was twirling her hair wistfully, watching the horizon for the changes. Urban to rural, rural to urban, England in the summer and autumn just can't be beaten she thought. The music was evoking memories of summer days lying in the grass, a world away from the trauma of adult life, the best thing about being a child, not having to pay bills Alex thought. Responsibility sucks.

The hospital in Southampton, a behemoth of a building. Drab, miserable and utterly soul destroying. Yet miracles are performed every day in the four walls that contained the most amazing of people. The building wasn't important, but the people, abused by the state, went about their jobs with dedication and brilliance.

They made their way to the fourth floor, cardiac intensive care. Armed police were flanking the doorway.

Alex flashed her warrant card.

"Thanks, Sergeant, can you guys sign in please?" Alex signed both Ricky and herself in. The gunner opened the door.

Harvey sat in a chair watching something on a tablet. He clocked Alex. He hadn't seen her since meeting her in the carpark.

He placed the tablet on the table next to him and jumped up. He walked over to Alex.

"Harvey, how are you?"

He shrugged and hugged her, he looked at Ricky.

"This is my partner, Ricky," Alex breaking the embrace, Ricky offered his hand, Harvey took it and shook violently, almost pumping Ricky into orbit.

"He's my actual partner, Renton wasn't."

"Yeah, I heard that it was his funeral today, how did it go?" Trailing off at the end of the sentence, knowing that asking how it went with regards to a funeral was a bit stupid.

"It went fine, emotional, but it went ahead okay." Alex nodded to the bed Lucy was in."How is she?"

"She's comfortable. They only wake her for one hour a day, they are doing the best they can, we laugh when she's awake, can't shut her up really."

Alex smiled and touched his arm. He felt it. Placed his own hand on top and squeezed.

"I want to thank you, Alex, Sergeant Cuthbert filled me in, to what had happened, you must 'av bin right through it for Lucy. I'll remember you for the rest of my life." Tears filled his eyes.

"That's cool, Harvey, she is worth it."

Alex walked to her bed, wires coming from Lucy's body, the ECMO machine whirring dark blood to the unit with brighter, oxygen enriched blood back in to her. She looked cleaner, more angelic. The soft glow of a bulb above her head gave her a peaceful appearance. Apart from the wires and tubes coming away from her body, you wouldn't think there was anything wrong with her. Though Alex had seen her at her worst. An image that will stay with her always.

"There's a guy here, some suit. He was askin' after you if you had arrived or bin to visit."

"Who was that?" Alex asked.

"Dunno, still around I think."

Liz came into the room, deep in conversation with the ODP looking after her. She sensed different people in the room, looked up and shut the clipboard and handed it to her ODP.

"Well bugger me, Alex right."

She walked over and shook Alex's hand.

"You look a bit better than when I last saw you," Liz said.

"Hi Liz, this is Ricky."

"I'm her tonto," Ricky said with a smile, his teeth the brightest thing in the room.

"Who's your dentist?" Liz asked. Ricky looked perplexed.

"Doesn't matter." Liz said, both women laughed.

"How is she?" Alex asked.

"Well, considering she has no vital organs, she's doing okay. The board are still struggling with the ethics about sticking her on the registry for new organs."

"Why?" said Ricky.

"What he said." Alex chimed up.

"Well, the chances of her surviving a transplant are very limited, until the board makes their decision, we can't even put her on the registry."

"That sucks, the very least Haemomatch can do is save her," Alex said.

"To be fair, she's lucky to be alive. You have to thank Broc for that. Our surgeons have looked her over and his work is perfection. One or two know him."

"If it weren't for Broc, she wouldn't be here in the first place, Liz," Alex said.

"Touché" Liz responded, leaning and adjusting a monitor.

They didn't notice a man had entered the room and was standing back from the bed, in the shadows of the room.

Liz turned, "Oh hello again."

Alex turned, he didn't have to speak. His appearance oozed spook. Simon Broadstone came into the only light available. Wearing a snappy charcoal tailored suit. Regimental tie and a wristwatch the size of a satellite. The signet ring on the small finger was either Masonic or his boarding school house. Probably Eton.

"Doctor Cranshaw" Nodding curtly.

"Sergeant Brown, how do you do?" He said. His voice powerful, deep and somber. A voice you would instantly trust and a voice you would never forget.

"Mr Broadstone," Alex said. Weirdly she felt sheepish and coy, she blushed. Damn, he was good-looking as well.

Ricky leaned in, "Told you I hated him," he said.

Alex smiled.

"Please call me Simon," He said. His voice reverberating right through Alex.

Liz leaned in, "Feel my sweater," She said.

Alex looked at Liz, "Why?"

"Boyfriend material, you know what I mean girl," Winking.

Alex smirked, "Enough."

Alex walked towards him, "Simon, how do you do?"

"Can we chat?" He said shaking her hand.

"Course."

He led Alex out of the room, and into the corridor.

"Have you located Broc?"

"Gosh, straight out of the blocks, that's why I like you, Alex," Simon said.

"You've probably read my file. I don't mince."

"You're right and I am aware that you don't…mince your words," He said leaning against the window.

"We have located him, unfortunately, he's in the wind."

"You let him get away first, you mean," She said.

He ignored the jibe, "The Villa was empty, he was there alright, his prints were everywhere."

"How did you know where to go precisely?" Alex asked looking out of the window, there was a guy in a wheelchair trying to get up the ramp, while people just walked past. Seemed odd at a hospital to see it she thought.

"We brought Ng in. He gave himself up. Acknowledged the syndicate, he won't be a problem anymore."

"How come?" Alex said.

"We massaged his tax returns in China." Hands in his trouser pockets, his physique athletic.

"The Supreme People's Court in China might seem to allow pedophilia, murder and other nasty crimes but evade tax, now that's a different matter. He won't see the light of day," He said looking at the floor.

"That doesn't shut the organization down, though."

"Indeed, but for now, it will. We have taps on this Triad branch, if they start again, we will know."

Alex was nodding.

"Also, I have spoken with the board. We have the organs that Lucy can have, ask me no questions and I will tell you no lies, I'll speak with Doctor Cranshaw in a moment. She will be having surgery tomorrow morning, I hope."

Alex turned, "You're kidding?" She said.

"We applied some pressure to Ng, he might need walking aids and soft food for a few weeks, but nonetheless, he gave us what we wanted."

"I'm impressed," Alex said.

"Also, we took this from his possession."

Alex took the clear bag, in the bag was a sealed jar with a vicious milky substance in it.

"What's this?" Alex asked holding up to the light.

"Orlov's ejacualte, I'm sure you can connect the DNA material in the jar to few unsolved sexual crimes." Simon said, grinning.

"Now we've solved pretty much everything for you. I am going to give your second strike at the ball Alex, will you join my organization."

Alex looked out the window, the guy still struggling up the ramp in the wheelchair. "Why can't anyone help that guy?"

Simon turned and looked down.

"We live in a different world, Alex and it's changing immeasurably. Something that we are struggling to keep under control. Healthcare related crimes are the new face of evil. From pharmaceuticals to fat-cat CEO's trying to inflate the bottom line. Care for cash we like to call it," He paused. Saw Alex deep in thought, the cogs almost audible.

"I'll let you run an investigation to bring Broc to justice, too. I am sure he will be up to his old tricks as soon as he is able."

"Give me some more time Simon, it's..." She paused, thought about the Mile End nick, Frank, Simon and her children "...Kinda comfortable, you know?"

"I get it Alex. But if your comfortable, you're stagnating, you're not moving forward. Things happen for a reason. That's why our paths have met. I am sure of it."

Alex slowly nodded, give me a day or so.

"Like I said, that's your second strike. I will only ask you one more time."

She nodded again.

"Alex it's been smashing to meet you." He stood erect and offered his hand, Alex took it. The tailored suit, expensive cologne and sun-kissed skin were all betrayed by the rough, calloused hands. This man was a worker and had a lifetime of getting them dirty, Alex felt it. She felt safe by his touch. She liked it.

He turned and left.

She watched him walk through the doors, Ricky waiting in the wings on the other side.

Her phone rang, withheld number wanting to video call. Unusual.

She hit the green button.

Blood drained from her face as if she had seen a ghost, staring at the image of Broc, grinning at her.

"Hello, Alex," He said.

She couldn't find any words.

"Cat got your tongue, Sergeant?"

He smiled again.

"You have royally fucked my life up, Sergeant. I must commend you. I didn't think you would."

"Fuck you Broc!" Alex said, Ricky stopped, he knew who it was.

"I'm amazed you're alive. Carmen really let me down not

shooting you, then disabling the charge in the barn, how is Lucy by the way?"

"That's none of your business, although she is still alive… just."

"Good, the surgeons in Southampton, some of them have been my *underlings*. Will no doubt do their best for her, I suspect that the ravages of infection will take her first though."

"You're a bag of chuckles, Broc," Alex said.

"You nearly got me too. Ng managed to tip me off after they had tortured him. Managed to get away to another hideaway before your friend found me."

Alex nodded "I love the fact that you call your next house a hideaway, for someone so astute, you need to hole up in a hideaway. I am surprised you can fit into anything on this earth with an ego like yours."

Broc laughed, "No need to get personal, Sergeant. Jealousy is a sin, don't you know."

"Things became personal when you had a friend killed, not to mention the other people that have filled up the morgue, all in the name of money." Alex sneered.

"Not true," Broc said. "I'd have done it all for nothing. Ng gave me the means. I would have done it gratis. The killing was my thirst."

"Why did you not just kill and not be so weird with it?" Alex said.

"People have to see what becomes of them, that in itself is a privilege for the dying, is it not. If you were to die today, you wouldn't know anything about it."

"For someone so educated, you're really stupid, Broc," Alex said as he cocked his head.

"You're no Bond villain, Broc and never will be. You're a sexually inadequate moron, that is probably still a bedwetter. If your dad were still alive, he'd probably put you over his knee, that might even give you an erection, you piece of shit," Alex said.

Broc's face was red, "How fucking dare you!" He said through his teeth.

"How dare I? Your days on this earth are numbered, Broc, I

am coming for you."

He laughed. The image went dark then a live video stream came up. Alex squinted, trying to dial into the picture, then it dawned on her what she was looking at, suddenly feeling helplessly nauseous.

Alex's daughter, Devon was sat on a bus, the top deck. She always sat on the top-deck. Alex's blood ran cold, sat behind her was the nonchalant assassin Ji-Yeon, smiling at the camera. With her thumb, she traced it across her throat, leaned forward and offered Devon a sweet. They sat for a few seconds laughing.

Alex was clicking her fingers to Ricky and holding her thumb and forefinger up to her ear. Ricky pulled his phone out. He was already on it, scrolling for Devon's number and hitting call.

The video feed was live. Devon answered the phone.

"Hey, mom, how you doing, just on my way to a lecture."

Alex was trying to be cool, "Who are you sat with?"

Devon looked around, "No one you know."

Ji-Yeon had left.

"Who was the Chinese women that gave you a sweet?"

Devon searched around looking for her mum. "How the hell did you know mom?"

Still looking, "I dunno, she introduced herself on the bus, she was nice, another student I think."

"Listen to me Devon, closely, look up." She looked up.

"There's a camera there, can you see it?"

"Yeah, are you looking at me through there? Wow that's a bit weird mom, why are you doing that?" she asked.

"Mom, I am feeling a bit funny." She slumped to the seat, her hand let go of the phone, trying to hold her head up, fear in her eyes, Alex could see that she was trying to talk.

Alex was powerless to do anything, Devon finally succumbing to whatever she had ingested, fell against the window, legs jerking.

The Korean came into view, smiled and spray painted the camera lens black. "DEVON!" Alex shouted as she disappeared from view.

The video feed went blank and then Broc came back into

view.

"You motherfucker Broc!"

He laughed. "Lucy was number 27. Devon Brown will be number 28. I'm going to take my time on Devon. What is she, 18, 19? Doesn't matter, the skin is perfectly pliable. Cuts beautifully, like a spring lamb. I shall send you a video when I am done."

The feed went blank, the call ended.

Alex sank to her knees, "My God, what have I done?" Alex said. Ricky stood with one hand on his forehead. He had known Devon most of her life. This had hit him just as hard.

The doors opened, Broadstone walked out, he stopped. Sensing a moment.

"What's happened?"

Alex looked up, face stony and ashen. "I have two conditions."

"Name them," Simon said.

"First, Ricky comes with."

He looked at Ricky, looked back at Alex, "Okay, agreed, and the second?"

"Broc is my number one target, my first job."

Simon squinted, "What's happened?"

Alex held up her phone, "Shit just got personal."

THE END

This is not where it ends or even where it starts, find out about the case of the Troll! Since you bought this book, you can get your copy for FREE.

There is also the question of Chapter 40. Alex visiting Lolly's Nightclub.

Type this link and find out how to download this novella from Jon A. Biddle and the extra Chapter to The Harvester, but don't press it with your finger! It won't get you anywhere and you'll look stupid.

Hypnos is the second episode of six in the Broc series, released early spring 2019. If you want your copy, click this link too.

Get Troll for free and Chapter 40 by typing; https://jonbiddle.uk/troll/ into your phone right now…

Authors Note.

I have spent many years in primary healthcare. Working at the front line of surgical care. Working with some of the most amazing people that walk this planet, including the surgeons, of which I call my friends. The beginning of the book mentions 'The first law of anaesthesiology,' something that we use in jest. Its something is true, and we seriously wouldn't want it any other way. It takes a certain kind of someone to take a knife, and cut into a person and 'rummage' around in their cavities to be considered normal.
Being a surgeon is something I wouldn't do for all the tea in China. When I go home and shut my front door, I want to keep that world outside, as a surgical assistant, I have that luxury.
Healthcare is going through some major radicalizations in the western world. The ageing population is burgeoning in a system that isn't fit for purpose with a management hell bent of screwing every ounce of sanity the doctors and healthcare practitioners can give. Before, it was about patient-centered care. Now under the same guise, the strap-line ought to read 'Care for Cash' because that's what modern healthcare has been reduced to.
I am very proud of the people I work with and very proud of the small vocation I represent professionally. I love every one of them, and there is not enough room in this book to mention all of them.
But I want to take this opportunity to mention a debt of gratitude for getting this book on to the shelves.
Casie L. Williams, Editor, Texan woman with a brain bigger than a brain pie, and feisty as fuck to boot.
Paul Hobby, ODP, Proofreader, and Welsh, I love the Welsh so I won't hear negativity towards them!
Dr. Chris Sellar, Consultant anesthetist, and all round

top chap. I don't know how I get through some of my list's without the sanity and humor this man provides. My family for not rolling their eyes when I had a silly question or 'hang on a minute, just one more sentence' when dinner was ready.
The 101 beta readers that kept it real through the editing phase. Constructive, challenging and truthful was what I needed to make this book the best book I could have written along with making the skin on my back thick as an old boot. Running and licking my wounds was a regular thing. And thank God for my wife Sam with her nonsense approach to 'getting a grip.'

The theory of ECMO being used in the way Broc uses it would most likely be impossible. Speaking to a cardio-thoracic surgeon, they said it would be impossible, speaking with a perfusionist, who operate one of these machines says it would.
In all honesty, nutrition and infection would be the major challenges in keeping someone alive on bypass not to mention the high standard of nursing care that would be required to ensure the patient made it through the whole process.
That said, Extra corporeal membrane oxygenators are life savers and used extensively throughout the western world. Without it, some patients just wouldn't stand a chance. Having seen them used in the clinical setting quiet a lot, one was for organ harvest, which was the genesis of my story many years ago. The surgeon though, was a delight, and incredibly competent, a far cry from the piece of shit Dale Broc is.
Click the link or visit my website for more information about the Broc series. Hypnos, the second episode in this series will be released early spring on 2019.

35150066R00202

Printed in Poland
by Amazon Fulfillment
Poland Sp. z o.o., Wrocław